# PASSIONS MEET AT...

## CHECKPOINT ORINOCO

## Also by Alice Ekert-Rotholz

Rice in Silver Bowls
The Sydney Circle

Published by
POPULAR LIBRARY

# CHECKPOINT ORINOCO

A Novel by

## Alice Ekert-Rotholz

Translated by
Catherine Hutter

**POPULAR LIBRARY**

An Imprint of Warner Books, Inc.

A Warner Communications Company

# 1

## The Chatelaine

Pilar Álvarez had just come home from the office when the phone rang. She frowned. After spending the whole day at the firm of Álvarez & Sánchez coping with computers and consulting engineers for the industrial plans in the Orinoco area, she was looking forward to a quiet, pleasant evening. For a moment she sat motionless and let the phone ring. It could only be her stepsister Teresa, five hundred kilometers away in Mérida. Teresa was impossible. She only called when she wanted something, but she wanted something all the time. Pilar picked up the receiver; her voice was surly. But it wasn't Teresa; it was Juana Álvarez in Mérida.

"Is that you, Pilar?"

"Who else could it be? I'm the only one here, as usual."

"Where is Teresa's husband?"

"Carlos is not in Caracas."

Juana Álvarez wanted to say something, but evidently her twin sister, Antonia had taken the receiver from her. It always annoyed Pilar when her aunts fought each other for the phone. Antonia's voice was weepier than ever, but she wasn't given time for more than a greeting. "Give me back that phone, Antonia! This minute! *I* am going to talk to Pilar!"

"Is it that important?" Pilar asked wearily. "I've just come home from the office and I'm dead tired."

"It isn't right that you should be so tired, Pilar. You're

1

not *that* old. Look at the two of us! You should take Antonia's pills. Since she's been taking them, she has so much vitality, it's unbearable!"

"I can just barely drag myself around," Antonia interrupted. "The pills only help the pharmacist!"

"Are you calling me just to tell me that?"

"Don't be so disagreeable," said Juana, in command again. "Pilar, I've got to speak to Carlos."

"He's still in Ciudad Bolívar. On business. I have no idea where he's spending the weekend."

"I don't know another husband who's so hard to find," said Juana Álvarez. "For heaven's sake, Antonia, let me talk! You're usually happy to leave all the unpleasant news to me."

"May I please know what Teresa's done this time?" Pilar asked. "Is she too cowardly to call me herself? Tell her to come home at once! Then she can settle whatever it is with Carlos in person."

"She can't go home."

"Is she pretending to be ill again? Don't take it seriously, Aunt Juana. She's a fraud!"

"She is dead," said Juana Álvarez.

". . . Dead?"

"She took too many sleeping pills. By mistake. Unfortunately she was always careless about things like that. She died three hours ago. At five o'clock."

Five o'clock . . . five o'clock in the afternoon . . . Pilar pulled herself together. She was more exhausted than she had ever been in her entire life, except perhaps for the day eighteen years ago when Carlos Sánchez had become engaged to Teresa. My blood pressure's too low, she thought. Juana Álvarez asked irritably if Pilar was still listening, or had she fallen asleep? Didn't she want to know how Teresa had died?

"I've got to attend to everything," said Juana, a note of satisfaction in her voice. "You know Antonia. Falls apart at the least provocation. Without me this house would collapse. But I must say, when I found Teresa in her room, dying, *I* nearly collapsed. Fortunately our doctor just happened to be here, with Antonia, and he got Father Alcázar . . . I'll be the next one to go, you'll see. And what's to become of Antonia then? The way she gets on everybody's nerves..."

"Calm down, Aunt Juana!"

"What would your father have said to this tragedy? And such a senseless thing! Teresa was Juan's pride and joy. He spoiled her so. But nobody could tell your father anything. Like you."

"I'm going to hang up now. I'll be in Mérida tomorrow."

"Thank you, child. As I've always said, you're no ray of sunshine, but you can be depended on. That's more than can be said of some people."

"You mean Carlos."

"My dear Pilar, I meant in general. You're ready to jump down the throat of anyone who dares to *think* anything bad about Carlos."

"Good night."

"Just a minute, please! What about the funeral? Should ... should the body be moved to Caracas? How are we going to find Carlos? After all she's ... she *was* his wife!"

"Everything will be taken care of. I'll call Ciudad Bolívar. Salvador Paz may know where Carlos is."

"Thank God we have you, Pilar! Dreadful, when someone dies suddenly like that! Last night Teresa ate almost a whole fish all by herself! She never could control herself where food was concerned. The dear Lord bless her soul!"

"Good night."

"Wait, Pilar! I don't often take your precious time. Oh, why did this have to happen just when she was with us? People always talk when there is a sudden death."

"What do you mean?"

"Nothing." Juana Álvarez sounded embarrassed. "One should only say good things about the dead."

"Why?"

"Why? A question of tact, my dear. I regret Teresa's death to the depths of my soul, but I wasn't blind or deaf or feebleminded. There was a lot of talk about Teresa here in Mérida. She made herself rather conspicuous lately—and don't pretend you don't know what I'm talking about. You were thankful that I took Teresa off your hands so often. But she was a darling. Aside from her shopping orgies and her pathological appetites."

"Must we discuss all this now?"

"We're going to miss Teresa. She always gave us a decent amount of money for the household, although she really wasn't with us very much."

"That's the first I've heard about that."

"Well, there's a first time for everything. Teresa was simply too young to be left alone in Caracas all the time."

"When she was here she had visitors nearly every evening."

"Just the same—she was abandoned. She needed her husband, Pilar. Like every young wife. She was only thirty-one."

"She was thirty-five a few months ago."

"Really? On her good days she could look incredibly young. Unfortunately those days were becoming increasingly rare. Pilar, there's something I've got to tell you, and it's *very* unpleasant. I only hope Carlos doesn't find out."

"And what is it?"

"You know Teresa always had secrets. Well, she disappeared for weeks in the Andes and she asked me to forward her letters to Carlos from Mérida. She didn't want him to know that she was traveling around alone."

"And you agreed to that, Aunt Juana?"

"I can only be surprised that you're surprised. Carlos would have beaten Teresa half to death if he'd known that for weeks and weeks ... He's as strong as a horse, and when he beats anybody ... Teresa told me a few things. She was terrified of him!"

"He was too good to her. That was the only trouble."

"Just the same, she was terrified of him. She simply couldn't handle him."

"That may be."

"He of course lived according to his own laws." Juana Álvarez's voice was sharp. "He couldn't see that a neglected wife had to go astray. That right he concedes only to himself."

Pilar's hand was cramped around the receiver. She didn't

feel like diving headlong into the past. She asked Aunt Juana for some details about Teresa's excursions into the Andes. She suddenly had the feeling that they were talking about a stranger rather than her stepsister. Although Teresa had sometimes wrung her hands in despair in the Villa Acacia, Pilar had looked the other way. She couldn't bear the sight of those soft, fleshy hands with the pointed fingers and a short thumb, greedy for pleasure, avid and weak.

The evening wind blew restlessly, threateningly, through the trees outside, through the branches of the acacia, under whose leaves Carlos had often sought refuge from Teresa's tirades. There was a taste of ashes in Pilar's mouth. Now it was she who didn't want to end the conversation. She had to find out more about her stepsister before Carlos heard it from someone else. With unusual gentleness she begged her aunt to tell her everything.

"It is dreadful, Pilar! One tells someone the truth because one has to, and then she drops dead. On our last evening I reproached Teresa about her behavior with the American in San Cristóbal. I didn't want to spoil her appetite so I told her after dinner... And what did she do? She went into one of her rages and threw a cake plate at my feet. An heirloom from great-grandmother Álvarez. Irreplaceable! Of course I asked her to leave the room. If I had known that she would take too many sleeping pills... but who knows what one should or shouldn't say?"

"The best thing is to say nothing."

"But I couldn't remain silent any longer! The reputation of our family was at stake! Things simply couldn't go on like that! The whole hotel was talking about Teresa and the Yanqui. I don't know whether she wanted to follow him to Chicago, but during her last weeks here she was absolutely crazy and wrote him endless letters. Manuela kept having to run back and forth between Teresa and the mailbox. Teresa! Who never wrote to anybody! Except the required letters to Carlos."

Pilar was silent. What would happen when Carlos found out about this scandal? Pilar was certain Teresa would never have separated from her husband. She had always looked upon him as her possession. And no other man could possibly have treated her to the luxury that her industrial tsar, Carlos Sánchez, had been able to offer her? Teresa's soft, greedy hands . . . Pilar thought of Carlos, of his pride, his problems, his generosity wherever help was needed. What if Teresa had made her husband's name the object of ridicule? Or had fallen into the hands of a blackmailer who knew that Sánchez was enormously rich? Had Teresa, for some reason or other, not known where to turn and swallowed the overdose of sleeping pills on purpose? Who knew anything about this stranger in the Andes? Pilar asked what was the Yanqui's name?

"In all the excitement, I've forgotten it. I couldn't take the letters out of Manuela's hand, and without my glasses I don't read too well. And what difference does the name make now that Teresa . . ."

"It makes a lot of difference," Pilar said slowly. "Can't you remember? Somebody must have spoken to you about it."

"That's right. Señora de Villegas. She was living in San Cristóbal at the time and saw everything. I can ask her."

"No! Please don't!" Pilar said quickly. "We mustn't mention this to anybody!"

"No. You're right. You'd think the Yanqui would have answered Teresa's letters just once, wouldn't you? She watched for every mail delivery like a hawk . . . in vain. The gentleman chose to remain silent. Like all men when women become difficult. Of course Teresa was utterly uncontrolled. But she was truly beautiful, although she got fatter all the time."

"What does that matter?"

"That's where you're wrong, my dear Pilar. Men don't care about anything else! Why was Carlos so crazy about that girl from Berlin two years ago? Because of her blond hair? No wonder Teresa had temper tantrums. She knew all about it."

"She knew nothing," said Pilar.

"I've never trusted Carlos Sánchez. You know that, Pilar.

He's so inscrutable. And he would never let anything stop him. Forgive me, I don't want to . . ."

"I've got to hang up now and you've got to calm down. I'll be with you tomorrow. And I'll pay for the call."

"Thank you very much, my dear. Now at last Carlos will realize what our Teresa meant to him . . ."

Let's hope not! thought Pilar Álvarez.

She sat down on the terrace with its view of the woods and thought of Teresa. The household triangle had never been idyllic. One of the women was always an outsider. Pilar had assigned the role to Teresa, and Teresa to Pilar. But Pilar had inherited her father's thick skin—as well as the partnership in the firm of Álvarez Sánchez—and she was hardly one to give up her rights. She was an excellent partner for Carlos Sánchez, and every now and then he told her so. Unfortunately she was not very outgoing, and in the office Sánchez had to smile for them both. But he wasn't the friendliest person either, and he relaxed at home by being obstinately silent. Teresa took this as a personal insult.

"So say something, for God's sake!" she screamed at them. Their silence frightened her, and during the last years she had fled to Mérida more and more often. There she had created a little cosmos that revolved around her alone.

Pilar sighed. Now Teresa was dead. For years she had wished Teresa nothing good. Not death, but something or somebody that would remove her from the Villa Acacia. And that was just what the Yanqui in the Andes had turned out to be. It would be like Teresa to disgrace herself and her husband openly. Still, had she really done so? The only tangibles in the whole business were her letters to the Yanqui and his silence. Had Teresa sent a cry—no, a scream—with no echo out into the mountains?

Pilar called Ciudad Bolívar. Salvador Paz, one of Carlos's oldest friends answered. He sounded sleepy, and Pilar gave him the news bit by bit. Salvador always liked things in small portions—good fortune, bad fortune, news.

"But that's unbelievable! Why didn't you tell me Teresa

was ill? Carlos has no idea either! We are totally unprepared..."

"She wasn't ill, Salvador."

"But one doesn't die when one's healthy!" Paz sounded impatient.

"Teresa took an overdose of sleeping pills. That's all."

"How stupid of her! Well, Teresa was careless. I suppose she thought the pills were candy."

"Anything is possible," said Pilar.

"Please let me know when the funeral is. I'll come to Caracas, of course. Fortunately Carlos is still here. He wanted to take a look at his house on the Orinoco again. I'll try to reach him right away. He's at a party. Americans. Where did Teresa die?"

"In Mérida. At our aunts' house. Juana and Antonia Álvarez."

"Wasn't she sweet, our little Teresa? I remember those old aunts. Carlos calls Juana 'the Fury' and Antonia 'the Goat.'" Paz coughed, embarrassed. "You know his little jokes."

"I know."

"Carlos will be inconsolable," said Paz, in an appropriately grave tone. "He worshiped Teresa. Dreadful, how quickly one can die! Mostly one has a thousand plans before it happens. Senseless to make plans, don't you think?"

"I don't know, Salvador. After all, one's got to have something planned. One never knows how long one's going to live."

"Never long enough, my dear. One clings to life quite without reason, but one does cling to it. Are you going to be very lonely without Teresa? She was so fond of you. When she was a child, she followed you everywhere."

"I know."

"Lately I haven't been feeling too well myself, Pilar. This news has just finished me. I know I'm going to have a sleepless night. Teresa's death is a warning to all of us."

"In what way?"

"I mean in as far as our medication is concerned. One can't be careful enough. Unfortunately I suffer from insomnia. At night the malaise of our world creates such a turmoil in my mind."

"I'm sorry I had to disturb you so late, but..."

"Don't be silly, Pilar! Carlos is one of my oldest friends. I don't know how I'm going to break the news to him, but it's got to be done."

"Yes."

"Lucky for you, Pilar, that you have such a robust constitution. I know you'll look after everything and keep visitors away. Practically everybody gets on his nerves. My wife has spent half the day turning down invitations for him. But just tonight he accepted one."

"It's always like that, Salvador. Teresa only died at five o'clock this afternoon, and of course I was told at once."

"When Teresa was at home," Salvador Paz said gloomily, "she gave the best parties in Caracas. Do you remember her big garden party two years ago when that young lady from Berlin suddenly put in an appearance?"

"Yes. I remember."

"As far as I know, nobody had invited her. Teresa behaved admirably. By the way..." Señor Paz coughed again, "I'll be flying to Caracas alone. The doctor has forbidden my wife to go to funerals. Maria will pray for the soul of our dear departed one at home."

"Of course, Salvador. Give Maria my best regards."

"Thank you, my dear. I'll tell her tomorrow. And once more—be careful with pills, do you hear?"

"I don't need any. Good night."

Pilar was still holding the receiver in her hand, although the conversation was over. She had a premonition of danger. Once Salvador Paz had called her "the chatelaine." If she hadn't been caretaker of this house, or hadn't been able to, now she certainly had to protect it!

A car drove through the large entrance gate and halted abruptly in front of the terrace where Teresa used to receive her guests. A young girl began to walk slowly up the steps. It was Carlos's private secretary, Rosa Martínez, Pilar had detested her ever since Rosa had decided that she was Carlos's "right hand." She treated Señorita Martínez coldly, almost rudely, although the woman's only crime was that she was the best secretary Carlos had ever had. "What do you want so late?" Pilar asked. "Where have you come from?" She didn't ask Rosa to come up but addressed her from the dark terrace.

"I've come from Mérida. Señor Sánchez sent me there."

"To Mérida? What were you supposed to do there?"

"Señor Sánchez asked me to attend to some private business for him," Rosa Martínez said haughtily. "I have something important to tell you, señorita, and I think it will be in your interest to listen to it. May I come up?"

There was a humming in Pilar's ears. Since when did Carlos give his secretary private business to attend to? And in Mérida of all places! How much did she know, or was she perhaps just making herself important? Carlos couldn't possibly intend to push his chatelaine to one side in favor of this upstart.

Pilar felt she knew Carlos better than anyone else in the world. Or did she? But she had imagined for years that she knew all about Teresa.

The secretary made herself comfortable in her boss's big wicker armchair. It had been constructed to accommodate his long legs, so Rosa's dangled above the ground, but that didn't seem to bother her. She tried to appear at home in the Villa Acacia, though actually this was her first visit.

She had had to travel a long way—from the hill slums of Caracas—to be in a position to have this confidential conversation with Pilar Álvarez. Kitchen maid in a tortilla shack, chambermaid in a harbor bordello, beat up by her pimp, bar girl in a place called Palm Forest, in the same port city where Carlos Sánchez had discovered her and had her educated to be a secretary. He had noticed her intelligence, and her past was a guarantee for eternal gratitude. She passed her business-school examination with honors and hid her maltreated ego carefully from all eyes, and, whenever possible, from herself. Her jobs hadn't lasted long, a few weeks or months, but she had been working for Sánchez for two years now and would have gone through fire and water for him.

Rosa Martínez had inherited her intelligence from her Portuguese father and her wide mouth from her mulatto mother, but her doggedness and passion for money were her own. So was her deadly fear of having to return to the hovels on the hillside one day, a fear not shared by the other members of her family. They, especially Maria, all felt fine up there. On the hill there were maize cakes, dirt, beatings, lethargy, and a cozy lightheartedness. Sánchez's secretary was through with all that.

She stared wide-eyed at Pilar and handed the señorita a letter. Rosa didn't want power over her boss's formidable sister-in-law, nor did she want to flaunt her position with him. All she wanted was what she always wanted—a lot of bolivars.

Pilar read the letter, her back turned on the deliverer. It was from Teresa and was addressed to a man whose first name was Elliot. The letter had been written in the Andes, and was not on Teresa's notepaper with the engraved letterhead. Moreover, it was signed Teresa Álvarez. The name Sánchez was not mentioned. Teresa had evidently been slyer than Pilar had given her credit for—slyer and wilder.

Pilar read the letter twice, astonished at Teresa's shamelessness. At last she turned around. She had drawn her black mantilla tighter around her shoulders, but her face was expressionless, except for a slight twitch at the corners of her mouth. "What were you doing in Mérida?" she asked coldly.

Rosa Martínez looked up, surprised and innocent, and replied that she had been in Mérida to see the Sierra Nevada. And to pay a few calls. Pilar's lips tightened. Didn't Rosa know that Teresa was dead? How had she come into possession of the letter?

"Mérida is beautiful," Rosa said dreamily, switching her chewing gum from one side of her mouth to the other. "I saw the university, Señorita. I might have studied there if my father had been luckier in this country. He was a slow European, not suited for the rat race of Caracas." Pilar was silent. "I was only twelve years old when he died. I have my intelligence from him."

"Where did you get this letter?" Pilar's tone was threatening. She had had just about enough of Rosa's prattle. Involuntarily Rosa shrank from Pilar Álvarez like a fearful, beaten child of the hill slums. She ducked from beatings as her mother had ducked from her father. Her forehead was beaded with sweat and her linen dress stuck to her body. But she murmured that the letter wasn't going to please her boss.

"This letter is a forgery," said Pilar. "You may go."

Rosa stared at Pilar, speechless. Her glittering black eyes lost their glow, a deep frown became visible under her Hollywood makeup. Her supple body with its full breasts suddenly was at odds with her bitter mouth and hollow cheeks. Her face bore the stamp of the earlier years of starvation. At that moment Rosa Martínez again became the daughter of an uprooted sardine fisherman and a merry, slovenly mulatto.

Pilar noticed the change and for a moment felt sorry for the girl. But then she saw the secret triumph in Rosa's sly eyes. Rosa sensed that Pilar was determined to have this letter and was bluffing, otherwise she would have had the blackmailer thrown out.

Señorita Álvarez was still holding the letter in her hand and still hadn't asked for the price. It made Rosa nervous. The letter was no forgery. It had been written a few days ago by Teresa Sánchez, who went by the name of Álvarez when she was traveling. Rosa had got hold of it quite by chance. Sometimes chance was the benefactor of the poor. But how could a lady write to a strange man like that, a lady who had everything a woman could possibly wish for: jewels, a magnificent house in a beautiful park, a husband like Señor Sánchez, and—the most important thing of all—this lady could eat as much as she liked! She had never walked through narrow, stinking alleyways in washed-out cotton rags. She had never worn sandals full of holes or been bitten by vermin. Had she ever housed with a lot of people in a dilapidated hut, or nearly suffocated when the sun beat down on its tin roof?

And now Rosa Martínez, who had experienced all this, was holding the peace and honor of Teresa's house in her hands.

"The letter is *not* a forgery," she said.

"How much?" Pilar showed no sign of how Teresa's letter had shocked her, but she didn't have the presence of mind simply to tear it up.

Rosa looked at Pilar. Then she mentioned a big sum and was annoyed that her voice trembled. Her thoughts raced feverishly through her tired brain. Perhaps she was doing the stupidest thing of her entire life. What if Pilar tore up the letter or told Sánchez about her visit? Rosa would stand before him as a shameless liar. Sánchez would never believe that she had actually held such a letter from his wife in her hands. She could hear the señorita saying that it was a clumsy forgery. Sánchez would fire her and send her back to the hovels on the hill. Without a reference she would never find another job in Caracas in spite of her proficiency and diligence; she would be branded a liar, a blackmailer. The rare praise of her boss and the basket of fruit with the shiny satin bow on her birthday were all Rosa had lived for during these last two years. The satin bows lay wrapped in tissue paper in her trunk, in the clean, furnished room that her boss paid for. He paid for her little car too. Suddenly Rosa was hungry for unattainable treasures: a small house with a patio and a funny parrot whom she would gently silence for the night by covering his cage. And she would become a respectable, settled person, the chatelaine of her castle-in-the-air.

"How much?"

Rosa shrank. Pilar was looking at her so strangely. She had just given the price. She couldn't utter another word; all she could see were the hovels on the hill, her slovenly, jolly mother. As a child she had always seen her with a swollen stomach. And beside her mother stood her father with his dark, straggly mustache, and his hollowed-out, careworn face. The missing teeth, the superfluous toothpick . . . He didn't live to see his fifteen-year-old son steal a bicycle (Rosa was twelve) nor did he hear Enrico laugh aloud as he repaired it. A good thing his father hadn't been there to thrash him. Mama and Rosa were afraid of Enrico. Once he had thrown sacks across a deep hole behind the hut. Rosa had fallen into it and broken a leg. When she was tired, she limped a little. Enrico was wild and liked to torture people. "If he had had everything, he wouldn't have had to steal," she said.

"Whom are you talking about, Rosa?"

"Nobody."

"Are you crazy or drunk?"

Rosa rubbed her wet forehead with her forefinger as she always did when she was unsure. She sighed. Whenever she tried to throw stones up to heaven they fell down on her head. Pilar said that she would go and get the money, but Rosa got up and held her back by her mantilla. "I don't want any money!" she cried. "The letter is a forgery!"

"That's what I thought," said Pilar, although she hadn't thought anything of the sort. "Please don't tear my mantilla. Sit down again." Pilar handed Rosa a glass of lemonade and casually asked her why she had changed her mind about the money.

"Because I don't want it." With a wild motion Rosa snatched the letter out of Pilar's hand, tore it up, and threw the scraps into the garden. Pilar told her that the garden wasn't a wastepaper basket. Rosa didn't move. The evening wind swept the pieces away. The rain would look after the rest.

"Blackmailers must have strong nerves," Pilar said amiably. "You don't. You should steer clear of anything like that."

Rosa's instinct told her that Señorita Álvarez hadn't believed the letter to be a forgery for a moment, but nonetheless, would never have handed over any money for it. No one could invent a letter like that. Even she would have been ashamed. "Señor Sánchez must never find out about it. Swear to it!" she said.

"I swear only in a courtroom. But there is nothing to tell him. By the way, what did you really want in Mérida?"

"Round bricks for Señor Sánchez's new house. And some private business. He has a lot of secrets. He is planning . . ."

"So for heaven's sake, *talk!*"

"I've forgotten. Good night, señorita."

At that moment the defeated woman seemed stronger than the unassailable one on the terrace. Rosa Martínez laughed, for no particular reason then she pressed her lips together so that no further sound might escape them, and crept off to her little car.

Watching her go, Pilar had to think of a snail who had dared to crawl out of her house only to dive quickly back into it. Rosa posed no threat but she possessed dangerous information. What had Rosa been up to in Mérida "on private business," and how had she got hold of Teresa's letter? Pilar looked around as if someone on the terrace were reading her thoughts and was suddenly disoriented. She saw things double—the moon, the lemonade jug—and she saw Carlos with a Janus head. Was she suffering from optical illusions? Nonsense! Carlos had only one head, but possibly a double persona. Only I am always the same, she thought grimly. Carlos must find her rather monotonous. Yet he was devoted to her and looked upon her as the rock of his existence. He had told her so once. She would do her best to secure his peace in the future. His life was restless enough. Not only his life—the whole world was restless and confused. There was no certainty, especially not for Carlos Sánchez. She would continue to try to protect the Villa Acacia from intruders, even though she had little hope of succeeding. Were faithfulness and reliability already ridiculously atavistic in these times?

Pilar stared out into the garden. She wondered how many letters Teresa had written to this unknown Yanqui and who beside Rosa Martínez had read them. Would anyone else come, wanting to sell Teresa's letters? To her, or to Sánchez, or to one of his enemies? She stifled a groan. Today's been just too much, she thought. I'll take one of Teresa's sleeping pills.

The ringing of the telephone brought her back into the house. It was Carlos Sánchez in Ciudad Bolívar.

# 2

# Memento Mori

Carlos Sánchez stood on his terrace, greeting those who had come to condole with him. He listened politely yet seemed absorbed by his own thoughts.

He is an obelisk, thought his friend Salvador Paz, with thoughts like hieroglyphs. Paz was a sculptor. He worked in stone, bronze, and tin. He worked for big corporations. Sánchez had placed several of Salvador's very modern sculptures in the lobbies of his offices in Caracas and Puerto Cabello.

Pilar stood beside Sánchez, afraid that at any moment he might disappear in the surrounding woods. She was always afraid that one day he might disappear altogether.

He had come back to Caracas as quickly as possible and had not yet spoken to anyone privately. Pilar looked at his motionless face. Teresa's death had already changed the atmosphere in the Villa Acacia. Sánchez was suddenly an inaccessible stranger. Pilar wondered if she had ever really been his confidante. Now he seemed to regard her merely as a business partner. It was as if Teresa's shadow stood between them.

Carlos gave her an enigmatic look, then greeted Señor and Señora de Villegas, who had come from Mérida with Pilar's aunts. They were the oldest friends of the Álvarez family. Señora de Villegas was robust, virtuous, and nearsighted,

16

and she was squinting because she wanted to see Sánchez clearly. Juana hadn't told her how handsome he was.

Ramón de Villegas was a business colleague who went fishing with Sánchez and had great respect for him. The feeling was mutual. Villegas was the director of an important banking house and a hard, tough worker like his Andean peasant forefathers. He was short, stocky, and feared. Nobody had ever seen him laugh. Now, he stood beside his wife and her friend, Juana Álvarez, and listened disapprovingly to their conversation. "This is *not* the place for gossip," he told his wife. "This is a house of mourning. Sánchez is exhausted, and no wonder. Teresa was a beauty."

"How did you happen to know her?" Señora de Villegas sounded threatening.

"I met her somewhere or other. What does it matter? She was a real woman—gentle and patient."

Juana Álvarez was speechless. Señora de Villegas said, "Unfortunately she got very fat. In San Cristóbal I thought she looked absolutely bloated. Don't step on my foot, Ramón!"

Señor de Villegas turned to talk to a banker from Caracas. Who cared about the body weight of a corpse? Teresa Sánchez had been a charmer, and anyway he liked soft, round figures. His wife was all muscle and frigidity. As he conversed with his colleague he thought, without self-pity, how little pleasure there was in his life. His only delight was fishing in the crystal clear lakes of the Andes. Sometimes, in the middle of the night, with his wife snoring beside him, he planned desperate flights to the Sierra Nevada, and in the morning, over his paper and the celebrated Mérida coffee, he would smile. All he ever embraced was the air. Secretly he envied Sánchez for his experience with Teresa.

Sánchez was astounded over how many people there were who wanted to shake his hand. The parade of wealthy Venezuelans seemed endless. Most of them had come to receive sympathy, not to give it. Teresa's death had touched them like a breath of decay, and their only consolation in gathering at the Villa Acacia was to convince themselves that most of

them were still alive. Death didn't differentiate between young
and old. That also consoled many middle-aged people. Proudly
they watched the aged, sharp-tongued Señora González in
her wheelchair. As long as she held out, they too could hang
on to the illusion of immortality.

The old and very influential woman took both Sánchez's
hands in hers. "My dear Carlos, what is there to say?"

Sánchez leaned over the old lady. "There is nothing to say,
my dear. I am grateful that you came. How are you?"

"Unfortunately I can't die."

"And you mustn't die. All of us would miss you terribly."

"Wasn't his grandfather Emilio Domingo Sánchez, the
freedom fighter from Margarita?" asked her grandniece, as she
wheeled Señora González past the reception line.

"I'm glad to see you know our history. I shan't disinherit
you after all!"

Sánchez almost smiled at the girl. She was really quite
pretty, but too green. In the next moment he had forgotten
her. He became aware of a strange noise in the garden—a
high-pitched, tremulous, hysterical sound. Teresa's laughter!
Perhaps she was laughing at him behind the bushes. That was
how she had laughed two years ago when he had offered his
hospitality to the girl from Berlin, an absolute stranger. It
had been late in the evening and Carla Moll hadn't found a
place to stay in Caracas. On the following day Teresa had
already forgotten her. Or pretended to. Sánchez frowned. The
laughter was silenced. Perhaps nobody had laughed. Sánchez
fought down anger and nausea as he always did whenever he
recalled the journalist, Carla Moll. How could he possibly
have been taken in by her? He wasn't a novice. The devil
take her!

But the devil hadn't done Carlos Sánchez the favor. Carla
Moll was in Venezuela again. The newspapers reported that
she was somewhere in the Orinoco area. Carla Moll! Once
she had seemed his ideal, now she was an embarrassing
memory. At least that was the way Sánchez saw it today, and
he liked to shake off the dead weight of past experiences. A
man couldn't go on living otherwise. Sánchez needed quiet,

clarity, and again and again the liberation from himself and the past. Women didn't seem to need things like that. They burrowed like moles into the earth of their memories. Teresa and all her friends had been like that. Pilar had had no experience with men. *Memento mori!*

Bankers. Oil magnates. Statesmen. Members of the Chamber of Commerce. Entrepreneurs. Artists. His staff, with the exception of Rosa Martínez, who had a sore throat. Señor Obon (aluminum magnate and co-owner of a paper factory) was talking about industrial methods with a North American guest, Mr. Myers, who found the industrialists in Latin America patriarchal, eccentric, and in any case, mistrustful of the Yanquis whose methods were so different. Mr. Myers manufactured pseudo-Victorian furniture in Montgomery, Alabama. "Do you find us very slow over here, Mr. Myers?" asked Señor Obon.

"A little slower than in the States, señor. A friend of mine, a management consultant, has some very interesting opinions on the subject. He is just now traveling through Venezuela. A member of a very important firm in the United States."

"I'd like to meet him. I have a paper factory in Caracas. What's his name?"

"Cooper. E. J. Cooper of Smith & Stone, Chicago. He looks as if he couldn't count to three, but he can twist bank directors and corporate managers around his little finger."

"Where can I reach him, Mr. Myers?"

"He's on vacation in the Andes. I just got a card from him from the Hotel Táchira. Crazy about fishing in his spare time. If I'm not mistaken, he met our unfortunate little lady there."

"Whom do you mean?"

"Mrs. Sánchez. What a tragedy, isn't it?"

"Yes. It certainly is," said Señor Obon. "May I ask what business you are in, Mr. Myers?"

"Decorator furniture. But I'm not in Caracas on business. My daughter is getting married here. Lemonade factory. A nice little business. Yes . . . I've heard that Carlos Sánchez is very progressive. He's been to the States often. A great man. A little too serious for my taste . . ."

"Well, after all, his wife just died, Mr. Myers."

*Memento mori!*

"You must distract yourself, Carlos," said Salvador Paz. "It *is* a tragedy, but Teresa..."

"I wasn't thinking of Teresa."

"You can't turn your back on the world, my friend." Of course Carlos was thinking of Teresa. Constantly. Otherwise why did he look so grim?

Sánchez looked at his friend, astonished. Turn his back on the world? Had Salvador drunk too much of Teresa's fruit punch? "I'm only turning my back on the illusions of this world, Salvador. And the sooner I've done that, the better." Sánchez patted his old friend on the shoulder.

"When are you coming to Ciudad Bolívar again?"

"Very soon, Salvador. The new buildings, the engineers..."

"Work is the best medicine, Carlos."

"You think so?" Sánchez shrugged. He hated all such well-meant phrases. If Salvador knew... but the sculptor couldn't know. He was happily married.

Pilar was beginning to nod to all questions and statements like an automaton. "Where is Consuelo Márquez, Pilar? I only see her parents."

"She isn't here."

"That's strange. She was Teresa's best friend, wasn't she?"

"Maybe it's strange. I wouldn't know."

"Poor Pilar. You're going to be very lonely without Teresa. Please come and see us often."

Pilar nodded. The last thing she'd do would be visit Teresa's friends. They had nothing in common. Not even Teresa. Why hadn't Carlos said a word to her? Her feeling of insecurity grew as the twilight deepened. The perfume from the gleaming bushes and flower beds Teresa had loved aggravated it. She was all alone. The thought filled Pilar with a sense of desperate satisfaction. She had never possessed Carlos; in this respect nothing had changed. She was still stretching her arms out for fruit that eluded her grasp. Sánchez was becoming more inaccessible from minute to minute. It was Teresa's night.

Sánchez suddenly found himself alone with Juana Álvarez in the empty reception room. In the garden the lights were being put out. So far Juana hadn't said a word. She felt uncomfortable with Carlos, although he had obviously made a point of being pleasant all day. She studied his bold features, but could see no sign of emotion in them. Perhaps he mourned for Teresa when no one was watching. Was he reproaching himself for having neglected her? Was he lonely without her after all? Perhaps he missed her as one misses the coffee pot that always stands in a certain place and which suddenly, one day, is missing. She shivered. Sánchez was standing beside her, silent and far away. Juana groped for words. He gave her no help. "I am devastated, Carlos. A tragic loss for all of us," she said hesitantly. It sounded as if somebody else had said it. She excused Antonia's absence. "She needs rest. You know, dear Carlos, what nerves can do to you."

"I don't have any." Sánchez was icily silent again. Juana wondered how often Teresa had had to capitulate to this silence. Juana didn't know that it was not Sánchez's intention to be unfriendly to her; he just had exhausted his ability to be sociable.

A Cadillac blew its horn at the entrance gate. The strident noise irritated Sánchez even more. "We grow increasingly numb," he said aloud. "I mean, we feel nothing deeply enough to be able to learn from what we experience."

"Nobody could mourn for Teresa more deeply than my sister and I," Juana said stiffly. "If you happen to be without feeling, you shouldn't draw the same conclusion for others."

The fury, Sánchez thought, amused. He replied that he probably didn't know what he was saying in his pain. "If I may give you some advice, Juana—don't listen to me."

"I don't think this is the right time for ironic comments. Please don't contradict me, Carlos. You were always a cynic. I regret that I have to tell you so today."

"I do too. Please be careful. One word leads to another. But I am for peace. What can I do to placate you?"

"Antonia and I have done our best to create a relationship between us. A picture of Emilio Domingo Sánchez hangs in our living room. But you never visit us. And after all, we are Teresa's closest relatives."

"It is all my fault. I beg to be forgiven. But you mustn't think that I have no family feeling. After all, I am a Venezuelan." He smiled, and she tried hard not to smile back. She had never understood what women saw in Carlos and why they put up with how he treated them. But when he smiled...

"Please visit us in Mérida if you ever have the time," she said, appeased. "You will always be welcome."

"Thank you, Juana. I wanted to express my gratitude to you anyway."

"For what?"

"For all the trouble you took with Teresa."

"Don't mention it. I was glad to."

"I'm sure of that. Still, you could have spared yourself a lot of trouble."

"We loved the poor girl."

"Let me finish... Thank you. I am referring to Teresa's letters to me."

"Teresa's... letters... to you?"

"Yes. Of course. Teresa had the very natural wish to keep me informed as to how she was feeling. And what she forgot to tell me, I could read between the lines. My wife was easy to read. She lived for the moment. Like a child... a trapeze artist."

Juana tried to control her trembling. Now her heart was actually beating as fast as she sometimes declared it did. Sánchez spoke softly, in an almost flattering tone, like an adroit investigator who destroys his victim piecemeal.

"A trapeze artist?" said Juana. "Really, Carlos—Teresa was much too fat to..."

Sánchez's probing eyes checked her. "You mustn't take me so literally, my dear. I mean Teresa didn't see the abyss under her wire. When I couldn't keep an eye on her, she did stupid things."

"You should have kept an eye on her! It was your duty!"

"The world would be a monotonous Garden of Eden if all of us did our duty, don't you agree? Little sins are a lot more fun than the practices of duty. Not that I was amused when Teresa sought a change. I worked so that she could amuse herself."

"It sounds touching, I must say."

"It is touching. Tell me—why did you send Teresa's letters to me from Mérida when she was in the Hotel Táchira? Why this circumlocution?"

"I don't know what you're talking about, Carlos!"

"You mean you want me to put it more clearly?"

"I mean that this is a senseless conversation. I would like to go to bed now."

"Just a moment, Juana. I have one more question. Why in the world should I object to my wife staying at the Hotel Táchira? It's a first-class hotel, in beautiful surroundings."

"I was never there."

"Teresa should have taken you with her once. Too bad. But why this secrecy toward me? Did you think I begrudged my wife such a stay?"

"I didn't think anything. The whole world knows that you were a model husband."

"I did my best," Sánchez said modestly. "But perhaps it wasn't enough for Teresa."

"I can't be a judge of that."

"Stop it, Juana. It may come as a surprise to you, but I don't like to be made a fool of. And as far as I know, until now nobody has been able to do so. How could you imagine that you and Teresa could succeed?"

"Your wife asked me to forward the letters, and that's all I have to say about it. You know better than anyone else how Teresa behaved when she was refused anything. She raved!"

"You don't say. As far as I know she acquiesced fairly quickly when faced with the inevitable."

"Not with us in Mérida. Believe me, Carlos, I forwarded Teresa's letters to you reluctantly."

"Why did you encourage my wife in such ridiculous and simpleminded maneuvers? I want an explanation!"

"And I refuse to be spoken to like this! If you can't respect the dead, then at least have some respect for my white hair!"

"If I didn't respect your white hair, my dear, I would express myself much more drastically. Do you smoke? No? Perhaps a glass of Teresa's fruit punch?"

"You don't have to trouble yourself further as far as I am concerned."

"As you wish. I was only speaking in your interest when I said that you took a lot of trouble and spent a lot of money unnecessarily. The number of photos Teresa sent in every letter . . . the post office must have grown rich!"

Juana made a face as if she wanted to sneeze but couldn't. She tried hard but in vain to find justification for her behavior. What sort of an impression was she making on this fox? "Please, Carlos, let me explain . . ."

"That isn't necessary, dear Juana. If it made our poor Teresa happy to keep you busy forwarding her mail—all right."

Juana Álvarez looked at her hands. Once they had been beautiful. Now the knuckles stuck out like little blue hillocks. Gout. I am too old for such discussions, she thought, exhausted. Nobody can get the best of him. Poor Teresa . . . Juana really had not liked to forward the letters, but now, in spite of the fact that she felt conscience-stricken, she was filled with an almost righteous anger. Sánchez had made a fool of her! "I've had enough," she said brusquely. "Why didn't you give your wife a piece of your mind since you knew all about it?"

"All about what? Now I don't know what you're talking about!"

"I have no intention of saying anything more. But I am happy for Teresa that you can no longer torment her. Whoever gets to know you better, Carlos, can understand that the poor thing sought consolation . . ." She coughed, horrified. The eyes of her Grand Inquisitor had evidently robbed her of the little sense she had left!

"Please go on talking, Juana. I am finding out something new all the time, and it is all very interesting. So our dear Teresa sought consolation with another man. I wouldn't have given her credit for so much initiative. Who was this fortunate one?"

Juana wanted to leave the room, but Sánchez held her back by her arm. "Let go of me! At once!" she gasped.

"You must calm down, Juana, and I must go back to my guests. Drink this. It will refresh you." He handed her a glass of pineapple juice. "Now you'll feel better. And now I may ask one more small question? How did you ever get the idea that I am one of those husbands who is the last to find out what half the city knows?"

Juana was utterly confused. This is the way one starts to go crazy, she thought. Soon she would be stammering or weeping nervously like Antonia. That would be the end—to exhibit weakness in front of this man! She, who looked upon the weak with a compassion that only masked her scorn.

"Are you all right, Juana? Do you want me to call Pilar?"

"Nonsense! I ate too much, that's all."

"The black beans," Sánchez said thoughtfully. "They do lie heavy in one's stomach."

You lie heavy in my stomach, thought Juana Álvarez. Sadist!

"We should really get to know each other better," Sánchez said thoughtfully. "Thank you again for the invitation to Mérida. We can talk more about Teresa there, undisturbed."

Juana said nothing.

"Teresa will be with us in spirit, I hope. She still has a lot of things to confess to me."

"Have you gone crazy, Carlos?"

Sánchez laughed. Juana wasn't so bad. He had a certain weakness for Furies. They at least defended themselves. "So, good-bye until Mérida," he said cheerfully. "It was Teresa's headquarters during the last two years anyway."

"The dead are silent."

"The dead speak, dear Juana. And what is even more amazing, they force you to listen to them. They have no consideration for the fact that we need more peace in life than in the grave."

He drove Teresa to it, thought Juana. But she didn't know whether he had driven her to adultery or death. She was too exhausted to think. She went to her bedroom and looked at her peacefully snoring sister, whom she had spared everything again. Who really knew Sánchez? In her mind's eye she saw him with Señora González—sincerely kind and affectionate. Whomever he loved was well off with him. Whom he hated ... Had he hated Teresa because she had hurt his pride, or had she merely become unbearable? Juana didn't know and didn't want to know. Her instincts told her that Teresa had not taken the fatal dose of pills by mistake. She had known what she was doing. But why poor Teresa had taken this mortal sin upon herself would remain a secret. Juana Álvarez hoped Sánchez would never find out.

She went to the bathroom and took a sleeping pill, something she never did.

# 3

## Teresa's Redux

Although Teresa had still been a young woman during the last years of her life, Sánchez had known exactly how she would age. He had already noticed at certain times and under certain circumstances a subtle rigor mortis of the emotions. Teresa's hectic chatter at social events had misled everyone but him. In long marriages, the masks fall away.

For several weeks now he had been staying on Margarita Island in his grandfather's house. The quiet life did him good; still he could not find peace. He thought often and intensively of Teresa, to whom he had paid practically no attention during the last years. Now he couldn't understand why she haunted him. During the day he scarcely thought of her. He fished, sunbathed beside the lagoon, and chatted occasionally with his friends, the pearl fishers. These old men still saw him as 'young Señor Carlos,' and secretly it pleased him. That was during the day. But when the sun sank into the sea and the precipitous rocks rose up into the evening sky, then Teresa appeared and accused him of being hard, indifferent, unfaithful, and having no desire to comfort her. Women needed comfort. It was more effective than sleeping pills.

Whenever Teresa crossed the threshold of his consciousness, she disturbed the tranquility of the island. Sooner or later he would have to rid himself of her. Teresa had always been powerless when she had faced him in person, but every night this vexing phantom appeared. *Leave me in peace, Teresa!* Don't keep dragging me into the chaos of your death! And don't bring the empty baby carriage with you next time. You lost my son out of pure negligence before he was born ... as you lost everything: your youth, your husband, your life.

You never wanted to live on the island. You found the shadow of my grandfather too powerful and the house too primitive. You needed the mundane things: night clubs, neon lights. I forgave you your poor taste because you were beautiful and young; you were like springtime.

Poor Teresa! You were stubbornly determined to remain eighteen years old. You were riddled with vanity; it ate you up as moths eat beautiful clothes. There is no escape from old age, and we must accept growing older, which is more difficult when one still feels young. But for you facts were only handicaps or irritants. Before you took too many sleeping pills, you still wanted to be a butterfly. Poor Teresa! You had become an overweight butterfly long ago, but you chose to ignore this too.

When we got married, you were seventeen. I was enchanted. I was fifteen years older than you, but my experiences had made me fifty years older, especially after that one year in Berlin. Did you know that it was really my intention to marry Pilar? Then you turned up in Caracas and I saw nothing else. Your fiery yet innocent eyes flattered me. At the age of thirty-two a man is susceptible to things like that. And I didn't know that above everything else you wanted to take your stepsister Pilar's man away. Later I realized that you begrudged every woman her man. Pilar would have been better suited to me. In those days she still had it in her to be a companion for life. She was twenty-five and would have given me the son I wanted.

On your thirtieth birthday you cried. I didn't console you. I tried to console myself because you saw your duties as a wife as a burden. From then on you persecuted me with your hysterical jealousy. Not because you suddenly loved me or wanted to sleep with me. You raved because no other woman was to have me. I was your possession, although we had had separate bedrooms for some time already—at your wish! In the morning you were always ill-humored; your eyes were swollen, your appetite was barbaric. Nobody could do anything right for you because you couldn't do anything right for yourself. I read the paper while we breakfasted, Pilar looked at the mail. Nobody spoke. Then Pilar and I drove to the office.

You were in good spirits only when you could give a party. Then you made yourself beautiful and were radiant. Pilar and I scarcely recognized you. Once, when you had drunk too much of your fruit punch, you came to my room in the night. You had on a robe I detested. The color of running blood. Your face was shiny with cream or sweat, and you stank of cigarette ash. You were already chain smoking, and it befogged the little understanding you had. I pretended to be asleep. A week later I took the young girl from Berlin to Margarita Island with me. Carla Moll smelled of youth and freshness, and she had a mind. She could think. For a few weeks I was a happy, grateful man. The idyll dissolved like a shallow puddle.

You were afraid of the dark, Teresa. Wherever you were, the lights had to be on, and you needed to hear voices. At night you had the record player on in your room, and you sat hunched, your mind a blank, under the lighted lamps. You were terribly afraid of being snuffed out, alone in the dark. Poor Teresa! Dying is a lonely and silent business, and no electric light illumines the way into that darkness. We leave the world just as alone as we entered it. What is worse, so many people seem to be dead long before their light goes out. Your flowers and your hummingbirds will mourn your going; your relatives and friends will only pretend to do so.

I don't think for a moment that you took an overdose of sleeping pills by accident. Don't try to tell me that my letter from Ciudad Bolívar was responsible for your death. Of course I knew that you had been living in San Cristóbal for weeks instead of looking after your aunts. An acquaintance told me about it, quite by chance, the way things like that happen.

Naturally I then had you watched. I gave that repulsive order not out of jealousy but because I had to save my reputation. And besides, I didn't like to be ridiculed. But I asked you, very politely, to return to Caracas immediately, because I wanted to talk to you. I didn't threaten you—that would never have occurred to me. I admit I didn't write: come home, all is forgiven. I can at best forget bad things, but never forgive. God knows, I wrote a temperate letter. I didn't want to frighten you because *I* would have had to pay for that. So why did you do it, Teresa?

You are silent. You smile in your shroud. I shall find out the truth and I know where: in Mérida.

# 4

# Sánchez in Mérida

After her stay in the Villa Acacia, Juana Álvarez was afraid Sánchez would drink coffee with her in Mérida until the dead began to speak. She needn't have worried—Sánchez never did what one expected of him.

Juana read in the paper that he was staying at a quiet, colonial-style hotel in the city of Mérida. The firm of Álvarez & Sánchez intended to modernize this hotel without destroying its historic, old Spanish atmosphere. There was no reason why Sánchez shouldn't acquire a hotel in the Andes, since Teresa's presence in this area could no longer disturb him. Now he was negotiating under the tiled roofs of this honorable university city which his secretary, Rosa Martínez, had recently inspected for him.

Juana waited in vain for Sánchez to call. Had all of them died for him with Teresa? Frankly, he didn't merit her interest, and she didn't know why she thought about him so much. Perhaps he was finding out things about Teresa here that hurt his pride, his sense of honor. Not that one could prevent it. Sánchez could look after himself!

Actually Juana had sympathy for Sánchez and his situation, even if he would never know it. And he would never know it if he never called up. I am too old! Juana thought angrily. Old women don't interest him. She had never thought of herself like that before. A Fury? All right. Furies had to be reckoned with. Teresa had told her that this was what Carlos called her. Teresa was not discreet. That was why Juana knew a lot more about Sánchez than he was aware of.

The telephone rang. Juana jumped up. At last! But it was only the wife of their doctor. Dr. Borges would not be able to see Antonia until tomorrow; he had visitors. "That's all right," Juana said irritably. It really was all right. Juana had never understood why her sister constantly needed a doctor to soothe her nerves. The phone rang again. It had to be Sánchez. "Go away!" Juana told her sister. "This must be Carlos."

Antonia stared at Juana, mouth agape. Why shouldn't she hear what this dreadful man had to say and what Juana would reply? Antonia stayed on the veranda and listened, but all Juana said was "yes" and "no" and finally, *"Bon voyage."*

"What did Carlos say? Is he coming?"

"It was Señora de Villegas. She is going away." Juana had banged down the receiver.

"Why doesn't Carlos call us?" Antonia mused. "It would be such a nice change. It's so quiet in the house without Teresa."

"Isn't that what you always wanted? Quiet in the house?" Juana's tone was sharp. "You're very hard to please."

One day more and she gave up her place beside the phone. "So much the better," she told her sister. "He'll regret it!" Antonia wanted to know why Sánchez would regret what, but got no reply.

Juana shrugged. She had never liked Sánchez and fortunately remembered this at the right moment. The more she thought about him, the more incomprehensible he became. It was strange that he had so many more friends than Teresa, in spite of her charm. Besides Consuelo Márquez, Teresa had no friends. Juana even doubted that Consuelo was sincere. Friendship with Teresa had offered her too many advantages to be an indication of true affection. Teresa's thoughtlessness might easily have made Consuelo resentful. Teresa could be so tactless. Juana and Consuelo's parents had been friends for years. They had never said anything nice about Teresa, although the latter had often invited their daughter to stay with her in elegant hotels. "Whoever has money is a dragon," they said in the Andes.

When Juana came home, deep in thought after visiting a sick cousin, she was told that Señor Sánchez from Caracas had called. He regretted that he had no more time for a visit and could not be reached anymore today in the hotel. He was leaving Mérida tomorrow, very early in the morning. Juana shook her head angrily. Today he was visiting all sorts of people, but he had no time for his relatives.

Antonia appeared on the veranda, all excited. "A car, Juana! I do hope Carlos is in a good mood!"

Juana didn't reply. To her astonishment Consuelo Márquez got out of the car. Juana's eyes squinted behind her glasses. "What does she want here?" asked Antonia. "She never visits us."

"So she's starting to this afternoon. *Good!*" Juana rang for coffee. In a flash of clairvoyance it became clear to her that Sánchez was visiting Professor Márquez in order to question Consuelo. That was the way he did things. Clearly, Consuelo was visiting Teresa's aunts to escape Sánchez.

In Mérida Sánchez thought more kindly of Teresa. In the silence of the mountains he listened to the wind. Teresa had lived here. Here was where she had fled from her prison. Here she had wanted to hunt the stars and the hummingbirds. Guilt without atonement, lust without joy, life without a goal. This was also where Teresa had died. But nothing could wring an answer from the mountains. Gigantic, alien, and stony, they looked down on the people of the Andes from a majestic distance.

Sánchez only permitted himself to think thoughts like this at night. In the morning he was dynamic and locked up his tendency toward introspection in his desk. He had a lot to do in Mérida. First he went to see Teresa's lawyer, who had looked after the affairs of the Álvarez family for generations. Señor Parra coughed constantly and liked to interrupt his clients. But with Sánchez he didn't have much luck. The

gentleman simply talked on unperturbed. As a result, Sánchez
got what he was after fairly quickly. He wanted to transfer
Teresa's share of the Álvarez coffee plantation to Juana and
Antonia. Señor Parra found this very noble, but didn't express
his admiration in any way. Unusually silent, he got the papers
ready to be signed.

The Álvarez family in the Andes was descended from
coffee planters. Juana and Antonia lived from the revenue of
coffee plantations, modestly. Sánchez felt that they could do
very well with Teresa's considerably larger share. And what
the Fury and the Old Goat needed, they should have!

The modernized coffee plantation of the Álvarez family
in the western Andes, which today was cultivated in part by
seasonal workers from Colombia, was, to its city descendents,
a legendary place in the mountains where boring coffee shrubs
were transformed into amusing stocks and bonds and bank
checks. Teresa Sánchez had always used up her share; Pilar
had saved hers. She had no husband who earned money for
her. No Andean peasant could have lived more frugally. All
her dresses were alike: a black or brown shell for a disappointed body. And her face, brooding darkly, twitched with
thunder and lightning.

In the preceding century, coffee had become one of the
most important factors in Venezuela, and until the First World
War, the Álvarez family had made enormous profits. They
had become wealthy. They had lived in an atmosphere of
security that later generations were not to enjoy. Juan Álvarez,
Pilar and Teresa's father, was already a wealthy man when
Sánchez married his daughter. He was ahead of his time. He
lived in Caracas and founded the internationally known firm
of Álvarez & Sánchez with his coffee money from the Andes.
Cannily he had watched the growth of the petroleum industry
and had leaped into the Venezuelan stream of black gold
before others were aware of the boom to come. Hardy, sly,
and tough, like his ancestors, Juan Álvarez could drink his
coffee for his pleasure when production and export sank dramatically. Later he explained to Sánchez that captains of

industry had to plan audaciously but proceed cautiously. They had to listen attentively to what others said but say little themselves. And of course they had to marry the right women—women with good sense and capital. Pilar's mother had met these demands; Teresa's mother had been a deviation from this ideal of practicality. At the time Juan Álvarez had been in a position to indulge himself. This was not to say that Doña Isabella hadn't had good sense, but she had been an adventuress; her gifts had been intuition and imagination, and this had delighted Juan Álvarez, the resigned widower, who couldn't or wouldn't pay any attention to little Pilar. Teresa's childish, carefree chatter had made a hopelessly foolish father out of serious, stony Juan Álvarez. He did his duty to Pilar as a father, but he loved Teresa, the spring of his autumn. He cradled her in his arms. He, who never laughed and only joked when business demanded it, laughed and joked with Teresa. Pilar didn't recognize her father any more when she saw him with Teresa. Pilar needed love too. Was she too obedient? Too diligent?

Juan Álvarez accepted Carlos Domingo Sánchez as a son-in-law with reservations. He considered him too old for Teresa. Pilar would have suited Carlos better. Teresa's father still thought in terms of dynasties. But since he could deny his younger child nothing, he submitted. Later he and Sánchez became friends, not only partners. They understood and trusted each other. Sánchez had a famous grandfather, so one could overlook his father. Juan Álvarez had found out long ago that one could only live relatively contentedly if one overlooked unpleasant things. Sánchez spoke about his father once, then never mentioned him again. Juan Álvarez kept the knowledge to himself. Trust for trust! No man was responsible for his father. In any case, Sánchez had behaved honorably and revealed his family conflict to his father-in-law. *Basta!*

Juan Álvarez had always been on the side of the victor, and the growth and increasing importance of his firm proved what a prize this son-in-law of his was. Sánchez admired his father-in-law, and took such a lively interest in his interests, that he too began to study the exciting geology of his country.

This led him to plan new industrial projects in Ciudad Bolívar on the Orinoco River. Now, years after the death of his father-in-law, these plans were beginning to be realized.

Right now, however, Sánchez was still in Mérida trying to solve riddles. While he waited for Consuelo in Professor Márquez's reception room, he asked himself whether it wouldn't be better to let sleeping dogs lie. His business appointments were over, and now he could do as he pleased. His lips tightened. Consuelo Márquez knew Teresa's secrets. He would get a few of them out of her. That was why he was here. He needed to know what sort of a man this fellow Cooper was. Teresa must have enjoyed his company uninterruptedly during the last months of her life in the Hotel Táchira and Consuelo had been there and witnessed it all.

The big room was humid and its stone walls exuded a damp smell. A bare, polished table stood in the middle of the room, four stiff carved chairs around it. Book shelves on all four walls. Sánchez read the titles: *The Colonial History of Venezuela. The Lives of the Saints. Latin America—A Historical Perspective.* Biographies. Memoirs. Professor Márquez was a historian.

Sánchez looked around cautiously, then took the book about his grandfather off the shelf. *The Freedom Fighter of Margarita.* His heart was beating fast, like a young man's, as it always did when anyone honored his grandfather. Emilio Domingo Sánchez gave his restless grandson a sense of calm, homeland, identity. Even the shadow of this extraordinary man enriched the spirit and soul and transformed this formal Spanish room in Mérida into a living room. Professor Márquez had come in softly. Sánchez put the book back hastily.

"My dear Carlos! What a pleasure to see you in Mérida again at last!" The professor really seemed to be delighted. "You must excuse my wife, dear friend. She is lying down. She isn't well, alas."

"I don't want to disturb you, professor. I only want to speak to Consuelo for a moment."

"I know, I know. Consuelo was just called to a sick friend. But I'll get in touch with her at once."

"That isn't necessary. I shall give you a piece of jewelry to give to Consuelo. It belonged to my deceased wife."

"Your visit honors us, Carlos. My daughter will come home right away," the professor said angrily. "Unfortunately she is not always as considerate as she should be."

"She is young."

"Not all that young, dear friend. Consuelo isn't an innocent anymore where social graces are concerned. She was just thirty-three." He coughed. "Bad habits are rarely transformed into their opposites as the years go by."

Sánchez laughed, but the professor remained serious. "I mean that only saints are transformed. They work indefatigably for perfection." He coughed again. "My daughter is unfortunately the last person from whom one can expect such a transformation. I shall telephone right away, my friend." He bowed and gestured to an armchair in a bay window, then he left for his study.

Sánchez lit a cigarette and crossed his legs. He had time. The professor's harsh voice, giving orders, penetrated to the reception room. Sánchez stuck out his chin. It gave him a grim look of determination. He knew very well why Consuelo hadn't accompanied her father to the funeral reception in the Villa Acacia.

"My daughter is coming as soon as she can," said the professor. "She is very sorry and apologizes."

Sánchez smiled politely. Of course Consuelo wasn't in the least sorry. But she was coming, and that was all that mattered. Márquez didn't say whom he had called and Sánchez didn't ask.

"May I offer you anything, Carlos?"

"No, thank you very much. I ate with Teresa's lawyer. People are frightfully hospitable in this city."

The professor smiled for the first time. "A little wine? . . . Now, that's better."

They drank slowly and peacefully. Suddenly Márquez said, "Teresa's aunts are truly very unhappy. The other day Antonia wept. They must really have loved your wife."

"Yes. The old take everything harder."

"Don't you think that's more or less a question of disposition? My daughter, for instance, isn't moved by anything. As for old age, my friend, you can't use that as an excuse. Not yet!"

"I can return the compliment, professor. You haven't changed in years."

"I am an *andino*. Tough as old leather. Apparently indestructible. Our politicians are proof of that."

Sánchez nodded. Bernardo Márquez came from the province of Táchira in the far western Andes. Numerous Venezuelan presidents had come from this harsh, forbidding region. Juan Vicente Gómez, for instance. "He was a true dictator," explained Márquez. "He considered himself the nation. In many respects he reminds me of Adolf Hitler. He hated the intellectuals, just like the Führer of the Germans. Gómez never married either. But he was tougher than the man from Austria. And he talked less. Much less."

"And he understood a lot about business," Sánchez said drily. "Of course Gómez was incredibly lucky with the oil boom. But he controlled the profits, slyly and prudently."

"An *andino*, my dear Carlos. Yes, Gómez was tough. That's why he was able to manage. Look, as a boy I wanted to study. Everybody in Táchira was astounded. Young Bernardo, the son of a farmer! Yes, people in the country are conservative. But nobody in Táchira doubted that I would make it. And when I finally did go to the University of Mérida, you should have seen the people at home! They came to my parents in ox carts, in automobiles, on foot, and on horseback, and brought presents: fruit, vegetables, and everything the fields and woods could contribute . . . yes. Ah, and here comes Consuelo! So may I leave you now, my friend? I have to work on a lecture."

"You work too hard, Papa."

Sánchez had risen and bowed to Teresa's best friend. She was tall and thin, and her smooth black hair fell from a middle part down to her shoulders as in old pictures of the Madonna. But her ironic smile and owlish eyes, that seemed to want to fathom everything and betrayed a restless mind, were of today. That Consuelo Márquez had chosen to play the part of Teresa's modest companion was a mystery. She was independent and crafty, a daughter of the Andes.

"Let's go to my studio," she said brusquely.

Her studio was a spacious attic room in the beautiful, old, slightly neglected colonial house with its typical tiled roof. Consuelo stood in the bleak room like a lonely tree and pointed to her paintings. If anything could have appeared more out of place here than Consuelo, it was her paintings. Whirling objects and symbols, mythical marginal figures and spirits, toyed with legitimate commercial articles. "Strange," said Sánchez.

"A girl must have a sense of humor," said Consuelo Márquez. "I paint advertisements."

"With success?"

"No."

"Then why don't you do something else?"

"Why should I? After all, it doesn't matter what one does."

"You don't think so?"

"No. Why should I put on an act for you?"

"That's something I couldn't possibly tell you."

"So what can you tell me?"

"First of all, you have far too much imagination for commercial art. A lemonade factory isn't going to buy a demon in a cola bottle. Why don't you paint your own picture?"

"That would be too indiscreet."

Sánchez looked at the grotesque designs. What on earth could Consuelo and his wife have had in common? She fitted better into her studio than into an elegant hotel. She wouldn't starve at home, and Consuelo Márquez had not been born to be a voyeur. She had been in San Cristóbal with his wife twice, perhaps three times. She was the key figure in Teresa's tragedy. Except for Cooper, of course. Sánchez studied her clever, ugly face. Something deep inside her was twisted, distorted. And the expression around her mouth . . . Consuelo didn't look at him. She erased every expression from her face as if cleaning a slate. For a moment she looked like someone who had drowned.

Without being asked, Sánchez had sat down on a hard chair and stretched his long legs. Then he wanted to know in what year this house had been built.

"Did you come here to ask that?"

"My interest in architecture happens to be irrepressible."

"Do you intend to build in Mérida?"

"What makes you think that?"

"Teresa told me on our little vacation that you suffered from a building mania. You had just built a house on the Orinoco, but nobody had been allowed to see it yet."

"The kitchen and the ballroom aren't finished." Sánchez half closed his eyes. "Did my wife betray any more highlights of my life?"

"A few. They were very revealing. You may recall that discretion was not one of Teresa's strong points."

Sánchez asked if Consuelo would like to smoke and lit a cigarette for her. He could see an angry light in the fierce eyes behind her thick glasses. What did she know ... if she knew anything? As far as he knew Teresa had never talked about whom he had established in his remote house on the Orinoco. That was a family secret. It isn't possible, thought Sánchez. Teresa couldn't have done that to me.

He forced himself to calm down and looked at Consuelo from the side. The mere mention of Teresa's name had obviously heightened her bitterness. On her face was a grimace of hatred. But in the very next moment she was smiling again, that ironic smile. There she sat, in her empty world, in her snake's nest, watching for catastrophes with cold, glittering eyes. Sánchez could sense its emptiness, the failure, the ineffectuality of her secret efforts for a little happiness. The sketches on the wall too—strident, glaring records of revulsion—were as ineffectual as pots with holes. What did Consuelo Márquez know?

He handed her a heavy gold bracelet of cacique coins, the heads of Indian chiefs imprinted on them, chiefs who had fought against the Spanish conquistadors in the sixteenth century. It was a valuable collector's item that had belonged to

Teresa. Consuelo thanked him without looking at him. Both were silent. There was nothing to say about this bequest.

Consuelo was called to the phone downstairs. Sánchez's eyes fell on a half-open desk drawer: letters and bills, a letter postmarked Venezuela lay on the top. All Sánchez could read was the name Cooper. When he heard Consuelo's steps, he hurriedly started looking at the paintings again. They betrayed an inimical world, a soul afire with resentment. A rosy, deformed child in a lacy gown, wearing a gas mask. Was it supposed to be an advertisement for lingerie or for the next war? An elegant caballero with a head of clay, half-covered with a cloth, as if the death mask were to be kept damp for Ash Wednesday. Three women with fish heads on a hotel terrace wearing bloodstained Paris fashions. Consuelo explained that the three women were really very pretty. Lately she had been painting a lot of people with animal heads. There was a robust young person who reminded him vaguely of Teresa. She was picking flowers for a well-known flower shop, but had wound snakes instead of ribbons around the bouquets. "I am the illustrator of the unexpected episode," Consuelo explained.

"Would you like to run around with a fish head?"

"I am running around with one. Haven't you noticed? And how do you like Teresa with the snake ribbons? See her unsuspecting expression? Teresa never suspected danger."

"Perhaps because her life was too protected."

"Perhaps she lived too thoughtlessly. She understood nothing," her best friend said harshly. "And she was too simple-minded to be happy."

"You don't need intelligence for that."

"I must say you arouse my respect, señor."

A note was pushed under the door. Consuelo picked it up and read it, looking bored. "A message from my mother. She doesn't talk to me."

"Why not?"

"I haven't the slightest idea. Mama has been sending me messages like this for years: 'Wash your hair!' 'Buy me some fish and coffee drops!' 'Don't paint!' Things like that." She smiled wryly. "A happy family, aren't we? Mother tells me to be exceptionally nice to you. In case I have forgotten to."

Sánchez smiled for the first time. "I'm waiting," he said. ."You are much more amusing than I expected from what Teresa told me. I don't know why she was so afraid of you."

"I don't know either. As you can see, I'm harmless enough."

"I can't be a judge of that. I hardly know you."

"Well, then you're in for a good time," said Sánchez. "Tell me, when did we meet last?"

"I think it was at your garden party two years ago. I lived in Puerto Cabello for a long time."

"Did nostalgia bring you back to Mérida?"

"Mama sent another one of her messages. She needed the money I was spending for herself. My father spends the rest on books. Would you happen to know where I could get a job?"

"What do you have in mind?" Sánchez managed to hide his astonishment. Had this girl lived on Teresa's money?

"I'm a good photographer. I could be a secretary. Anybody can be a secretary."

"You think so? Very well, I'll give it some thought."

"That would surprise me."

"Why? Do you think I don't think?"

"Not about me. You're not interested in helping me."

Sánchez laughed. "If one only helped those in whom one was interested, one would help hardly anyone at all."

"You're very kind, Carlos."

He was watching Consuelo with utmost concentration. She was breathing fast. A deep frown lined her forehead. "Why did you do it?" he asked suddenly.

Consuelo licked her dry lips. "I don't know what you're talking about."

"I think you do."

Consuelo was silent. Her face had turned a splotchy gray-white.

"Why did you write me such an unfriendly letter about my wife?"

Still Consuelo said nothing.

"What did you have against her?"

"Is this an interrogation, señor? You can't play that game with me the way you did with Teresa. She still idealized you!" Consuelo was blazing. "Even if Teresa did detest you, she trusted you blindly."

"Perhaps my wife had her reasons for trusting me in certain important respects. But that she trusted *you* . . . that I find incomprehensible!"

Consuelo was silent.

"How could you write to me, whom you scarcely knew, things about my wife that were utterly untrue?"

"Untrue?" Consuelo began to tremble.

Sánchez repeated, *"Untrue!"* in order to rob her of the rest of her composure and perhaps find out something only she could reveal to him. He was not as composed as he appeared to be. He was hoping against all hope that Teresa's relationship with Cooper had been harmless and only blown up by gossip. Consuelo's letter to him had been a classic example of malice. To be sure, he had had his wife watched after that, but outsiders can't know what goes on between two people. They remain on the periphery of events. Consuelo, on the other hand, had been in the center of what was going on. He said calmly, "You made a fool of yourself with that letter, Consuelo. My wife could drink coffee with whomever she pleased."

*"But not with Cooper!"* Consuelo screamed. "He was mine! Mine! Do you hear, señor? I knew him from Puerto Cabello. We were going to be married! Now that surprises you, doesn't it?"

It did surprise Sánchez. Consuelo Márquez was in her own private hell in the Hotel Táchira. Teresa had thrown herself at the only man who had ever taken a serious interest in her, Consuelo. It was not Elliot Cooper's fault. He was only a man.

"I wrote you the truth!" she said hoarsely. "Your wife forgot all caution and consideration. She begrudged anyone else a man—you must know that! I wrote to you because I wanted you to take Teresa away. That would have been best for all of us!"

Now Sánchez was silent. Suddenly Consuelo said, "I am not guilty of Teresa's death."

"Women do dreadful things to each other all the time," Sánchez said grimly. "Why?"

"Teresa had you. She had no right to Elliot."

"Elliot James Cooper of Smith & Stone. An excellent firm. Knows a lot about business. I know the company."

"Do you know Elliot Cooper?"

"No. But you'd better forget about any marriage with him, my dear. He is already married. To a woman from Berlin."

Consuelo stared at Sánchez.

"I asked my friend, William Stone, about Mr. Cooper," Sánchez told her. "In connection with Teresa. Married men usually set certain limits. In short, Mr. Cooper didn't leave his wife alone any more than I left Teresa."

With great effort, Consuelo managed a frosty smile. She was staring at Cooper's letter. "It would be nice," she said, "if you didn't visit me again." Her voice was dead. "Goodbye, señor. Thanks for the bracelet."

"Thank Teresa. Goodbye."

On the way to Teresa's doctor, Sánchez was still thinking of Consuelo Márquez. She had obviously been shocked by the news that Cooper was married. Carlos had watched her without sympathy. All he had thought was: she doesn't sleep enough. She is poisoned by exhaustion. Perhaps she would fall to pieces and the next man would have to pick them up. Nearly everybody had to make do with what had been pieced together. Human relationships were nourished either by beautiful errors or the ability to patch up what was broken. It seemed to Sánchez as if this ability was a dying art; it demanded patience. Again he saw Consuelo in her studio. It was unfortunate that passion disfigured her. Perhaps a woman's true charm lay in moderation.

Had Teresa told her best friend anything about the house on the Orinoco? Sánchez pushed the thought away. Right now

Consuelo was absorbed by her disappointment. Nobody could look into the future. Whoever tried became a nervous wreck. Sánchez couldn't afford nerves. If he believed in anything, it was in the preservation of his own strength.

Had Consuelo loved this Yanqui, or had she talked herself into it? Perhaps she had wanted the experience; perhaps she had wanted to get away from home. She was past thirty, an overage house daughter. In Latin America, girls married young. Marriage was a status symbol. Undoubtedly Consuelo's encounter with Cooper had brought her little joy. What sort of a man was he? A man who took advantage of female dissatisfaction? Gambler, bluebeard, victim? A husband who needed to make up for a deficiency? A Puritan gone crazy on his travels? A man at odds with himself? The mountains were silent. Even if Consuelo could have conjured up a picture for Carlos, it would have been distorted by her pain and rage. What had Teresa experienced with Cooper on her way to her death? She had been one of those women who made something beautiful of passion, even if only a fleeting or deceptive fire had kindled her. But passion had nothing to do with happiness. No one knew that better than Sánchez.

Dr. Julio Borges, the doctor of the Álvarez family in Mérida, received Sánchez with murmured condolences. What a tragedy! A healthy young woman! A little too fat, true. The doctor was very thin, his movements were stiff, as if he spent his nights at his desk. With his long neck he looked like a giraffe.

"What did my wife die of?" asked Sánchez, his expression stony.

Dr. Borges didn't answer right away but leafed through his files and pushed the ones that had been attended to aside. Then he coughed, a short, bronchial cough, and went on looking. "Dreadful, dreadful," he murmured. Did he mean Teresa's sudden death or his cough?

"Your wife took too many sleeping pills," he mumbled finally, putting the rest of his papers aside. Now only Teresa's file lay in front of him. He looked at Sánchez, his eyes sharp but not without sympathy. "I warned her that she was taking too many, but she was in a constant state of excitement and, in her condition, needed sleep."

In her condition. Sánchez felt a pressure on his chest and his heart began to beat fast. He stared at Dr. Borges. The desk lamp flickered before his eyes: light, dim, suddenly bright again, then dark. The doctor read the report of Teresa's death, wiped his glasses, and looked at Sánchez with genuine sympathy. "I am very sorry, señor. Juana Álvarez told me once that you had been longing for a child for years. Very understandable. I know your wife had an unsuccessful pregnancy years ago. Well . . . and . . ."

Sánchez said nothing.

"Unfortunately your wife was very fearful. Very nervous. She was really a little old for a pregnancy, wasn't she? She was in her fourth month. She implored me not to tell the Álvarez ladies anything about her condition. Naturally I respected this slightly hysterical wish. A joyous event is usually reported happily, but some women in this condition . . ." He cleared his throat. "All very unfortunate, Señor. When I was called to your wife, it was already too late. She couldn't be saved. Well . . ."

The doctor rose and silently shook Sánchez's hand.

She couldn't be saved.

Sánchez stepped out into the night and tried to accept the fact with equanimity. Everything that had been confused and incomprehensible was now laid bare. The shock didn't stupefy him; on the contrary, he was agonizingly aware. It awoke an additional energy in him, the energy of a pain that produces unbearable physical tension. He began to run. His steps echoed in the empty streets and plazas, and the moon shone on his face. The aroma of baked bananas wafted across to him, and suddenly he was furiously hungry. But he couldn't have touched food because in his thoughts he was with Teresa's doctor again. In a vacant park a fountain sprayed silvery drops. Somewhere he could hear Teresa's laughter, her special, shrill laughter for another man. Had Cooper been able to stand it?

Sánchez kicked a rotten melon rind with his foot. A house with shuttered windows. The owners were either dead or traveling . . . like Teresa . . . like him. Did Cooper know that he was to become a father? Sánchez felt a shock deep within him, like a plane landing. At this moment he felt neither love nor hatred, only the indifference that dulled all feelings. But he would wake up again and look the monstrous fact in the face—that Teresa had been expecting a child by another man. Was Cooper the father? Clearly, Sánchez knew nothing about these strangers from the Andes. He knew nothing about the lawless powers that ruled their souls. Only one thing was certain—every human being needed someone with whom he could share his thoughts and his deepest emotions. Teresa was no exception to this rule, even if her thoughts and feelings had been shallow and fleeting. Perhaps only he, Sánchez, had been incapable of binding her to him. Had he ever tried? Suddenly Sánchez felt as unsure as he had felt as a young student in Berlin. His world was trembling. Again he felt pressures on his chest and made fists of his hands. Then he breathed deeply. The night wind cooled his forehead and his senses. More than ever he needed to put Teresa behind him. Here in Mérida, with Consuelo and Cooper. What had taken place between those three was their drama, not his. This was how he had parted from Carla Moll two years ago, and her drama, too, was no longer his. One constantly had to let go and save oneself. There was no other way.

Sánchez got back to his hotel room late that night and fell asleep at once. Tomorrow, when he would leave Mérida early, he would again be cautious, stubborn and unflinching. A man on his own. A man on firm ground, surrounded by drifting islands.

In Caracas a letter was waiting for him from the journalist Carla Moll from Berlin. Postmarked: Venezuela.

# 5

# Barren like the Furies

Consuelo Márquez could no longer remember a night that she had slept through. Instead of relaxing after Sánchez's visit in Mérida, she spent the nights interrogating Cooper and was surprised when in the mornings she vomited. Not that she was expecting a child. Cooper had respected her far too much to enjoy himself with her that intimately. At any rate, that was what he had told her several times. There wasn't much a girl could do in the face of such lofty morality without cheapening herself or seeming ridiculous. Until Teresa had burst in on this platonic idyll, Consuelo had resigned herself to the situation. Had Cooper mentioned marriage out of the blue or had Consuelo hinted at it? Anyway, Cooper had had nothing to say against it, and had certainly made no mention of his wife. Cooper would only have made him unpopular, and popularity was something he needed to live. It didn't always matter with whom.

His cardinal sin had been that he had found Teresa suitable for passion. Consuelo, having to continue to be satisfied fulfilling his spiritual needs, had finally gone home—but not before Teresa had described to her friend the details of her own relationship with Cooper. From then on Consuelo had joined the ranks of the insomniacs.

She wandered restlessly through the empty house in her bare feet. Or she settled down on one of the steps, saw hideous

48

objects in every corner, and went back to her studio in the morning where it stank of fresh oil paint and old suffering. Then she painted the horror pictures she had seen in the night, and went on interrogating Cooper. Or she wrote him one threatening letter after the other, or a pitiful letter begging for a sign of life from him. The letter Sánchez had seen in her desk drawer had been written months ago. She went on writing letters to Cooper, but like Penelope, who each night had destroyed what she had woven that day, every morning Consuelo tore up her letters to the Yanqui, which she had addressed: "Please forward." Cooper, a bird of passage, never revealed his address in Venezuela.

Finally, after lengthier and lengthier wanderings through the house and about a dozen torn up letters, Señorita Márquez wrote a letter which she mailed on the following morning to the United States. The letter was not addressed to Cooper this time but to his wife. Since Consuelo didn't know the lady nor Cooper's private address in the States, she sent the letter to Cooper's firm in Chicago with a request to forward it. An act of revenge by mail.

Mrs. Naomi Cooper, née Singer, from Berlin, received the letter somewhat delayed because she was recuperating in Europe from Chicago, or Cooper, after sticking it out for years in the United States. Consuelo's letter reached her in the Swiss sanatorium where she was taking a cure because Cooper's firm knew where she was staying. She read the letter from Mérida several times. In spite of the fact that it was written in English, it sounded Spanish. There were a lot of things wrong with Cooper which she had pointed out to him repeatedly throughout the years, but Naomi had always taken for granted that she could depend on him. Whoever could have become *so* enamored of him that she would write such a crazy letter? Mrs. Cooper did not answer the letter because she had an insuperable distaste for people she didn't know. She didn't even answer Cooper's letters and, after all, she knew him. Knew him well. She was absolutely sure that Cooper had never offered to marry this woman in Mérida because he did not like to get married, but she would write to him as soon as her nerves were in better shape. She had chosen this sanatorium near Zürich because she could speak German with the head doctor.

After lunch Naomi Cooper was still thinking of Consuelo's letter. Naomi had looked upon Cooper for ages as being as firm as the Rock of Gibraltar and created for her to lean upon. That was what he had assured her before their marriage. Cooper's mother had imagined that her daughter-in-law would be an American. An American girl would have been more suitable.

Naomi hated news about unknown people. Teresa Álvarez was no concern to her. Nor was the writer of this letter. Cooper seemed to be having a very social time in Venezuela, much more so than at home. Naomi wondered what she could do to spoil Cooper's sociability. Almost at once she came up with a plan. Her plans rarely went well, though, because she liked to reverse them at the last minute. Cooper said she was her own worst enemy. He was his own best friend. Narcissus in Chicago. Only not so beautiful. Narcissus cannot be an ideal husband. Cooper was hiding from her in South America. Before his marriage he had lived with 'Mother' in Chicago. He had many friends, old and new, but he didn't introduce them to his ladies at home. Where he found those friends and how he got rid of them was a secret. He didn't like permanency. A change of decor, a different woman, different food— that was what he thrived on. Nevertheless his checks arrived in Europe with faithful regularity. He who does not want love, must pay! An old story. Mrs. Cooper brooded.

The flood nurse brought her another letter. Cooper was asking with obvious impatience when she was going to be well enough to come home. He always liked to have a reception committee waiting for him, or his homecoming was nothing more than an arrival. Gratitude should reside in the heart and not be only a word in the dictionary. (And didn't his wife have every reason to be eternally grateful?) Naomi read her husband's letter cursorily and without sympathy. Cooper wrote that business complications were keeping him in Venezuela longer than expected. That was the bloody end! Consuelo Márquez's letter sounded as if Cooper were engaged in an endless round of festivities. Nonalcoholic orgies, granted. He never drank anything stronger than lemonade. At parties he drank it in wine glasses. But with Mother and his wife he drank milk. Naomi, on the other hand, drank enough alcohol for both of them, at times enough for a whole regiment! Couldn't they dig up a tiny glass of brandy in this fruit juice establishment?

A: *Psychiatric Report* Dr. Andres Sprüngli. Sanatorium See-blick. Switzerland.
*Patient:* Mrs. Naomi Cooper, Chicago, U.S.A. Age 49. No children.
*Pathological symptoms:* Occasional alcoholism.
Hyperfunction of the thyroid gland. (Slight goiter.)
Insomnia. Nightmares.
Unsociable to the extent of persecution complex.
Hallucinations. Flights of fancy.
*Body type:* Slender.
*Temperament:* Depressed.
*Father:* Dr. Lothar Singer. Journalist. Died 1936 in the concentration camp Oranienburg, Germany.
*Mother:* Margaret Singer, née von Strelitz. Mark Brandenburg. Died in Berlin 1937.
*Siblings:* None.

B: *Biography* (according to the patient)
*The patient left Berlin in 1938 at the age of seventeen. Her father was a well-known journalist until Hitler came to power. He was arrested in 1934 for his political beliefs. After his arrest, his wife, Frau Singer, practically impoverished, with Naomi, moved in with her brother, Werner von Strelitz, on his estate in Mark Brandenburg. After evidently bitter political quarrels, Frau Singer, with her daughter Naomi, moved for a short time into the Tiergarten villa of the banker, Ludwig Mandelbaum, the brother-in-law of her missing husband. After the arrest of the banker, Frau Singer died of a*

*heart attack. The villa was requisitioned by SS Sturmbann-führer Carl Friedrich Bonnhoff, and Naomi, an orphan now, went to live with a friend of her mother's in a quiet villa in Grunewald, until she emigrated. Werner von Strelitz had asked her at once, after the arrest of her Jewish uncle, to come back and live with him and his wife. She rejected his offer but was grateful for his goodwill. In spite of her youth she withdrew completely from the world and learned how to cook, for which she had neither talent nor inclination. It was during this time that she developed melancholia and a tendency to inactivity and brooding. In 1938, with the help of friends and a refugee committee, Naomi Singer, who had wanted to study philosophy, found a job and a place to stay in the United States as a domestic. First she tried to find work as a baby nurse because she loved children, but she could find no work in this area. She wandered as an all-purpose maid from household to household. In between jobs she lived with a German friend who had married an American, and who arranged for her to move to Chicago, where she again went from job to job. At night, dead tired after doing housework all day, she studied her old German books, and Kant and Hegel, which may have induced her insomnia.*

*Finally, after many job changes, she was engaged as housemaid by Mrs. John Elliot Cooper, the wealthy widow of a Chicago industrialist, and married her only son, Mr. Elliot J. Cooper, management consultant and industrial expert. Mr. Cooper is rarely in Chicago since his business takes him constantly to South America.*

*The patient proffers no information whatsoever concerning her marriage of many years. We therefore cannot judge from her report what psychological pressures led to her alcoholism, and to what extent her marital relationship is responsible for it. The couple live with Mr. Cooper's mother in the family mansion on Lake Michigan. According to a photograph it is an impressive house. Naomi Cooper refers to it either as "the labyrinth" or "the family mausoleum." She has no photograph of her husband with her and offers no information as to his character, his habits, or his relationship to her. The*

*fact that there are no children has undoubtedly contributed
to the estrangement between her and her husband, who is
younger than she. A few years ago Mr. Cooper accepted a
job as business consultant with the firm Smith & Stone, Chicago, after which he visited various Latin American countries. He spends his vacations in the United States with his
wife and mother. At the moment, after a holiday in the Andes,
he is in Ciudad Bolívar on business, and recently wrote a
letter with the following revealing remarks about his marriage:*

In my opinion, normal people and neurotics are
separated from each other by nothing more than a
thin glass wall through which they observe each
other constantly, to the detriment of both parties. I
think we normal people also have moments of absolute madness and behave accordingly; the only
difference between us and your patients may be our
capacity to control ourselves.

Of course my wife is not mad. When she doesn't
happen to be drinking, she displays a brilliant understanding of things and controls her hypersensitivity
with a certain severity. In no way does she seem to
me crazier than aging film stars, politicians unfit for
their jobs, amateur artists, or some managers of industrial corporations.

I am afraid that my wife is probably overexcited,
as she usually is during withdrawal, and I hope she
isn't suffering too much in this condition between
heaven and hell. I am grateful to you for proceeding
gradually with the withdrawal. It is difficult for me
to empathize with my wife's trying condition, since
I drink nothing but milk or lemonade.

In answer to your question as to whether I suggested a legal divorce to my wife five years ago, the
answer is a definite *no*. It would never occur to me
to leave a helpless woman, although she makes my
mother's life especially difficult. After all, my mother

can't help it that she has always lived in orderly circumstances and was never a victim of National Socialism. And with that I come to what is worrying me most.

For several years now my wife has been living, in her thoughts and dreams, in the days of her youth in Berlin, although she has been domiciled in the United States for years and formerly rarely spoke of her family's tragic situation. I thought she had got over it long ago. It seems to me that most Europeans live much too much in the past, and my wife has quite suddenly, after decades, settled down again in the Berlin of the thirties. This began five years ago, and since then she drinks. Unfortunately my mother can't understand this because she herself is a teetotaler. I mention this only as a clarification of the situation. If you could heal my wife of her flight into the past, she might very well give up drinking. But you will be a better judge of that. Too much proximity and the condition of suffering with my wife, which marriage brings with it, tend to dim impartial thinking.

As soon as she is fit to travel, I shall fetch my wife and will be pleased to meet you and get to know beautiful Switzerland.

Sincerely yours,<br>E. J. Cooper

We have no further letters from Mr. Cooper. In my reply I explained to him that his wife's regression is a defense mechanism in the subconscious as the result of a shock. Our efforts have therefore been expended to effect a reconciliation with the present.

I did *not* tell Mr. Cooper of the existence of "August" and "Minna." Furthermore I saw no reason for pointing out the reason for this regression, namely a strong feeling of frustration in her own failure to adjust to her surroundings, which have remained strange to her in spite of all efforts and her marriage to an American. A reason therefore for her insistence on a mental institution where German was spoken. Alcohol is the means she has chosen to forget her failures in the present. Naomi is not actively vengeful. She takes revenge only in her dreams. A lack of scruples and decisiveness prevent her from *any* sort of action! She admits that in spite of her precarious position as the daughter of a Jewish Marxist, she would never have left Berlin without the active assistance of her friends, since everything had become a matter of indifference to her. She exhibits the same indifference now toward her husband and mother-in-law. Recently, however, she received a letter from Venezuela that seemed to excite her. She asked me if I had ever heard such a funny name as "Consuelo!" After which—silence.

Mr. Elliot Cooper writes to his wife regularly. The head nurse has noticed that the patient reads his letters aloud to her two 'companions' whom she brought with her: a stuffed bird, August, and an old armless doll, Minna. When she thinks no one is watching her she speaks clearly and animatedly to them. With us she speaks only in a whisper. During her periods of silence she uses sign language. Occasionally she calls the stuffed bird "Cooper" and reproaches him in rapid English.

She has never been back to Berlin. After lengthy questioning she murmured that she never wanted to see "that brute Bonnhoff" again. This former SS officer, who took over the villa of her uncle, L. Mandelbaum, appears again and again in her dreams and conversations, but I have not been able to find out yet whether she ever met Carl Friedrich Bonnhoff personally. All she did was explain that she had read in the papers that the German authorities were still looking for him. According to the article he is probably in Venezuela, but Mrs. Cooper says she is afraid of meeting up with him in Berlin. During our last conversation she said she had asked Cooper to look for Bonnhoff in Venezuela. Mr. Cooper had ignored her request, as usual, since he preferred to run around with South American women rather than try to find "the murderer of her father and uncle." We had difficulty calming her down.

Naturally I did not mention this man Bonnhoff in my letter
to Mr. Cooper. I take it he is another one of her numerous
nightmare figures, although she declares firmly that a man
called Bonnhoff had taken over her uncle's Tiergarten villa.
She couldn't tell me in what paper she had read the notice
about the former Sturmbannführer, but she whispered, "He
had terrible eyes."

C: *Tests*

> *Single tests:* Intelligence. Memory gaps. Mirror test
> according to Neumann-Giese: positive. High
> intelligence quota.
>
> *Group tests:* Complete failure.
>
> *Crafts (hobbies):* A tendency to destroy things con-
> structed in wire, cotton reels and screws.
>
> *Suitcase test:* Patient quickly broke down and wept
> while packing a suitcase with large and small
> objects. "Packing is one of my weak points,"
> she explained later. We stopped further tests.
> She is still unstable.

D: *Tapes* (during several sessions) Speaker: Mrs. Naomi
Cooper, Chicago. Highlights:

*"Why do you say 'Mrs. Cooper' all the time, doctor. Why
don't you call me Naomi? I'm still playing with dolls and
talking to my bird. I always wanted a child. By the way, are
you related to the bakery Sprünglis in Zürich? . . . If you'd
let me have a brandy, you'd be surprised what I could tell
you about Cooper and Berlin. No sympathy? Do you want
to be the death of me? Not that I care. I don't care whether
I vegetate here or whether Cooper treats me to a state funeral
in Chicago. . . .*

*Did you know that Elliot John Cooper wouldn't have found
a wife easily in Chicago? I must admit that this wasn't Mother's fault, but his. To make a long story short—mother and
son were thankful to heaven when we got married, even if
they behaved as if I should go down on my knees and thank*

*them. To some extent they were right. After all, I'd been kitchen maid and butler for quite a while and had opened the door for guests, and suddenly I was in a position to slam the door in their faces! 'Mrs. Elliot John Cooper regrets...' That was the best thing about the whole marriage! August thinks so too. Where is he? Oh yes, in my room. It is really lucky that penguins like August can't fly, or the little beast would have flown away long ago. He doesn't like it here in your sanatorium. Told me so last night. Excuse me please, have I said already that refugees from Germany were not welcome in Cooper's circles? Arrogant and totally lacking in understanding, the whole bunch of them. And so sure of themselves! They're the ones I'd like to have seen go through one of Bonnhoff's interrogations.*

"You have no idea how quickly I'd recover if only you'd offer me a glass of red wine! My uncle, Werner von Strelitz, had some good wines in his cellar. That was comforting. He really knew a lot about wine. Only not about his sister, who was my mother. But after they took Father away to the concentration camp, Mother said red wine reminded her of blood. Uncle Ludwig's feelings were hurt. Quite right, too. If Mother had drunk red wine she might have got over Father's death more easily.

"When I think that Bonnhoff inherited the Tiergarten villa and Uncle Ludwig's red wine—but inherited is hardly the right expression. Because first he threw my uncle out. And then...where were we? Everything's turning around in my head. I never knew that you could get drunk on memories....

"Do you also treat people with high blood pressure? Uncle Ludwig had high blood pressure. No wonder! First he had to worry about the inflation, then about the Nazis. No blood pressure can take that. Everything was first class in his villa. No imitations. Original paintings—a real Liebermann—good wine, orientals, and he had a heart too, Uncle Ludwig did. He behaved wonderfully toward Mother and me, although he didn't really like us very much. He had been against my father's marrying my mother. Uncle Ludwig had been a widower for a long time when we moved in on him. According *to the portrait in his bedroom, my aunt must have been very beautiful. By the way, when I went to see Sturmbannführer Bonnhoff, the Führer's picture hung where Uncle Ludwig's Liebermann used to hang. A good thing my uncle didn't live to see that. He fell over dead after the third or thirtieth interrogation. Of course Uncle Ludwig had money in Switzerland. What else was he a banker for? After all, for God's sake, it was his money. After that everything was confiscated. Good evening. Good night."*

"Have I told you already how beautiful Uncle Ludwig's house was? The Cooper family home in Chicago is an unholy mixture of Italian Renaissance, Swiss chalet, and a touch of slaughter house. Not much local color. And the paintings! I must say in defense of Cooper that he too finds the paintings on Mother's walls ghastly.

"When I heard that our Tiergarten had been bombed—I was in America at the time—and the last trees had been used for heating in the first winter after the war—I cried like a baby. Crazy, after so many years, no? Today they say it looks fine again.

"When I'm sad, my bird, August, is my only comfort. If you find that crazy, Doctor, I can't help it. August is hopelessly underrated. You should really analyze him some day. You would be surprised to find out what an inner life he has. As a young penguin he used to stand on Grandfather Strelitz's mantel. Grandfather gave him to me on my tenth birthday. I was never so happy again. August is beautifully crafted. Just take a good look at him once in my room. He's held up much better than I have, or my doll, Minna. She's very frail since I tore out her arms so that she couldn't open doors and run away.

"Help! ... What's the matter? doctor, you mustn't scream for help. That makes me nervous. You know, it was August's fault that I went to see Bonnhoff. So, if I was the one who screamed and not you, that's all right with me. Perhaps it would be best if I confessed that I really did visit Sturmbannführer Bonnhoff. But not today. Now I'm going to my *room. August and Minna are crying for some bread. By the way I would be grateful if the head nurse wouldn't keep offering me warm milk. Milk is Cooper's thing. Please tell her that."*

"Hello, doctor. Today I'm going to tell all! I'm in a giving mood. Maybe then I'll sleep better and dream something nice for a change. Of course it wasn't exactly cautious of me to visit Sturmbannführer Bonnhoff in Uncle Ludwig's villa, and I didn't do it because of him but because I wanted to get my August. We were all orphans now. I was living with Wilhelm and Rosemarie Schilling in Grunewald. They were friends of Mother's, and by now Mother was dead. When I packed my things in the Tiergarten villa before Bonnhoff moved in, I forgot stupid old August. I was in such a hurry. He really could have spoken up, the dumb animal! Even the Schillings asked why he had stayed with Bonnhoff. There you can see what a famous personality August was in Berlin. I really should have written to the Schillings. After all, they hid me and behaved as if it were the greatest fun in the world to hide Lothar Singer's daughter in the Third Reich. So I moved to the Tiergarten villa. It was my right, wasn't it? I mean, to pick up my August. Don't you agree?

"An elderly woman opened the door and asked what I wanted. I didn't dare to tell her what I wanted, not in this strange house. As I stood there like a bump on a log, a man's voice called out, 'Is that you, Ludwig? Why so late?' He couldn't possibly have meant my uncle Mandelbaum. The elderly woman called out that a young fräulein was there. The man's voice bellowed, "I am not at home for fräuleins!" And then, not quite so loud, 'What's her name?' And with that a man appeared in the hallway. It could only have been Bonnhoff. He was wearing the black SS uniform. He looked me up and down without saying a word. Perhaps he was surprised that anyone would visit him of their own free will. I had seen his picture in the papers several times, but he didn't look like them. He looked much more terrifying than his pictures. I said I was Herta von Strelitz.

"Actually I looked a lot like my cousin, who at the time was studying Swedish massage. Massage would have done a lot for Bonnhoff, he was so fat. He could cast two shadows. Who ever said that fat people are good-natured? If Sturmbannführer Bonnhoff had smiled at you, Herr Doktor Sprüngli, your feet might have turned to ice too. He asked what I wanted from him. Well . . . I happened to be in Berlin again to shop and just wander around, and Grandfather Strelitz had given me greetings to distribute to old friends. He had known Bonnhoff's father in Potsdam when they had been young. They had been in the same regiment. And so on . . . If Bonnhoff was surprised over these greetings from the Ice Age, he didn't show it. He asked me to come into the library, and used the house phone to order coffee. I sat in Mother's armchair, and he sat in Uncle Ludwig's place. He looked at me, then at the picture of the Führer, as if he expected some sort of inspiration from it. Formerly the Liebermann painting had hung there. That had been relegated to a corner, but it was still there. So were the etchings of old Berlin. And my August was still standing on the mantel. He was looking at me bug-eyed and was standing at attention. For a minute I didn't know whose side he was on. His beak was a little dusty. Apparently nobody ever touched him. Thank God! The familiar surroundings were no help. Bonnhoff was no help either. The room was darker than it used to be. The light green, brocade drapes had been changed for heavy red ones. So ostentatious and bloody! As I tried desperately to think of something to say to Bonnhoff without hanging myself, a model-type blonde and a handsome, tanned young man appeared in the doorway. The young man said brusquely, 'Christina and I are going riding.' The blonde asked if Bonnhoff wanted anything. Bonnhoff growled, 'I want to be left in peace!' He didn't introduce us. The young people left after nodding politely to me. Nobody said 'Heil Hitler!' It was all perfectly normal, only nothing was right! I don't know why. . . . The housekeeper came and asked if Herr Carlos was coming back for dinner. For some reason or other this question infuriated Bonnhoff. He reddened, and his light, fixed eyes became *lighter and more fixed. The woman repeated her question. All she wanted to know was for how many people to prepare dinner. Wasn't one allowed to ask anything like that now in the Third Reich? Bonnhoff yelled, 'Bring the coffee Frau Schulze! Don't ask damned fool questions!' For a moment he looked lonely and tired.*

"Over coffee he grewer livelier and asked about Grandfather Strelitz and Uncle Werner, and whether we still had the magnificent dairy cows. Of course we did! And George Strelitz was a great young fellow. Of course he was! Or why was he in the SS? 'How come you look so pale, little girl?' he asked pleasantly. 'With your good air up there, and riding! Don't tell me you're a bookworm.' God forbid! I raced with George, on horseback. Right now I was busy in the dairy, but I wanted to be a ballet dancer. 'A Strelitz on the stage?' he asked, his eyebrows raised. Conservative from birth! 'That's what Father says,' I answered quickly. I should learn massage first, Bonnhoff suggested gently. 'And then get married, young lady. Still the best thing for you chicks.' Was he married? Bonnhoff didn't say that the Führer needed soldiers. He didn't mention the Bund deutscher Mädchen. That's the Women's Corps. The sly old dog played an aristocrat who strayed from the flock because he was talking to a von Strelitz. Grandfather said once that Bonnhoff's old man came from a first class stable.

"Actually it would all have been very pleasant if it hadn't been so weird! Bonnhoff shouldn't have smiled. When he did, August's feathers stood on end! Always a warning sign. I walked over to him and said, 'He's cute.' 'He's yours if you want him, Fräulein von Strelitz. I can live without him,' and he laughed. I thanked him profusely and took my August in my arms. 'He's lucky,' said Bonnhoff. . . .

"I am not tired, Dr. My head is perfectly clear! I've simply got to talk! I haven't forgotten a thing. I . . . I live with that afternoon. Something like that sticks . . . sticks in one's memory . . . something so . . . so terrible!

"So there was Bonnhoff, standing in front of me, as faithful as Albrecht the Bear. He understood a little about art, and *explained Uncle Ludwig's prints to me. August listened. He was at my side and was hiding my treasures inside him: Father's manuscript about a Russian Marxist. If Bonnhoff had dissected him . . . I said I was crazy about art and things like that. 'But you prefer that stupid old penguin, my child. Well, you're young. Sixteen? Or seventeen already?'*

"Then we talked about the Murano glass. Museum pieces! *'Would you like to see them?'* I said I'd love to. Bonnhoff said politely, *'Ladies first,'* and I walked through a side door as if in a trance, along a passage and into the dining room, and headed straight for the Venetian glass. Uncle Ludwig had given it to his wife on their honeymoon. *'See Venice and then die!'* said Bonnhoff. What did he say? I should look at the Murano glass and then . . . and then . . . He was standing behind me. I felt dizzy. I knew that I had to do something important, but I didn't know what. Like in a dream. The glass glittered in the cupboard because Bonnhoff had turned on the lights. Now he was standing beside me and his eyes were glittering too. Everything was quite different. Even the air in the dining room smelled of a canal and death in Venice. *'Beautiful, isn't it?'* Bonnhoff murmured in a soft voice. I managed to choke a word out of my dry throat. *'Miraculous!'* Now I knew what I had to do: run away, with or without August. But I was stuck to the floor in front of the glass cupboard. The few steps to the door and through the passage were too much for me. And the passage which I could see through the open door, grew longer and longer. There seemed no end to it. I repeated like an idiot, *'Miraculous!'* Bonnhoff was staring at me. *'Yes,'* he said, even more gently, *'truly miraculous.'* I began to tremble. I realized too late that he had set a trap for me with his *'Ladies first.'* How could I have found my way to the Venetian glass in the dining room in a strange house? Bonnhoff laid one hand on my shoulder. In a second he'd say, *'You're Singer's daughter. Come with me.'* But he said, *'What you need is a schnapps, my child. You're as pale as a ghost.'*

He took my arm and led me back to the library. *'You young creatures have no guts,'* he growled. *'Let's go to the Mark*

*Brandenburg Museum next time.' 'I'd love to,' I said, my voice hoarse. 'Don't forget your stupid August!' He called Frau Schulze. 'Wrap the bird for the young lady.' I couldn't understand. He knew that my bird's name was August! He knew everything . . . he had interrogated Uncle Ludwig at the Alexanderplatz police headquarters.*

"In the evening he called Werner von Strelitz to find out how I was feeling. I don't know what happened after that. I've got to scream . . . scream . . . Please give me something for . . . for . . . (laughter) now, I'm having hysterics? (laughter) . . .

*Yes, Uncle Werner was no coward. He brought a forged passport to the Schillings for me . . . and shipped me off to Switzerland, to the Quakers, where I stayed . . . and . . . c . . . c . . . cooked. And after that, horribly far away. What did I want to say? Thanks for the schnapps, even if it's only apple juice. Minna is dying. My doll will soon need a funeral. She never did get over the trip. I want marble on her grave. Nothing is too expensive for my daughter. Even if you think it's old-fashioned . . . Soon I'll stop dreaming. . . .*

"You know what's made me so sick, beside the Nazis? That I am being deceived by everybody. *By humans and inhumans. It gives me the feeling that I'm constantly crossing the Atlantic in a nutshell. For years I thought Uncle Werner was a weakling, and then he turns up with a forged passport for me and visits me in Switzerland and can hear the grass growing! Like all the Strelitzes. He told Bonnhoff on the phone that his daughter had come home completely exhausted because she spent much too much time running around Berlin visiting their friends! I stared at him. 'Uncle Werner,' I stammered, 'how did you know that I went to see Bonnhoff?' He laughed. 'Who but you would go to see Gestapo Bonnhoff of her own free will? My daughter and you looked exactly alike when you were children, and one was stupider than the other!' I wept onto the roast goose. Uncle Werner went to see Herta in Sweden, and she wrote Bonnhoff a postcard thanking him for the nice afternoon! There was a general in the Strelitz family and Uncle Werner said that rubs off. He threw his*

*handkerchief across to me and said gently, 'It was too much
for you,' and then, 'For God's sake, laugh, silly!' And I had
to laugh. I was only seventeen. When I left he said, 'My son
sends greetings. He'll keep his mouth shut, and if Bonnhoff
asks anything, he'll get the story just the way I told it. But
up to now he hasn't asked.'*

*'You see, doctor, I am constantly deceived. What did I
expect of Cooper? That's too big a subject to tackle now. I've
written to my husband again. I want him to look for Bonnhoff
in Venezuela in his free time. He won't even do that for me.
He considers himself a benefactor of mankind—of female
kind, rather—but in spite of it he is definitely disobliging. I
shall fly to Venezuela. I'm going for a walk in the park now,
with August. Cooper, I presume, is right now taking a walk
with the lady Consuelo. I may be a slob, but I don't write
crazy letters to other men's wives like Consuelo. Perhaps
Cooper has dropped her already. In fact I imagine he has
. . . and has taken on another miserable wretch! Got her by
smiling at her. Cooper can smile, but Bonnhoff was better
at it. I would like to know if Bonnhoff smelled a rat, but
wanted to keep on the good side of the Strelitz family, or even
more important, Cousin George. Or maybe I imagined that
dreadful hour in the dining room. I used to say, 'You are so
compassionate, Elliot. Don't you notice how unhappy I am?
How much I want a child. Better two, so that they can grow
up together.' And do you know what he replied, doctor? . . .
Forget it! It still hurts . . .*

"Once he said, 'Stop drinking and I'll pay more attention
to you.' But I said in that case I'd rather drink. When he
heard that, he stopped smiling. He said he was known at
home and abroad for his patience, but now he'd had it! I got
so frightened I begged him to forgive me for not sufficiently
appreciating my brilliant marriage, for having wanted children, for the fact that he didn't mean a word he said to me.
After I waited for quite a while, pardon was granted, and
the monthly checks were paid into my account again. If I had
gone on worshiping him in spite of everything, he'd never
have stopped the payments. Not that I was after his dollars,*

*but I owed money at the liquor store. I hate to leave a benefactor waiting. Then one day Cooper took off for South America. I'd like to see his face if I turned up unexpectedly in Venezuela! Couldn't you give me a new head, Dr. Sprüngli? Mine is a garbage pail. Everything all piled up together. I am a garbage pail. . . . He'll be pop-eyed when I turn up on the Orinoco. . . . Will you come along, doctor?"*

# 6

# Cooper's Dilemma

Cooper put his letter in an envelope and cleared his throat as if he had just given his wife an oral lecture. He was sitting all alone on the terrace of the hotel, cleaning his glasses. He wore very strong glasses because he was nearsighted, and they were tinted against the tropical sun. One could scarcely see his eyes behind them. When his eyes brightened they were rivaled only by his smile. Cooper had several different smiles on tap: a smile for business associates, radiant as the tropical sun; a fleeting, pleasant smile for employees and mailmen; a slightly muted smile for Mother; and a martyr's smile for his wife. Also in his repertoire was the compassionate but optimistic smile that encouraged unfortunate females. Why was it that so many women wanted to weep on his shoulder? They probably sensed that E. J. Cooper was a worldly father confessor. He was forty-five years old now and a specialist in flotsam and jetsam, martyrs, and weeping willows. Naturally he couldn't have ladies leaning on his shoulder and bemoaning their fate without cease; he had to ration them. Unfortunately certain types couldn't grasp this and tried to cling. Egoism like that shocked him. And what did he get in return for his efforts? Foolish letters, reproaches, sometimes even threats.

This startling female devotion was only one aspect of his dilemma. Beneficent E. J. Cooper tended to tire in the midst of his beneficence and feel bored to death. Actually it was understandable. Real tragedy and misfortune are made interesting only by the charm of being fresh. Just like imaginary suffering and melodramatic bad luck. A normal person can only stand the penetrating aroma of misfortune for a limited time, after which he flees back to his bed of roses. Thus Cooper experienced time and again that a touching sacrificial lamb seemed after a while more like a raisin cake without raisins! With his wife he had had the experience that after her first enthusiasm over his kindness, she had one day criticized, even reproached him—he who had done everything for her, and only because of her hadn't married a girl from one of the wealthiest families in Chicago. He had already been engaged when Naomi had still been serving his fiancée at table! . . . Yes, in the course of time everything had changed. Only his thirst for the praise and recognition of women hadn't!

Even if the facts spoke against it, he was a born Puritan, not a Don Juan. His sexual needs were secondary. He sought the company of women because their flattery and gratitude did worlds for his self-esteem. He grew in stature with every word of praise. The need to be popular rather than loved had developed in him over the years into an absolute addiction! In his youth Cooper's achievements attracted little attention neither at school nor at home. His pragmatic intelligence and personality had developed much later. Today, when his mother admired him because of his success in business, he smiled sadly. Her praise came at least twenty-five years too late. She had expected too much from him too soon. He had been less a son for her than a racehorse that balked just before the finish line out of sheer nervousness. Yes, Cooper, like everyone else, had his own retired story of suffering.

He looked around him on the terrace of the Hotel Amazonas. He hated empty terraces. Next to his glass of fruit juice lay a letter from his wife. He looked at it without smiling. That was all he needed, that Naomi should visit him here. He watched an army of ants creeping busily along a wooden beam. Nice little creatures. They always had something to do, Cooper brooded. The hotel parrot shook him out of it in Spanish. Cooper shifted his glasses into position and wrote two of his slick, cautious letters.

Puerto Ayacucho, Venezuela, Hotel Amazonas.

Dear Naomi,
    Thank you very much for your letter of last month. It was high time that I heard from you. I would have liked to hear that your cure has been successful, but I am satisfied with small blessings. I am only surprised that you don't mention my bird pictures, which I sent to you in Switzerland, air mail. I had expected a word of thanks for them. I would like to have back the picture of the big bird that the Indians call devil-bird, since you are evidently not interested. (Rust-brown, white spots on its feathers, and a hooked beak.) I would like to send the picture to two friends I met traveling. They would appreciate it. Right now the gentlemen are following the trail Humboldt left in the Orinoco area. Professor Locker and press photographer Hanns König from Berlin were good enough to assist me in my research into the unique fauna along the Orinoco. Believe it or not, both gentlemen congratulated me on my crocodile pictures and could hardly believe that I am only an amateur. I'm sorry to say that the two moved on yesterday. Now I am alone again. Of course the quiet does me good; my negotiations in Ciudad Bolívar were fairly exhausting. The Venezuelan *caudillos* speak English fluently, but fall back into Spanish, which they speak very fast whenever consulting each other. I am therefore studying Spanish harder than ever on my quiet evenings. I understand a good deal more already than the gentlemen realize! I bring this up in order to make clear to you that I have bigger and better worries than the two señoritas you have attributed to me.

Your letter was confused, as if you had drunk a bottle of whisky before writing. If this is the result of Dr. Sprüngli's treatment, then either Freud or I have misunderstood the blessings of psychoanalysis. Please spare me your wild ideas. My firm sends me to South America to study the chances for industrial development, not to look for an old Nazi called Bonnhoff, who probably exists only in your imagination. You thought you saw him a few years ago on the streets of Chicago and another time on a Mississippi steamboat. Let us draw the curtain of brotherly love over the act you put on on that occasion in front of my friends. But I have had enough, Naomi, really, of this nonsense.

Uncle Tom's youngest son, Richard Cooper, has offered to spare me a time-robbing trip to Switzerland and will come to get you as soon as they release you. Naturally I shall have to reimburse him for the plane fare and a week's stay in Zürich. My money doesn't grow on trees, Naomi, but I do what I can for you. I hope you will realize this at last and show me a friendly face when I get home. That's all I ask of you. Or let's say, I have grown used to the fact that I cannot expect you to give me what other wives give to their hardworking husbands: a fond kiss, a kind word—in short, the *recognition* I have the right to expect.

What would have become of you without me? Shouldn't you at some time or another ask yourself this, my dear Naomi? But what do you do? You make me scenes in writing! Señorita Márquez from Mérida is a casual acquaintance, an excellent photographer, by the way. We went bird-watching in the Andes together. You must have misunderstood her letter completely and got everything mixed up. I sent you a postcard once from the Hotel Táchira while I was with her and her friend, Teresa Álvarez, or am I mistaken? Anyway, *I* have never heard

from either of the ladies again, nor have I written
to them. If I were to correspond with all the people
who cross my path during my extended travels, I
would have to give up my business activities entirely. Why did you tear up Señorita Márquez's
letter instead of sending it to me? I can tell you
why: you made things up as you went along, as
usual, to irritate me. Don't worry, my dear, I have
no intention of marrying Señorita Márquez or anyone else. Before I go to the altar again hell will
have to freeze over. Besides, I *am* married, am I
not? I can't for the life of me explain to you why
Miss Márquez chose to send you greetings from
Mérida. But it was very nice of her, since we didn't
really know each other that well.

Mother wonders why you don't answer any of
her letters. Please drop her a few friendly lines. I
think she has it coming to her.

That you want to visit me here is a joke, surely.
As soon as my vacation in Puerto Ayacucho is
over, I travel on. And the unaccustomed climate
would finish you off. On the Orinoco all you get
is tough meat with the strangest vegetables, dust,
Indians, parrots, dwarf trees on the llanos, and
swarms of mosquitoes. Please put this idea out of
your head at once. I can only explain your sudden
longing for me by the fact that you want to find
Herr Bonnhoff. I am writing to Dr. Sprüngli by
the same mail. He will take care of you until
Richard comes for you.

God willing, we will be celebrating a happy reunion with Mother in Chicago in a few months. After
that I have to visit various countries. The six to eight
months I am spending in Venezuela and Colombia
will pass quickly. By then you will be feeling at
home again in Chicago. Mother will help you.

All the best,
Elliot

P.S. Many thanks for your picture. It would have given me more pleasure if you had had your hair done for it and put on a pretty dress. I know that sloppy robe from Chicago. Other women would like to look as attractive as possible, whereas you seem to want to achieve the opposite effect. Why? Have you lost more weight? That worries me. You must force yourself to eat. All of us have to force ourselves to do some things.

Then Cooper wrote his second letter:

Dear Miss Márquez,

It was my intention to send you greetings from the Orinoco long ago, but unfortunately I have been very busy. Your friendly letter, sent to Ciudad Bolívar, also reached me only after a long trail of forwardings. I have an industrial bird of passage; I never stay long in one place. How nice of you to remember me!

I was sincerely sorry to hear that your friend, Teresa Álvarez, died so suddenly. It must have been a shock for you. Was she ill? Or in a car accident? She drove too fast and without sufficient concentration. I warned her about it in San Cristóbal, but she only laughed. She was so carefree and gay. I like to remember my vacation in the Andes when we were such a merry trio. The poor young woman!

Are you still photographing? I shall be bringing treasures back to the States from the Orinoco. Above all, pictures of birds. The water birds in this region are more remarkable than the people! I can't get very far with the Indians. They laugh at or ignore any efforts to get acquainted.

I remember the Hotel Táchira in the Andes so fondly that I would like to spend a few weeks there with my wife when I am through with my business in Venezuela. How about your coming back at the

same time and we could enjoy a holiday *à trois*
again. I'll let you know in good time if anything
comes of the plan. Here's hoping!

With best wishes,
Sincerely yours,
E. J. Cooper

And that takes care of that! thought Cooper, and read the
letter through again with satisfaction. How could this Consuelo woman have dared to write to his wife? And how had
she found out that he had one? *Who* had betrayed the fact to
her? He frowned. Another unpleasant riddle. And Teresa was
dead. In the end she had become a nuisance, even violent,
and he had been glad when she had gone back to Mérida. Of
course he had torn up her letters, unread. On leaving she had
made a scene worthy of Naomi. Only Naomi spoke English
well, and he had understood only a third of Teresa's tirade—
like arias in an opera of which one understands only a word
here and there from the upper tiers. Right now Cooper had
had quite enough of melodramatic South Americans. At first
they pretended to be unapproachable and then . . . good God!
Teresa Álvarez, with a flower behind her ear, had raised his
adrenaline and plunged his mood down to zero. That was
why he hadn't read her numerous letters from Mérida. And
now she was dead. How fast things like that happened. She'd
probably rammed her car against a stone wall. Just the same,
now he felt slightly embarrassed that he had never read any
of her letters. One always lost the game against the dead.
Strange . . . as if they suddenly became the judges of life and
read secret ledgers of guilt in the beyond. On the other hand
they became harmless as suddenly as a burned match. Not
the right partner for a busy man. She had told him her husband
had died during a gallstone operation. It didn't surprise Cooper.
He had only been surprised that Teresa had had no picture of
the dead man. That was something widows always took out
of their pockets at the most inappropriate moments. Now it
was too late for arguments, excuses, much less remorse!

Cooper wasn't quite as alone in the hotel as he had led

his wife to believe. The two Berliners had left, true, but the
journalist, Carla Moll, still kept him company in the evenings.
He found her very attractive but a bit too self-assured and
aggressive. Where was she anyway? Cooper approved of
absolute punctuality because to him it seemed to be a bulwark
against chaos. He read Naomi's letter again before tearing it
up. Had he perhaps overlooked a word of praise or thanks?
No. She really doesn't like me, he thought, and it hurt. In
the course of the years Naomi had developed into a wolf in
sheep's clothing. Cooper had torn up her letter, but scraps
lived on in his mind:

> I can translate words and sentences into English,
> but will you ever understand my thoughts and feel-
> ings?

> Did you hide a snake in Consuelo's whatever-her-
> name-is bed? Or why is she so furious? Of course
> you will want a divorce to marry this person! Does
> she like to drink milk too? Why do you preach morals
> to me all the time, Elliot? Why? . . . Excuse me. I
> see white mice on the meadow.

> Why is Chicago so much better than Berlin?
> (Joke.)

> Can't your mother move into a widow's home?
> My Uncle Werner had a place like that on his estate,
> and his mother lived there and never complained.

> You say I've made a Strindberg marriage out of
> our union. Have you ever seen a play by that Swede?
> Let me tell you, compared with a Strindberg house-
> hold, ours reeks of lilac and Chanel No. 5!

> I'm coming to Venezuela soon. Bringing August
> with me. Minna died. Unfortunately. I feel awful
> . . . feeble and gray in spirit. Why does one live on

and on and on? Dumb! *Bon voyage* . . . meant to say
*Bon nuit*, Mr. Cooper. You could be so nice if you
were nicer . . .

Again he felt a stab in the region of his heart. Either gas
from the Spanish food or gas from his German wife. But he
couldn't bear the thought of an evening alone. A man without
a woman is a beggar. Spanish motto.

He walked across the patio to the swimming pool that lay
in a tropical park behind the open dining room. Whoever was
looking for Miss Moll could find her before supper in the
pool. She swam like a fish. He would have liked to photograph her, but then he would again have to answer Mother's
and Naomi's questions: "We thought you were so alone in
Puerto Ayacucho, or whatever the place was?" He couldn't
explain that he *was* pretty much alone with Carla Moll.

"Hello, hello!" he said with false jocularity. "You swim
beautifully, Miss Moll. May I order the fruit punch?"

"That's a good idea, Mr. Cooper. Thanks," and she went
off to her room and kept him waiting. Don't spoil them.
Don't be the one to wait for them! That's what she'd learned
from her affair with Carlos Sánchez. It was useful knowledge,
but no fun. Everything she had experienced with men since
Carlos Sánchez had been shining failure. Sánchez had created
for her a world of enchantment. She hadn't been able to find
a new El Dorado.

"Well, you certainly took your time, Miss Moll! I was
beginning to pine for you!"

Like hell you were, she thought. She found Cooper, with
his constantly apologetic smile, amusing, but right now he
wasn't smiling. "Anything wrong, Mr. Cooper?" she asked.

"No, no. What could be wrong when I'm with you?"

Since Carla Moll had no answer for that, she declared the
fruit punch to be a little too sweet. "I'm devastated, Miss
Moll!"

"Would you like me to console you?" .

Cooper looked at her quizzically through his glasses. Who
would have thought that the evening would start off like this!

Until now, Miss Moll had been fairly arrogant. He told her his name was Elliot—E-l-l-i-o-t.

She ignored the statement, which annoyed Cooper. Not that he showed it. She seemed to be moody. He had enough of that at home, thank you! But in her white dress with a string of pearls she looked so beautiful that he smiled at her. Carla Moll looked at him from the side. Was he telling himself a joke? His full sensuous lips twitched with restrained amusement, but his eyes, enlarged by his strong glasses, didn't join in. The journalist Carla Moll knew eyes like that. Men who were secretly looking for a companion for the night and who, in the morning, rode off on their saddle horses, self-assured. Not for me, thought Carla Moll. She had finally reached the point where she wanted someone who would also find use for her during the day. There was a frown on Cooper's high, clever forehead. He seemed to object to the fact that she preferred rum. What did she know about him anyway? Probably he was as indifferent to her as she was to him. Why didn't I stay in Berlin? Carla Moll asked herself.

Because Sánchez is living in Venezuela.

Cooper was silent. Both of them were stranded in the Hotel Amazonas, pretending to be enjoying themselves. She sensed that Cooper's cheerfulness wasn't real. Perhaps because both of them were caught in a dilemma. But Cooper was a lot better than no man at all!

Carla Moll earned her living like her male colleagues, but when she took her meals alone in hotels and restaurants, surrounded by happy couples, her inferiority complex grew, however much she hated to admit it. Only at home did she like to be by herself. In public, at the theater, on outings or at a concert, a man had to be with you. It was a law. She hadn't invented it.

Cooper went about in the right way. At first he pretended that he preferred to be left alone with his notes rather than to have her company, knowing very well that a man by himself aroused interest, whereas a woman alone, whatever age— teenagers excepted—aroused distrust or malice. *Something* must have gone wrong if a smart young woman like Carla

Moll sat alone! Cooper seemed to be so utterly satisfied with his own company that Carla's colleagues, Locker and König, hadn't dared at first to start a conversation with him. All bluff!

The open dining room with its tropical plants was three-quarters empty. This pioneer city was situated a little too far away from the tourist Edens of Venezuela and the Caribbean Islands. Here, on the east bank of the Orinoco, you could find only naturalists doing research or bird-watching, painters, film directors, Indians, missionaries, pillar saints—and Cooper! "It's terribly humid tonight, isn't it?" said Miss Moll.

"Yes. It's a trying climate. But we won't let that spoil our evening, will we?"

"Of course not! In a gyp joint like this, cheerfulness is obligatory!"

Carla Moll didn't laugh easily because she lived in a state of chronic dissatisfaction with herself. After a long period of indecision she had sent her successful book, *Caracas for Beginners*, to Sánchez, but had never received a reply. Today I'll hear! she had told herself this morning, too. Didn't the señor know that one said "thank you"? Or did he despise her? Ass! she thought in her despair.

Since Cooper was eyeing her like a hawk, she forced a radiant smile. But at just that moment the hotel parrot screeched so scornfully that she winced. "What's wrong with you tonight?" Cooper asked, sounding like a nurse. Miss Moll wanted some more rum.

"Are you going to continue to travel in Venezuela, Miss Moll?"

"I'm waiting for my colleagues to get back. Then we pool our various impressions, and back to Berlin!"

"Are you looking forward to getting back?"

"As soon as I land in Tempelhof."

"I'm already looking forward to getting home." Cooper smiled broadly and artificially. "There's nothing better than a family."

"You think so?" Carla Moll wondered why he wasn't married if he enjoyed being home so much. Cooper looked at her thoughtfully. She was neither a sacrificial lamb nor a weeping willow for his collection, but something was wrong. He asked hopefully if she was worried, and ordered a second fruit punch. This *was* a gyp joint. She was quite right. "But less sugar, please," he said in Spanish.

The waiter closed his Indian eyes in an expression of unbearable pain and ignored Cooper's request. For him every guest was a threat to his repose, and he paid as little attention to any extra wishes as a waitress in a mediocre London restaurant.

Miss Moll downed her strong drink fast. Almost like Naomi, thought Cooper, slightly irritated. Did all Berlin women have an aversion to milk? But she was beautiful, especially when her shiny blond hair fell to her shoulders. Loose hair hadn't looked nearly as nice on Consuelo Márquez. Ugly girls had no right to a romantic hairdo. Consuelo at least brushed her hair, though; Naomi had given up anything like that long ago. Naomi. There was gray in her blond hair. That didn't bother her either. Soon she would look like his mother, only in as far as her fading was concerned of course. Mother, with grim determination, still put up her iron gray hair in a beehive hairdo on the top of her head.

She was altogether a hard woman, a pillar of society. It tired Cooper to think of his mother, although he loved her and she was tirelessly interested in him. And if she hadn't encouraged him sufficiently in his formative years, he had forgiven her. He forgave practically everything. Naomi never ceased being astonished about it because she couldn't forgive Mother anything! Her antipathy wasn't a question of taste but of instinct. Nor could she forgive her husband for the fact that, in spite of all the money he had inherited and made, he insisted on continuing to live in the 'family mausoleum.' Besides, he was more often than not away, and anybody was bearable from a distance. Anyway, he seemed to prefer to upset his wife rather than his mother, and that was a real dilemma.

Cooper shook himself out of his brooding. "You're looking tired, Miss Moll," he said, sounding worried.

"What he means is I look old," thought Carla Moll. After all, she was thirty years old. She could feel Cooper looking at her. Cautiously, yet indiscreetly, he was feeling his way toward her. In his greed for other people's trouble, he was searching for her wounds. She had never met a man so avid for wretchedness. Knowledgeable, and never at a loss for an answer, Cooper wallowed gently in the mire of alien souls. Funny man, thought Carla Moll. But he wasn't boring. She wondered if he too inhabited a loveless universe. If only he weren't so damn curious, one could have a great time with him—conversationally.

Miss Moll's cool, smooth face betrayed nothing. Only her rather shrill laughter was a symptom of hidden frustrations. Of course she needed advice and consoling like any other lonely girl. Cooper had been ready for some time to give her both. That would make her more vulnerable and him unassailable. In the end she would be eating out of his hand—a fascinating prospect!

"What are you brooding about so tensely, Mr. Cooper?"

"About the lasciviousness of misery," he replied.

"That's above my head."

"Or beneath it, Miss Moll."

A big fat mulatto with a faded white European woman sat down at a table beside them, although the room was half empty. He wore an enormous diamond ring on his middle finger, which he kept looking at with the joy of a rich man who has long been poor. His wife began to play solitaire and paid no attention to him. Typical, thought Cooper. The poor devil married so as not to be alone. He asked Carla Moll if she missed her colleagues.

"Locker and König? Colleagues aren't men as far as I'm concerned. I rank them together with my doctor and fortune-teller." She laughed again. "Why are you staring at me?"

He leaned forward. "Won't you tell me what is torturing you, Carla?"

She looked at him, flabbergasted. It made him feel a little unsure. Then she told him that she felt fine.

"All of us have our sorrows, and sorrow shared is sorrow halved. According to the laws of bliss and mathematics."

"I always got an A-plus in mathematics, but aside from that I am principally against sorrow shared. A super mess. You get someone else's misery on top of your own."

"How can you be so enchanting and so pessimistic? Don't you really believe in the good of mankind?"

"No," Carla Moll said simply. "And on no account in our contemporaries. That would be idiocy. Who on earth can have any illusions left after Hitler and Stalin? Or the assassination in Dallas? Vietnam? That little invasion of Czechoslovakia? I couldn't believe in the goodness of mankind in the cradle! World War II happened to be going on at the time." Carla Moll stopped to catch her breath. "Where have you spent the last thirty years? In a greenhouse?"

"In various hells. Like everyone else," said Cooper, not quite as gently and sweetly as before. "In spite of Korea I went on hoping for world peace."

"I envy you," Carla Moll said drily. "So you're sailing through the atomic age in a dream boat."

"Where would we be without our dreams?"

"Maybe you can dream better with dollars."

Cooper's eyes half closed to slits, a sign that he was annoyed. Why had he let himself in for this kind of argument? Now he was smiling only for the gallery. "I am sure you went through very difficult times when Berlin was destroyed," he said. "The times are cruel for a delicate young woman."

"I have the constitution of a horse, and believe me, you need it in journalism. One is constantly being sent out on assignment to the most ridiculous areas."

"Does your private life suffer in consequence?"

"The boss doesn't give a damn about that. He pays me to describe what I see, not what I feel. Whom on God's earth would that interest?"

"Me!" said Cooper. "Very much so. Yes, your inner life would interest me enormously, Carla."

"But *not* me! May I have another rum, please?"

* * *

The huge mulatto rose cumbersomely, rattled the table settings, and finally, with a practiced gesture, swept his wife's cards together in a heap. She let out a feeble cry and he held his broad hand over her mouth. Then he dragged the washed-out looking woman behind him by the hand. He had trained her long ago not to walk beside him.

"Nice customs," said Carla Moll. "Why does she put up with it?"

"Since she is apparently dependent on her husband, she has to put up with everything. Sad, sad...." Cooper's eyes behind his glasses gleamed, eerily animated. Carla Moll wondered if this lemonade jerk wasn't perhaps a sadist. He should marry. Then he wouldn't have time to snuffle around in other people's tragedies.

"Do you find Venezuela changed in the last two years, Miss Moll?"

"All I know is *Caracas For Beginners*."

"And is *Caracas for Advanced Pupils* to follow?"

"I don't know. Right now I've been left high and dry," she said with brusque honesty. "My colleagues moved on into the wilderness without me because they felt the going would be too rough. In the Hansa district things are of course a lot more elegant. Do you happen to have ever heard of Berlin?"

"My wife comes from Berlin."

*"You're married?"*

"Yes."

"Well, you've certainly managed to keep it a secret until now."

"You haven't told me either whether you're engaged or divorced."

"Neither," she said. "Didn't your wife want to come along?"

"No. She isn't strong enough for Venezuela. And by the way, she still has an old uncle in Berlin. Baron von Strelitz. It is supposed to be a well-known family."

Cooper was slowly losing his interest in Miss Moll as a sex object. She validated herself, not him. She wasn't even a mirror that reflected his picture. A decorative, disagreeable woman, with her feet on much too firm ground.

"I never heard of Baron Strelitz," said Miss Moll. "Too fine for where I come from. My father was an idealistic socialist. He lost his life in East Sector."

Cooper gave it a thought. Naomi's father must have played a similar role because he had died in the Oranienburg concentration camp. He said slowly, "When I was in Berlin in 1964, I didn't meet an idealistic socialist on either side of the wall."

"*You* were in Berlin? There seems to be no end to your surprises. What were you doing there?"

"I was taking part in an economic conference. I took the opportunity to have a look at East Berlin also. It was very instructive."

"What do you mean?"

"The Berliners are normal, only the city is schizophrenic."

"Would you give me an exclusive interview?"

"Alas, no," Cooper replied with offensive gentleness. "It wouldn't interest your readers."

"I'm a better judge of that. I know the readers of *Comet*."

"I read the paper several times while I was there."

"And what else did you find remarkable in Berlin?"

"What I found remarkable in Berlin was that everyone there carried his story on his face. Only you don't. Why?"

"Probably because I have none."

"That sounds very unlikely."

Miss Moll asked what sort of an impression Berlin, 1964 had made on his wife.

"She stayed in Chicago. Tell me, Miss Moll, are there still any old Nazis in Berlin or surrounding areas?"

"I'm afraid I can't tell you that, Mr. Cooper. I am a nomad with a typewriter. West Berlin suddenly became too confining."

"But doesn't the political situation interest you as a journalist? It must be particularly interesting in Berlin."

"There is an old Chinese blessing, Mr. Cooper. 'May you not have to live in interesting times.' Good night, Mr. Cooper."

\* \* \*

Carla Moll felt vaguely uncomfortable. The conversation with Mr. Cooper had led onto a wrong track. He probably knew Berlin much better than he pretended to. What am I supposed to know about old Nazis? She knew better than anyone else that she knew nothing. Her editorial office had sent her to Venezuela two years ago to look for former Sturmbannführer Carl Friedrich Bonnhoff of Berlin, who presumably was hidden there. She hadn't found him.

Cooper also experienced a slight feeling of discomfort. Conversation with Miss Moll tended to end abruptly and resulted in estrangement rather than rapprochement. This young lady was amusing, though, much more amusing than Naomi. Yet both came from Berlin. Miss Moll had undoubtedly spent her childhood among ruins, black markets, Allied gods, and exploded German myths. Ten years before that, Naomi's youth had been poisoned and threatened. She had experienced brown headhunters, death masks, experiments on corpses and the living, and fear as a folk sickness. At that time she hadn't needed psychoanalysis; everyone had known where the fear came from and that one couldn't get rid of it by talking on a couch. She was still startled every time the doorbell rang, and she saw the mythical Bonnhoff in all sorts of men. They only had to be blond and look dangerous. Cooper's Berlin of 1964, on the other hand, had been a metropolis where people had joked about the constant peril from the East, but his German hadn't been good enough to understand them, or to enjoy the cabarets in the West as the Berliners did. Somebody had told Cooper at the time that Berlin had invented irony. At any rate, one had laughed there over different things and situations than in the United States or South America. Cooper found the latter too melodramatic. He preferred Berlin.

He was just going to leave the dining room when the wife of the mulatto came storming in. She was wearing a faded robe and her braid hung, Indian style, to her waist. She was panting as she sank down on a wicker chair. Her pale tongue hung sideways out of her mouth, like a sick dog's, a rattling sound issued from her throat, then she groaned. The waiter didn't move. He stood between Cooper and the groaning woman like a statue. For a moment the emaciated European woman hid her head in the protective darkness of her arms. Then she looked up and stared at Cooper out of her red-rimmed eyes and murmured in Spanish, "Help!" And then in English, "Help!"

Cooper stepped up to her. She needs a good scrubbing from head to foot, he thought. She's dusty all over. He looked with disgust at her dangling breasts under the wildly checked Indian cotton of her robe. Her cotton belt was dangling too, like a tired snake. He asked what he could do for her. She looked at him, dazed. A benevolent, elegant American, who had been sitting with a beautiful girl, wanted to do something for her? She knew nothing about beatings and abuse. Her husband had scratched her face with his diamond ring. In her total debasement she was humble and ridiculous, and tragic. Cooper gave her his handkerchief, and she wiped the sweat and traces of blood off her face. "I had fine handkerchiefs like this once," she murmured, then she jumped up abruptly and her wishy-washy blue eyes were ablaze. "He tore up my cards. The dirty nigger!" she screamed. "I'll kill him!"

"You'd better not do that, señora," Cooper said in fluent Spanish. "You must calm down, please."

She gave him back his handkerchief, and he suppressed his repugnance as he put it back in his pocket. Disgusting—her blood, her sweat, her tears.

"I brought the cards with me to this country," the woman said solemnly. "I dusted them every evening. They stayed clean like everything else at home." Her pasty face was hollow-cheeked, and there were deep, dark rings around her eyes. "He has taken everything away from me, and now my cards!" she said, with the same absurd solemnity. "Good night sir. Perhaps you will think better of me if I tell you that we used handkerchiefs like yours at home." She staggered off, but turned around once to face Cooper. Her fine nostrils were quivering. "Women are always wrong in this accursed country. But I am a coward, sir. A soiled swan, so to say." She was breathing with difficulty. "In Yugoslavia I even had a

German governess. That surprises you, doesn't it? She used to sing me to sleep. My parents paid her to look after me. She told me fairy tales . . . as white as snow . . . as red as blood . . . The governess waited on my mother too. Sometimes I vexed her. Excuse me, Señor Americano. I found your name in the hotel register and I thought to myself, that is a happy and compassionate man. I must know what his name is and where he's from. Forgive me, sir. I babble. An old, bad habit from East Europe."

"You need rest, señora." Cooper wanted to leave, but the strange woman held onto his arm. Her fingers clawed him, then let him go again.

"Rest? How good that sounds? One breathes slowly, one listens, one outwits the noise, the screaming pain. 'Rest in peace' is written on grave stones." With a trembling hand she made the sign of the cross. "Stay, sir! Please stay! Please, please, don't leave! Have pity on me. Give me some money so that I can get away. I won't touch your arm again. I know . . . you don't like it. Just the plane fare to Ciudad Bolívar, Señora Americano! You are rich. I can smell it from way off. A pleasant, comforting smell."

"I must go now, señora, and you must get some sleep."

"There is no sleep for those who can't sleep, sir, and no rest for them. He is—a naked, neighing stallion when he isn't weeping or beating me. You saw him with me a while ago. Don't deny it. My cards used to pacify me. My faithful, clean cards. To play solitaire is a genteel way of passing time. My whole family used to play solitaire. It doesn't harm anything. As I just said, a genteel . . ."

Her husband came into the dining room, but he didn't go up to her. He waited, big, massive, and authoritative at the end of the room. She crept over to him, bowed and mute, and didn't look at Cooper again. Señor de Padilla grabbed her roughly by the hand and dragged her off behind him. His round face was grim, but his full merciless lips were smiling: he had thought of a new punishment for his wretched bitch!

Cooper was upset. Señora de Padilla was desperate, to be sure. Just the same she could wash herself and have a hand-

kerchief with her. Her misery had such a penetrating smell
that he hadn't been able to feel sorry for her. Didn't she use
a deodorant? In this tropical climate?

An hour later Cooper felt deeply depressed as he sat alone
on his little balcony, breathing the night air. Some fool had
once declared that the proper breathing dispelled melancholy.
One breathed in nothing but alien misery and couldn't exhale
it again.

He could see Señora de Padilla following her lord and
master, her head bowed, her braid swinging. She had reminded him of someone. With a shock he realized that Naomi
sometimes ran around looking just as shabby and chattering
in her despair. Also a soiled swan. No. His wife washed
herself with absolute fanaticism. She simply didn't attend to
her hair. She had never run around the dining room half naked.
But this unappetizing, long-suffering woman with her fine,
snuffed out features and her Indian braid had at least expressed
respect for him—even admiration! Naomi never even thought
of anything like that. On the contrary . . . Cooper didn't want
to think the thought to the end. His displeasure grew. Miss
Moll's room was dark. She neither wanted to be comforted
nor to comfort him. That was the sort of person she was.
Women always exaggerated in one direction or the other.
More often than not they gave too much or too little, and
never the right thing at the right time.

But Cooper wasn't alone; Naomi touched his shoulder. Or
was it Señora de Padilla? No, no—it was Naomi! He thought
much too much about her here, and her sister in misery was
all he'd needed right now! He took his dirty handkerchief out
of his pocket and again could smell shameless intimate
wretchedness. But this he could steer clear of by simply
throwing the handkerchief away. Naomi's misery, however,
clung to him. She was an old wound in his healthy body that
kept breaking open. It had nothing to do with duty or his
eternally lurking compassion that caught fire only at unfamiliar misery. He knew Naomi's suffering and his whole
marital drama *ad nauseam*. Why couldn't he shake her off?
Why had he suddenly asked Carla Moll about former Nazis?

Because of Naomi. He was a ghost, a witness from the past, who existed probably only in her imagination. He should have divorced Naomi and gone on caring for her financially. He parted constantly from other women. Teresa. Consuelo. A part-time secretary in Ciudad Bolívar. A chance meeting, a fleeting fire, and ashes . . . the time-robbing ritual of seduction whereby the seducer always became the one seduced, or the other way around. Dove, tigress, soiled swan, or an icy virgin like Carla Moll. They were of no concern to him. And why did he always have to think of Naomi when a human wreck crossed his path? Señora de Padilla, in her ignorance, had called him a happy, considerate man. He didn't stay with Naomi out of consideration. He stayed because one couldn't flee from the weak and the helpless. That night Cooper realized this for the first time. They ran after one or one went back to them. Unwilling. Or indignant. Or resigned. Because the weak and the helpless were for some reason stronger than the strong.

Bats whirred through the dark. The patio of the hotel, with the guest and social rooms all around it, lay deserted in the moonlight. A muted cry could be heard coming from one room. Dogs howled and a hen cackled sleepily in its dream of a proud cock.

"Tomorrow I go fishing," Cooper said aloud, and was startled by his own voice. He should leave before the heavy rains started. Crocodiles and boa constrictors lurked in the river slime, waiting for the rain, and for humans who dared to come too close. One never knew what was waiting for one on the Orinoco.

# 7

# Five O'Clock in the Afternoon

Five o'clock in the afternoon . . . a fearful hour. A rotting bridge between daytime and evening. The day is dying, evening is still hiding somewhere in outer space so as not to encroach on the day, because dying is catching. Five o'clock in the afternoon is the no man's land of the soul, the hour between awakening and going to sleep.

Five o'clock in the afternoon . . . limbo in Caracas, in Mérida, in Puerto Ayacucho, in the primeval landscape along the Orinoco, on which the great German naturalist, Alexander Humboldt, sailed once in a small boat, to verify the joining of the Orinoco with the Río Negro. And limbo in the harbor of Samariapo, which Cooper reached at five o'clock in the afternoon, alone, like the first Indian in the region; like the Indian woman wrapped in cloth, on her donkey; alone like the forests on the horizon, like the great rocks that stuck out of the waters of the Orinoco like islands; alone like every civilized human being with his worthless properties and symbols.

At five o'clock in the afternoon, everything and nothing happens. In Caracas thousands of men and women wait for death and many children are born, baptized, and condemned to live in pile dwellings or luxurious villas. People live or

87

die or watch the light fading because they have nothing better
to do. In the Upper Orinoco, a pair of twins are born and the
happy mother gets a beating from her husband and a barrage
of hoarse insults because he has two more mouths to feed
and he can't catch more fish. The mother doesn't object. She
is still quite young, but her skin is as leathery as the shell of
a turtle's egg. "Yes, yes," she mumbles, resigned and ready
for the next blow. Then she tickles her twins with a palm leaf
and drags herself over to the hearth. Such is life.

At five o'clock in the afternoon corporation presidents and
managers drive away from the skyscrapers in the business
district of Caracas to their ostentatious homes with their large
gardens and their mechanized happiness. They are dissatisfied
with their employees and fear creeps up on them like the
poisonous snakes in the primeval forest—fear of competition,
of cheap imports from Colombia, Peru, Chile. Fear of new
governments and constantly changing administrations. Fear
of the guerrillas who are biding their time all over Venezuela
and have learned their lesson in Cuba. Fear that one day the
oil will be used up, that the silent mountains will give forth
no more iron ore. And what will happen then? In Venezuela
death is preferable to a return to poverty.

That's what Señor de Padilla was telling his wife over and
over again while she was playing solitaire and not listening.
Camilo de Padilla, having risen from miner to capitalist and
co-owner of iron mines, was also afraid at five o'clock in the
afternoon, when old wounds burned like the sun. The only
thing to do then was fish or sleep, or think of a young woman
with voluptuous breasts and smooth skin who never played
solitaire and had never had a German governess. At five
o'clock he would consider throwing his wife into the Orinoco
with a stone around her neck. If only there weren't the police!
If only there weren't always witnesses! Señor de Padilla hated
witnesses just as much as he hated his wife with her gray
skin and hair like withered corn. For instance, that smiling
Yanqui, Cooper, in the Hotel Amazonas, was a witness. Señor
de Padilla wanted something from his wife very much like
what Yanqui Cooper wanted from Naomi: recognition, praise,

an attentive ear. Since he couldn't get this, his disappointment had turned into a desire to murder. Sometimes, at five o'clock in the afternoon, he felt that he had to murder her or go mad!

This was not Cooper's case. At best he felt the discrepancy between the real Elliot Cooper and his ideal image of himself, that insane image from his mother's hope chest. If anyone had a tendency toward madness, it was Naomi. What Cooper felt in this fateful hour was a half-conscious fear of nothingness, a vacuum, a world without banks, checkbooks, conferences, and women. His old wounds, too, burned like the sun. The memory of how, as a student, he had had to run around with a hearing aid because scarlet fever had affected his hearing and sight. Until he had admitted to his mother that he couldn't hear what the teacher was saying, he had been the disgrace of the Cooper family—a failure, without ambition or honor. Five o'clock in the afternoon was teatime at home, and Mother had used this hour of refreshment and relaxation to ask her handicapped son what he had achieved that day and then drawn devastating comparisons between him and more accomplished students. These teatimes must have penetrated so deeply into the subconscious of the successful consultant that at five o'clock in the afternoon he was transformed again into the apprehensive student.

At five o'clock in the afternoon, Carlos Sánchez said to his secretary, Rosa Martínez, "That's all for today. Have a pleasant evening, Rosa."

He doesn't need me anymore, she thought every afternoon at this time as she got into her little car and drove to her dreary, orderly rented room that stank of emptiness and insecticide. Thousands of secretaries and salesgirls did the same thing at this fateful hour. Since Rosa had nothing to expect from the evening, the day rotted away, and the hope for a companion for the night died like an exotic flower on a coffin. Rosa rubbed her forehead with her forefinger and told an invisible Señorita Álvarez everything that she didn't dare to tell her to her face.

She found herself staring at the only picture on the walls

of her room. It depicted, without any surrealism, the Savior
at the wedding in Cana when he had changed the water into
wine. On this old stained print, peppered with mold spots,
he looked Portuguese, and there was a certain resemblance
between him and Rosa's father, who had brought the picture
to Venezuela. Rosa crossed herself hastily. But she was still
absorbed by the insults Pilar Álvarez had subjected her to
this morning. Her boss's sister-in-law insulted her constantly.
If Rosa was utterly honest with herself, she was more afraid
of Pilar Álvarez than of the devil who constantly stalked her
in the shape of her brother. She had let Enrico go to jail a
while ago by destroying Teresa Sánchez's love letter instead
of selling it. She hadn't been able to give the leader of the
gang money to keep silent about Enrico. What would he do
to her when they let him out? She was ready to love all her
enemies, with the exception of Pilar Álvarez.

At five o'clock in the afternoon Pilar was drinking coffee
alone in the Villa Acacia. Sánchez had gone straight from
the office to La Guaira, the Palm Forest, and she owned a
house in the mountains in which Sánchez intended to spend
the weekend. Pilar never asked him if he visited the nightclub
on these weekend visits, and he was silent about it. But she
was sure that he spent an evening now and then at the Palm
Forest because that was where he had found Rosa Martínez.
"Carlos is unique. He gets his secretaries from bordellos,"
Juana Álvarez had told Pilar over the phone. Pilar had banged
down the receiver. For this, she paid her aunts' telephone
bills! It was five o'clock in the afternoon, that horrible hour!
The hour Teresa had died, missed by no one.

At five o'clock in the afternoon, Señor de Padilla was
fishing in the so-called fisherman's paradise on the Orinoco,
not far from Cooper. He squinted across at this representative
of American industry and frowned. As far as he was concerned, there were too many Coopers in Venezuela.
Cooper was enjoying a peaceful siesta in a makeshift rest
area on the shore. His guide had put up a hammock between

two palm trees and was crouching patiently on the ground. Cooper had hired this Indian with the severe, birdlike head and rented a canoe in Samariapo. A tin roof protected the boat from the sun, and a roof of leaves protected Cooper's valuable head. What does a man need for his contentment? Cooper asked himself lazily. A patched hammock, a roof of palm leaves, and an Indian who is silent because he has nothing to say to a gringo. This Indian was an admirable fellow, but not as congenial as Cooper would have liked. Instead of occasionally entertaining his employer he was chewing something. The muscles in his cheeks were in constant motion. His body, however, was motionless yet lithe, like a jaguar before pouncing on his prey. When Cooper finally got up, the Indian rose simultaneously and accompanied him to the shore. He was paid to protect the gringo from predatory fish, from the afternoon sun, from people with evil designs—thieves, murderers, hunters.

Cooper took pictures of the no man's land on the river: the distance between the clouds and the fishermen, three swimming turtles, the wooded labyrinth on the opposite shore. A pity that one couldn't photograph the silence. When Cooper wanted to take a picture of the Indian as a symbol of this silence, the man immediately turned his back. A picture would bring misfortune on him and his entire tribe. Everybody on the Orinoco knew this, only the gringo didn't. In spite of his four eyes, he saw nothing. Glasses also brought misfortune. That was why Zongo kept a cautious distance.

Cooper surreptitiously took a picture of Señor de Padilla. The man sat alone on the shore, absorbed in his fishing, rigid as a stone statue. At that moment he was dreaming of wild orchids and freedom and dignity, without too much hard work. He didn't notice that Cooper took several pictures of him. Señor de Padilla was wearing pajamas with a fish pattern, high-water boots, and the usual straw hat, big and round as a sun dial. There was a hole in the top of the hat. He had stuffed a bunch of grass into it. The Padillas presented themselves to their astonished public in highly eccentric dress. Soon the evening would swallow up all masquerades, and the dolphins in the river would start their strange trumpeting. The sound always reminded Padilla of the trumpeting to be expected on Judgment Day, of those mysterious instruments of God's Divine Justice, sounding from far, far away. Let the dolphins trumpet! Until now Padilla had only chastised his wife, not drowned her. He had left her behind in the Hotel Amazonas in order not to be tempted. In his own way he was a fearful Christian.

He looked grimly at the wide blazing sky. Soon the sky's rays would run across the river like trails of blood. His head ached. Five o'clock in the afternoon was the dangerous hour when present and past flowed together and confused him, and what he saw at this hour wasn't good. He saw the body of his wife floating on the ochre-yellow water. Her head disappeared in the jaws of a crocodile. He could hear bones cracking. Only Anna's braid circled on the water, reddening, either from her blood or the setting sun. Blood was always red, whether people were white, black, or brown. Padilla swept the vision away with his big hand as if it had been a swarm of mosquitoes.

He wondered if the Yanqui could read his thoughts. What had Anna whispered to that damned lady killer? In spite of threats and a double portion of beatings, Padilla hadn't been able to get it out of her. Perhaps she had betrayed him to the gringo. In his youth Padilla had been jailed for attempted murder. Camilo could still see the grinning face of the overseer who had bullied him in the mine. Padilla's narrow-minded, withered wife still considered her white skin superior to his powerful body, wild black curls, and blazing eyes, and in the beginning, she had tried to treat Camilo's African mother like a servant. She had greatly underestimated Señor de Padilla. Camilo's mother was a colossus with the temperament of a tiger. "Throw her into the river, the miserable little slut!" she had screamed, after which Anna had paid fearful attention to her manners when faced with his mother-in-law. And she thinks she can look down on us! thought Padilla.

As a young man he had had no time to learn to read and write. He had had to break his back hauling iron ore out of

Cerro Bolívar. Ore had been discovered where the Caroní River joined the Orinoco, and a new industry had been created. Camilo's European father had been a victim of the mine. The Yanquis had been the first to exploit the business; the Venezuelan government had got into it only much later, and today it was the new Sánchez Mining Company. Camilo de Padilla stared at the river. He had been lucky. He had escaped the mine. He had won in the lottery. An enormous sum of money for a poor beast of burden who had glared enviously at the exploiters in their Cadillacs. Today he was a capitalist too, and he considered this perfectly fair. He had bought stock in the Orinoco Mining Company as his dying father had advised him to do. "Don't spend the money for fleeting pleasures, my son!" With his last breath the elder Padilla had explained the nature of stocks to Camilo. "Little paper rabbits that increase all by themselves. A miracle of the Almighty! A little piece of paper that doesn't have to be fed, yet gives you power and dignity. A little piece of paper!" After listening intently to this explanation, Camilo had allowed the prayers for his father's soul to begin. Father Gonzalez, from the mission, had implored Camilo to spend the fortune he had fallen heir to in a way that would please God—to benefit the church and the poor who increased like swarms of mosquitoes in Venezuela. Camilo had listened to the exhortation gloomily, and after considerable hesitation had given the priest a sum for the salvation of the Padilla family. Once, but never again! Nobody wins the lottery twice. He had moved, with Mamacita, out of the family hut into a stone house in Puerto Ordaz, and with delight had watched how the trucks brought iron ore to the harbor to be loaded without his help. There, in the big harbor city, he had met Anna.

Padilla went on watching the Yanqui Cooper. He despised the capacity for work of these foreigners. They had no idea whatsoever of the meaning of the siesta. Padilla got up and walked over to Cooper. The latter felt a shadow on his back and turned around. Padilla was looking down at Cooper darkly. He asked, "What did my wife tell you in the Hotel Amazonas?"

Cooper was astounded. He squinted sideways up at the powerful giant with his curly black hair. "Won't you sit down?" he said, as if they were at a reception.

"What's going on between you and my wife? I surprised you in an intimate conversation, mister. Yes or no?"

"Your wife was looking for a handkerchief, señor." Cooper never lied when the truth did just as well.

Padilla opened his glittering eyes wide; a whole world was mirrored in his pupils. "Why did she want a handkerchief-conversation with you, mister?"

"I really don't know, señor. And frankly, I don't care."

Cooper's tone angered Señor Padilla, proud owner of a stock portfolio, a bank account in Puerto Ordaz, a house with a roof that didn't leak, and a wife from Europe—slightly damaged but still white, and therefore a status symbol for old-fashioned mulattoes. Cooper's tone was polite, yet shamelessly arrogant. Padilla changed his tactics; he would take his revenge some other time. He leaned over Cooper and whispered without a trace of anger or aggression, "Some men watch whatever their wives are up to silently. I am not that kind of a man. Take the advice of a friend. My wife isn't worthy of you. She was a prostitute in Puerto Ordaz."

"Oh," said Cooper. Señor de Padilla did not appear to be joking. His dark round face was serious and somehow comical in its arrogance. "She had nothing but a few torn dresses and her cards when she landed in my country. The bordellos in Puerto Ordaz may satisfy modest demands, Mister. I imagine that you are accustomed to better things in the States. Avoid Señora de Padilla. I am giving you good advice."

Cooper, baffled, said nothing. Señor de Padilla spoke about his wife as if she were a stranger. "I took pity on her, a Christian act, mister. She was doing it for money, in spite of her cards and handkerchief collection."

He bowed, got into his canoe, apparently satisfied, and paddled away. Cooper watched him. He thought he had lost his sense of astonishment on the Orinoco, yet the sudden candor of this corpulent blackguard surprised him. Everything was so absurd. Cooper decided to ask his friend, Gilbert

Preston in Puerto Ordaz, for information on Camilo de Padilla. The railway Preston worked for connected Cerro Bolívar with the harbor, and Preston had known the line and the people working on it for years. Preston had settled in Venezuela with wife and children. Cooper didn't know why he was so interested in Padilla, but his instinct seemed to tell him he should be. He remembered suddenly having read the name in a newspaper in Ciudad Bolívar, but in what connection escaped him. Business? Stocks? Distinguished service medal? Murder? Cooper racked his brains. He knew only one thing—the article had not been concerned with "Christian acts."

Cooper was suddenly very sleepy. The disturbing confrontation with Padilla had drained him. Cooper had rarely felt so uncomfortable as he had in the presence of this giant chameleon who could alternate so suddenly between icy rage and phony friendliness. He wished he could remember what he had read about Padilla. He felt so exhausted that his customary attentiveness seemed to have sunk like a stone into the river. He had the dark feeling that his ready wit, adroitness, and pragmatic mind were powerless toys of civilization in a world of primeval forests and streams. How helpless an expert in industrial progress could become in these backwaters of the Orinoco! Stupefied by the oppressive humidity, Cooper watched a delicate white river heron. The bird reminded him fleetingly of Naomi. He closed his eyes and sank down onto the grass. He was on the edge of consciousness, on the edge of a great darkness at five o'clock in the afternoon. Too much nature and silence; too many new animals and threats.

Suddenly somebody grabbed his arm and his body was flung to one side. The shock woke him. Beads of sweat collected on his upper lip, his heart was beating fast, and he wanted to scream, but couldn't. He wanted to curse and beat up the Indian who, with a strength Cooper would never have attributed to him, had shoved him away from the spot where he had been dozing. There, in the grass on the shore, the tip of a long, sharp arrow was embedded in the earth. It must have been intended for him and would have found its mark had Zongo not seen the danger and acted with lightning speed.

Cooper's breathing was labored, and his eyes filled slowly with tears. His glasses had fallen off and were lying beside his camera. Zongo didn't move. He was perfectly willing to save the foolish gringo's life—that was what the hotel paid him for—but he wouldn't touch Cooper's four-eyes.

"What happened?" Cooper asked in Spanish. Zongo knew enough tourist Spanish to qualify for his job, but he didn't answer the stupid question. The arrow in the grass spoke of death much more convincingly than the tongue of any man. In his incomprehensible curiosity, the gringo stretched out his hand for the arrow but Zongo grabbed his hand away. "Perhaps poison, perhaps no poison," he explained to the majestic river. Now the gringo was white and trembling. He looked all around him, still in a daze, but everything was swimming before his eyes, and he sat down on the grass without saying a word. Wasn't there somebody over there, running away? Had the arrow been shot at him from a canoe in the river or from the top of one of the tall palms? *Who* had shot it? Someone hated him so much that he wanted to kill him. The thought was unbearable because the belief in his popularity was so deeply rooted. 'I have a fever,' he thought hazily. Or was he even crazier than Naomi, who thought the man Bonnhoff was in this area?

But Cooper's enemy existed, and the arrow in the grass was real. He tried to regain his composure, drank his fruit juice, and felt better. Perhaps the arrow had been intended for Zongo, or for a bird, or for a predatory fish. He, Cooper, was more popular than any of the men he knew. Even Miss Moll sought his company every evening, whether she liked to admit it or not. He wanted to get back to Puerto Ayacucho as quickly as possible, even if the Padilla couple were there. Nobody shot poisoned arrows at the Hotel Amazonas.

Zongo didn't move and waited for the gringo to give him his orders. Cooper wanted to pat him on the shoulder in recognition of what he had done for him, but Zongo instinctively drew back. All right, skip it, thought Cooper. When they parted, he would give the Indian the flashlight he coveted. And glass beads for a girl. Surely Zongo had a girl.

Every man had a girl except Cooper. Perhaps he had forgotten how to make a woman happy? At first Naomi had been happy with him, then everything had fallen apart: love, trust, contentment. The last woman who had cared for him had been Teresa Álvarez. Some people made one appreciate loneliness.

Cooper wiped his glasses and saw the world along the river sharply again. An old man and a young Indian had appeared from somewhere and settled down to fish not far from Cooper. The old man was white, no doubt about it. Cooper could see his red face clearly, his bulging, light-blue eyes, his unkempt white hair under his old Panama hat, and his big flabby stomach. The Indian cast his net into the water with classic grace, and the old man, who was holding a fishing rod in his hands, was humming to himself. The river was suddenly in motion. A green light suffused the ochre-yellow water. The glittering fish surfaced and dived like fleeting dreams. The captive prey wriggled in the net and changed color.

"*El viejo,*" whispered Zongo. "*El capitán!*" Zongo often brought gringos to the fisherman's paradise and seemed to know the old man. Cooper asked from what country the old man had come, but Zongo didn't know. Now the old man was singing, but from the distance Cooper couldn't understand the words: *Das war in Schöneberg, im Monat Mai . . .*

Cooper got into his canoe without looking at the old man again. He had solved a mystery but didn't know it. By chance he had come within touching distance of the man for whom the German authorities had been looking in South America for the better part of three decades: Carl Friedrich Bonnhoff, last residence the Tiergarten villa of a banker in Nazi Berlin. There he sat, Bonnhoff, the fugitive on the shores of the Orinoco, singing happily! He was not a figment of Naomi's imagination. He was just as real as the arrow stuck in the ground. Bonnhoff was so old now that his mind was wandering back to Schöneberg in the month of May, and had forgotten the Nazi Horst Wessel song.

The worst enemy of the refugee was coincidence. Thus the journalist, Carla Moll, had looked for old Bonnhoff two years ago in Venezuela and hadn't found him; while Cooper had caught sight of *el viejo* at five o'clock in the afternoon without having looked for him, and had forgotten him in the next moment. Much later he remembered him, but late, more often than not, is too late.

At five o'clock in the afternoon, the journalist, Carla Moll, at last received a letter from Carlos Sánchez in Caracas. She opened it so hastily that she tore the envelope. She read the letter twice because in her excitement she could only assemble her Spanish word by word. Then she said aloud, "I don't believe it!"

# 8

# Carla Moll's Exile

Carla Moll:

When I have nothing better to do in the evening, I look at myself in the mirror, not to admire my beauty but to get to know Carla Moll better. Mirrors are not supposed to lie— at any rate not as often and stupidly as humans. I take off my makeup meticulously before subjecting myself to this scrutiny. I step courageously out of the dark of my dream factory into the light of truth, and see all sorts of things. The other day, in a moment of bravado, I tried to see myself as others see me, for instance, as Mother sees me, or editor-in-chief Wendt, or my colleagues, Locker and König. All of them can live very well without me. I've never been in jail for larceny nor do I have a contagious disease, yet I spend most of my days in splendid isolation. Mother says I've grown sour in the last two years. She should talk! Perhaps I was sweeter with Sánchez on Margarita Island. Right now I am the most expendable person on two continents: Locker and König left to follow Humboldt's trail, and have apparently forgotten me.

I am a slave to my memories. Sánchez is different; he is the master of his. When they don't suit him, he pushes them away. As he did me.

Shall I forget faster in the Hotel Amazanos than in the Berlin Hilton? Hardly. Here, parrots are all over the place, as they were then, and peculiar dogs are running around. If Locker would only send me his notes to work up, then I'd have something to do. With all due respect to factual information, one can't subject the average reader to what that scholar is going to put down on paper. His style is as dry as Venezuelan llanos grass.

Why in heaven can't I write here? Wendt will be furious. He's not paying me for a vacation.

Perhaps Locker has been eaten by termites. He wanted to marry me once. In Berlin. I was nineteen. But just before taking the plunge, he thought it over once more, and told my friend Lotte that I asked too many questions. There can't be a better preparation for the career of a journalist, but at the time I was studying philosophy. Lotte passed on Locker's "declaration of love" to me, which was her duty as my best friend. Still, I resented it. At the time Lotte was afraid I had a father complex, and that I wanted Professor Locker as a surrogate father. Only a psychology student could have come up with that sort of reasoning. Anyway, at the time, I really wanted to get married, if only to get away from Mother without a scene. Lotte wasn't aware of that—she had probably slept through the course on motivation. Today I congratulate myself that nothing came of it. You never know where you stand with Locker. He thinks in whispers. He'd never tell his wife the truth to her face. There would have been no point in trying to change him.

Lotte married long ago. Our psychologist now darns Kurt Sommer's socks and washes his shirts. She says nobody can wear out clothes like Kurt. Lotte isn't as communicative as she used to be, perhaps because Kurt does most of the talking. Just the same, she still tells me, straight to my face, with the same old honesty, what she thinks of me, and that changes all the time. Sánchez always told me what he thought of me, and it also kept changing. And when he threw me out of his house on Margarita Island two years ago, he also told me precisely why he was doing it. He looked like an enraged statue. I break out in a cold sweat whenever I think of it. And in sleepless nights I hear his voice again; "Tell your employer in Berlin that Carl Friedrich Bonnhoff died years ago in Venezuela, deranged and under a false name." And the way he looked at me as he said it! "You inveigled your way into my house, Fräulein Moll! You wanted to expose my honest name to the sensational press. If you dare to come near me or my family again, I shall have you deported as an undesirable alien. Is that clear?"

It could hardly have been clearer. The trouble is, you can't make anything clear to Sánchez. He is implacable. He inscribes sins on marble tablets. And idiot that I am—I sent him my book, *Caracas for Beginners*, from the Orinoco. The Spanish edition.

I should have gone fishing with Cooper. He was willing to pay for everything, even my rum. He invited me at the last minute, true—probably had to fight it out with himself first. I might have found something to write about in Samariapo. If Wendt knew how I neglect my chances! Must be the climate. When I told Cooper, no, I must have thought I'd be my own best company. That made even the woman in the mirror smile. Most people never know me long enough to discover the angel inside me. They see only the icy bitch. Sánchez was just about to get past the facade when the bomb exploded.

There must be a reason why everybody forgets me as soon as I'm out of sight. I don't even hear from Cooper, in spite of the fact that he used to wait avidly for me every evening and paid for my drinks regularly, even if he didn't approve of them. He wasn't the worst kind of guy. Friendly. Sánchez could learn something from him. I find it nice that Cooper wants to share everything with me, except his checkbook— his impressions, his thoughts, his tastes, and if possible, his bed. Perhaps even his secret sorrow if he were sure I wouldn't laugh at him. It's not very funny that his wife doesn't write to him, with him constantly on the lookout for a letter from her. But when one comes, it upsets him.

I say to the woman in the mirror: you went too far, Moll! Congratulations! Sánchez has his secretary thank you for your book and wishes you a pleasant visit to Venezuela. Signed,

Rosa Martínez, Private Secretary. A miracle that he didn't return it. It probably wasn't worth his while. Does he sleep with her?

I have such rotten luck. I am not bad looking. Even Mother says so. I have naturally blond hair and a good figure. I should think of Lotte's hips and rejoice! Instead I submit myself to a brutal examination in the mirror and, with masochistic bravado, use a bright light. The person in the mirror looks cross, pale, unsympathetic, and every bit of thirty-five. Why the dark shadows under her eyes? If I'm not mistaken, we haven't spent any wild nights with Sánchez recently.

Come to your senses, girl! Count your blessings! You have an iron constitution, so at least forty enchanting years still lie ahead of you. Professionally you're in great shape. *Caracas for Beginners* wasn't nearly the bad idea that some people thought. After my departure from Margarita Island I had plenty of time to nose around in Caracas. I was living in exile, and in exile one frequently sees ten times more sharply and ten times as much. One is a person without a face and has a room in a hotel somewhere or other. One stands to one side, completely isolated, while the others eat, drink, and laugh together, or kiss each other. One stands behind a wall, punching holes in it to watch the strange country and its people, little partial views, but in the end they form a pattern, a mosaic. I should be satisfied with my hole punching. I have a fur coat, several gold bracelets, a chain of Margarita pearls, and money in the bank, which so far nobody has wanted to rob me of. In spite of Mother's whimpering, I have my own apartment and shall stay in it. After a long period of opposition, she has grown accustomed to visiting me only after phoning that she is coming. I know how she hates to be alone, but I can't help that. I've tried, but when I'm with her, she nags. Or she is surprised that nobody at the office wants to marry me. That I don't want to marry anybody at the office never occurs to her. I do what I can for her. I'm sure it's not enough, but Mother is one of those people for whom nothing one does is right. Father said so too. In her presence one is always somehow tired. I don't know anybody who is so good at making one feel guilty. Even me. Her rheumatism, her cold—all my fault. Before that it was Father's. But since I'm on my own, things are a little better, even if she continues to work on my guilt feelings until I'm bleary eyed. She likes what I cook and I've relieved her of all financial worries. She should be envied.

A lot of people in Berlin envy me. I can do and leave undone whatever I please, and I can dress well. That's something Lotte can't do since she got married. Her Kurt needs too much money for himself, and there doesn't seem to be enough left over for Lotte. So go ahead, think of all those who aren't as well off as you are, millions of them. But the human mind has its limitations. Naturally one should never think of all those who are better off. Then it's curtains for gratitude. Gratitude is a popular virtue but, like most virtues, not much fun. You're unique, Moll! You want to have fun too? Forget it, and you'll be able to bear anything. That's what I always tell myself when I'm in a bind and find the position I'm in unbearable. One goes on living, even after the most embarrassing episodes.

After Sánchez I was surrounded by dwarfs. With my involuntary departure from Margarita Island, a period of my life began which, on looking back, I call the period of being despised. Sánchez despised me because he saw me as a spy. And I despised my editor-in-chief, Wendt, because he gave me the assignment to look for Carl Friedrich Bonnhoff in Venezuela. Most likely in Caracas. Most likely in the Villa Acacia in Altamira. Most likely in the private apartment of Sánchez. All because of a rumor! There wasn't a thing in the world less likely. Wendt should have known that and not given me the assignment, especially since he constantly reproaches me: I'm not reliable; I veer from the track; I lose sight of my objective; which I did promptly, and lost track completely of old Bonnhoff. Instead, I fell in love with Sánchez.

\* \* \*

Frau Katharina Moll (West Berlin) to Carla Moll
(Puerto Ayacucho)

Dear Carla,

Why haven't you answered my three long letters?
Can't you spare ten minutes for your mother? I sit
here as usual, in my empty apartment, all alone,
waiting for a sign of life from you. Moreover I beg
you to answer the questions I have asked in my four
letters. I know you don't want me to worry about
you, but I do anyway. Who is going to worry about
you if not I? I seem to be the only person in the
world who worries about you; how you behave to
me seems to make no difference. I am not complaining; just stating facts. It's simply disgraceful
that you haven't even sent me a postcard from that
place with the unpronounceable name! The Schneiders agree with me. Dr. Schneider has given me a
new medicine for my rheumatism. It hasn't helped
yet.

Everybody asks me what you're writing about in
Venezuela, and I stand there like an idiot. That's
why I don't play bridge very often now. I simply
don't know what to say! I can't tell my friends that
you never write! At least send me some pictures I
can show.

Yesterday I went to your apartment to see if Frau
Frosch was keeping it clean. It's been my impression
for weeks that she drinks too much coffee and doesn't
dust enough. She wasn't very friendly. How can you
afford her? It's none of my business, but do you
want me to look for somebody nicer? As soon as I
hear of anybody, I'll let your friend Lotte know.
Perhaps Frau von Hahn knows of somebody suitable.
She got somebody very good for the Friedrichs.
Comes twice a week and does light laundry. But
things like that don't interest you. Frau Friedrich has
given up hope of ever getting a card from you, and

you know her little grandson collects stamps. If only you liked children, you'd send something to the little boy—or if only you had children of your own. Are you aware that you're the only one of your whole university crowd who sits there without a husband? Why are you so forbidding? Nobody dares to go near you anymore. That's what Frau von Hahn said the other day. I always hoped you'd marry her eldest son. He married a perfectly impossible woman three weeks ago. Frau von Hahn is beside herself.

Can't you start things going again with Professor Locker? Now would be your chance while you're all working together on that river. I'm sure Herr König is so busy with his pictures, he wouldn't bother you. I like Willy Locker a lot. He has a very good job in Berlin and is a serious man. I don't know why you never fall in love, Carla. It's ridiculous that you want to keep that expensive apartment in the Hansa district. There's plenty of room in my apartment, and the faucet in the bathroom doesn't drip anymore. As I remember it, that's why you moved out. I promise not to disturb you if you should decide to move back in with me. If you did marry Locker, he has a wonderful apartment, all furnished with antiques. He sent me an airmail postcard from Venezuela, which is more than I can say for my daughter. The palm trees on the picture look dusty. Is that possible?

I took your blue suit to the cleaner. Frau Frosch broke two of your coffee cups, the good set, of course, and didn't apologize to me. Next week I'll go and inspect your apartment again.

Are you eating enough? You really shouldn't get any thinner. It makes you look old. Fondest greetings, also to Professor Locker, and all the best! Write at once!

Mother

Wilhelm Locker, (Professor of Ethnology,
Berlin University), to Carla Moll (Hotel Amazonas,
Puerto Ayacucho)


San Carlos de Río Negro,
Venezuela, 1970

Dear Carla,

I know you haven't heard from us in a long time, but Hans König and I have been traveling on lonely waterways. For weeks we saw nothing but Indian huts, ghost towns, and a few forest missions.

San Carlos de Río Negro is a village-like city on the periphery of civilization: a military fort, motor boats, ranches, shops, and a few *haciendas* in an empty countryside. I do hope you are all right. Hans and I are so-so. Right now we're rather worn out. For most of the trip, I felt like nothing but eyes, a target for the insects. I imagine you're already working on your own impressions of the Amazon area. Unfortunately I don't have your gift for description. I know you could do more justice to it all. I can only approach the Orinoco scientifically. Without König's magnificent photos we would have to call the whole thing off. The Indians call his camera "glass-eye." They also make curare poison out of plant juices.

On the Río Ocamo we were grateful for the hospitality of some missionaries. These priests are the indefatigable link between the Indian tribes and our culture. You should have met these men! But the exertion of the river trips and the wandering through the grasslands would have been too much for you. Hans König is used to things like that from his Africa tours, also to the heat. The color pictures he is taking here will be a sensation in Europe. Even my dry commentary won't be able to spoil them.

And with that I have come to the purpose of my letter. In San Carlos we found mail from Dr. Wendt. After seeing König's first pictures he has decided on an illustrated series. He'll be writing to you himself about this change of plan. In the meantime he seems to have come to an agreement with a well-known publishing house to present the picture series all over the world. The text is to be strictly documentary. I am sorry that this means you won't be participating in this project anymore. Wendt's decision surprised us just as much as I am sure it will surprise you. He'll certainly find something else for you.

More news: König and I are going on to Brazil from here. It's not very far from the Río Negro. There we'll use the same method. The illustrated series will cover both countries. Interesting, no? So we won't be coming back, to Puerto Ayacucho, and won't be seeing you again. Too bad! But you know how plans change in this business. The Brazilian wilderness would be just as exhausting for you as our expedition in Venezuela. Our only company here were tapirs, crocodiles and swarms of mosquitoes. The Indians probably wouldn't have interested you. You really are a city person.

Finally, a bit of private news. After my return to Berlin, I am going to be married. Lisbeth Wendt and I have been friends for years. She is Wendt's cousin. I met her at his home. She is a fine doctor, clever and warm. Before we left I suggested to her that we finally get married. Fortunately she wasn't nearly as astonished as I was afraid she would be. She doesn't seem to be afraid of anything, not even of a forty-eight-year-old bachelor with irritating habits! I have no idea how I came to deserve such luck. It became clear to me on this long river trip that I am not a completely hopeless loner. I miss Lisbeth dreadfully! I hope you two will become friends. She is looking forward to meeting you. Of course she's read *Ca-*

*racas for Beginners*. She admires your style and your
sharp eye. I hope you will be back in Berlin for the
wedding. Your dear mother and you must celebrate
with us. König sends his regards too.

Your<br>Willy

Dr. Herbert Wendt (Editor-in-chief of *Comet*, West
Berlin) to Carla Moll (Hotel Amazonas, Puerto Ayacucho)

Berlin, 1970

Dear Carla Moll,

For weeks now I haven't heard from you or read
anything by you. What's the matter this time? Are
you ill? (Impossible!) In a bad mood? Have you
fallen in love with a crocodile? Or have you left us?
Your postcard of Ciudad Bolívar's tin roofs and a
second one from Puerto Ayacucho were welcome
but hardly a substitute for reports and articles. Where
is the material you were going to send from Puerto
Ayacucho?

What are you doing anyway at the Hotel Amazonas? Conversing with the parrots? You can't possibly be waiting for Locker's reports, or for his return.
Can't you manage to live without him anymore?
Who do you think you are?

Since you, Locker, and König landed in Puerto
Ayacucho, a lot of water has flown down the Orinoco. You don't have to wait for Locker's material
because we are publishing an illustrated series, not
a journalist's report. Locker's short commentaries
will suffice for that. Your own reports about Ciudad
Bolívar, Puerto Ayacucho and Samariapo, where all
civilization cases, will of course appear. König has
taken marvelous pictures of these areas too. When
you get back, you could go on the air. Since Locker
and König have to go on to Brazil from Río Negro,

you'll be going back to Caracas alone. And as soon as possible, please. I can't imagine that you want to spend the rest of your days in the swimming pool of the Hotel Amazonas. We can let you have that cheaper in Wannsee.

If you haven't succumbed to one of your blank periods, you should have a lot of material by now. I'm worried about you, Carla Moll. You are not what I would call reliable. I want to know precisely: *Where are you now? What are you doing today?* You may recall that our feature series about former Nazies appears under this heading, and that two years ago you were supposed to look for Sturmbannführer Carl Friedrich Bonnhoff in Venezuela. I am still of the opinion that you go at things too superficially. I admit the result of that little expedition was *Caracas for Beginners*, but how long do you intend to rest on those laurels?

Since I am beginning to doubt that your experiences in the Amazon area will suffice for a new series, I suggest you do a documentary on the South American harbor cities. Cities are the right thing for you. You see, as usual I am thinking of what's best for you. I have in mind La Guaira and Puerto Cabello in Venezuela and Cartagena in Colombia. From there to Panama City and back to Berlin. With this itinerary you would be in your proper element again and not have to be a phony Rousseau on the Orinoco. I've read *Caracas for Beginners* again and like it even better this time. That's why I feel this new assignment is just what you need.

Locker is going to marry my cousin Lisbeth. When I was a student I wanted to marry her, but changed my mind and settled for Trude. She can cook!

I hope all of us meet again at Locker's wedding. Have you ever noticed that our good Willy laughs like a neighing horse? Main thing though is that Lisbeth likes to hear it. Locker told me once, in all seriousness, that he wanted to spread knowledge rather than happiness. I didn't pass these words of wisdom on to Lisbeth. That's me. Much too thoughtful, especially of you!

Please send each of my two kids a postcard from the Orinoco before you leave. In case you want to buy emeralds in Columbia (and knowing you, you will), I want to remind you that you can't put them on your expense account. I love you dearly, Carla Moll, but you're one of those persons who becomes increasingly dear the more you love them!

The longer this Sunday letter gets the more I wonder why I didn't fly to Venezuela myself and leave you in Berlin. As if I didn't know what happens when one doesn't do everything oneself!

The entire office sends regards, especially Frau Hannemann. My wife joins me in wishing you all the very best, and since we happen to be wishing, I wish you a speedy recovery.

Yours,<br>Wendt

Elliot Cooper (Samariapo Harbor) to Carla Moll (Hotel Amazonas, Puerto Ayacucho)

Dear Miss Moll,

I hope you received my pictures from Samariapo. They were intended to give you pleasure and show you what you missed. I think you would have liked it here: the quiet, the bird life, the river dwellers, the majestic river, the Indian calls. But I couldn't stand this paradise for any great length of time. It's too lonely. If I recall it correctly, Eve too was bored in the Garden of Eden, and she didn't have to put up with the surly silence of the Indians!

I am enjoying the fishing very much, in spite of the fact that the other day I was almost shot by an arrow. My Indian boy from Samariapo, who has accompanied me to this fisherman's paradise, jerked me to one side just in time. I praised him and said three times: *Bién hecho!* But either he doesn't understand that much Spanish or he doesn't like to be praised by a gringo. The friendlier I was, the more unfriendly he became. When I think that something like this might have happened to you too, I realize it is just as well that you stayed in the Hotel Amazonas. The arrow was poisoned, at least that's what my boy implied. Other countries, other customs!

I've had pleasant company during the last few days. While I was fishing I met a young compatriot of yours, a Mr. Bendix from Berlin. He was very impressed that I knew you. He knows your *Caracas for Beginners* and is an admirer of yours. But he'll get to meet you because he's coming back to the Hotel Amazonas with me. He is an engineer and works for a big American company in Cerro Bolívar. A nice young man. I found out a lot from him about the problems between Cerro Bolívar and Puerto Ordaz. You will recall that I am an industrial bird of passage. This brings me unfortunately to the fact of my departure from Puerto Ayacucho. I must move on to Puerto Cabello. I'm afraid you're going to feel exiled, all alone in the Hotel Amazonas, or am I being presumptuous? I won't forget our evenings there.

Fortunately I shall be able to fetch my wife from Switzerland in the near future. She is much better. I am sure you are happy with me. I shall be giving a farewell party in Puerto Ayacucho, and I want you to be my guest of honor. A friend of mine from Puerto Ordaz is coming too, and an important industrialist from Caracas.

I'm afraid I shall miss the fishing and the rain forests when I get back to Chicago, but to enjoy family life again, which I can do so rarely because of my profession, will be adequate compensation. My mother is already impatient.

It is somehow frightening when one doesn't speak to anyone for so many days. While I was fishing I didn't see a soul from our western world except for Mr. Bendix. Oh, once I saw an old white man whom the natives call "*el capitán*" or simply "the old man." A strange figure: big red face, bulging blue eyes, and unkempt white hair under a shabby old sombrero. He was humming something and holding his rod in trembling hands. My Indian didn't know from what country the strange old fellow had come to this desolate region.

Beginning next week I'll be back in the Hotel Amazonas. I hope you are having a good time. By the way, I advise caution where the Padilla couple are concerned. The señor was here one afternoon too and told me absolutely wild things about his wife. I was nice to the poor woman in the Amazonas because I felt sorry for her, but my compassion may have been wasted. I'm afraid the Padillas are not what they pretend to be. I have no proof, but I'm recognized in business for my instinct. I have a nose for that sort of thing. I don't trust them, and you shouldn't either. Just friendly advice.

*Auf Wiedersehen*, and my best wishes,
                                   Yours very sincerely,
                                       Elliot Cooper

Cooper's letter didn't lift Miss Moll's spirits. I really am the most expendable person in the world, she thought. The door to her room opened softly and suddenly someone was standing beside her, a little behind her, someone who had crept into the room on silent feet. How long had Señora de Padilla been standing there, perhaps reading Cooper's letter over her shoulder?

"It's time for afternoon coffee, Fräulein Mull."

"My name is Moll."

"Am I disturbing you, Fräulein Mull?"

Carla threw Cooper's letter on the bedside table. "I'll be right down," she said brusquely, ignoring the woman's imploring expression.

"Fortunate lady. You get letters. Men adore you." Señora de Padilla handed Carla the envelope with Cooper's name on the back. She had thrown it on the straw carpet. She always threw envelopes on the floor; it drove her mother crazy. She looked at the señora thoughtfully, but couldn't tell: was she being nosy or had she just done something polite? Cooper's large handwriting was clearly legible. It didn't really matter.

"I'm always so happy to have an opportunity to chat with you, Fräulein Mull."

Carla closed the door behind the woman. She looked at Cooper's letter. It may not have lifted her spirits, but it hadn't bored her. On the contrary, she felt she had to see Samariapo before she left. Cooper had given her the necessary clues for Wendt: Silence, birds, poisoned arrows, Indians, the big river, *el capitán*, big fish, little fish . . .

Señora de Padilla was waiting. Everybody kept her waiting. For a moment her gray wrinkled face was distorted, then she waved when she saw Fräulein Moll. A horrible, arrogant, lucky woman! "Here I am," said Carla Moll. "Why are you staring at me?"

"I admire you. You are beautiful, young, and . . . and . . ."

"And?"

"I've forgotten what I was going to say. Please forgive me. My memory is failing. And no wonder. I often forget who I am. Where I am . . ."

"You are in Puerto Ayacucho. I see you've ordered coffee for us. Good."

"I wait all day for this hour. I think of you all the time. You are the only friend I have in this terrible world."

"Would you like a shot of rum in your coffee, señora?"

"Please. Rum makes people talkative and they tell each other secrets." Señora de Padilla was staring at Carla Moll again. "I want to warn you," she whispered. "I was laying cards yesterday afternoon. The Yanqui is not your friend. I mean Mr. Cooper."

"One or two pieces of sugar?"

"We can tell each other secrets," the señora said darkly. "How would I dare to speak so intimately with such a rich, fortunate lady if we weren't both exiles?"

"I don't know what you're talking about."

"You heard me, señorita. Two European women in exile. Far from our homeland, surrounded by invisible enemies with a thousand eyes and ears. Even the fish in the Orinoco don't wish us well. We must make ourselves small and inconspicuous so that they don't catch us."

Señora de Padilla looked around her fearfully, then poured some rum into her coffee. "You like rum?"

"It's not bad."

"It fires the blood; our thoughts chase each other like racehorses. My papa always went to the races, but he lost his head and his shirt every time. I come from a respectable family of losers." The woman coughed. "A confidence for a confidence. Fräulein Mull, are you in love with the Yanqui Cooper? Yes or no. Don't ignore my warning. Mr. Cooper has many faces. He smiles, he writes you love letters, but he won't marry you. The cards don't lie."

"Have you got a fever, Señora de Padilla?"

"You are mocking me, Fräulein. I say again: don't ignore my warning. One day you will weep on my shoulder."

"I don't think so, señora. But if I may tell you something in confidence: watch what you're saying when you've put rum in your coffee."

The señora leaned forward. "I forgive you your youthful impertinence. You are nervous, lost. I see more sharply than you realize. In exile one stands on one leg, like the rainbirds."

Carla Moll rose. "I'm going swimming."

Señora de Padilla rose too and bowed formally. One of the tame parrots perched on her shoulder as she walked slowly across the patio. When Carla had withdrawn into the pool area, Anna de Padilla walked up and down, talking to the parrot. Then she walked into Carla's unlocked room and read Cooper's letter. An arrow that missed its aim, a couple one shouldn't trust, an industrial bird of passage . . . how long will he still fly, she thought, and laughed. The parrot laughed with her. A married bird of passage! That was why Fräulein Mull had looked so dispirited. The devil take the lot of them! He wouldn't find it difficult because all the angels had wandered away . . . High time that something happened, she thought.

While Carla Moll was dressing for dinner, she felt uneasy. Her chat with Señora de Padilla hadn't agreed with her. Cooper's letter lay on the bedside table, but it seemed to be folded differently. The woman wouldn't have dared . . . or would she? Carla shook her head. Being alone wasn't really doing her any good. Wendt was right. It was time that she got away from here. Cities. Life. People who spoke the same language. How long was it since she had heard German spoken? It was as if Locker and König had been exploring the Orinoco for years! She thought suddenly of Berlin. Even when she was walking by herself on the Kurfürstendamm, there were people all around her, uncommunicative society with whom, however, she could converse spontaneously whenever she wanted to. There was a certain warmth in the air, even when it was snowing or hailing. Strange . . .

Carla Moll put Cooper's letter in her small suitcase. It didn't make any difference if Señora de Padilla had read it or not. Soon all of them would be leaving. Only Cooper's farewell dinner and the trip to Samariapo, only the geographical separation from Sánchez, that was all. Then it was done. She shrugged. Venezuela was a hard nut to crack. So was life.

# 9

# Cooper's Farewell Dinner

Cooper's dinner took place under an unlucky star. Actually it should have been a success because his guests came from such different milieus: Chicago, Caracas, Río de Janeiro, and Berlin. Cooper believed in the melting pot as long as white was what was being melted. He would not have invited a mulatto like Señor de Padilla if the man had had the disposition of a lamb and the manners of a Boston Brahmin! In spite of his considerable experience in South America, Cooper had not yet grasped that the prestige of a man in this corner of the world depended to a great extent on his wealth and how he used it. A rich man was always acceptable. That was why Padilla couldn't understand why he hadn't been invited. Of course he hadn't counted on his wife being asked to attend. Anna didn't have a bank account, an evening dress, or a bosom, and her collection of handkerchiefs was no help.

Heaven only knew why, but Cooper's guests didn't seem to take to each other. Perhaps they didn't know each other well enough. Even Cooper didn't know them well. What did he know about Miss Moll? Or his friend of long standing—Gilbert Preston? Or Gilbert's Brazilian wife? He had met Mr. Bendix recently while fishing, and he didn't know his guest from Caracas at all. Had never met him before Preston had invited him to give Cooper a chance to talk to one of the most influential Venezuelan industrialists. In the beginning the evening seemed promising. His guests had smiled at each other in the proper fashion, told stale jokes and anecdotes, and talked about Venezuela, the United States, Vietnam, economic miracles and catastrophes, the Brazilian carnival, fruit diets, fishing on the Orinoco, the guerrillas in Venezuela and Colombia, football, Indians, the moon landing, and Berlin pancakes versus *tostadas*. Everything was as it should be. But a hidden meaning seemed to lurk behind everything that was said and critical reservations behind every smile. Ungrateful and egotistical, Cooper's guests had brought their prejudices, vexations, and inner conflicts with them. On top of that there was a barely hidden distaste to listening patiently to one's neighbor. The later the evening, the more tense the atmosphere became, and Cooper began to feel the same pressure in his stomach as he had as a schoolboy. The farewell party was a grotesque distortion of his favorite dream—Elliot J. Cooper, the unrivaled master of every situation, a symbol of personal success, center of attraction of the international elite. In a few days he would be leaving the Hotel Amazonas forever and this made him feel melancholy. Only the hope that he would never see his guests again cheered him. At the moment all he longed for was the party's end.

How could his guests dare to persist in their gloom while he was smiling at every one of them radiantly? Their laughter sounded false. Perhaps he only imagined he was among friends. The thought startled him. Cooper had asked himself that once already, when an unknown enemy had shot a poisoned arrow at him in the fisherman's paradise. No poisoned arrows were flying around at his party, but Cooper was faced with a riddle, and he hated riddles.

Even Carla Moll had changed in the course of the dinner so conspicuously that Cooper scarcely recognized her. The former Carla Moll was frank, always in good spirits, and frequently entertaining. She didn't seem to realize that as guest of honor it was her duty to be amusing. Cooper had often been guest of honor at business dinners, and on such occasions had smiled his heart out, even though his wife hadn't written to him for months. Or perhaps because of it.

Actually Naomi wasn't nearly as well as he had led Miss Moll to believe in his letter from Samariapo. He had invented this happy family picture to bolster his self-esteem, because a healthy and loving wife was part of the image of a successful man. Since reality always tended to limp behind one's wishful thinking, Cooper helped it along a little. The head doctor of the Swiss sanatorium had reported Naomi's relapse into the old dreary habits. They would have to start treatment all over again from the beginning. Cooper had *not* smiled when he had read the letter. The horrendous bills would start all over too. That was *not* going to happen! Cousin Richard would have to fetch Naomi from the sanatorium as soon as possible. Naomi had gone too far.

Sometimes spontaneous contact takes place between strangers, intensive, enchanting, and brief. But this takes place only when people are interested in each other. The only person who was avidly interested in the others was Anna de Padilla, and she hadn't been invited. She was sitting in her cotton dress in a dark corner of the garden, peering with the dull, solemn eyes of a cow at Cooper's festive, well-tailored gold birds. How wonderful it must be, she was thinking, to dine in an expensive dress and wavy coiffeur, and to converse with strangers and sun oneself in their benevolence. That Cooper hadn't invited her mulatto husband Anna found perfectly all right. But she could have been a credit to his party if Miss Moll had loaned her an evening dress. Cooper would get his punishment. Not every arrow missed its mark, and death didn't keep visiting hours. Death could give Cooper what was coming to him any minute. The peasants at home said, "Today a man, tomorrow black earth." Anna crossed herself and ordered pineapple for her lonely meal on the balcony. *Where was Padilla?* Perhaps he had carried out his frequent threat to leave her. At the thought she panicked. She couldn't manage without him. She was in a country that was still strange to her, and the bordello in Puerto Ordaz was the only home she knew. She couldn't go back to it; she was no longer young and pretty.

Padilla turned up eventually in a foul mood. He knocked

over the basket of fruit and threw himself on the bed. Anna didn't dare to ask where he had been. He came and went as it suited him. Anna picked up the fruit from the floor and crept out into the garden to enjoy Cooper's dinner from a distance. She had a good nose for danger and was seized suddenly by a vague apprehension, all the more frightening because of its vagueness. Padilla was cautious only when it was too late. He constantly ran into trouble. Like the Indians, Anna believed in omens.

Gilbert Preston from Washington, in spite of his white hair, was not an old man. Anna was afraid of him for a very specific reason. He knew too much about Padilla. Preston had been living in South America for decades, and knew all there was to know about the people of Cerro Bolívar and Puerto Ordaz. Wherever he turned up, Padilla was in danger. Anna walked back to her room slowly in the semi-darkness. Cooper's guests were illuminated by colorful lanterns that created a gold-framed world in the dark forests of the Amazon.

Padilla snored and groaned as he dreamed. Anna shook him awake. "You've got to get away. Preston is here. He'll have you arrested."

"Shut up!" Padilla yelled at her, but his big dark face had paled. The pupils of his eyes hopped up and down like little black balls. The gigantic mulatto was trembling like a volcano before an eruption. He walked up to Anna and raised his heavy hand like a club.

"So kill me!" she screamed. "Then you'll have nobody left. And who'll help you, you bandit! Your mother can't even read!"

Padilla wouldn't tolerate anything said against Mamacita. Certainly not by this worn-out cow. But when she wasn't chattering with gringos and wasn't boasting about being a European, she could think for him. She still had a little common sense left.

"She can't read," Anna repeated maliciously. "She can't even write her own name! She has to make a cross."

"I said shut up! Pack my suitcase. Don't forget my prayer book or I'll wring your neck!"

Padilla read the mass on Sundays when circumstances prevented his going to church. He moved his fat forefinger from word to word as he had done as a boy. Sometimes he trembled with excitement and fear. He bowed his head, crushed, as he listened to the priest. Every reference to sin and hellfire was directed at him. Secretly he was angry with the Savior from setting him down in a much too tricky world where he was constantly being torn between Christian effort and his hatred of Anna. Sometimes he supported his aching head with his hands as if it might fall off.

He put on dark pants and a dark shirt and carefully brushed the dust off his old sombrero, the one he had worn fishing in Samariapo. He looked like a bandit chief in an old opera.

"Where are you going?" asked Anna.

He threw a small bundle of bills at her and said roughly, "You go to my house in Puerto Ordaz. My mother will tell you what to do."

"What?!" She stared at him. Her eyelids itched and she rubbed them with her bony forefinger. It had a knob that kept growing and becoming more and more painful. "What are you planning to do, Padilla?" The words choked her as if she were swallowing stones. "What . . . what will she tell me to do?"

"This and that." Padilla swung his sombrero, picked up his suitcase, and disappeared into the night. She watched him go, mouth agape, which didn't look pretty because she had very few teeth left. This time Padilla hadn't told any of his cruel jokes. This time he had abandoned her. She had a so-called Caribbean marriage, as was customary in this part of the world—no papers, no legal protection. Padilla might have married her if she had borne him sons, but perhaps not. All over the Caribbean world women ran around with fatherless children, in spite of the exhortations of the church which Padilla faithfully spelled out to himself.

Anna's lips swelled slowly, like her loneliness. Room and balcony were empty. Padilla took up so much room. She

dreaded Mamacita. This was the end. Today a human, tomorrow the black earth. She picked up a pineapple that had
rolled under the bed and peeled it with a rusty knife Padilla
had forgotten to take in his hurry. Or had he left it behind
on purpose? The juice ran down her dress, and she didn't
wipe it away. Everything was sticky, like herself. Cooper had
been right in not inviting her to his dinner. She could hear
guitars playing. She sat hunched on her balcony, ate the
pineapple, and counted the money Padilla had tossed at her.
She got up, shook herself like a wet dog and locked Padilla's
money in her shabby suitcase. The hotel guests were asked
to deposit any large sums of money at the desk, but Anna
trusted nobody. Faded, crumbling family pictures from
Dubrovnik were in her suitcase. Fräulein Steinmeister, her
German governess, also smiled ironically at her from a lost
paradise. Anna wept while Cooper's dinner took its course
across the way from her under a bright light.

The unknown gentleman from Caracas had not put in an
appearance yet. Had the man forgotten the invitation or chosen not to come? Suddenly Cooper pulled himself together
as he saw a tall, elegant gentleman approach his table. He
examined the dark, fiery eyes, the cool smile, and the proud
Spanish profile, an unpleasant fellow who radiated energy,
power, and distrust. Preston shouldn't have invited him. "Señor
Sánchez from Caracas," said Gilbert Preston. "Why so late,
Carlos?"
    Carla Moll stared at Sánchez for a few seconds, then looked
away at the palm trees. She thought: this can't be true!

Cooper's guests were talking about Brazil. "We have races
of every color in our country," said Señora Preston, "and all
of them are welcome. My grandfathers had slaves on their
sugar plantations. Everybody was happy."
    "Especially the master of Casa Grande," Preston, the ju-
rist, remarked drily. "Besides all his rights and privileges, he
had the *jus primae noctis*. Those were the days!"
    Everybody laughed. Walter Bendix's eyes were open wide.

He'd have to write that to his family in Berlin. Bendix was a fanatical family man. Now he looked shyly across the table at Señor Sánchez. The man was so silent, his brows raised. It gave him a fierce look. It reminded Bendix of his interview in Sánchez's office in Caracas. A failure. The picture of a stern Venezuelan had hung on the wall. Bendix had found later that it was a portrait of Emilio Domingo Sánchez, the freedom fighter of Margarita Island. Sánchez's grandfather. Sánchez's face expressed the same distrust and stubborn unwillingness to give any information beyond what was absolutely necessary. Or did Sánchez look so somber because his wife had died recently? Young Bendix had read it in a newspaper but hadn't dared to send a note of condolence. The señor would certainly have forgotten him.

The inscrutable señor had just noticed the Margarita pearls around Miss Moll's neck. Her face burned and she turned to Preston. How stupid of me, she thought.

"Miss Moll is a famous journalist," Cooper explained. "Have you read *Caracas for Beginners*, Señor Sánchez?"

"The pleasure still lies ahead of me. Tell me, señorita, haven't we met once before in Caracas?"

"Perhaps a hundred years ago."

"If that is so, you've kept very well."

"Thank you, señor."

"You know each other?" Cooper asked, astonished.

"That's saying too much," said Miss Moll. "Señor Sánchez is a friend of a friend of a friend of mine."

Sánchez smiled. "That's too complicated for me, señorita. We are simple people here. What are you doing on the Orinoco?"

"Looking around."

"There's nothing to look at here. Are you intending to stay much longer?" He was staring at her.

"I don't know. That depends."

Sánchez raised his brows and turned brusquely to Cooper. "Thank you for your kind invitation, Mr. Cooper. I've heard a lot about you."

"I hope nothing too bad, señor."

"In that case I wouldn't have mentioned it. My friend William Cornerstone in Chicago spoke about your business in Venezuela in the most glowing terms."

"He's a top ranking officer in the firm."

"A very good firm, Mr. Cooper. This fish is delicious. On Margarita Island I catch my own fish."

"How interesting," said Miss Moll.

"It would bore you, señorita. You need a lot of patience to fish. One has to wait a long time for results." Sánchez's voice was cold.

An unpleasant silence. Mr. and Mrs. Preston and Bendix ate their fish without saying a word. Cooper looked from Sánchez to Miss Moll. They had conversed like enemies and paid no attention to the other guests. Cooper was indignant and therefore smiled more radiantly than ever.

Sánchez asked Cooper about his impressions of Venezuela. Cooper replied cautiously. "I haven't been here very long, señor. I wouldn't like to give a hasty opinion. I am an industrial bird of passage."

Sánchez asked Cooper to give him a bird's-eye view of his impressions.

"Everything is very different here, especially the work tempo."

"Perhaps we like to catch too many fish, Mr. Cooper."

"Come on, Carlos!" Preston laughed. "Our friend Cooper is doing his best in a very difficult sector. You don't tell him what you really think either..."

"You're wrong, Gilberto. I say what I think much too often."

"Are you fishing for compliments, señor?" asked Miss Moll.

Sánchez smiled. "If you would like to pay me a compliment..."

"Unfortunately I can't think of one."

"I thought a journalist could always think of anything."

"Why don't you pay me a compliment, señor?"

"Unfortunately I can't think of one either."

"May I ask—how is your wife? Isn't she here with you?"

"My wife is dead."

Carla Moll had violated a taboo. Nobody mentioned Teresa Sánchez, not even Pilar anymore. Except for Cooper, who knew nothing about Sánchez's private life, everybody looked somber.

"I'm sorry to hear that, señor," Cooper mumbled, but received no reply. Cooper couldn't understand why Sánchez seemed to have taken such a sudden dislike to him.

Sánchez pulled himself together and asked whether Cooper was encountering any difficulties as an economic advisor in Venezuela. Cooper cleared his throat. He always did when he had to be cautious. Sánchez was like an inquisitor. "Venezuela is an immensely rich land," he said finally. "But if I may speak frankly..."

"Please do."

"Venezuela's industry seems pretty patriarchal to me, at least for our times. Or am I wrong?"

"Not at all. In Latin America paternalism is an established industrial strategy. Our people adapt very slowly to today's industrial structure. We still have so many illiterates. The contrasts with the United States are tremendous."

"We have difficulties of other kinds," Cooper said politely.

"You mean your racial problem? We don't have any of that here."

"That is only one of our problems. Life in the States may be too mechanized; in your country on the other hand it seems too individualistic. If I may say so, you have too many eccentrics here."

Sánchez laughed. "That's possible."

"I have met nothing else," said Miss Moll.

"In spite of the contrasts between our continents," Cooper said diplomatically, "I think they can be bridged. Much too much is made of them. The human being is the same everywhere."

"Without a doubt," said Sánchez. "I too wish sincerely that we could learn to understand each other better. But I am afraid we are basically very different. We like bullfights, you have a society for the prevention of cruelty to animals."

Preston laughed, and Sánchez joined in, not exactly heartily. Carla and Mrs. Preston were excluded. Carla hated conversations exclusively between men, whereas Yolanda Preston was used to them. She began to talk about her seven children. Carla hated conversations about children even more than exclusive conversations between men. She felt pushed into the background. That was what Sánchez had wanted. She choked over her steak. She glared at him and thought: bastard!

Preston ate with concentration. He had high blood pressure and discussions excited him. Every now and then he looked surreptitiously into the garden. It was growing dark. He hoped to catch a glimpse of Padilla. He had read his name in the hotel register. Had the bird flown?

The more depressed Carla became the more Sánchez's spirits rose. Smiling amiably, he turned to Bendix, who had been listening to him with rapt concentration.

"I would like to talk to you tomorrow, Señor Bendix. I am sure you have gained a lot of experience with United Steel."

"Oh yes, a lot, Señor Sánchez. But unfortunately I have to go back to Berlin. My contract has expired."

"I may be able to offer you a position."

"You mean it, señor?" Young Bendix's face had turned a fiery red.

"We can always use good engineers, young man. Haven't we had a talk once in Caracas?"

"Yes, señor. But nothing came of it."

How young he is, and how honest, thought Sánchez. No, this man never had anything to do with Carla Moll's search for Bonnhoff. "Our head office is in Ciudad Guayana," he said.

"United Steel works there too!" Cooper said quickly.

"I know the managers," said Sánchez. "Very capable men. Yes, our country is vast and to a great extent unexploited. There is plenty of room for the firm of Álvarez & Sánchez on the Orinoco. You see, Mr. Cooper, private enterprise is still flourishing in our part of the world."

Álvarez & Sánchez? thought Cooper. His Teresa, who had died so suddenly in Mérida, was called Álvarez. Had she perhaps been related to Sánchez? Or was Álvarez a common name in Venezuela? Probably. He looked across the table at Carla Moll. "You're not eating anything, Miss Moll. Isn't it to your liking?"

"The rum is excellent, Mr. Cooper."

"Your health, señorita!" Sánchez looked at her with the eyes of an esthete. A composition in gold and white. But the melancholy way she was watching him left him cold. "The rum is too strong for you," he said. "Why don't you try a whiskey and soda, señorita?"

"I happen to prefer rum, especially with fruit."

"That's not the point," Sánchez said sternly. "You'll have to be carried to your room, my dear, if you go on like this."

"I can take a lot, señor."

"As you wish."

Cooper stared at the two. Miss Moll was undergoing a startling change. Right now she was a strange combination of Fury and Camille. She was acting in a way he couldn't stand in women: one way of behavior for men, another for those she considered neutral, and no way of behavior at all for women. Yolanda Preston didn't exist for her. Very rude, thought Cooper.

Carla felt utterly miserable. I'm headed for a padded cell, she thought. She felt exposed, at the mercy of Sánchez's eyes. With his smiling cruelty he was suggesting that she wasn't as young as she had been on the island. She could no longer fascinate him. Suddenly she saw her future with her mother's eyes: nothing but work, colleagues, and empty Sundays. Soon she would see love as a children's illness.

"Let me have the waiter bring you a wrap," said Sánchez. "You are cold, señorita. You're very pale." He looked into her eyes for a moment, then called over a waiter. Carla told him where he could find her woolen cape. Quite a while later he came back with a red shawl. He hadn't been able to find the wrap. She's still so untidy, thought Sánchez. Certain characteristics never change. Once her untidyness had amused him. Her red shawl was blood on snow. His eyes flashed. Then he turned to Cooper again. He said that small successes meant a lot in Venezuela; in the States big successes were quickly forgotten. Why, he wanted to know.

"We are obsessed by success." Preston joined in unexpectedly. "And you're getting to that stage gradually too, Carlos."

"I hope not, Gilberto. Contentment is more important."

"Where can you buy it?" asked Carla Moll.

"We've read too much Freud," said Gilbert Preston. "I'm afraid we've become a nation of thinkers. I don't like it."

"We don't think as pragmatically as you do in the States. At least not yet," said Sánchez. "Even in our growing industrial world we tend to create myths rather than to believe in electronics. It's a great nuisance!"

For a moment Sánchez was in his own private universe, and Cooper looked at him, astonished. Sánchez was a devious fellow. Was he making fun of the United States? Of Cooper? Of women? Something very odd was going on between him and Miss Moll.

"How does the Orinoco impress you, Miss Moll?" asked Preston.

"Not as exciting as a bullfight but better than bridge."

"What do you have against bridge?" Yolanda Preston asked irritably. "It's a good game. You have to think."

"That's what I have against it," said Carla, squashing her cigarette angrily in an ash tray and reaching for another. Sánchez asked what harm the poor cigarette had done to be treated so violently, and received no reply. Carla felt dizzy. All around her Preston, Cooper, and Sánchez were conversing about the era of technology, natural resources, chemistry. She knew a thing or two about chemistry. How illusions could turn into vinegar and love into bitter tea. I'm stoned, she thought. Carlos, can you hear me? What do I care about steel, petroleum, cement? And you? Are you a mourning widower, Carlos?

"Yes. I am chairman of the chamber of commerce in Caracas," said Sánchez. "We have a businessmen's club, Mr. Cooper. If you would like an introduction . . . any time. Unfortunately I don't know when I'll be in Caracas."

Once, on the island, he had said, *"Basta ya!"* thought Carla, when I made a scene because he wanted to go fishing alone. He looked grim, as he does now, standing up. He looks like one of El Greco's gentlemen. What good does it do me? Carlos, stay! Don't go away. He's had enough . . . *basta ya!*

Sánchez walked over to Carla Moll and picked up her shawl. She hadn't noticed that it had fallen off her shoulders. Everything was turning around and around . . . Cooper, the Prestons, Bendix, the fruit bowl. The ground beneath her opened up, the Orinoco overflowed Cooper's dinner, a naked couple embraced in the clouds . . . there was no Hotel Amazonas, only a primeval landscape: cacti, sharp as knives; feral animals; trees with long, sinister roots; and snakes, hungry crocodiles, night birds with hooked beaks. The wild primeval animal world of the Orinoco swam, crawled, and flew closer . . . closer. She saw it all in the glow of her drunkenness, and between it El Greco's gentleman, without his lace collar, without his seal ring on his middle finger, without his Vandyke beard . . . only with his deep-set eyes and an expression of disgust playing about his lips.

"You are not feeling well, señorita. You drank too fast," murmured Sánchez. He was frowning. He had warned Señorita Moll. Rum didn't agree with her.

She looked up at him drearily. She would have liked to upbraid him, but she was too tired and too drunk. Horrible that he should see her in this condition. He was supposed to have seen what he had lost on this evening.

"Come, señorita. I'll take you to your room."

"I must explain . . ."

"That isn't necessary. I understand. *Please* come! Can you stand? Good. Slowly now."

She was sobbing.

"Tears won't help. What on earth's the matter with you?"

"I . . . I . . . feel sick."

"Yes."

"I can't walk, Carlos."

"Yes you can. There. That's better. Where is your room?"

"Back there . . . I've got to . . . for just a minute. Excuse me, Carlos."

"Sit down here. I'll get somebody."

"No, no! I can walk. Only I must hang onto you. Forgive me. I . . . must hang onto you. Can't do it otherwise. I've forgotten all my Spanish. All I can remember is *policía* and *un médico* . . ."

"You don't need a doctor. All you need is . . ."

"All I need is you. Nothing else!"

"You need rest. Good night."

"Stay! Please stay! Please!"

"Please help the señorita," Sánchez told a maid to whom he had gestured from the patio. He gave her some money.

"Thank you, señor. What is the matter with the señorita?"

"She is overtired."

He walked up to Carla who was sitting motionless on a wicker chair, listening to the conversation. "Goodbye," he murmured.

She didn't look up or reply.

# 10

# Coming to Terms

Carlos Sánchez:

I should never have slept with Carla Moll. We were completely incompatible. But there is a mixture of brashness, irony, and sudden submission in her that is hard to resist. At any rate, I couldn't resist it two years ago. Since then so much has changed. It is important to cure our passions. They reduce us to slaves.

Carla Moll is too young to understand this. She is dissatisfied and unhappy, and feels nothing but emptiness. I sensed that last night as I walked up to Cooper's table. She was pale and depressed, and her thoughts were elsewhere. But then she came alive, and her eyes held an invitation she didn't express in words. She tried desperately to control herself, but for a moment she looked like a child dreaming her favorite dream. It would have touched me if it had been any other young woman. On the island she enchanted me. Of course both of us were thinking of the island. I have Pilar to thank for the fact that I didn't go on living on Margarita in a fool's paradise.

Carla's blond hair reminded me of Christina, my first sweetheart in Berlin. I was eighteen years old at the time, studying at the Polytechnic and living in Bonnhoff's Tiergarten villa. And then, thirty-two years later, Carla Moll came storming into my house in Caracas: intelligent, just as deceitful as Christina, just as blond, and from Berlin, too. I carried her off to the island, and she let me do it because she needed a man. And on the island I behaved like an idiot. I introduced this *Fräulein* to a Caribbean paradise, a world ruled by Eros, with no duties, no pain, no reality. Actually I think I lied more thoroughly than she did. She was unspoiled and quite possibly truly in love with me. At any rate, for the time being she forgot her Berlin employer and her absurd search for Bonnhoff. Just the same, she watched me constantly, not to find out what my relationship was to Bonnhoff or get information out of me as to where he could be found, but to gain control of me and bind me to her. She didn't succeed. She has a lot of healthy common sense and wit, but in her soul there is as much disorder as in her bedroom on Margarita.

There was a certain magic about our nights on the island. A very young man doesn't sense something like this because he is too curious about his body. After forty he lets himself be surprised. The night transformed Carla into Carlita, a nymph with no home and no family. On the island I encouraged such moments, but her behaviour last night was disgusting. She doesn't know when something is over. For a moment, when I saw her at Cooper's table, I admit I envisioned a grand reconciliation in bed. Besides, my Carlita offered herself freely last night. Her ironic manner couldn't hide her desire. Cooper's guests didn't notice anything, but I know this lady more intimately. She wanted to sleep with me.

She did her best. She turned to Preston and began to talk to him, to remind me of her beautiful profile. She let her evening dress slip further off her shoulders. This exhibitionism was new to me. Carlita had dressed like a cloister novice in the evenings on the island (probably only because she wanted to be undressed), but it delighted me. Now she behaved as if she would have liked to take off everything. She drank too much and laughed too shrilly. Her shoulder straps slipped down still farther. Cooper wiped his glasses. Her tricks were too primitive. They didn't suit Carlita. By the fish and rice course I had decided not to play along. When we spoke of iron ore, the technological era, and the latest forms of mass hysteria, Carla Moll sat there like a Pallas Athene who had seen better days.

When she walked into our house in Caracas, she was conspicuously pale, in spite of her boldness—a northern household plant among wild orchids. In my mind's eye I could see the fräulein from Berlin in front of a burning bush, and the flames casting a red glow on her face. Then Pilar came in and she grew pale again. Suddenly Bonnhoff, out in the garden house, let out a scream. I said it was a night bird. At Cooper's dinner Carla's shawl again cast a red glow on her face. No one screamed, except Yolanda Preston, who must have grown up among deaf people. Cooper speaks softly and cautiously, as if he is constantly afraid of saying more than he intends. He seems just as lost on the Orinoco as my fräulein. He certainly resented Carla Moll for not paying enough attention to him. He thirsts for attention. I realized that as soon as I spoke to him. Preston tells me that Cooper is married to a woman from Berlin whom nobody ever sees.

The more I think of it, the more I realize why I can't forgive Carla, something I might have been prepared to do, if she hadn't got drunk. With that she shattered the image I still had of her—a young woman who, in spite of all passion, was reserved to the core of her being. Never had she implored me as she did that night. Never before had she shown me her tears or her fear. Pure tears can move me, but not an outburst fueled by alcohol. Carla reminded me of Teresa in her dreariest moments: without dignity, without beauty, strapped in a straitjacket of desire. I could see her despair clearly. In her light eyes there was the fear of being abandoned. I pitied her.

They say that pity evokes love. Nothing ruins the relationship between a man and a woman so quickly and finally as pity. I want a partner, not a heap of misery. I felt sorry for Teresa and it enfeebled me. In the end I hated her. And last night, for the first time, Carla was a heap of misery. Her hair hung bedraggled over her forehead as she sat on the wicker chair in front of her room. I should have taken her in my arms and comforted her, but I stood there, motionless. A slovenly woman with a ridiculous lemon-yellow braid and a parrot on her shoulder was staring at us. Her loose dress was closed with safety pins. She might have been a model for Goya in one of his gruesome moods, when he was inspired by ugliness and decay. Carla had the hiccups. They make all suffering comical. I said, "Goodbye." She looked up at me and said nothing. Her eyes glittered in the dark, meaningless as the luminous numbers on a broken watch. I looked away. I remembered just in time what women can do to one when one lets them.

I hate Carla and myself. However, I really have nothing against Cooper. I even feel an ironic compassion for him. There he is, this intelligent, well-mannered man, messing up my private life, with no idea that Teresa Álvarez was my wife and Carla Moll once my Carlita. It's really very funny. But if an unsuspecting mind is the eighth of the deadly sins, then things don't look good for Cooper.

Perhaps, if I continue to turn my back on love I will gradually petrify and turn to stone. When the angel Lucifer no longer recognized love, he became the devil. I'm not complaining. I'm freer than I could be with the best wife. But there is still a void. I am not gentle, but I need gentleness. Perhaps I am looking for an angel.

Elliot Cooper (Venezuela) to Naomi Cooper (Switzerland)

Dear Naomi,

I have waited long enough for an answer from you. I could have died in the meantime—which almost happened—and I'm sure it would have made little impression on you. Now at last you have pulled yourself together and written to me, and I almost wish you hadn't! If you had kept silent I would have remained philosophical about it instead of writing a very annoyed letter to your doctor. I hope he will forgive me. You seem to see me too as an (unpayed) psychiatrist, because every third sentence in your letter is an insult. I don't expect any thanks for what I have done and still do for you, but I may ask for a somewhat politer tone. Your doctor writes that you are withdrawing more and more into your shell, and you are drinking. He doesn't say how you manage to get the stuff; evidently he doesn't know. All he knows is that alcoholics and dope addicts are extremely sly when it comes to their habits. I know this too from bitter experience, as do Mother, Cousin Maud, and Richard Cooper. If nothing else, you have presented my family with unending drama.

I have written to your doctor by return mail that I refuse to pay for any further treatment; that is to say I will not pay for the whole thing all over again from the beginning. I don't know of any cure for your condition, but psychoanalytical chats at astronomical prices no longer come into question. Mother was against this effort in Switzerland from the start, and she has been proved right again. I should have told myself the same thing after your efforts with Alcoholics Anonymous in Chicago ended with double doses of whiskey and gin.

In case Dr. Sprüngli informs you of my decision too gently, I repeat: I do *not* agree to your going to Berlin. As I arranged a long time ago, Richard will fly back to Chicago with you whether you're seeing white mice or not. It is absolutely incomprehensible to me that your doctor thinks a visit to Germany might be successful therapeutically. In Berlin you will see your imaginary Sturmbannführer Bonnhoff in every third pedestrian, whereas in Chicago this will happen less frequently. Even granting that this man did exist in pre-World War II Berlin, he must be dead by now—or very old, and certainly powerless. The world is full of men who have left their evil deeds behind them and are living out their old age peacefully. They don't interest anybody. The only important thing is what happens now. What is behind this flight of yours into the past? Tell me, for God's sake, and without any psychological nonsense. I am beginning to detest all aspects of psychology. Why aren't you like other women: pleasant, polite, and content? Do you think dreadful things have happened only to you? All sorts of people all over the world have lost their savings, their families, and the respect of the people around them, yet manage to recover and lead useful lives. Moreover, everyone has certain memories that are torturous. I have too, believe it or not. But I push them away, like a sensible person. No one can live under constant pressure. You are destroying yourself. And for what? You are not the young girl any more who suffered hard times in Berlin. Look in the mirror. It will tell you. I did all I could to make an American of you, and you have experienced only good things from my family. Well, we've given up on you. I am gradually becoming a ridiculous figure, a married bachelor. I'm afraid some day I'm going to have had as much of it as I can take. Your indifference is unbelievable! A poisoned arrow nearly cost me my life. And I didn't mention my infected corn, although in this climate one always has to be careful of blood poisoning. A young friend gave me a salve. When I get to Puerto Cabello I guess everything will be all right again. I mean my corn, not my marriage.

One more thing. Mother can't possibly have written to you that I am considering divorcing you. In the condition you're in, you only half read letters and misunderstand half of that. Mother is the last person who would get herself mixed up in my affairs. I imagine Maudie is at the bottom of it, as usual, in her inconspicuous way. Her opinions on marriage are strictly theoretical. In order to be able to discuss marriage one has to have experienced it. Maud Cooper hasn't done that. She prefers to be a burden to Mother.

I can't imagine what you see in her. She was a handsome girl, but now she looks like a stuffed laundry bag. I am surprised that she writes to you so often. She hasn't written to me in all these months.

They're starting work in Puerto Cabello again, thank goodness. Unfortunately I have too much time to think in the Hotel Amazonas. The other day I gave a farewell dinner for my friends. It was a huge success. A very important industrialist from Caracas was one of my guests and he offered me some valuable introductions. My old friend Preston and his wife (whom I can't stand) came from Río and are staying at the Amazonas. They have five or seven children now. It saddened me. My guest of honor was a Berlin journalist, Miss Carla Moll, whom I have mentioned in earlier letters. She is a little in love with me, but idiot that I am, I have done nothing about it, as usual. Anyway, she is elegant, amusing, and very circumspect when it comes to alcohol. Her book on Caracas is a huge success.

Why don't you do something useful? For instance, interior decoration. Then you could renovate Mother's living room. You would enjoy it, and we could save a lot of money. You have good taste when you set your mind to it. Or you could visit old and poor people with Mother. But for God's sake *do something*! Find your way back into reality! What you've talked yourself into about my friend Roger Brown is absolute nonsense. Of course he is my lawyer. But he is also a friend of our family. When Mother invites him to dinner, that's her business, surely. Did Maudie tell you that I would like to marry Roger's younger sister? How did you get that idea? Maudie must be crazy. Is any one of you still sane? Anyway, right now I am married. I informed Maudie to this effect. What would you do without me?

I forbid you to write my Mother objectionable letters. She sent me your last one. She almost had a heart attack while reading it. It left me speechless. It must have been difficult for Mother to send me that letter because she is very discreet and has resigned herself to you long ago. But after all, she *is* my mother! Perhaps in a sane moment you will grasp that she can't exactly be happy about my marriage. But as I just said, she is resigned to it. Roger Brown also sent me a letter from you—as my friend, not as my lawyer. What goes on in your mind when you throw all these complaints at poor Roger? He hasn't done you any harm, nor is he even against you. Is he supposed to drown his sister so that I can't marry her? You have *delirium tremens*, my dear. Roger knows this as all of us do, and is ready to overlook your behavior. Your sudden writing craze is something that doesn't help to make me more popular. I don't want you to write to my friends and relatives as long as you are so excited and confused. I have asked Dr. Sprüngli to influence you in this respect.

That's all for today. Richard will cable Dr. Sprüngli when he can fly to Zürich. Please be nice to him. He is making a sacrifice to do this for us. His time is limited. Fortunately he loves Switzerland. I hope you come to your senses. Then nothing will stand between you and a normal family life. *Auf Wiedersehen* in Chicago.

Yours,
Elliot

Naomi Cooper:
Perhaps there are people who are healed when they look into their past. I only get sicker and sicker the deeper psychiatrist Sprüngli digs into my childhood. Now he has dug up my rocking chair complex and I feel dizzy. Grandfather Strelitz had an old rocking chair, and I was allowed to rock in it. August would watch me. Grandfather laughed, and I screamed my head off while he rocked the chair faster and faster. I thought it would never stop. It gave me my first

feeling of insecurity. If only Dr. Sprüngli hadn't dug so deeply! Now I am rocking back and forth again as I did when I first came to Chicago, when Richard Cooper and I . . . I have told Dr. Sprüngli all sorts of things, some true, some not, but I have never told Dr. Sprüngli about Richard. Dr. Sprüngli would raise his fee immediately if Richard were dragged into the daylight. I'm dreading Richard's arrival in Zürich. Meanwhile I go on playing crazy and drunk, and Dr. Sprüngli tapes it. After all, he's got to do something! He's very nice and knows his Freud and Jung, but he is much too credulous. And he costs too much. Elliot is right about that, no matter how much I hate to admit it.

My psychiatrist hasn't noticed that gradually, very gradually, I have stopped drinking. I started drinking again because I thought that would keep me from being sent back to Mother Cooper in Chicago. Stupid of me. Richard is coming and that's that!

Elliot never suspected anything about Cousin Richard and me. He surpasses anyone I know in gullibility. I would never have thought that so much blindness could go with such acute business sense. Richard said once, "Elliot is one of those people to whom dreadful things happen without their noticing it. He sees every shipwreck as a successful pleasure trip." I asked if that was American. Richard laughed and said, "That's Elliot Cooper." Richard always laughed at my questions. I wonder if he's laughing now over Mother Cooper's efforts to marry Roger Brown's youngest sister off to my husband. In all dishonesty, of course. With a legal divorce from me and legal orange blossoms for them, and a reception in the family mausoleum on Lake Michigan. As usual Elliot knew nothing about it until I wrote to him. Richard, of course, knows all about it because his wife is also one of Roger Brown's sisters. Richard's wife loves everything that brings money into the house, which includes Richard. Horrible person! Richard is a dog, but he still deserves a nicer wife. Not me—I was never nice, and that's no secret. Perhaps with Richard I might have turned out differently. As a young man he was so . . .

so *real*! When he came into the kitchen, someone was actually there. Not like Elliot, who is so artificial.

Richard Cooper is the only man of whom I was never afraid. He would have laughed at me. With him I probably wouldn't have needed a psychiatrist. I don't know. Today I'm so many Naomis: Elliot's wife, an alcoholic, a case for mind probers, and a child in a rocking chair. And then there is the young girl who went to see Bonnhoff of her own free will, and the old woman I am going to be some day. It's difficult to cope with all these different images. Dr. Sprüngli can't do it. He thinks I'm Naomi Cooper from Chicago all the time. He also believes that I'm drinking more, when actually I'm drinking less. Otherwise I would never be able to carry out my plan.

Shortly before they took my father off to Oranienburg, he gave me his poems and his notes on the Russian revolutionary, Michael Bakunin, friend of Wagner's youth, to keep for him. Politically controversial notes. He couldn't have given them to Mother or any of the other Strelitzes. Even Father realized that. He was a romantic, slightly tinged with red, and for that he died in the Oranienburg concentration camp. Richard said once that in Europe you died for your ideals, in the United States you lived for them. That was years before Vietnam. My father considered dying for one's ideals the thing to do, even in the Third Reich. So there I was with his notes on Bakunin's Pan-Slavism, and Father looked out of the window to see if the Gestapo had entered the house yet. In spite of his youth he was already a little stooped as he stood there, watching and listening. I have never since seen such an unbowed man with such a bowed back. I swallowed hard, and my penguin was perched on Father's desk that afternoon and never said a word. August was ready to do his duty because, after all, he had once belonged to Grandfather Strelitz and was a Prussian penguin. Nor did he say a word when I cut him open and stuffed Father's poems and his notes on Bakunin inside him, and sewed him up again. To this day I can't sew, but I did all right that time because I was so frightened. So when August was standing stiff and straight on the mantel in Sturmbannführer Bonnhoff's room, he still had Bakunin and the world revolution of those days in his stomach. I would have laughed if Himmler had found out about it and had hanged Bonnhoff for secretly being a Marxist and a traitor. That would have been funny, or, as Father would have put it, poetic justice. But nothing funny ever happens to me. I find that very funny.

When I cut my clever August open again after my flight to the United States, the papers were as yellowed and brittle as Father's ideals of long ago. I wept, and August made himself very small. He is sad when I am sad. We've been through a lot together.

My big plan keeps me awake at night, but the head nurse must know nothing about it. Otherwise she'll come with a hypo and my head won't be clear. Richard will soon be arriving in Zürich. August, don't you dare say a word!

Richard was my first man. I was nineteen and cooking for Mrs. Jane Warren Cooper. Son Elliot was away on vacation. So there was a long time with just Mother Cooper and cousin Maudie; and Richard came often for a weekend because he wanted to marry one of Roger Brown's innumerable sisters. I didn't know that, and Richard didn't say anything about it. Nobody confesses anything to the cook. Even Maudie, who found out everything, knew nothing about Richard's marriage plans. He was a sly one. Maudie was always nice, but she had little time for me. At the time she was a private secretary in a big company, and wasted her spare time trying to seduce her boss because that always happened in the movies. It didn't work for Maudie because she pounces on men, like Uncle Werner's hunting dogs on their prey, and I don't think men like that. Most men run if women are too aggressive.

Richard didn't run. He was big and athletic. In those days his stomach was flat, and he had a loud, hearty laugh. He laughed most at my cooking efforts. Maudie used to go out to eat, as a matter of principle, because she liked good food—and it showed on her. After the death of her parents in a plane crash, she moved in with Elliot's mother and rented a floor of the huge house. So she is in no way a burden to Mrs.

Cooper, as Elliot always claims, but pays her way. Mother Cooper was glad to take her in because she likes people around her who agree with her. Maudie says yes, yes, to every foolish thing Mother says, and keeps smoking her cigarettes. But she'd rather be with Mother Cooper than alone. Until my marriage to Elliot, Maudie was my only consolation. When Mrs. Cooper expected guests, Maudie would come home from the office at noon and secretly do the cooking for me. Whatever she does, she does well. Today she's a real estate agent and she's good at that too. She has offered Elliot a suitable house for us a hundred times, but he wants to stay with Mother. Of course he's rarely home.

Richard would come into the kitchen and help to cook when Mrs. Cooper was playing bridge. Very often he yawned loudly, and that offended me. I had learned at home that one didn't yawn in the company of ladies, but then, after all, I wasn't a lady anymore. Richard knew that just as well as I did. Usually he cheered me up with nonsense, so that I became young again and forgot Berlin for hours. He worked in a family business on the Mississippi, and he had a lot of hobbies, mainly unattached girls, horse racing, and ventriloquism.

His little dummy was Charlie. He had a stiff white collar, a wooden head with big round eyes, a dirty grin, and told dirty jokes which would have shocked Elliot. I didn't understand enough English yet to appreciate Richard's and Charlie's jokes, but it was all very funny, and in the end we became friends—Richard and I, Charlie and my August. Richard said we were a quartet and had to do all our foolish things together and never part. Mother Cooper didn't have to know about it. Elliot was always away, present only on her sewing table as a photograph.

One day Charlie made me a declaration of love in Richard's name—my first! Well, I was young and lonely and lost. At the time I would have welcomed anybody who assured me that he loved me. Besides Richard said I was a very sweet girl, which was all wrong, and Charlie waggled his head and I had to laugh again. Richard was standing beside the stove, tall, full of vitality. He was wearing a red sports shirt, white trousers, and an alligator belt with a gold buckle. I had on my apron and my hair was dangling over my face. "You have beautiful hair, Naomi. Is it dyed?" croaked Charlie. As if I had money to dye my hair! Richard said, "Why not? Everybody's doing it." He went on to say that he'd never come across such a child of nature as myself. His dark hair was always wild—his eyes too—and he had a strange expression around his mouth: moody, spoiled, and a little bored. The boredom disappeared once he got his way. And he got his way often, also with me. And when it happened for the first time, August fell off the table. Richard said, "My God! You're still a virgin. I should have known. Stop crying! So it's happened." Whenever Richard came into my room, August had to be put in the closet. Charlie waited in Richard's car.

Elliot must have been on an endless vacation. Once I asked Maudie when he was coming back. She mumbled something about some sort of scandal he'd gotten himself involved in, and Mother Cooper had sent him off on a trip. After his return he was to become an economic advisor. His picture showed a young man with a round, soft face, wearing glasses, with greedy eyes and an insincere smile. "Elliot likes to save lost girls," said Richard, whereupon Mrs. Cooper lost her party smile. I spilled a little soup on her hair. It was a charming evening. After supper Richard went out and I lay in bed with August in my arms and wept. His feathers got wet. Maudie brought me some hot milk and said, "That's Aunt Jane for you. She's worried about Elliot too."

It made no impression on me. I was worried about Richard, but I asked about Elliot because I was bored. Maudie said, "This is what happened. A while ago Elliot..." Then she paused and said, "Oh, I can't tell you Naomi. It's a secret." Maudie was a specialist at dark insinuations, and when things were getting really interesting she would suddenly remember her promise to be silent. She could drive you crazy. But she's the best soul in the world. It's the little things that are so annoying. For instance, Mrs. Cooper would rustle the newspaper as if an autumn storm were raging in the room, or she would try to initiate me into the American way of life. That was when I began to hate her, long before she became my mother-in-law.

Richard was my afternoon demon. In the evening he went out and didn't take me with him. If I asked where he was going, he'd say, "To the singers, the heathens, and the speech-makers." His only resemblance to Elliot was his reluctance to give any definite information. He couldn't stand dismal moods. He would often ask me if I were going to a funeral. Or he said I shouldn't be so sulky if I wanted to be successful in life. That was the last thing I wanted. I already hated the word success as violently as the word mother. But I said nothing, just looked at him wide-eyed. Then he would relent and take me in his arms and rock me like a baby. I was as serious as a child in those days. I grew out of that. "Richard's not good for you," Maudie grumbled.

I read Kant and Hegel less and less and drank more and more whiskey with Richard. Whiskey was really the only thing that kept him home. When it grew dark he became restless, as if he were about to miss the best things in life if he stayed with me. In the end he gave me a fleeting kiss or yawned unabashedly, and stormed off. Sometimes he left me his whiskey. That's how it all began. Then I felt warmer, almost happy, if happiness means simply freedom from pain. Richard was genuinely fond of me and had the best intentions about cheering me up. But he said often that after a while good intentions stank like a fish. I bored him. And then he was about to become engaged to a suitable lady. Shortly before the end, our relationship broke like a cheap pocket comb.

Today, after so many years, I still tremble when I think of the scene Richard made when I was in my third month. He changed so mysteriously that I shrank from him. In the kitchen, on a perfectly ordinary afternoon, he became a total stranger, an ice-cold gentleman in evening dress. Maudie had gone to the movies and Mrs. Cooper was visiting Richard's father in Mississippi—these were the only merciful aspects of the whole story. I stared at Richard, horrified at the things he had said to me in his first shock: that I was a cunning, scheming creature who had played the innocent, that I was out to get him to marry me, but nothing was going to come of *that*! He, Richard Cooper, was going to marry a . . . a . . .

"Go ahead, Richard," I said. "Spell it out for me."

He tore off to his singers, heathens, and speechmakers. I walked into Mrs. Cooper's living room and Elliot's picture caught my eye. I remembered what Richard had said: "He likes to save lost girls. God only knows where he finds them today." All my ideas about Elliot came from Richard.

But the first one to save me was Maudie, not only because she loves secrets but because she's always there in an emergency. She took me to a doctor and waited in the waiting room. I was then put in a clinic on a street with no lights. An old, eternally new thing. Not worth mentioning. Richard was right. Something to yawn over. I stayed in the clinic for a few days, and Maudie brought me flowers, chocolates, and August. That's something I'll never forget . . . that she brought August Strelitz to me. Maudie was wearing a silk suit that fitted her nicely, and a new hat with flowers that didn't go well with her long thin face and sharp eyes. "Why are you all dressed up?" I asked crossly. "Do you think this is a wedding?"

Maudie gave me a look and her long nose got even longer. She always looked like an alert bird, especially when she held her head sideways and stopped talking. "I'm going on somewhere else from here," she said, sounding embarrassed. "The Roger Browns are giving a party."

"For Richard and Clarissa Brown?"

"You're crazy. That's still a secret. No. Just cocktails." She began to smoke, and I told her she should strew some ashes on her good silk suit.

"What are you going to do, Naomi?"

"I am going to try to get Elliot Cooper to marry me. Then I can . . . I can . . ." I wanted to say that then I could carry my child to birth, but swallowed the words. My throat was closed tight. I probably needed a schnapps.

"In four days I'll take you home, Naomi. Then you'll be ready."

"Ready for what?"

"Hush!" she said, as if to a naughty child. "I don't want to hear another word about it. Elliot Cooper is not for you, do you hear?"

"He's the only one around. Tell me, Maudie, what was that scandal about? After all, I've got to know why his mother sent him on this endless vacation."

"You'll find out soon enough." Maudie gave her flower hat a push. "Is there anything else you want, Naomi? Anything I can do for you?"

"You can lend me that hat for the wedding."

"Will do. Now sleep a little, silly girl."

"Stay a little longer, Maudie. Please! Do you like me just a little bit?"

"Any more questions?" Maudie was blushing. "I like your August better. So now behave yourself until I come to get you."

"Thank you, Maudie. A thousand times, thank you. I'll pay everything back when I'm... when I'm Mrs. Elliot Cooper. You want to bet that..."

I won the bet and lost the game. Gullible as ever, young Elliot had become involved in a disgraceful scandal. A murder, in fact, involving a prostitute who was available to the most prestigious men in Chicago. Elliot's name was in her telephone book. He had probably wanted to save her. She was his first experience. And someone or other tried to pin the murder on him. It was highly embarrassing for Mother and all the Coopers. They were in the social register, and Elliot—young, trusting, intimidated—had to appear in court. The murderer was found a while later, and the case was closed, but people now saw Elliot Cooper as the soul mate of a venal Venus. His engagement was broken off. He married me with his mother's consent. Maudie was astonished. I wore her flower hat at the wedding. I was grateful to Elliot. I didn't know that he hated gratitude.

\* \* \*

I never understood him. Now, years later, I understand him even less. He wants to be honorably married—please God not another scandal! But actually he can't stand being with his mother or me for any length of time. I don't bore him as I bored Richard, still it seems to suffice to send him away. Richard is, and remains, a snake in the grass. It was he who introduced Elliot to prostitution because at twenty Elliot was still a virgin; Richard didn't approve. Once he said, "Life is stupid when one does only what one's supposed to do. I want to leave traces behind me." I asked him what he meant. "Forget it!" he said irritably. Then he yawned and walked out. Perhaps he has finally given up this nonsense of leaving traces. He has married suitably, is a father, and a millionaire. But Richard Cooper left his traces on me.

Maudie writes regularly. I love her and she doesn't mind. Richard describes his affair with me as a negative experience. Actually Maudie didn't tell me this. It was one secret that she kept. I read it in a letter Richard wrote to her after my wedding. Everybody writes to her. Perhaps because she answers.

I am very calm and as sober as I can be. I even think kindly of Elliot. He hasn't had an easy time of it with me. Dr. Sprüngli calls my depression "traumatic imbalance." That seems to be a very complicated way of saying I don't enjoy life very much.

I begged Maudie to look after Elliot when he gets back to Chicago. He won't like being alone, never mind the scandal. Poor Elliot! He doesn't deserve someone as wonderful as Maudie, but certainly someone better than me. I read and hear all the time that one may change one's husband for the better. You can change no one, not even yourself. No beast of a human being ever develops a heart of gold. Maudie keeps asking me what my plans are. I have only one big plan, and that is a secret. Only August will go with me. Wherever I go, he comes along.

Gilbert Preston:
I have known Elliot Cooper for years. He is a man I can

find plenty of fault with, but that has never disturbed our friendship. At his dinner I began to draw comparisons between him and Sánchez. Doing so wasn't exactly loyal, but for me it clarified Elliot's character to some extent. Carlos Sánchez would never run away from the truth. On the contrary, he seeks the truth and faces it squarely. That makes him strong. Perhaps seeking and enduring the truth is the essence of manliness. How simple the world would be if a man's potency was enough to make a man of him. In youth it's sufficient to make one feel like a man. But later one learns that isn't enough. I hope I'll remain as rigorous in my search for the truth as Sánchez. Only the truth prevails. I take a dim view of Cooper's private life. He should separate from Naomi, who separated from him long ago. I have never met Naomi Cooper. I saw her only once seated at a table in a restaurant.

Elliot Cooper and I are at a strange point in our lives. In the thirties we were schoolboys. In the bloody forties our idealistic fathers died for democracy. In the fifties we were still young and had faith. We had faith in the American way of life, not only for America but for the whole world. Even at the beginning of the sixties, we still believed in that way of life. But then came Vietnam and the American way of death. The Kennedy brothers, Martin Luther King. Murder in the jungles of Asia, murder of people known and unknown. Our civil war between black and white. New evangelical doctrines: Black is beautiful. Why not? It doesn't automatically make white ugly!

So much happens in the world yet we experience so little of it intensively. Everything is thrown at us, mass produced: more and more sex, more and more happenings, *la dolce vita*, plus! And our inner reserves shrink. Disgust wherever you turn, regardless of the fact that at the end of the sixties we reached the moon. The drugs, the hippies, the poverty, the true and the false revolts. Dramas, melodramas, absurd plays. *It is too much!* Where will it all lead?

I asked Cooper if he had any idea who could possibly have aimed the arrow at him. Didn't he have any idea who his enemy or enemies might be? He looked at me, astonished.

He didn't have any enemies. I have my own thoughts on the matter but keep them to myself. Always the best thing to do. Cooper ignores the fact that we are becoming the target of the guerrillas to an ever greater extent, but it's wrong to ignore it. You can hire a murderer cheaply anywhere today. He doesn't even have to know why he's killing. Padilla remains a man on whom we can't pin anything. For years now he has had a reputation for being willing to assassinate Yanquis. Not long ago, in Puerto Ordaz, he was mentioned and interrogated in connection with an assassination, but they couldn't prove anything. When I entered the Hotel Amazonas, Padilla had disappeared in the woods; only his wife with the blond braid remained behind. In his youth Padilla almost beat a mine overseer to death. I have read his file and I have friends at police headquarters in Puerto Ordaz. I am sure Padilla won't be going back there in the near future. I have nothing against him. Actually I feel sorry for him. He is only one of the millions who are victims of the ideologies they espoused in their youth and poverty. Today Padilla is a capitalist and a landowner, but he hasn't lost a thing to the guerrillas except perhaps some money for propaganda and weapons.

The revolutionary medicine must lie heavy in his stomach. His instincts make him sly and taciturn, but his powers of thinking are primitive, and he isn't equal to the intellectual leaders from the middle-class and landowner families. Padilla—a dangerous believer in blind force, a camp follower of the Ché Guevaras in Venezuela. The police are looking for him right now as an accomplice in the arson of American property in our settlement at Cerro Bolívar, a workers' settlement. Perhaps he participated in it, perhaps not. I'm not writing his biography, but I do know the people between Cerro Bolívar and Puerto Ordaz pretty well. They ignore the fact that we have invested good dollars in their partially developed, backward land on the Orinoco, and are developing it industrially. Facts like this would only confuse Padilla's simplistic mind.

In this century we have experienced many dictatorships and rebellions. Every twenty years or so, all the angels wander away and the new tyrant stays. In Venezuela this takes place in shorter intervals. But for every new leader we get millions of scapegoats and martyrs. It disgusts me. The sacrificial lambs are born with their mouths wide open so that, like Padilla, they can swallow anything: new programs, half truths, fat lies, jokes that make them tremble, threats, demands, bans . . . what irony! Padilla is not a victim of the present government but of its enemies. The government hasn't taken his bank account or his property from him—yet. What will his comrades do? I know there are idealists and selfless fighters in all groups and parties, but what the guerrillas in this country overlook is that it is easier to rebel, to shoot, and to destroy institutions, the property of others, or their lives, than to keep one person alive, comfort him, listen to his tiresome complaints, and stop him from sinking into the morass of the times. I heard once that Carlos Sánchez keeps an old refugee from Hitler's Germany hidden somewhere and protects him. I don't know how much truth there is in it, and it's really none of my business, but I could believe it of Carlos. I could also imagine him not being very pleasant about it.

Cooper performs only the duties that convention and common sense prescribe, but in spite of his little weaknesses, I consider him of much greater importance and value to society than Padilla, with his readiness to destroy for half-baked ideologies, and, when he wishes or he's given the order, to kill. The only thing that stands in his way is his religion. My wife has seen him at mass in Puerto Ordaz, praying furiously. A Latin American phenomenon. A priest from Bogotá was recently taken blindfolded to a band of guerrillas to baptize their children and to bless their marriages. I read about it in a paper.

It is quite possible that Padilla is nearby and will attack Cooper and me as we drink our coffee. I never drink Venezuela's magnificent coffee without a loaded pistol in my pocket. Perhaps I look a little grim about it. My dear wife wonders why I'm not as cheerful as I used to be, God bless her! Why am I using my siesta hour to think about our lousy times? I need rest. The siesta is a very wise tradition. Cooper has never known the meaning of a rest period. High time that he left here. On the Orinoco the climate of the soul is dangerous.

What's that noise in the middle of the holy hour of the siesta? Yolanda is screaming. "Gilberto! Something's happened! Come! Come quickly! Cooper . . . He's dying! They've poisoned him!"

# 11

# The Truth Lies in the River

"Isn't it dreadful, about Mr. Cooper?"

"I've heard funnier things."

"Another cigarette, Fräulein Moll? Who could have wanted to poison such a nice man? A ghastly business. How do you like the fisherman's paradise? Marvelously quiet and peaceful, isn't it?"

"There must be a lot of snakes here, but except for that, it's paradise. Nice of you to drag me here."

"It's an honor for me, Fräulein Moll."

"I'm glad, but up till now I haven't discovered anything to describe. Only nature. A pity that Mr. Cooper didn't drink his poisoned lemonade here. That would have been something for my paper. What do they have against Cooper anyway?"

"I thought he was exceptionally nice," Herr Bendix said stiffly. "I have the feeling that the waiters at the Amazonas are careless. Or treacherous. Possibly the half-caste..."

"Could be."

"Poor Cooper. Who would want to die that way?"

"You rarely get to plan that sort of thing. You'll find that out one of these days, Herr Bendix."

"I feel sick when I think of Mr. Cooper."

"So think of something else. Anyway, Cooper was recovering when we left."

"Who knows what will happen to him next?"

"Do you know what's going to happen to me next? Or to you?"

"My instinct is to get out, get out! I'm beginning to take a very dim view of Venezuela."

"That must take some doing in this blazing sunshine."

"My whole attitude toward the country has changed." Young Wally Bendix looked grim.

"And high time too. You astonished me the way you saw the country with rose-colored glasses. For foreigners Venezuela is a dead-end street with palm trees."

"That's above my head, Fräulein Moll. What a shame that Señora de Padilla knocked over the lemonade glass. What was she doing there anyway?"

"You never know with Señora de Padilla."

"If she hadn't knocked over the glass they could have analyzed the lemonade."

"Well, it doesn't matter. Of course, it would have been horrible if Cooper had died, but it would really have been horrible only for him. The rest of us have had to live without Cooper all our lives, and that is what we would have had to go on doing."

"But Fräulein Moll . . ."

"You have to face facts, Herr Bendix. Why are you looking at me so horrified?"

"I . . . I didn't think you were so callous."

"Unfortunately I don't improve on closer acquaintance. Runs in the family. Don't you want to fish now?"

"I know a wonderful place. Not far away. I was there with Mr. Cooper."

"And I'll have a nap. Please leave your Indian with me . . . in case of poisoned arrows."

"Of course Zongo stays with you. I wouldn't dream of leaving you here alone. I won't be long. *Ádios*." He turned around once more before he disappeared. "I'm a funny man, Fräulein Moll. I always want to know what *really* happens. It was lucky that a doctor had just arrived. But we'll never find out who the culprit was. I like clarity and truth, but the truth lies in the river."

"May I borrow that little saying sometime?"

"Not my invention. It's what the Indians on the Orinoco say."

Herr Bendix departed. Carla Moll watched him go. Funny, how worried he looked when she was cynical. She stretched out in her hammock under its protective roof of leaves. Zongo had thrown a mosquito net like a giant sheet over her. The grass on the shore prickled, as inhospitable as the river. She was killing time again. She leafed through her German-Spanish dictionary: Where is the pain? Do you need an enema? Would you like a hot drink? She closed her eyes and composed various versions of her life.

First version: Carla Moll, wife.

Born in an air raid shelter during the Second World War. Sweet baby. Content. Blossoms out to become a student of philosophy but decides she'd rather marry the young graduate student, Willy Locker, from the Free University of Berlin. Mother Moll ecstatic, but tries to rearrange the marriage by nagging. Finally through tireless efforts achieves the separation of the Lockers' bed and bank account. Willy has his meals at the bachelor's club as before; Carla has nothing.

Second version: Carla Moll, martyr.

In the Second World War, hungry baby. Refuses nourishing food so that Mother Moll may have more to eat. After her father's departure—Professor Moll wandered off to East Berlin of his own free will—Student Moll hangs up her studies on the nearest available nail in order to act as surrogate husband to her mother. Moils and toils as typist in drab offices with exclusively nasty bosses. Chances of seduction: zilch. Neither she them nor they her. Typist Moll bears her virtue and her cross with patience and spends her evenings exchanging confidences and playing cards with her mother. No future worth projecting because imagination on strike.

Third version: Carla Moll, houri in Caracas, Venezuela.

Instead of looking for former Sturmbannführer Carl Fried-

rich Bonnhoff on *Comet* editor-in-chief Wendt's money—
Bonnhoff presumably in Venezuela—Moll spends a slightly
flawed honeymoon on Margarita Island with Carlos Sánchez.
After this idyll, she is thrown out of his famous grandfather's
house because Señor Sánchez discovers secret correspondence between her and editor-in-chief Wendt. Pilar Álvarez
manages somehow to dig up these letters in Moll's pension
in Caracas and personally brings them to her brother-in-law
Sánchez on the island.

Moll holes up in the Hotel Potomac in Caracas and waits,
with her customary stubbornness, not for Bonnhoff but for
Sánchez. After a long wait, Sánchez appears at the hotel,
throws himself at Moll's feet, and begs for forgiveness.
(Imagination doesn't even balk at that!) After a reconciliation
in bed he offers her a well-paying position as his houri read
goddess and private secretary. Moll plays the *belle dame sans
merci*, and at first, except for the reconciliation in bed, turns
him down on all counts. Absolute mistress of the situation.
(At this point the imagination finally balks.)

The sun stood high and motionless in the heavens. Carla
sat in the shelter of her big straw hat and Zongo refused to
answer any of her tourist-Spanish questions. Half-naked people glided by on the river in canoes and motorboats with
awnings, slowly, measuredly, indifferent to anything that
wasn't connected to a floating existence. It was much more
peaceful here at this hour than at the Hotel Amazonas, but
also much less comfortable. Cooper had had more luck in
the fisherman's paradise. Beside fish and birds and greenery,
he had at least seen an old European whom Zongo had called
"*el capitán*." Carla would have welcomed him with open
arms. She yawned. There was a stillness in the air. Even the
clouds hung like motionless tufts of cotton over the water.
Sánchez stood somewhere on the horizon, a statuesque shadow.

Where was Bendix? With her luck a crocodile had got him
and Zongo would leave her to find her own way back to the
harbor of Río Samariapo. Weren't there any people at all on
this shore?

She asked Zongo where the señorita might be. In two hours

it would be twilight. The cotton clouds would be drenched with blood by the setting sun. Just then three men climbed down to the shore. They must have come out of a house behind the palms and shrubs: a young Venezuelan, who looked like a priest in civilian dress; a husky Indian; and a very old man who leaned heavily on the priest. He was wearing an old, shabby sombrero, and had unruly white hair, strange, staring, light blue eyes, and a big red face. Carla could see it all through her binoculars. The old man also had binoculars attached to a leather strap around his neck. They bounced around on his big, flabby stomach. He was wearing high rubber boots as protection against the mosquitoes and snakes, and held a fishing rod in his trembling hand. He swung it like a whip, or at least tried to, until the Indian took it away from him. The Indian had a fishing net in his free hand; the young man with the Spanish profile was carrying a prayer book.

The Orinoco was suddenly alive. Green lights glittered in the water. The canoes and motorboats had moved on to far away villages, wooded coves, mission settlements. The fish gleamed beneath the glassy surface. Suddenly there was motion everywhere. Even Zongo had wakened out of his morose silence. *"El viejo,"* he murmured. *"El capitán."*

Carla asked where the *el viejo* came from. Zongo shook his birdlike head. *"De ninguna parte,"* and turned back to his fishing. So *el viejo* came from nowhere. But whenever Zongo had seen him, he had waved his rod wildly like a whip, or sung. Sometimes he yelled across the rushing river like a parrot. But he wore wonderful shoes, like a general. Zongo envied him those shoes. He didn't want to wear them, he just wanted to stand them up and admire them.

Carla Moll was still wondering where Bendix was. She could not remember if they had driven fast or slowly to the fisherman's paradise or what the name of their hotel was. Bendix had the name, address, and the money. The devil take him with his clarity and truth.

"Hotel? Samariapo? *Nombre?*" she asked softly, because the Indian didn't like a loud voice. And the worst part of it was, the more one asked, the more silent he became. After thinking it over for a long time, Zongo murmured, *"Su sombrero."* The yellow-haired woman should put her hat on again. Carla repeated her question about the name of the hotel. As far as stubbornness was concerned, she could match hers with any Indian's on the Orinoco. Zongo's whispered information consisted this time of only one word: *Insolación.* Carla Moll sighed. The name of the hotel had not been "sunstroke!" Slowly the river changed to a dull metallic color. She saw everything as if through broken glasses—teetering, fragmentary, spectral.

Not everybody was looking through broken glasses. *El capitán* looked at the girl with the blond hair through his binoculars, an old glass but a good German one. He turned the screw until he had brought the blond female into sharp focus. He didn't see as well as he used to. His age or the tropical sun or both . . . Well now! He knew that girl! From Berlin! What was her name? Ullstein . . . no . . . Ullmann! Christina Ullmann. His housekeeper in the Tiergarten villa. But she had committed suicide! He had seen her death certificate. Engelbert Schmidt or Ludwig—all SS elite—had brought Ullmann's death certificate to him. Bonnhoff had had the woman arrested. Those were the days! Bonnhoff waved his rod. The Ullmann woman was over there and his head was suddenly clearer than it had been for a long time. He felt twenty, no, thirty years younger, just as in the year 1938 when the Ullmann woman had started an affair with his son Carlos. The young fellow had turned up in Berlin from Caracas to study for a few months, and Ullmann had started right off with him. He had been eighteen years old, and strictly brought up by his grandfather Sánchez. *El viejo* gave the girl another sharp look. Ullmann had survived her suicide! Anything could happen in this crazy world. He would simply walk over to her, tap her gently on the shoulder, and say sweetly, "Hello Ullmann. Tina Ullmann. I thought you were dead." And after a little pause he'd say, a shade cooler, "What the hell are you doing here?" I'll bowl her over, he thought.

\* \* \*

*"El capitán!"* Zongo whispered.

He took a stand between the old man and his señorita. The hotel paid him to watch over her. Of course *el viejo* couldn't do the blond señorita any harm. He was as old as the hills and his stomach wobbled like an overloaded canoe. Zongo would have liked to chase the old man away like a big stinging fly, but didn't dare touch him. The thick blue veins on his old hands were branched like the roots of a tree. Zongo planted his calabash as a symbol of distance between the blond señorita and the old European. Or was he a Yanqui? After having taken this precautionary measure, Zongo sat down contentedly on the sandy shore. He could still throw a mosquito net over *el capitán's* head and strangle him if this confrontation proved dangerous. What wild eyes the old man had! Zongo was careful not to look into their horrible blue light. Evil magic issued from those eyes. Bonnhoff's Indian, Tucu, watched and waited at an appropriate distance. He too knew what to do if the yellow-haired woman attacked his old señor or tried to bewitch him. Señor Sánchez from Caracas had given Tucu a canoe as a present, so that he could look after the old man better. He was *never* to talk to strange people, those were Señor Sánchez' orders. He had meant men, of course, and this was only a woman. Tucu wasn't worried. He drew closer to Bonnhoff. The young man with the prayer book had closed his eyes and was enjoying his siesta. The sun wasn't as fiery as before, but it hadn't fallen into the river yet. The river was holding its breath. The air trembled between yesterday and today. Bonnhoff tapped Carla on the shoulder. She jumped up and Zongo rose. Carla stared at the strange old man. He looked wild, neglected, and treacherous. Where was Bendix? Like every man, he wasn't there when he was needed. *"Que hay?"* she asked brusquely. "What do you want?"

Bonnhoff began to laugh. The laughter burst from him like a clap of thunder, and both Indians winced. Bonnhoff's heavy body shook with crazy, incomprehensible merriment. His eyes rolled like an epileptic's. Tears and sweat ran down his flabby cheeks and wrinkled neck. He gasped, groaned, swallowed his laughter, and pushed Tucu, who wanted to assist him, aside with unexpected strength and brutality. "Down!" he shouted hoarsely. Tucu stepped aside obediently, but remained on the alert.

Fräulein Moll asked for a second time what the old man wanted, and if he needed help. Now the señor shouted with glee, and she asked him if he didn't think enough was enough. She spoke quietly but with suppressed impatience. She wished he would go away, and take his Indian with him. They should all go away, and Bendix should come back. Such simple wishes. Bonnhoff's laughter ceased abruptly. What had Ullmann asked? Did he need help? He'd help her! In spite of her bad behavior in Berlin, she'd never been that fresh. For seconds the old, crazy, lost Berlin, all ruins and ashes, stood like a *fata morgana* on the horizon, and he looked at it silently and with superstitious delight. In a minute it would disappear again as it always did. But Ullmann had better stay so that finally, after thirty-two years, he could arrest her. It was her fault. He hadn't invited her. He straightened out to his full height and raised his hand for the Hitler salute, or had the man's name been Hirtler? Or Himmler? Didn't matter. He'd better just raise his hand and say nothing. Nobody was going to make a fool of him, least of all Ullmann who had always trembled before him. In bed, too. Mainly in bed. She hadn't liked him. Had only done what he'd made her do. All water under the bridge today. She wasn't going to make a fool of him. His big moment had arrived. What else had he wanted to say? Oh yes, he wanted to say: "Don't put on an act, Ullmann. How did you happen to get here anyway? What are you looking for on the Orino...noco?" That's what he wanted to say. And: "Come along." "Where to?" "You'll soon find out." But there was something else he'd wanted to say, something that'd damn near kill her! Courage she'd never had. Only pretended to. Jesus, what else had he had in mind? He was over eighty and his thoughts ran away from him like race horses. His tortured soul fluttered like a wing-clipped bird. Cold sweat broke out on his forehead. His big red face was distorted by exertion, and his pupils grew large like softened-raisins. He stared at Ullmann gloomily and, in a way, helplessly. Suddenly he managed to say, "I thought you were dead."

Carla Moll stared at him, speechless. The crazy old man had spoken German! Now she'd heard everything. She said in German, "I beg your pardon."

Bonnhoff nodded. She didn't look Spanish to him anymore. He said softly, "Come clean, Ullmann. I want a total confession, if you please. And stand up when I talk to you. Or you'll be sorry."

"My name is Carla Moll. You must be mistaking me for somebody else."

"Hear, hear!" Bonnhoff laughed. "I don't remember everything. But you, you bitch, I remember. Now don't tell me you don't know who I am!"

"I have no idea who you are, and that's the truth. Come Zongo, we'll find somewhere else to wait for Señor Bendix." Zongo didn't move. Suddenly he didn't understand that much Spanish. He had promised the young German to wait for him with the señorita on this spot, and this was where he would wait with her and the mosquito nets.

"I have no idea, and that's the truth!" Bonnhoff said, in a mincing imitation of what she had just said. "You want to know where the truth lies? In the river. And it lies well there." He raised two fingers to his sombrero in an arrogant greeting, bowed awkwardly, and said, "My pleasure, Fräulein Ullmann. Strumbannführer Bonnhoff from Berlin. Heil Hitler! Well . . . does that ring a bell?"

"You are . . ."

That surprises you, doesn't it? Fresh bitch!" He stepped closer to Carla Moll, but the forehead and eyes of the old fighter were suddenly clouded. His lips trembled. He raised his heavy right hand to his ear and whispered, "Did you hear me, Tina? Death, the old beast, is neighing again. Stay! I'm not going to do you any harm. What harm can an old man like me do? I'm telling you, death has forgotten me. In Berlin he'd have come for me long ago, but here, in this lousy country, they're slow about everything. Stay a little while, girl. When do I ever get a chance to speak German? Most of the time I'm counting the fish. Or the boats. A man's got to do something. That's what I'm always telling my son." He whispered, "I'm a prisoner here. Caught and hanged, we used to say. Those were the days! I invite my only son to visit me in Berlin in '38, and nothing suits him. You remember? *I and you and Carlos?* Of course he was younger than I, and that's what did it."

Carla Moll didn't say a word. Although Bonnhoff was standing in front of her, he was separated from her by his total isolation from the outside world. He possessed nothing now but his memories and his rage. She could sense his impotence, his love-hate for Carlos Sánchez, his burned-out brutality. A horrible man and a pathetic one. He staggered back three steps. "How long can you stay?" he asked, trembling.

"Not much longer."

He nodded. He might have known. Who would stay with him? He would have liked to tell her so much more: the things that made his heart heavy in the night. But for what? After his visit to Nazi Berlin, his son had taken the name of Carlos Domingo Sánchez and discarded the name Bonnhoff. He had gone over to his mother's side of the family. That hurt a father, regardless of the sort of father. Christina had lived through it all. She had seen how he, Sturmbannführer Bonnhoff, had waited patiently for Carlos when he was playing around instead of coming home to the Tiergarten villa. He had forgiven the young rascal for his affair with Ullmann. All he'd wanted was to eliminate Ullmann. But here she was, under his very nose. *So he was not a murderer!* So he rated mercy rather than justice. Oh, the hell with it! He was gasping. He was too fat. Funny that with all his misery he could be so fat . . .

"There's too much water here," he mumbled mournfully. "And the heat all the time. And nothing happening, ever . . ." No answer came from Tina. Should he swallow his anger and again ask her to stay? He looked at her from the side.

Hard to believe but she was more beautiful than she had ever been. *Was she really Ullmann?* Or . . . was she just pretending to be? An icy fear ran down his back. Oh, God in heaven! She wasn't Tina Ullmann at all! Ullmann would be past fifty today. And this woman with the cold face and the long blond mane of hair and her silence was young! Nineteen perhaps! Or twenty-four. She had said her name was Moll or Toll or Kroll. Said it loudly and clearly. But he was in the middle of an interrogation and wanted a full confession from Ullmann.

"Are you Ullmann or are you not?" he wanted to ask. That would be the sensible thing to say and then he would know. If only fire would break out in the river or it would rain poison! A permanent eclipse of the sun would do, too. Something, anything that would destroy him and this treacherous person before Carlos came. If she told his son that he had betrayed everything, told her his name and God only knew what else . . . He began to tremble and had to cling to the palm tree nearest to him.

"You must calm down, Herr Bonnhoff," the strange girl said. That did it. He had still hoped dimly that he hadn't mentioned his name. If the woman passed on the information to the German authorities . . . oh, God in heaven! The dogs never stopped searching. There was a rushing sound in his ears. His blood pressure rose when he got excited. He swayed slightly, or was the river making that horrible noise? He felt as if he were dissolving like a wax hero. Others, when they were afraid, had teeth that chattered; he burned. Was it possible to be afraid of one's own son? Or was he really as crazy as people made him out to be? No! He shook himself. Even if he never opened his mouth again, he did have one thing to say to this fresh girl who had pretended to be Christina Ullmann, only one thing more, but it was important.

"I hear the name Bonnhoff all the time," he said, clearly and slyly. "That idiot is dead, Fräulein. I was just playing a little joke on you. Old Bonnhoff is asleep in his grave. Died years ago."

"That's what I thought, señor."

"What did you think?"

"That you were joking."

"I was a big joker in my day. Word of honor. Sometimes even the runt laughed. I mean that shrunken Teuton. What was his name? Goebbels. Always laughed sweet-sour, Herr Goebbels did. Listen, Fräulein . . . in the Berlin zoo the hippopotamus opens its mouth wide. And Party Member A says to Party Member B, 'Poor animal . . . the hippopotamus. Such a big mouth and no chance of advancement . . .' Why don't you laugh?" He mumbled curses, oaths, abuse, obscenities to himself. His fat sweating body sagged. She hadn't laughed. When his jokes didn't work he became unsure. He had experienced all this as a cadet in Lichterfelde. "Where do you come from?" he asked suddenly.

"From Berlin."

That was all he needed. From Berlin. Not from Düsseldorf or Munich or Hamburg. Such nice cities. It was the last straw. His breathing became labored. "They have horrible birds here," he managed to say finally. "I like thrushes best. Thrushes, blackbirds, finches, birds like that. Do they still have blackbirds at home? Come, Tucu."

He leaned heavily on his Indian. He felt wretched. He turned his broad back on the treacherous woman from Berlin without a word of farewell. Oh, God, how tired he was! Wasn't there a place to sit down anywhere? He lifted his massive head as if trying to catch the scent of something. There was an eerie silence, as if someone were going to shoot him in the back at any moment. Pistols, tanks, whips, swastikas, gold teeth, broken hearts, were flying wildly among the clouds. There were planes, a unicorn from the Bonnhoff family crest, blackbirds, and motorbicycles with side cars, but Ullmann wasn't sitting in the side car, letting her hair flutter in the wind. A machine gun was in the side car, and somewhere on the horizon a lilac bush was growing. Bonnhoff closed his eyes because he couldn't take anymore . . . not the lilacs blooming in Potsdam. Quick, think of something else! Suddenly there was a roaring in the air that startled him. He couldn't stand noise anymore either, but he heard dogs barking, orders being given, shots, laughter, cries, screaming. All he really longed for was peace, shade, music . . . there was something eternal about music, something comforting. Bach . . . Schubert . . . Chopin . . . Ullmann had fallen asleep once in Berlin at *The Marriage of Figaro*. For that alone she had deserved to hang. Bonnhoff thought again of the woman from Berlin who had pretended to be Ullmann. He wondered what she looked like naked. It was funny, even when no feelings were left, the curiosity about a woman's body remained. She had said her name was Moll. And what if she told his son about their little conversation by the river? Why should she? He had told her Bonnhoff was dead. If he kept his mouth shut—and his head was usually pretty clear where his safety was concerned—nothing could happen to him. And the fellows in the new Berlin could look for ex-Sturmbannführer Bonnhoff until Judgment Day. The Fräulein had probably swum off already. She had better things to do than denounce an old man. She had been waiting for some young man. Right. One was only young once.

Bonnhoff punched Tucu in the side. He was dumb like all natives, but he had a heart. Hard to believe there could be someone so ignorant, but that's the way it was. Sometimes Tucu looked at him, silently of course, but there was something in his dark eyes . . . worry, or a slow dawning of understanding and . . . and compassion. Bonnhoff raised two fat trembling fingers to his lips. "You keep your mouth shut, understand?" he shouted in sudden fury. *"Silencio!"* Tucu nodded. Nobody could accuse him of being talkative. He took a sidelong look at his old señor. *El capitán* not only looked furious, he also looked scared, and no wonder . . . they were expecting Señor Sánchez in a few days. They were cleaning, cooking, baking. The servant José was catching fish. Brother Fernando was praying, and he, Tucu, was watching over his master.

Bonnhoff's rage passed, but he couldn't get the young woman from Berlin out of his mind. He brooded. Should he perhaps turn back and, if she was still nearby, beg her to forget the "joke"? He shook his head disconsolately. What good would it do?


Brother Fernando was about to get into his motorboat when Bonnhoff came back with Tucu. He looked at the old man sharply. Bonnhoff's watery eyes were tearing, the thick veins on both sides of his temples were pulsating. Brother Fernando was worried. "You are excited, my friend. That's not good," the lay brother said in a gentle reproach.

"You're leaving?" Bonnhoff sounded startled.

"I told you I was two days ago."

"That's right," Bonnhoff mumbled. "When will you visit me again?"

"As soon as I can arrange it. They are waiting for me." He suppressed a sigh of impatience. He was in charge of many people on the Orinoco, and all of them needed his assistance, medicine, and sympathy in their isolated Indian villages. Fernando López was impatient by nature, and he prayed daily for forbearance. He prayed at length and dramatically for the old man with the roaring voice and the occasional confusion of mind. He couldn't change him, neither with severity nor kindness, but Brother Fernando was also quite stubborn and possessed the dignity of his Spanish ancestors. On top of that he had an unquenchable thirst for holiness, and broad shoulders that were capable of dragging the crosses of his charges with ease. He waved once more to Bonnhoff; in a few months he would visit him again.

"There goes the praying brother who doesn't sing anymore," said Bonnhoff in a Spanish of his own invention. Tucu nodded. He looked worried. Things were so much easier when Brother Fernando was living with them. Now el capitán would start raving again. Only Brother Fernando could calm him. He was even better at it than Señorita Álvarez. Pilar visited the house on the Orinoco twice or three times a year to see Carlos Sánchez's father. Everybody in the house knew that Señorita Álvarez was strict but just. She intimidated everyone and saw to it that they worked—the servant José, his mother, the gardener, Tucu—all of them. Nobody loved

Señor Sánchez's sister-in-law, and she didn't seem to expect them to. Brother Fernando admired her, yet sometimes he also pitied her. It must be hard to be unable to arouse any sympathy in one's fellow men, especially when one did so much for them. Brother Fernando couldn't complain about a lack of sympathy. Everybody loved him except Carlos Sánchez, and there was a reason for that.

Brother Fernando—naive and unafraid—had insisted that the señor respect the white-haired old man, but he hadn't felt exactly comfortable when the great financier from Caracas had looked at him with his cold, sharp eyes. Yet Señor Sánchez, in spite of his dark looks and sneering smile, was a good man. He did much for the Franciscan mission, visited Father Alonzo regularly, saw to the well-being of *el capitán*, and had given Tucu a canoe. But arrogance was a sin, and Brother Fernando said so to the señor. Trembling, but resolutely, he had exhorted him to behave with Christian mercy toward the unfortunate old man. He didn't know what the relationship was between the old European and the great man from Caracas, and it was no concern of his. All he had grasped was that *el capitán* was to talk to nobody and was in some sort of danger. It was evidently a secret. Señor Sánchez had listened to the sermon of the young lay brother with astonishing patience, but in the end it had become too much and too religious for him, and he had said, "Basta ya!" On his departure he had given Brother Fernando a check for his charges, but he hadn't said a word about *el capitán*. He seemed to hate the old man, and it worried Brother Fernando. He had prayed for Señor Sánchez because the rich were always tempted to buy their way out with a check.

Brother Fernando sailed toward the setting sun and the silence. Why had the old man been so excited? All he had done was talk to a woman on the shore, and a young woman like that couldn't possibly pose any danger for an old man. Or shouldn't he have let the old man speak to the strange young woman? Brother Fernando felt a strange uneasiness. It had nothing to do with the mind. Maybe he should visit the old man more often. He had never known him to be so excited. Perhaps he was just having one of his bad days again. He had bad days now with increasing frequency, and Brother Fernando knew why. The old man lived in a vacuum, and that was bad for the heart.

Reality is incredible, thought Carla Moll. I wouldn't believe it if somebody told me he'd found Bonnhoff without lifting a finger. Suddenly she was glad that Bendix hadn't come back yet. She had to think. Think hard. The long search for Sturmbannführer Bonnhoff was over. His outburst of passion, his brutality, and then his fear, had touched her. Yes, he had survived everything, even himself. A witness of yesterday, a madman, a fossil. What could a court do with such a wreck? But that wasn't her responsibility. Let the authorities do something for a change. But hadn't she promised herself never to betray Bonnhoff's hiding place if she ever found it? Moll's word of honor. That was two years ago, and at the time she had loved Sánchez, even though he had driven her away from Margarita Island. Again she thought of Cooper's dinner and how Sánchez had rejected her.

Bonnhoff had turned up like a ghost. He lived on the edge of reality, and he had mentioned something that would be useful for her report. It reminded her vaguely of an early experience. What? She had to remember. It was important. The incident was buried somewhere in her memory. Did it happen before her first trip to Venezuela? In Caracas? No, no—in Berlin. Before her expedition with Locker and Hanns König. It seemed that way to her, but she didn't know exactly. All she knew was that it had somehow been connected with Sánchez, or rather with the mysterious story of his life.

The experience had to do with fear. But not her fear. The encounter—it could only have been an encounter—had been exciting, or exhausting, or unpleasant, and that was probably why it now rested in her subconscious. She tried to remember everything Bonnhoff had said, word for word. This was difficult because he hadn't been coherent, and she had been slightly dazed because of her discovery. Bonnhoff had not expressed himself clearly. I don't want to get that old, she thought. In the end he had scarcely been able to talk or walk. She hadn't felt sorry for him. She wasn't always so hard on people, but in spite of his deterioration, there had been an aura of brutality about Bonnhoff.

The river gleamed amber and yellow. Soon it would be bathed in blood. Locker and König were off to find buried cities, but she, Carla Moll, had found a buried man. Let anyone match that! Let them all be astounded, the whole editorial office! All Berlin! All West Germany! Sánchez would not be pleased, but he was a stranger now. Just the same, it hurt.

Suddenly a woman appeared out of the twilight of her consciousness, a gray-haired woman, in her middle fifties, unsure and entangled in the web of a dead past. In Berlin. Shortly before Carla's second trip to Venezuela. Now she remembered! Exactly! The unknown woman who had asked to speak to her in the editorial offices of *Comet*, was dressed like a nurse and was wearing ugly, sturdy, laced shoes. Carla had never seen her before. She didn't know what the nurse wanted because she was so indirect and asked superficial time-consuming questions about Venezuela. Her name was *Christina Ullmann*, and she was head nurse in Dr. von Hartlieb's clinic in West Berlin. Carla Moll had found her extremely irritating because she exuded embarrassment and didn't say what was really on her mind for a long time. And now, in this remote corner of Venezuela, Carla could hear her soft, hesitant voice again.

"Years ago, in Berlin, shortly before the war, I met a young Venezuelan. His father was a Berliner. The son went back to Venezuela at the end of '38. It was a strange time. All the foreigners left. After the war I tried to get in touch with him. His name was Carlos Bonnhoff. Did you perhaps hear his name mentioned in Caracas, Fräulein Moll? He comes from a very prestigious South American family. His father's name was Carl Friedrich Bonnhoff." No—Carla Moll had never heard the name.

Carla Moll lit a cigarette and, eyes closed, blew the smoke at the face of her silent guardian, Zongo. *El capitán* was standing in front of her again, wild, sly, crazy. "Do you remember, Tina? I and you and Carlos? He was younger than I, of course, and that did it."

That did it. Carla Moll had great perspicacity for anything she could see, hear, or grasp. And at that moment she saw young Carlos in Nazi Berlin, age eighteen, shy, torn between ecstasy and guilt, either completely silent or bubbling over with words. Christina Ullmann may have been his first girl. And she had also been carrying on with the old man. She must have been in her early twenties then. Blond like herself, but with that the resemblance had probably ended. Except for Bonnhoff and Sánchez . . .

Somebody was standing behind her, tapping her gently on the shoulder. She screamed. It was Bendix. He had a lot of excuses as well as fish in his net. His watch had stopped! "And you have been here all alone!" he said. "I hope you're not angry with me."

"Not at all. It was boring, of course, but I smoked and rested and thought a bit. Don't often get the chance."

"What did you think about?"

"*Not* about my love life, dear Herr Bendix. It isn't worth it. You know something . . . I've been racking my brains about that Indian saying I'd like to use."

"The truth lies in the river?"

"Exactly. That means, of course, that when it's fat it rises to the top."

"You're funny. I must tell that to Señor Sánchez when I get to Puerto Cabello."

"I wouldn't do that. I get the impression that your idol doesn't appreciate my jokes. I think Señor Sánchez fishes his truths out of the Orinoco himself, or grabs them out of the air. Maybe that's the custom of the land."

"When are you joking and when are you being serious, Fräulein Moll?"

"I'm always joking, especially when things get serious."

"I hope we meet again in Puerto Cabello. When are you going to be there?"

"I don't know. My boss decides that. But I'm certainly

leaving here. I've seen everything there is to see on the Orinoco."

"You can't mean that! You can explore the world along this river for years! Think of Humboldt! Or your colleagues!"

"It always depends on what you're looking for." She yawned. "Right now I'm dead tired. Perhaps I've had too much sun." The river held its breath. Steam rose from its depths. Carla Moll shivered. The Orinoco hadn't been her friend, not for a second, unlike the River Spree or the Havel. And Sánchez would soon be her archenemy. But she couldn't keep silent. She didn't want to and she wouldn't. She would never see him again anyway. Still she was torn, and horribly depressed. She had achieved what she had wanted to achieve. She had been so lucky that she could scarcely believe it herself.

# 12

# Dialogue in Puerto Cabello

"Señor Bendix from Berlin?"

"Yes."

"Welcome to Puerto Cabello. Señor Sánchez has sent me. He regrets that he can't see you until later. He is in conference at the Chamber of Commerce. They always seem to foul things up. I don't know why."

"That doesn't matter, señorita. Do you think Señor Sánchez will have time for me today?"

"I hope so. But I have a portfolio here with information for you. Señor Sánchez will have time for you in a few days when you've looked through this technical material."

"Thank you very much, señorita." Wally Bendix had a queasy feeling in the pit of his stomach. Was the great man going to let him down? But here was the material Sánchez had sent via this unknown señorita in her elegant linen dress.

"I am Rosa Martínez, Señor Sánchez's private secretary. His right hand." Rosa was astonished to see that the young man was blushing. Such light skin. She had imagined him older and more self-assured. She asked him, a little loftily, how he liked Puerto Cabello. His respectful reply and general humility gave her a fleeting feeling of security which she never felt in the presence of Sánchez or Pilar Álvarez. Pilar had stayed in the main office in Caracas. Here she, Rosa

Martínez, was in charge. With any luck she'd soon be in charge of this young man, too.

"I hope I'm not taking any of your precious time."

Until now no one had ever considered Rosa's time precious, and she decided to ask Sánchez for a raise. She assured this naive young man that he was not robbing her of any time, and smiled coolly, like Pilar Álvarez. Señor Bendix declared that he hadn't seen anything of Puerto Cabello yet. He was staring at the great entrepreneur's private secretary and was endowing her with all the dignity, influence, and importance to which she pretended. He even found her beautiful. Her smile did something to him. He didn't see the trace of slyness playing about her lips; all he saw was the same spontaneous feeling of friendship that he felt for her. This señorita, with her hair piled high, her skin-tight dress, and her large paste earrings, was the image of the typical Venezuelan woman he had pictured on many a lonely evening in the mine. The sharply defined features of her lean face and her full lips, the heritage of a mulatto mother, excited him. But perhaps he hadn't eaten enough today . . .

Wally Bendix was not a wildly passionate man. Normally, he let the girls seek him out, but the señorita's full breasts were so prominently thrust forward there was no overlooking them. Rosa's thin arms, which didn't go at all with her voluptuous bosom, were covered by wide lace sleeves, and her thin legs were hidden under her long skirt, which also protected her from mosquitoes. She was dressed according to Caracas's version of *Vogue*, and to a romantic like Wally, she looked just right. He never did find out about Rosa's blitz-career from cook in a tortilla shack to bargirl in a night club in Guaira. Moreover, Señor Bendix never found out that Rosa occasionally indulged in blackmail. She herself had forgotten that a while ago she had tried to sell a love letter of the deceased Teresa Sánchez to Pilar Álvarez.

Rosa Martínez was older than Bendix, and possessed of an alien temperament. He admired her without reservations because she was so different from any of his Berlin girl-friends, and he desired her shamefully and not without torment. He was ashamed because all she had to offer him was her body, and the torture came from the depths of his unrequited soul. "May I order coffee for you, señorita?"

"No thank you. I had coffee with Señor Sánchez. He is a hard taskmaster, but I admire him."

"I do too, señorita."

"How is that possible? You scarcely know him. Let me warn you: think it over carefully. Breaking a contract costs money."

"I have no contract, and if I had one, I'd never break it."

"You can't put anything over on Señor Sánchez. He won't tolerate excuses or lies, or any kind of deceit."

"I'm a lover of truth and clarity myself," said Señor Bendix.

"All of us are, señor. If you like, I can tell you a lot more about my boss. Nobody knows him as well as I do. And the way to him is through my office. But whatever I tell you about him must of course remain strictly between us."

"Naturally, señorita." He managed to tear his eyes away from the lady's bosom and ordered another coffee. "Do you live in Caracas, Señorita?"

"I was born in this witch's cauldron. My parents are Portugese. We brought our culture to this country. My father was in the hotel business."

"Isn't he alive anymore?"

"No."

Señor Martínez had really been in the hotel business. He had worked in a fish kitchen.

"How nice that you still have your mother," Señor Bendix said sympathetically.

"My mother is dead too," said Señorita Martínez, disregarding the fact that her mother was very much alive and living contentedly in the slums of Caracas. In answer to Wally's question as to whether she had any brothers or sisters, she said she had several. The oldest brother had a steady job, and that was an indisputable fact since he was still in jail for petty larceny. And her old nurse, a fat, easy-going mulatto, whom she visited frequently, lived somewhere in the hovels of Caracas. Señor Bendix found this touching.

He had to forget seeing Sánchez today (the Señor had evidently forgotten all about him), but perhaps he could hang onto Señorita Martínez. Could she have dinner with him tonight? She shrugged. She didn't know yet. It depended . . . On what? Señor Bendix never found out. "Here comes the boss!" cried Rosa. "He didn't forget you after all."

Sánchez patted Wally Bendix amiably on the shoulder. Rosa jumped up, and he gave her his briefcase. "Please sort these notes out for me, Rosa. Tomorrow we'll discuss business, Señor Bendix. Did you receive the information about our new projects?"

"Yes, thank you, señor. The portfolio is right here."

"Very good. What are you waiting for, Rosa? Before I forget—tell Señor Cortazar that I am dining with Mr. and Mrs. Moore tonight. The day after tomorrow I'm going out to Cumboto. I'd like to show you that modern city complex, Señor Bendix. We're participating in the building of a new residential section. Family homes. Would it interest you?"

"Enormously. Thank you very much!"

"Good! We'll drive out tomorrow afternoon. Here is a plan of it. You'll see another aspect of our country."

"All I've seen until now is the mine."

"That's what brought you to Venezuela, isn't it? But now you should gain some new impressions. It will help your work. You're very pale, young man. Are you hungry? I'll order something to eat for you."

"That really isn't necessary, Señor. I can eat later."

"Of course you can eat later, but I think now is a better time. What would you like to drink?" He called over a waiter. "How did you like the Hotel Amazonas?"

"Shortly before I left, I went to Samariapo. Wonderful! Truly the fisherman's paradise."

"Yes. Your Spanish has improved. Were you in Samariapo long?"

"No. A very short time. But the silence and isolation did me good."

"You're a little young for that sort of thing, aren't you?"

"Well, I wasn't actually all alone," Bendix said cheerfully. "I took Señorita Moll with me. You met her at Mr. Cooper's dinner. Do you remember, señor?"

"I never forget anyone I've met. How did Señorita Moll like the fisherman's paradise?"

Sánchez had half closed his eyes and his tone seemed somewhat cooler. Bendix began to feel unsure again. The señor looked slightly aloof. Or perhaps annoyed? Maybe he didn't like the journalist. "I'm afraid Fräulein Moll was bored," Bendix said hesitantly. "I think she prefers it where there are people and there's something going on. One doesn't see a soul for miles at Samariapo."

"I'm sorry, but I must leave you. We'll talk again tomorrow. Shall I ask my secretary to keep you company?"

"That would be wonderful!" Bendix blushed a fiery red. How young he is, thought Sánchez. How honest . . .

"That is if the señorita has nothing better to do," Wally stammered.

Sánchez raised his eyebrows. He gave orders and his employees obeyed them. "I imagine Señorita Martínez will be able to arrange it," he said drily.

"Welcome to Puerto Cabello! We met here a long time ago. In case you don't remember, I am Consuelo Márquez."

"How are you?" asked Cooper, with little enthusiasm. Consuelo, with her owlish eyes and a smile that was a question mark, was the last person he had wanted to see again in the port city. He had run into her, of all people, in a travel bureau and was trapped.

"How are you?"

"Barring the fact that there were two attempts to murder me, I'm fine. Why are you laughing, Miss Márquez? What's so funny about it?"

She was staring at him now with an indefinable expression on her face. "Whoever wanted to murder you?"

"The assassin didn't leave his name and address."

"Have you any idea who hates you?"

"No one hates me, Miss Márquez. On the contrary, I enjoy the goodwill of a great many of my contemporaries."

"That's enviable, Mr. Cooper. Just the same, I'd give it some thought. There are false friends and true friends. Don't you agree?"

"Since when have you been working here?"

"For a long time now. Things got too dull in Mérida."

"Have you given up painting?"

"It gave me up. What can I do for you?"

"Nothing right now. I've already asked about flight connections to Colombia. Please excuse me. I am not in Puerto Cabello for pleasure."

"Is your wife here?"

"She is waiting for me in Chicago. But unfortunately it will be a while until I get there. I am an industrial bird of passage."

"I know." She was staring at him as if he were one of her hallucinations. She reminded him of Teresa Álvarez, and he didn't want to think of the dead woman. Nevertheless Consuelo dragged him back into the mire of that memory. He forced himself to remain calm. It wasn't his fault that Teresa had died suddenly. He hadn't promised her anything. He had only torn up her annoying letters. After all, he was married, wasn't he? Why didn't Consuelo stop staring at him? Why didn't he simply walk out of the travel bureau? Suddenly he felt weak. Miss Márquez begged him to sit down. "You look green," she said cheerfully.

"It's nothing," said Cooper, his voice unusually sharp. His legs were trembling. Too much had happened to him recently.

"A good friend got me this job," she said. "Señor Sánchez. He's a prominent industrialist from Caracas. Have you ever met him?"

"He has invited me to dinner for tomorrow. And he was my guest on the Orinoco."

"So that was where you hid from Teresa and me!"

"I hide from no one, Miss Márquez. Moreover I should . . ."

"Perhaps you should hide after all. Especially from Señor Sánchez."

"I don't think that's funny."

"You don't? Have you forgotten? I am giving you some good advice. Steer clear of Señor Sánchez. Don't go to his dinner."

Cooper jumped up and wiped the sweat from his forehead. He felt dizzy. He asked Miss Márquez to stop talking nonsense, and turned to go.

"It is not nonsense, Mr. Cooper. After work I can explain it all to you."

"There is nothing to explain. Good-bye."

"Just a minute, Mr. Cooper. It would be better for you if you would let me explain before Señor Sánchez..."

"Then make it short!"

"Short and sweet. Isn't that what they say in the States?" Consuelo was enjoying an orgy of viciousness. "But I can't talk about it here. I'm expected to do something for the salary I receive. That's happening to me for the first time in my life. Teresa used to pay for everything. Her sudden death was a painful loss to me in every respect. But death is like that. Inconsiderate. No mercy for the living. How about coffee after I finish work?"

Cooper didn't want to call off the dinner with Sánchez. Their mutual friend, Cooper's boss in Chicago, had arranged it. Cooper would therefore go to Cumboto tomorrow evening. This vicious woman could say what she liked! But in order to be armed he did want to hear what she had to say. Armed? Was he going to a duel or to a dinner? Consuelo Márquez couldn't possibly have anything to reveal. He waited for her in the garden of the hotel. He really should have refused to meet her, but something had prevented him from doing so.

"Another coffee, Miss Márquez?"

"Why did you keep it a secret from me in the Andes that you were married?"

"I didn't think you were interested in my private life, Miss Márquez. I am flattered."

"You are? I didn't have any illusions about you. Poor, foolish Teresa did."

"Let's let the dead rest in peace. What did you want to tell me?"

"How you say that! Let's let the dead rest in peace! The dead don't let us rest in peace. Things aren't that simple."

She spoke in a monotone, but one filled with hatred. Cooper was silent, waiting for her to go on. Her eyes behind her horn-rimmed glasses were fixed and cloudy. She is a night creature, a bat, Cooper thought suddenly. As a little boy he had been terribly afraid of creatures of the night, and he felt the same fear in his bones now even if, as a grown man, he had tried to shake them off. As he looked at Consuelo Márquez he thought: she's after my blood. "Another coffee, Miss Márquez?"

"Thank you. I find coffee stimulating." Her face had a greenish tinge. From the palm trees? They stood around like skeletons with fringes.

"I often dream of Teresa," said Consuelo. "Do you? The poor creature loved dramatic effects. She always used soap that was too strongly perfumed. Her widower is in petroleum, among other things. Of course he is immensely rich. They call petroleum the black gold here. Did you know?"

"It's called that all over the world."

"Am I boring you? That would be too bad. In the Andes you hung on my every word until Teresa . . . what were we talking about? Oh yes. Black gold. In Venezuela we still have soulful millionaires. Like Carlos Sánchez."

Cooper decided he hadn't heard right. Teresa's widower? She had been a widow and he had consoled her! Why did Consuelo constantly include Sánchez in the conversation? Perhaps she was annoyed that he had been invited to dinner and she had not. She was looking at him greedily and curiously. But Cooper was too smart to ask any questions about Sánchez. He wasn't going to do her the favor. Nor could he throw her out of his hotel. Never had he found good manners such a handicap!

"Why so silent, Mr. Cooper?"

"I have had a very tiring day." He cleared his throat, always a signal that he was about to terminate a conversation. Miss Márquez chose not to get the message. I am too considerate. He sighed. He had always been a hesitant sort of go-getter. "A racer with a rattling old Ford," Richard had said of him once, after which he hadn't spoken to his cousin for three months.

"Teresa was too rich and too indolent," said Consuelo. "That was her misfortune. One of them. You were the other."

Cooper laughed, but even to him the laughter sounded hollow.

"I had to witness it all, and gradually I lost all respect for you. Before that I had respected you highly, Mr. Cooper, even admired you."

He said nothing. Surely she'd get tired of the whole thing in a while. She had nothing to tell him. She had made a fool of him again. She was adept at that.

"If there was anyone who knew Teresa Sánchez well, it was I," she said in a loud clear voice. "You didn't know her at all."

"Of course not. I never met the wife of Señor Sánchez."

"I think you don't want to understand me. Teresa must have told you that she was married to Carlos Sánchez. When she traveled she used her maiden name, Álvarez, because she was afraid of Carlos."

"You don't expect me to believe that!"

"It's the truth. You seem to be even more ignorant than I thought. And Teresa more cowardly. She was insanely afraid of Carlos. He is a forceful man in spite of his suave manners. If he loses his temper..."

Cooper was petrified. The woman was speaking the truth. He knew it. Teresa Sánchez... Álvarez... Sánchez...

"You don't know this country, Mr. Cooper. Not the women, and not the men. Honor and dignity are still more important than dollars. That may sound odd to you, but it's true. That is why our history is so heroic and bloody. What do you know about Carlos? His mother was the daughter of Emilio Domingo Sánchez, the freedom fighter of Margarita Island. You

have besmirched the honor of his grandson. You have sullied
his dignity with your dirty love affair. I am not mistaken. It
was probably Carlos Sánchez who was responsible for the
attempts on your life. He wouldn't sully his hands with them.
He has his people for that. And one more thing: he has a
good memory for insults. A Venezuelan virtue. May I give
you one more piece of advice for tomorrow evening?" But
to her disappointment Consuelo Márquez had to keep this
piece of advice to herself because Cooper had left without
another word.

"Welcome to Puerto Cabello, Mr. Cooper. Are you feeling
better?"

"Thank you, Señor Sánchez. I had another attack of fever
the other evening, and the rainy season hasn't even begun."

"But it's in the air. Always a threat for the visitors to our
country."

"Thank you for sending your car for me. It was very good
of you."

"Don't mention it." Sánchez was speaking English since
they were alone. "I sent the car for you so early so that you
could take a look at Urbanización Cumboto. How did you
like the new residential quarters?"

"I was very impressed. Especially after the wilderness
along the Orinoco. The Cumboto Hotel and the Caribbean
gave me a feeling of freedom. That sounds funny, I guess."

"Not at all. What would you like to drink? Coconut milk?
Very good. Cumboto is in the development stage. The city
of Puerto Cabello is fast becoming an industrial area, and the
harbor naturally grows with it. Puerto Cabello won't be satisfied until it is as noisy and hectic as Caracas."

"But aren't you contributing to this development, señor?"

Sánchez laughed. His teeth gleamed. He's a ferocious animal, thought Cooper. No wonder journalist Moll hadn't been
able to control herself at his dinner.

"I am basically a sentimentalist," Sánchez said gently.
"Tomorrow I'll show you the old coconut *haciendas*. They
lie north of the Avenida Salom. Parks and recreation centers

are springing up there. An uncle of mine had a plantation in that area, hence my love for these trees and meadowlands."

"Do you have a weekend house here, señor?"

"No. Things are already too lively for me in Cumboto. I built myself a small house in Palma Sola, far from the new villas. A living room, a few bedrooms, a veranda, a patio, a sun deck. In ten minutes by car I'm at the shore. I'm as alone there as in my grandfather's house on Margarita Island."

Cooper was silent. Sánchez was a completely different man. Was it the rural stillness, the smell of the sea? Didn't he like to be on the Orinoco? He could really be charming, Cooper admitted unwillingly, but perhaps, Sánchez was luring him into a trap. Consuelo might only have been trying to frighten him. She had called Sánchez a soulful millionaire. She must have known him and his deceased wife well. The closer Cooper wanted to come to Sánchez, the more this enigmatic man drew away. After all, they were only sharing a meal. They should be able to trust one another, but that was just what the situation made impossible.

"Our friend Preston writes that someone in the Hotel Amazonas tried to poison you, Mr. Cooper. What on earth was going on there?"

"Let's talk of pleasanter things."

"But what does that make my country look like?"

"Murders are committed in Chicago too. As a matter of fact, quite often."

"You're very magnanimous. I hope this fish isn't poisoned. Do you want me to taste it first?" Sánchez laughed. Cooper didn't find the remark funny. "I have compiled a temporary program for Puerto Cabello, Mr. Cooper. I suggest we start by driving through the industrial area tomorrow. Would that be all right with you?"

"I'm very interested, señor."

"This city has a history of war, like most cities in Venezuela. But we want to see the things of today, don't we? The modern installations of the petrochemical industry, the last stop of the oil transports, the dry docks. After that I'll introduce you to the heads of the Chamber of Commerce. They'll show you everything and tell you everything you want to know. Your work is highly thought of here, Mr. Cooper."

"I do my best as a go-between."

"May I thank you in the name of my country? We need greater interest on the part of the United States. Why is there so much hesitation when it comes to capital investment?"

"Uncertainty, señor. The influence of Cuba on the Latin American countries, and our ignorance concerning your economic situation. When it comes to big deals, I'm afraid we're provincials. We don't like to lose money."

"I share this dislike. Perhaps we too are distrustful. Here one really trusts only one's own family."

"Is that so in your case, Señor Sánchez?"

It was the first wrong question, and Cooper realized it at once. Unintentionally he had moved into an area that he should have avoided.

"I have no sons," Sánchez said harshly. "And my wife died recently. I suppose you heard about it." He was staring at Cooper.

"I'm sorry to hear that, señor."

"There's nothing one can do about it. In one's youth one looks upon life as a private carnival, and all one really does is move from cross to cross." Sánchez was silent.

Cooper wiped his glasses nervously. His impression at his dinner in Puerto Ayacucho had been correct: Sánchez was a mysterious man. What did he know about his affair with Teresa? Cold sweat broke out on Cooper's forehead, and he wiped it away with his handkerchief. His hand was trembling slightly. He took a sip of his coconut milk. Didn't it taste a little like . . . like bitter almonds? He went on drinking because Sánchez was staring at him unwaveringly. A fox, thought Cooper. *El zorro . . . Eplora el zorro la desierta via . . .* a fox on hidden paths . . . Miss Moll had read the Spanish poem to him in the Hotel Amazonas. It had surprised him at the time that she liked to read poetry. This one was by Rosalia Castro, of the nineteenth century. What could the poor creature do in those days, Miss Moll had said, but write poetry? Cooper wished she were there, drinking coconut milk for a change,

but she had said she wasn't coming until next week. She
hoped he would be able to show her Puerto Cabello. She
didn't know anyone there except Cooper and Bendix. Sánchez
called the waiter over, and Cooper was shocked by his com-
manding tone. Yet for Sánchez the tone was quite friendly.
He ordered the popular fruit salad for Cooper, without liqueur.
How thoughtful! It made Cooper feel uncomfortable. Apparently nothing escaped his host. And Sánchez was only
seeing him today for the second time.

"Do you like our coconut milk, Mr. Cooper? No! Then
please don't drink it. I'll order apple juice." Sánchez poured
some of the coconut milk into his water glass and tasted it.
"It's all right," he murmured. It sounded cynical, or so it
seemed to Cooper. He simply couldn't make this man out.
Was he harboring feelings of revenge because of his wife?
Perhaps Consuelo Márquez wasn't quite as crazy as he thought.
There might be a kernel of truth in her insinuations.

Sánchez had no intention of mentioning Teresa. He talked
about petroleum, Indian myths, oil refineries, the painter
Diego Rivera and his huge demonic frescos. He also mentioned his friend Salvador Paz, one of Venezuela's modern
sculptors and architects. It was in his house in Ciudad Bolívar
that Sánchez had received the news of Teresa's death. Cooper
had gone to an exhibition of Salvador Paz's works in Ciudad
Bolívar. That seemed to please Sánchez. He smiled brightly.
Salvador was a great friend of his, from the days of their
youth. He asked if Cooper had friends in Puerto Cabello. If
not he would be glad to introduce him to a few people. He
himself preferred to spend his evenings alone.

"I met Señor Bendix the other day," said Cooper. "Anyway
I shall soon have the company of a very charming young
lady. You know her, señor. You met her at the dinner I gave
at the Hotel Amazonas."

"Really? I don't remember."

"Miss Moll. The journalist from Berlin. She is coming to
Puerto Cabello on business, but her evenings of course will
be free."

"Of course," said Sánchez. "Have a good time, Mr. Cooper."

"Welcome to Puerto Cabello, señorita!"

"What are you doing here?" asked Carla Moll.

"I took the plane from Caracas. Is this your first visit to Puerto Cabello?"

"Yes."

"Puerto Cabello for Beginners?" Carlos Sánchez said, smiling. "You look adorable, as usual."

What's got into him? Carla Moll wondered. Why is he so charming? He can't put anything over on me anymore. He isn't so complimentary without some reason. He can't possibly know that in Samariapo . . .

"Did Señor Bendix meet your boat, señorita?"

"Anything wrong with that?"

"I sent him. He works for me and is a great admirer of yours. Or is your arrival in Puerto Cabello a secret?"

"I have no secrets."

"That's news to me. Could you have dinner with me tomorrow night?"

"I'm sorry, but I have another engagement."

"Too bad. I'm flying back to Caracas the day after tomorrow."

"Too bad."

"How long are you staying here?"

"I don't know yet."

"Two weeks? Two years?"

"Somewhere between two weeks and two years."

She threw away her cigarette. It missed the ashtray. Sánchez picked it up and put it out. He was as orderly as he had been on Margarita Island. "You smoke too much and too fast, señorita."

"I think I drink too much and too fast."

"Really? There you are . . . you're coughing. You ate your ice cream too fast too. Somebody should be looking after you."

"I'd soon get rid of whoever it was. I need my freedom."

"I don't like that cough."

"If I'm not mistaken, you don't like anything about me."

"You exaggerate, señorita. Tell me, how much longer are you going to tear around from place to place? You should explore fewer places more thoroughly. Don't you find this constant change trying?"

"As you make your bed, so must you lie."

"No doubt about it. *Good evening*, señorita."


Carla Moll took a deep breath, then she went to her room and called Wally Bendix. "Hello. This is Carla Moll. Can you have dinner with me tomorrow?"

"I'm sorry, Carla. But I have a date with Señorita Martínez. But the day after tomorrow would be perfect."

"That's when I'm having dinner with Cooper. I need you tomorrow only as an alibi. All you have to do is *say* we have a date. In case anybody asks you."

"Who should ask me?"

"The mailman, Wally! Or Santa Claus! The archangel Gabriel! Or Señor Sánchez! Everybody's asking things nowadays."

"Sure. But Señor Sánchez . . . he isn't likely to ask me whether you're going to have dinner with me. That doesn't interest him."

"You never know."

"But I know, my dear lady. You can take my word for it: I am the lowest man on his totem pole. . . . Are you still there, Carla Moll?"

"Just left."

"Just a minute, Rosa. I'm talking to . . . excuse me Fräulein Moll. Señorita Martínez happens to be here and she . . ."

"Who is Rosa Martínez? The name sounds familiar."

"The señorita is Señor Sánchez's private secretary, his right hand so to speak," Herr Bendix said with a note of pride.

"And who is his left hand? One more thing, Wally. Do you have a good memory?"

"No. Why do you ask?"

"You sound hoarse, Fräulein Moll. Is anything wrong?"

"Nothing's wrong. Do you have a minute's time? Is Señorita Martínez still there?"

"You don't have to worry about her. I don't have any secrets from her. So—what did you want to know?"

"Another time. *Ádios*."

Carla Moll put down the receiver. So she couldn't find out from Bendix if he had told Sánchez about their outing to the fisherman's paradise. He probably wouldn't remember anyway. But if he had mentioned it to Sánchez . . . Sánchez could smell a duck roasting from twenty miles away. That was the only certainty in a highly uncertain situation.

It was enough to drive one crazy! For years life had been uneventful, and now suddenly it was chaotic. On Margarita Island the world had consisted of Sánchez and herself, and now, only two years later, there wasn't room for them in the same universe. Very funny, she thought. She wouldn't see him again, not in two weeks, not in two years, not in eternity. She'd see to that. But what would Sánchez see to if he suspected something? Why had he asked her to have dinner with him tomorrow? He wanted to question her. About the fisherman's hell, but this time she held the trump card! Nothing could stop her, not even if Bendix had told Sánchez about the outing to Samariapo. But it didn't seem as if Sánchez held private conversations with Wally Bendix. Much too arrogant! He sat on Mount Olympus, as Cooper put it.

The telephone rang. She started. She wouldn't answer. No! Sánchez could keep ringing until Judgment Day. She didn't go to the phone. It went on ringing. She held her ears closed. She coughed. Smoke in the wrong windpipe. Go right on ringing, even if my eardrums burst! Go away! she told Bonnhoff's shadow. Go away, all of you!

"She must have gone out," Wally Bendix told Rosa Martínez. He looked worried. He had only wanted to tell Carla Moll that he would take her to dinner tomorrow evening,

even if Rosa didn't like it. And she didn't like it, he noted
to his sorrow. He had to make it clear to Rosa that, although
he loved her madly, he couldn't neglect his friends because
of it. Carla Moll hadn't sounded like Carla Moll on the phone.

# 13

# To Make One's Bed and Have to Lie in It

"I don't want you to go to Cooper's dinner!" Rosa Martínez said loudly and vehemently. Very softly Wally Bendix asked why he shouldn't accept Mr. Cooper's invitation. Rosa tried to estrange him from all his friends, and he found this distressing. He kept asking himself what Rosa could possibly gain if he lost all his friends. But he said nothing, for he couldn't imagine life without her anymore.

"Cooper didn't invite me," said Rosa, "and we belong together, Walito!"

"It's a business dinner, Rosa!"

"Is that woman from Berlin going to be there too?"

"Mr. Cooper didn't give me the guest list. Don't be silly, Rosa. You don't even know him. Have you ever talked to him?"

"I don't talk to Yanquis."

"Then everything's all right."

"Everything's not all right!" Rosa cried. "I could tell you stories about Cooper, about his women!"

"I don't want to hear them!" Bendix hated gossip.

Rosa spat out her chewing gum on the patio, a gesture left over from the hovels of Caracas. It irritated Bendix, but he took it to be the custom of the land. He lived and breathed in a smoky cloud of illusions. But Rosa had roused him. Unfortunately she wore old washed-out dresses or a shabby housecoat when they were alone. She had put away the long, glittering earrings that had captivated him, and her high hairdo wasn't neat and festive anymore. Stray strands of hair escaped the artistic structure and straggled down her neck. Bendix liked neatness, but if he complained he would be in trouble.

"Give me a kiss, Rosa."

She looked at him like a grouchy landlady, then she said, "All you want is sex, again and again and again." She added an obscenity, which shocked Bendix. He wanted love; sex just happened to be a part of it. Where had Rosa picked up language like that? In Berlin only prostitutes used such expressions. But he said nothing because Rosa's eyes were blazing with a cold anger. Bendix cheered himself by hoping that his Spanish was at fault and that again he had misunderstood her.

He had thought this weekend would be so beautiful, and now they were sitting opposite each other on the patio with nothing to say. Rosa was staying in a lodging house in the harbor area of Puerto Cabello. Bendix was staying in a good hotel on an expense account. He couldn't take Rosa there. She never ate with Sánchez and was alone every evening unless Bendix visited her. Then she told him a lot about her social life. She felt sure of him, but he wasn't rich enough. He had a good chance to advance with Sánchez, but his present salary was nothing to brag about. Besides, he sent part of his salary to his parents in Berlin. His mother had to go to a spa after an operation, and his father, according to Bendix's brother, shouldn't be working so hard. Nothing was too much for Wally's mother, and his sister wanted to get married soon, a student marriage. Wally translated his letters from home into Spanish for his beloved. Wally was a fool. If he weren't around, his family would have to get along without him. After Rosa and he were married, she would manage his life and what he spent. She would see to it that he gave her his salary. And of course she would never let him go back to Berlin! His family spoke neither Spanish nor

Portuguese, and Rosa felt sure nobody would think of learning those languages for her sake. And she didn't speak German. So what point was there in visiting them?

Wally had no idea what was going on in her mind when he translated the letters to her. He took her serious face to be an expression of compassion for his sick mother. What a wonderful girl. And what a wonderful bosom! But so far nobody at home knew anything about his marriage plans.

At the moment his future bride was showing little understanding for the Bendix family. An explosion was slowly generating. Wally's stomach was tied in knots. He didn't interrupt her with a single word. He had already found out that soothing words or a gentle admonition to be sensible could make his darling raving mad. Why, he didn't know. A custom of the land? No, he really couldn't ask Cooper to invite Rosa. That would have been forward. That wasn't done. Rosa shouldn't expect it of him. He was too taken aback to explain. He could only try to persuade her to give up the impossible idea. She looked at him furiously and said finally, "You are not a man!"

"Now listen, Rosa!"

Rosa sat in bitter silence. For bed she was all right, but he wanted to hide her from his fine friends. She looked at the patio: torn newspaper, banana skins, melon rind, beer bottles, wobbly bricks. Her patio wouldn't look like that. Right now it was a castle in the air, but not for long! Right now, though, she had bigger and better worries. Walito must not escape her. She had shocked him. A big mistake before the wedding. What was he thinking of right now? He was frighteningly quiet. Had he perhaps found out how old she really was? At the thought she panicked. She stepped up to him and threw her thin, tired arms around his neck. "Don't leave me, Walito!"

"I'll never leave you."

"I mean tonight," Rosa said irritably. They always meant different things and spoke different languages. Rosa dragged him into the room and pressed her body to his. Her robe fell to the floor. She was naked. Wally became confused. With his last remaining wits he told himself that in Berlin Rosa wouldn't be allowed to strip in the afternoon. What if his parents came for a surprise visit? His father would only be astonished, but his mother . . . Wally closed his eyes to the threats to his Eden. This was what he wanted. And anyway, they were still in Puerto Cabello.

"Will you stay with me this evening, Walito?"

He nodded. His throat felt tight. Happiness hurt. No one had prepared him for this. He was breathing with difficulty. "Do you really love me, Rosa?"

She chose not to hear this simple-minded question. She was dead tired after her exertion. Actually she was too young to be so used up already. But there was such a thing as a blitz-career, and she had been struck by every kind of blitz, and it had left her weary.

"I hope you still see me as your friend."

"Indeed I do," said Carla Moll.

"Please tell me what's troubling you. You're changed."

"Is the change an improvement, Mr. Cooper?"

"I'm worried about you, Miss Moll. You're so nervous."

"Really?"

"Really," Cooper sounded annoyed. "Seriously, Miss Moll . . . there, you see—you've just knocked over your cocktail. Fortunately not on your dress. And you're pale. I keep my eyes open."

"Very advisable after your adventures on the Orinoco. Did you ever find out who was trying to do you in?"

"I don't like to dwell on unpleasantness. The best thing to do is get on with one's business."

"Easier said than done."

"You should always wear white. Did anybody ever tell you that?"

Sánchez had told her just that centuries ago. On her first and last evening at the Villa Acacia. Pilar Álvarez had been listening in the bushes. She looked dully straight ahead.

"Do you have friends in Berlin, Miss Moll?"

"Mostly transients. I guess I'm too far away from where

the action is. You wouldn't believe how quickly one is forgotten."

"I shall never forget you."

"That's nice of you," Miss Moll said drily. "But it won't do you much good."

"I should be home more," Cooper said. "One loses contact. I have no idea when I'll see my wife again. Well . . . you'll at least be in Berlin in the near future. I can imagine how your mother must be looking forward to seeing you."

"I can too."

"What do you have against Señor Sánchez." Cooper asked unexpectedly. Again he was looking at her with burning curiosity. Since his dinner party in Puerto Ayacucho this question didn't seem to leave him any peace. Perhaps, it cheered him to know that his friends too had their problems.

Miss Moll said, "I have nothing against Señor Sánchez. Why do you ask?"

"I don't know, Miss Moll, but I got the impression that somehow Señor Sánchez spoils things for you. Not that this is his intention, mind you."

"God forbid!"

"Señor Sánchez and I have become good friends here. He is an exceptional man. A little difficult, a little too serious, but . . ." Cooper cleared his throat. "Every conversation I have with him I feel is something gained."

"I know nothing about finance, Mr. Cooper."

"You're very witty." Cooper sounded a little irritated, but he controlled himself at once. "Just between us, he was to dine with us this evening, but I'm glad for your sake that he couldn't make it."

"Here he comes," said Carla Moll.

Unpredictable as ever, Sánchez was neither enigmatic nor serious that evening. He had been able to arrange things after all, and here he was! A good evening to all! Cheers! thought Miss Moll. Cooper was beaming. He counted Sánchez's presence as a personal success. The great man had come only because of him, since Miss Moll's dislike was clearly mutual.

Perhaps he preferred Spanish fire to a cool blonde. It really was none of Cooper's business, but like many lonely people, he liked to be a part of his friends' lives, that was all. On the other hand, Cooper was very thankful that Sánchez had no inkling of Cooper's affair with his wife.

Meanwhile Miss Moll had been transformed into a sphinx. She was silent and smiling. A greenish shimmer lay over her light eyes. Sánchez was sitting in a glass house and would be careful not to throw any rum bottles around. But he remained a menace, and she had to be cautious. "What are you thinking of, señorita?"

She started visibly. Cooper had been called to the phone, and she was alone with Sánchez. "I wasn't thinking of anything, señor."

"At moments like that you are enchanting," Sánchez said.

"Thank you."

"It's not to your credit, señorita. You take the most touching care to displease me. But then you shouldn't make yourself so beautiful. Have you recuperated from your stay on the Orinoco?"

"I didn't have to recuperate. It was idyllic there."

Sánchez laughed loudly. "Idylls are not for you. I am sure you found it unbearably romantic."

"Where?"

"In Puerto Ayacucho, of course. Or were you somewhere else, too?"

"We paddled around in a canoe, here and there. I can't remember all the names."

"Your editor-in-chief will be delighted. By the way, do you still work for the same publisher?"

"Yes."

"And are you still looking for Venezuelan adventures?"

"My work isn't that exciting. Adventures would only be a handicap. All I'm supposed to do is report to our readers what goes on on the exotic shore."

"And what did you find on the exotic shore?"

"Nothing, señor."

"That's not much."

"It's enough for me. I am not a geographical gourmand."

"You tell me all the time what you are not. Wouldn't you like to tell me what you are?"

"You know very well what I am. It doesn't happen to be true, but you know everything better."

"I don't mind being corrected, but . . . as you wish."

"Mr. Cooper must be stuck to the phone," said Carla Moll, feeling very uncomfortable. "Do you think he's ever coming back?"

"Everybody comes back, señorita. You came back to Venezuela, too. Moreover, since you seem to like idylls, I could offer you one."

"I'd rather go to hell, señor."

"For that you don't have to travel, because you've already arrived. Why are you staring at me? I was only joking."

He's got that from his old man, she thought. He cracked jokes too on the Orinoco. If Cooper didn't come back soon, the conversation would deteriorate even further. But she hadn't counted on Sánchez.

"I have a weekend house in the Urbanización Palma Sola. You could rest there and at the same time write a charming report about the newest residential development in Puerto Cabello. Silence, palm trees, a highway to the ocean. Would you like to come with me on Friday afternoon?"

She was speechless. Was it his intention to silence her forever, there, among the palm trees? He *had* to know something. Perhaps Bendix had told him about their excursion to the fisherman's paradise. Wally was so guileless. But he didn't know anything abut her conversation with Bonnhoff, either.

"I am sorry, señor, but I can't possibly make it this weekend."

"Can't you or don't you want to?"

"I don't want to."

"That's the first honest answer you've given me."

"Why are you inviting me? What do you want?"

He was looking at her. "Don't you really know?" He got up and stroked her naked shoulders. "I want you and you want me. Afterward you can hate me again."

His lips were on her ear. Afterward . . . afterward . . . It was exactly what she would do, but her desire, her hunger for him—suppressed and scorned—was overwhelming. Sánchez let her go abruptly. His sharp eyes had seen Cooper returning.

"So, on Friday afternoon," he said, as Cooper apologized for his absence. "And don't forget your bathing suit, señorita."

Cooper's eyes widened. What was going on here?

"I'm taking Miss Moll to Palma Sola. Somebody's got to show her exotic shores for a change. How about it, Mr. Cooper? Would you like to come along?"

"How was it in Palma Sola, Miss Moll?"

"Very nice."

"Unfortunately, I couldn't join you," said Cooper. "I had visitors from Panama City. Is it really as idyllic as Señor Sánchez claims?"

"Compared with the gas tanks of Puerto Cabello, it is pure poetry."

"And his bungalow as modest?"

"Even more modest. Three bedrooms, each with shower and bath, a hall like Julius Caesar's, and half of the Palma Sola railway belongs to him too."

"A highway runs there, straight to Morón."

"I'm sorry, Mr. Cooper. Señor Sánchez's little train runs parallel to your highway. They're still working on it. It goes directly to his paper factory in Morón. Whatever fence you want to spit over in Venezuela, the land belongs to him."

"I happen to know all about the paper factory. The señor has only invested capital in it, that's all."

"I wish I could say the same of me. I think I'll lie down. I'm dead tired."

"I thought you went there for a rest."

"I have to take a rest after every rest. My mother is always furious about it. All that beautiful money . . ."

"Señor Sánchez must be a very generous host."

"Magnificent!"

"But a short pleasure, Miss Moll."

"Short and sweet."

"I must speak to Señor Sánchez tonight. Did he bring you back in his car?"

"His chauffeur brought me back. The señor drove to his paper factory."

"Isn't he coming back to Puerto Cabello?"

"Now you're asking too much, Mr. Cooper. He didn't say where he was going after that."

"Strange. You were together all the time, weren't you?"

"Nobody is with Señor Sánchez all the time. He wants his guests to rest."

Cooper laughed loudly, and Miss Moll laughed with him. He asked her if she had taken some good pictures in Palma Sola.

"Yes. But I either lost them in the sand or forgot them at the bungalow. No great loss. Palm trees look the same everywhere."

Cooper said nothing. After a while he asked, "Is there anything I can do for you, Miss Moll?"

She was so surprised, she didn't reply. She was even more surprised when she looked at him sharply. He was the same Elliot Cooper, but his dark eyes, enlarged through his glasses, were not smiling. They were looking with restrained melancholy at his own despair. No one can change in a moment, but for an instant Elliot Cooper was the man he might have been with a different mother, a different wife, and with a father at the breakfast table instead of in a grave.

Yes, undoubtedly, at this moment he wanted to do what he so often only pretended he wanted to do—help and console. This obdurate and eternal desire for warm human contact was very American. The cynical Europeans laughed at it, the East Asians despised it and the Latin Americans arrogantly ignored it. But Carla Moll did not. "Thank you Mr. Cooper," she said. "Everything's all right." Something seemed to be restricting her breathing.

"I regret to say I must take leave of you now, Miss Moll. Tomorrow morning I fly to Colombia. I am going to Bogotá."

"So suddenly?" she asked, feeling lost.

"The conferences are all set." He cleared his throat with

his standard farewell cough. "I want to thank you for the many stimulating hours you gave me." It sounded formal. The precious moment had passed.

"I have to thank you, Mr. Cooper. You were very kind to me. Unfortunately I am a moody person, but you were patient." She said it impulsively. She looked in her bag and took out a slightly crushed card with her Berlin address. "In case you ever come to Berlin."

"Thank you very much, Miss Moll. Anything's possible, isn't it? I will be happy to get in touch with you." He bowed and left. She would never see him again. He would have no time for her in Berlin, nor she for him. It was always like that.

From her balcony she saw him leave in a taxi. She hadn't eaten anything in hours, but she was still unable to eat. Her room was to the right. She could throw herself out of the window, either onto the street or into the hotel garden. With her luck she would probably get stuck in a palm tree and just break a leg. And then she would be in a wheelchair . . . it wasn't worth it. She had to forget everything, especially his smile. And his eyes. Had she really imagined he couldn't stand the longing for her anymore? He didn't know that she knew what he had been looking for in her room at four o'clock in the morning. She had pretended to be asleep.

She heard a scream from the street. A woman was screaming. The echo hung in the night air, a cry addressed to all human misery. A pair of lovers were walking arm in arm. "I know that man," Carla Moll thought, feeling infinitely tired. Of course. It was Herr Bendix. He leaned over Rosa Martínez and whispered something in her ear. Not even the nightwind could hear what he had to say.

# 14

## The Patio in the Air

Engineer Gustave Bendix (West Berlin) to Walter
Bendix (Venezuela)

Dear Walter,

Many thanks for your last letter. Mother is much
better. She will soon write to you herself. Luckily
the operation has had no bad aftereffects. It was
definitely a benign tumor and not what we were
afraid of, Dr. von Hartlieb assured me. Mother thinks
the world of both him and head nurse Ullmann.

We are looking forward immensely to your first
vacation in Europe. Berlin has not forgotten you.
Whatever makes you think that? Your girlfriends are
all lined up waiting for you. Ilse Wendt asks often
how you are doing. Do you remember Lisbeth's little
cousin? It would be nice if you were in Berlin for
Lisbeth's and Professor Locker's wedding. Didn't
that surprise you? Everybody always thought Locker
would marry Carla Moll. But, Lisbeth is a good
doctor and Locker is an old hypochondriac—a very
good match!

Your last letter sounded a little depressed. What's
wrong? If it's something that might worry Mother,

write to me at the factory. I hope you aren't working too hard. High time that you breathed a little Berlin air again. Have you made friends with people your own age? That you see the journalist Carla Moll often is interesting. You'll get there, Wally! All of us promptly read *Caracas for Beginners*! For you!

Herbert Wendt called me the other day and I told him that you had met Carla Moll. He must have been in a hurry, because he didn't say anything about her. Is she writing a second book about Venezuela? Mother is worried that you might fall in love with her! But she's always worried when you're away alone. After all, Carla Moll is a celebrity.

Actually I would be happy if you married soon. To be alone in a strange country isn't the right thing for a young man. A wholesome, capable girl, if possible from Berlin—that would be a great comfort to us. You are a young man who could easily make a mistake.

Mother is really getting along very well. When you come I know she'll bake an apple cake. The whole family sends greetings. Write soon. You know how Mother watches for your letters. Alfred is making a chair for her and is going to upholster it himself. Will she ever be surprised when she comes home! Nice of the boy. He doesn't have much time.

This is the longest letter I have ever written! Mother will soon be taking over again. Go on doing your best, my boy.

> Fondest wishes,
> Your Father

Wally received this letter in Caracas, where he had been sent by his boss to study the development of conditions in the mines on the Orinoco. The Caracas of the firm Álvarez & Sánchez was a new world for him. The South American employees were very different temperamentally and in their work tempo from the Yanquis in Venezuela. The Venezuelans

reacted quickly and keenly to the irritations and blows of the
outside world, but their work tempo was more languid and
erratic. In Sánchez's office, however, the atmosphere was
more high-pressured. Bendix was often called in to confer in
this enormous, almost empty, room where the street noises
of Caracas couldn't be heard. The office was in a modern
high-rise building. Here Sánchez was not the smiling caballero who had fascinated Bendix at Cooper's dinner in Puerto
Ayacucho. He was stern, concentrated, and taciturn. His eyes
were half-closed most of the time and he occasionally cast a
lightning glance from under his lids. When the person he was
talking to displeased him, the lines in his bold face seemed
to grow sharper, and the corners of his mouth drooped skeptically, almost threateningly. Sánchez's resemblance to the
grim Venezuelan whose picture hung on one wall of the room
was striking. It was the picture of his grandfather, Emilio
Domingo Sánchez, the freedom fighter of Margarita Island.
A second painting depicted the island with its rocks and the
sea, rich with fish. Sánchez thought only rarely of his idyll
with Carla Moll. The memory was as bitter as the Angostura
schnapps which was brewed on the Orinoco when Ciudad
Bolívar was still the old city of Angostura. One thing was
even more bitter than Angostura schnapps, and that was the
weekend in the Urbanizacíon Palma Sola. At the thought
Sánchez's face darkened so that Wally Bendix thought his
fabulous job was endangered. But his fear was unfounded.
Sánchez liked him, and Wally's *summa cum laude* diploma
was no reason to fire him. A German education was a good
thing to have in Venezuela.

Wally was deeply impressed by the elegance of his surroundings, but his own quarters would be a lot more cozy.
Could Rosa cook? In a month he was moving to the head
office of Álvarez & Sánchez in Ciudad Guayana, where the
iron ore deposits were. There was a residential development
there for Sánchez's employees, and what more could he and
Rosa ask? A small house, a tropical bungalow for them both,
and on top of everything—rent free! Sánchez pointed with
a stick at a map of Puerto Ordaz where the Orinoco Steel

Works were located; side by side with United Steel, which Cooper had visited and advised.

Wally pulled himself together; his boss was looking at him sharply. Sánchez encouraged him to air his ideas or express them in a memorandum sometimes, thus giving him a chance to contribute, although he was a newcomer. In his modesty, Wally hadn't noticed this, but Rosa Martínez had realized long ago that Sánchez had high hopes for Bendix.

"In a few days I am going to introduce you to three of my colleagues, Señor Bendix. We'll dine in my house in Altamira. My sister-in-law is looking forward to getting to know you better."

In his few fleeting encounters with Pilar Álvarez Wally had not gotten the impression that she wished to know him better. But it was a marvelous thought that he would see the Villa Acacia, and of course it was an honor. He must write home about it at once. Mother would be thrilled. Father wouldn't say anything, but he would be pleased.

Wally blushed with pleasure and almost got a smile out of Sánchez. Nice boy, young Bendix. Very good manners and a fine mind. Bendix took notes while his boss used the phone, stuck a new little flag on the map to mark another victory over the wild mountains, and dictated a letter to the secretary who had replaced Rosa. To Walter Bendix, Sánchez seemed like the great Caesar. What would Rosa say to the invitation to the Villa Acacia? He didn't know. Rosa was so unpredictable these days. Perhaps she missed her work at the office and regretted that she was about to marry the most unimportant man in the firm. Wally swallowed hard. Suddenly he felt dreadful. He was so crazily happy, but it frightened him that Rosa seemed to forget that they would have to save in order, years later, to have a beautiful apartment in Berlin, if possible in Charlottenburg, near his parents and brothers and sisters. All of them would admire Rosa. He was sure of that. But right now she was doing a tremendous amount of shopping in Ciudad Bolívar, and when he thought of the bills, he felt dizzy. She was buying vases and expensive furniture for a patio that didn't exist. And she became furious or she sulked when he gently remonstrated about what she was spending. That was something he couldn't stand. But he couldn't keep silent when she bought an expensive silver fruit bowl for this patio-in-the-air. He would have to pay for it in installments. That was another thing he didn't like. A respectable person either paid at once or did without. That was an iron rule in the Bendix family. Wally's only sister was going to be married soon, and it was unthinkable that Ulrieke and Gerhard would outfit themselves luxuriously on an installment plan. Rosa had grown very angry after this explanation. Wally felt awful about it, but he took the silver bowl back to the shop, whereupon Rosa had put him on a starvation diet for three nights. Why had she given up her good job at the office? There would have been plenty of time for that. Especially since Rosa wanted to stay in Caracas for a while. Nowadays all young wives worked. Rieke wanted to finish her studies after she married and then open an office together with Gerhard. When he had told Rosa this, she had sneered. Walito's sister had to be a real dumb girl. One got married in order to be able to do nothing and let the man work. Wally spoke less and less about his family, since Rosa now yawned quite openly when he did so. He could find an excuse even for that. It would change when Rosa got to know the whole Bendix family.

"That's all for today, Señor Bendix. Good evening."

Bendix pulled himself out of his thoughts with a start. There was something he had to tell his boss. He had promised Rosa he would. He blushed, then paled, as Sánchez looked at him, slightly perplexed. "Don't you feel well, Señor Bendix? Is it the air in Caracas?"

"No, no!" Wally stammered.

"Please sit down again, Señor Bendix. What did you want to tell me?" Señor Sánchez was smiling, which in Wally's eyes enchanced him enormously.

"It . . . it's something personal. I really shouldn't bother you with it, señor."

"Do you need advice?"

"Thank you very much. No. It's all settled. I only want to tell you that I . . . that I . . ."

"If you feel the job's too much for you, don't hesitate to say so, please. I would understand. Is it too much for you?"

Wally stared at his boss. His words were so friendly, so . . . so human. One could really confide in him. But what had he just said about the job? Did he already want to get rid of him and was buttering him up first? Wally's heart was beating fast. Sánchez was still staring at him.

"Do you want to get rid of me, Señor Sánchez?"

Sánchez laughed so loudly and so long, it shook Wally. Bendix's naive honesty was truly refreshing. "My dear young man, if I want to fire anybody, I don't need a musical accompaniment. Or do you think I am shy? So, out with it! What's troubling you?"

"I want to get married."

"Is that all? Congratulations. Is your bride from Berlin?"

"No. From Caracas."

"A Venezuelan?"

"Yes."

"Aha! A daughter of our land. Perhaps that's why your Spanish has improved so rapidly." Sánchez's smile was positively endearing. Wally's heart went out to him. His boss went on to say that he'd be happy to meet the young lady. Señor Bendix should bring her to coffee one day at the Villa Acacia.

"Many thanks, señor. But you know my bride."

"I do?"

"Yes. Señorita Martínez."

"Rosa Martínez?"

"Yes, Señor. I am so happy."

"Do you think Señorita Martínez will be happy in the primitive conditions on the Orinoco?"

"I hope so. Of course I know she is used to the luxurious way of life here."

Sánchez's smile was gone.

"Rosa wants to stay in Caracas for a while. She'll join me

when I'm settled. But we're going to get married before I leave."

Sánchez could see it all clearly. A deep frown of anger showed up between his dark eyebrows. Rosa Martínez had thrown sand into the eyes of this guileless young European. She would never follow him into the wilderness. She'd bleed him of every bolivar of his salary and would always have some excuse that prevented her from leaving Caracas. An old trick! Rosa Martínez hadn't exploited men just to lose her health, her innocence, and her conscience in the mire of La Guaira. Sánchez had dragged her out of it, and seen to it that she got an education, because at the time she had been ambitious and eager to learn. He had also paid for the operation ten years ago that had made it impossible for her to have children. Now she had suddenly retired and had naturally not said a word to Sánchez about this marriage. And here was this decent, diligent young man, radiant in his happiness and ignorance. It was cruel! And the cruelest part of it was that there wasn't a thing he could do. Except give a veiled warning. And she was ten years older than Bendix, too!

"Have you taken everything into careful consideration, Señor Bendix? What have your parents to say about it? Aren't you very young still to take a serious step like this?"

"My parents don't know anything about it yet, señor. Rosa wants to surprise them. We're going to be married very quietly."

I'm not surprised, thought Sánchez. Suddenly he appeared stern and aloof.

"It's a pity that my family is so far away," said Bendix.

"But the Martínez family is here, aren't they?"

Sánchez had visited Rosa's mother once, up in the hovels, and had found the old mulatto to be a nice woman, with none of Rosa's neuroses. She was honest, even cheerful. A woman with character.

"Unfortunately Rosa's parents are dead," Bendix told his boss. "All she has left is her old nurse, a mulatto, whom she's very fond of. But she's ill right now. And Rosa's brothers and sisters . . . I don't know exactly where they are."

Sánchez knew. Her oldest brother was in jail.

Wally Bendix couldn't explain his boss's sudden silence nor his fixed gaze. At last Rosa had agreed to let him reveal that they were getting married. Married employees could count on a raise in salary, but there Bendix had put his foot down. That wasn't right. Later, perhaps, when the children came. He wanted four, at least. But Rosa wanted to wait a while. First they would have to move away from the Orinoco to more civilized surroundings. Wally had agreed, hesitantly. Children were important to a marriage. Father and Mother hadn't really been able to afford Alfred, but suddenly he had been there. Mother still talked about how happy both of them had been, even when Alfred cried at night and Father had had to get up and carry him around. Fortunately Rosa liked children. She had assured him of that.

Sánchez was still silent. He probably wasn't interested in Rosa's old nurse. Bendix hoped the old woman would be well enough to come to the wedding. After all, she had brought Rosa up. Wally would have liked to visit her, but Rosa didn't have any time for that. All this shopping for the patio-in-the-air! And the storage cost. But Rosa was still paying for that. He looked shyly at the stony profile of his boss. Sánchez was standing at the window, looking down at the traffic. "Would you like a week's vacation after the wedding, Señor Bendix?"

"Thank you very much indeed. But I don't want to miss a day's work. I have a lot to learn."

"Not everyone realizes that in time."

A strange remark, but it didn't penetrate Wally's euphoria. "In two weeks I'll be an old married man!"

"I wish you all the best," Sánchez said quietly.

Shortly before the wedding, Wally turned up earlier than usual at Rosa's place. He had bought a pretty little gold chain for her in Ciudad Bolívar. It was to remind her of him until they met again on the Orinoco. Secretly he hoped he would be able to take her along with him right after the wedding.

After all, they belonged together. That she found it so easy to part from him so soon was a bitter pill for him to swallow.

Rosa's one-room apartment in a modern housing development, like dozens of others that had shot up out of the ground in and around Caracas, always made a dismal impression on Bendix. Sánchez had paid her rent for six months ahead so that Rosa could go on living there until she had recovered. She had explained that she was leaving the firm because of a nervous condition. She had never taken a real vacation. Actually her hysterical condition during the last months had been so noticeable that Sánchez hadn't asked for a doctor's certificate. For the first time in years her work had not been satisfactory. She hadn't told Bendix about her paid vacation. She had simply informed him curtly that she didn't intend to go to the office anymore. She wanted to live like other married women. Wally had nodded in silent acquiescence. Naturally he was ready to work himself to death for Rosa, but then she should be with him, like other wives. And he found the way he was nodding and saying yes to everything somehow replusive. He had never been afraid before, but now he was scared to death that Rosa might be displeased with him or that he might lose her.

On his way to Rosa's he had thought of her constantly. The more he tried to find an explanation for her moods, the more incomprehensible they became. In Puerto Cabello everything had been so simple and wonderful—only the two of them, and no hysterics about unimportant things. That she had no contact whatsoever with her brothers and sisters and wouldn't answer any questions concerning them had also become evident only in Caracas. It upset him. He wanted to get to know Rosa's family. But he had had to give up the idea because of her sulkiness and headaches. Whenever she had a headache she had to be absolutely quiet, and she would simply send him back to his hotel. "Leave me alone now, Walito. My poor head!" What could he do about it? He'd spend a sleepless night and have to drink a lot of black coffee next morning.

He reached her house feeling inexplicably depressed. Per-

haps her headaches three evenings in a row had something
to do with it. She wasn't ever tender to him anymore, and
he missed that. Although he desired her passionately and
painfully, he remained tender and still youthfully shy, and a
friendly look sufficed to make him happy. All he wanted was
to be with her, fondle her, and relieve her of all care. But
after dinner, which he usually prepared, she'd send him away.
"I need rest."

He nodded and nodded and nodded. Tomorrow he had to
write to his parents, but he was not going to tell Rosa about
it. That he hadn't told his family yet that he was going to
take such an important step was totally unlike him. He often
asked himself what on earth was going to become of him
way out here. He felt lost. He would write to his father
tomorrow and send the letter to the factory. Father could then
gently break the news to his mother that their youngest son
had married without their blessing.

Rosa evidently found this secrecy romantic; Wally, when
he was alone, found it embarrassing and unnecessary. But
when he was with Rosa and she didn't have a headache, his
accustomed world vanished. He found this somehow eerie,
as if he had taken a narcotic. On those nights he didn't belong
to himself but to Rosa. And he felt vaguely that this was
neither right nor good for him. But when they were married
things would calm down, and his marriage would be like
every other marriage. The thought cheered him up so that he
was almost like the old Wally.

Rosa wasn't home, and this at once acted as a damper on
his good spirits. Rosa was evidently still shopping for her
dream patio. Of course she didn't have the office car now;
her substitute drove around in that.

As usual her room smelled of emptiness and insecticide,
and the furniture was dismally functional. The elegant chairs
for the patio, instead of enhancing her room, were in storage.
The only picture showed the Savior at the wedding in Cana.
Rosa had explained that in this picture the Son of God bore
a strange resemblance to her father, and he actually did look
Portuguese. There was no picture of her mother, which had

surprised him. In his hotel he had a whole family album that went everywhere with him.

At last he heard steps and jumped up. He had already been waiting an hour for his bride. Why did she knock? Was Rosa expecting visitors? No. She hadn't been expecting visitors. The visitor walked into the room all by herself: a fat, frizzy-haired, older woman who moved ponderously into the room and stared, mouth agape, at the blond young man. She was carrying a dish covered with palm leaves that gave off a sharp Caribbean smell. She had round, friendly eyes and was obviously a mulatto. She was openly astonished to find a stranger in Rosa's room and asked in a deep voice where Rosa was. She had apparently taken some trouble dressing, but there was a tear and quite a few grease spots on her brightly-colored, shapeless dress. She was wearing worn, dusty sandals and enough false jewelry to decorate a Christmas tree. The sweat was running down her forehead, and she wiped it away with a clean, checked kerchief. The kerchief seemed to be her pride and joy, because after using it she folded it up again in its original creases. Wally found her very fat, very ugly, yet somehow someone he might trust.

"Rosa will be here soon. Please sit down, señora."

Groaning, the woman sat down on one of the high cane chairs. Her short fat legs didn't reach the ground. She couldn't have been sitting very comfortably because she groaned again. After a pause she asked Wally straight out who he was and what he was doing here. Wally was quite sure by now that the visitor was Rosa's faithful old nurse. She held the covered dish fast in her hands as if she thought he might take it away from her.

"I am engaged to Rosa. I am very happy to meet you at last. Rosa has told me so much about you."

"Rosa is engaged? To you? I don't know anything about it! Don't make fun of an old woman, señorito!"

"I am not making fun of you!" Wally said indignantly. "We are going to be married soon."

The little woman began to laugh. Her laughter gurgled

cheerfully in her throat. "You are going to marry Rosa? Why, you could almost be her son!"

Wally reddened with anger. First of all, he and Rosa were the same age, and anyway, what business was it of the old woman? But Rosa had told him that the old nurse was a little feebleminded. One shouldn't take offense.

"I'm very glad to see you are well again," he said amiably.

"I was never ill, señor. The Lord gives health to mothers," she said harshly. "What sort of fairy tales has Rosa been telling you? Is she wishing the seven plagues on me?"

"But señora, Rosa loves you. We've been meaning to visit you for a long time."

"But she never did. I haven't seen her for months. The sea could run dry in the meantime." She ignored Wally's position as Rosa's future husband. "Well, well. So Rosa made it at last. She is marrying a white man. Good! My little house protects me from arrogance." She put the dish down on a table and crossed herself. Then she said in a loud voice, "Rosa is and remains my daughter, do you hear, young man? And he who doesn't honor his parents, doesn't go far!"

"Unfortunately Rosa has so much to do before the wedding," he said apologetically. There was something touching about the old woman feeling so strongly that she was Rosa's mother. She was speaking quite sensibly, and didn't smell of rum. But she seemed strangely excited, so he said soothingly, "I know everything, señora. You were truly Rosa's second mother. I find that very touching."

"Rosa's second mother?"

"Rosa's parents died when she was a child. Don't you remember?"

The woman got out of the high chair clumsily, planted herself in front of Wally and said quietly, "Be ashamed, young man. You are a damned liar! God will send you to the hell of liars. And it isn't very cozy down there, you know."

Now one could reproach Wally for all sorts of things, but one couldn't call him a liar. He turned beet red. "I forbid you to speak to me like that, señora," he said, with a strange arrogance that startled him. "Rosa must know if her mother is alive or dead."

"Don't worry, señor. She knows," the old woman said harshly. Then she looked at him thoughtfully, and he knew she hadn't lied. He felt a stabbing pain at the back of his head. This was ridiculous. Rosa was the one who had head-aches.

"I didn't mean to be impolite," he murmured.

"You are not impolite, young man. Just innocent and naive. And too inexperienced for Rosa," she said firmly. There was sadness in her dark eyes, and pity for this young fool. Pity perhaps also for Rosa. She walked slowly to the window and looked out. But she didn't see the characterless street of a big city—she saw a quiet landscape in which daughters hon-ored their mothers and had their hearts in the right place. Suddenly she turned around and said to Wally, "Don't take it too hard."

She shouldn't let it upset her too much, either. Rosa had lied as a small child, and she had cried and prayed a lot for her. But right now she felt that in His endless wisdom and mercy He had sent her this daughter for her Christian puri-fication. She had been too proud of Rosa's quick grasp of things, and her car, and her big salary, and had spread herself like a peacock in front of her neighbors. She gave the petrified young man one last look, then she walked out of the door without another word—small, fat, grotesquely dressed, but, as far as Wally was concerned, with unforgettable dignity. He looked around him, stupefied. Only the palm-leaf—covered dish bore witness to the fact that the conversation had taken place.

Suddenly Rosa was there, staring at the covered dish, speechless. She had strictly forbidden her mother to visit her here, and her mother had always obeyed her. She must have had a reason for coming, but Rosa didn't want to know it. At last she managed to ask, "Did my nurse bring that?"

"Your mother did."

She paled under her lurid makeup. When he asked her

how she could have done a thing like that, she began to tremble and sweat. "Stay, Walito! I can explain everything!"

"I don't want to hear anything more, Rosa!"

He had never spoken to her like that. He looked at her again, and suddenly saw that she really wasn't young. But that wouldn't have been so important if everything else had been all right. But it wasn't, and Walter Bendix couldn't live with a liar.

"May I keep the furniture?" Rosa asked.

It was his first end-of-the-world experience. But he was a Berliner, and like a true son of this sober, heroic city, he accepted reality, whether he liked it or not.

"It's no use, the two of us, Rosa," he said, and knew exactly what awaited him: emptiness, the feeling of having been robbed, work and work and despair at night. But his voice remained firm.

He was on the stairs when he heard the crash. Rosa had thrown her mother's dish on the floor. Then he heard cries and sobs, but he didn't go back. No one could shake his decision, not even he.

# 15

# Five O'Clock
# in the Afternoon

Is it a dreadful hour? It is. One is tired of the heat, of work, tired of life in the chaotic and drearily organized city deserts. One's wounds burn blood red like the evening sun. Rosa Martínez swings on a trapeze of missed possibilities, because Señor Bendix does not return, and after office hours she again has nothing to do and no one to talk to. Of course she is back at the office, and Señor Sánchez again wishes her a pleasant evening as if nothing had happened. All the angels have wandered away, and likewise Señor Bendix, as already mentioned. Rosa Martínez is alone at five o'clock in the afternoon and she resents it because in her dismal room she has the old longing for the herd. The human being is a herd creature.

At five o'clock in the afternoon Señora Martínez thinks of her lost daughter, Rosa, her sinful lamb. She keeps looking for the smart little automobile that Sánchez puts at the disposal of his private secretaries, a consolation prize for jilted brides. But the car with Rosa in it doesn't come, and Señora Martínez weeps. She prays for Rosa, but Rosa no longer communicates with her. At around five-thirty, she dries her eyes and starts to get supper for her oldest son. Enrico has been let out of jail for good behavior, and has said good-bye to his gang of thieves. He has a job in a garage in Caracas and is a good son, a retired thief. That was what Señora Martínez had wanted to tell Rosa that afternoon, but then young Señor Bendix had been there, and Enrico was no concern of his. And as she sighs and cooks *arroz con pollo*, she thinks of Rosa again and the red snappers and the mushrooms and the wine she sometimes brought with her when she was still her mother's pride and joy, and a good daughter...

No one feels like singing at five o'clock in the afternoon. Especially not Cooper, the perennial traveler. He still has heard nothing from his wife, and doesn't know when Richard will move her from Zürich to Chicago. Richard was never one to write letters. Cooper in Bogotá is also alone at five o'clock in the afternoon. All conferences are over, so are the opulent lunches with the heads of industry, and there is no Miss Moll. Not that his longing for her prevents him from reading the paper, but he misses her. He frowns as he reads the Colombian daily and waits for further attempts on his life. There it is! "American diplomat kidnapped by guerrillas. Will be freed from their hiding place in the mountains of Colombia only with a guarantee that twenty guerrillas in the jails of Colombia will be let out." A simple and effective tactic, like the arrow in the fisherman's paradise. Cooper has left his smile in the hotel safe. It is well taken care of there. He recalls the American ambassador in Brazil who was kidnapped by guerrillas or thieves with no political program, and wasn't freed until several individuals with whom he had absolutely nothing to do were freed from a jail in Río. A Japanese and a German diplomat had also been kidnapped, and the German had been murdered. The kidnapping of diplomats seemed to have become a popular pastime. Cooper brooded. Was the United States giving the Latin American countries so much financial and technical aid toward this end? The third attempt on his life might be successful, and he hated to live dangerously.

For Señor de Padilla on the other hand, a life without danger was no life at all. He still hadn't put in an appearance at his house in Puerto Ordaz. His mother waited for him in vain, but she didn't weep. Her son looked after her and the other members of her household even when away. Only not Anna. She had been cast off. An empty old bag, as he called her, with an empty purse.

She arrived at five o'clock in the afternoon. She couldn't remember afterward how quickly she left the house again. Camilo had assured her before his flight from the Hotel Amazonas that Mama would explain everything to her. But there was nothing left to explain because the facts spoke loudly and clearly.

Mamacita: Who are you? What do you want here? Get out!

Anna Carlovac: I am Anna. Camilo's wife. Don't you recognize me?

Mamacita: Get out, you good for nothing garbage. There's no room for you here!

Anna Carlovac: This is my house. I always lived here and this is where I'm going to stay.

Mamacita (addressing the chandelier in the living room): Do you hear that? She's staying here? Get out you old whore!

Anna Carlovac: I am too refined to quarrel with a nigger. I had a German governess at home. Fräulein Steinmeister. She waited on my mother.

Mamacita: Get out, I tell you! Or do you need help?

Anna Carlovac: Ow! Ow! I'll sue you for assault!

Mamacita (to the chandelier): Do you hear that? She's going to sue me. I'll wring her neck! (Calls out) Gabriela! Come, my darling. Explain to this old bag how things stand.

Gabriela (a young black woman, very pregnant): I am Señora de Padilla. Marriage license and all, do you hear? I am in my sixth month, do you hear? Camilo wants children. Do you understand, you worn-out mattress?

The two women laugh loudly. Mamacita strokes Gabriela's swollen stomach. Anna de Padilla stands there, wide-eyed. So that is the explanation! Camilo got married. Mamacita chose the bride. Six months...

Anna: Where is my husband? Where is my money? This

is my house and I stay here. Go away! You'll hear from my lawyer!

Mamacita: Now listen carefully, you white shit! My son Camilo has made this house over to me. His bank account, too. Wherever he is, he doesn't need money. He can count on his mother.

Anna: Where is he?

Mamacita: He found you in a bordello. Go back to it! (She looks at her watch.) It's five minutes past five. Yes, I can read figures. Gabriela is teaching me how to read and write. Little grandson mustn't be ashamed. Get out, I tell you! I have the money and the house and everything.

Anna Carlovac, formerly Padilla, stands on the street. It is all over. She has always helped Padilla. She tried, on his orders, to poison the Yanqui Cooper. That it didn't work isn't her fault. Padilla has disappeared. Yanqui Cooper is alive, and she has nobody in the world now.

It begins to rain. The drops fall on Anna's tired, confused head. She walks like a somnambulist. The heavens grow dark. There is thunder. Anything is better than the laughter on the veranda. What does one do when it rains? A coffee bar. In the harbor. Taxi! Anna still has the money Padilla threw at her in the Hotel Amazonas. The many, many years with him. A series of misfortunes, abuse, without a moment of security. But there had been money. She knew where the rice and fish for the next day were coming from. Mamacita cooked—very well when her son was there. Otherwise Camilo bellowed and threw his dish at the wall. A dreadful family. In the rain all cats are gray, and so are all port cities. The taxi stops in a bumpy alley. The name of the bar is El Dorado. Anna stumbles and lies in the mud. A sailor helps her up and asks in broken Spanish if she's already drunk at this early hour.

It is shabby but cozy in the coffee bar. The wind howls, but it can't penetrate her lungs. Not here. What is she to do? Padilla shouldn't have done this to her. Perhaps he was tired of her contempt for him. Perhaps not. He wanted children even though he spent his life hiding in the woods. Sometimes he was nice. Everybody is nice sometimes.

In the bar there is a smell of the sea, of coffee and rum. Anna is alone in her corner. If only she could stay there always. It is pouring outside. If Anna goes out now she will drown in the puddles. *No importa.* Anna's raincoat is encrusted with street dirt. There is a crust around her heart too. That's nice: nothing hurts. She has fallen asleep in her corner. At some time or other, when the first lights are turned on in the harbor, she's got to go out in the rain again. Anna murmurs in her sleep.

"Throw her out!" says the owner's wife.

"Leave her alone," says her husband.

"She's dirty," says his wife.

"She is old. She's probably sick."

"So throw her out!" says his wife. "She'll bring us bad luck."

Pablo, the owner, doesn't want to do that. He shakes Anna by the arm gently. She asks who he is. Pablo. This is his coffee bar and this is his wife. "Can she find her way out alone?" Stupid question! She weaves her way back to the door of the Café El Dorado. Pablo says to his wife, "She is sick. Would you turn your mother out on a night like this?"

"She is not my mother," says Pablo's wife.

"She can sleep in the empty closet with the brooms. She can help you with the dishes. Be quiet, woman!"

"She'll bring us bad luck, I tell you!"

*"No importa!"*

Pablo leads Anna Carlovac to the broom closet. A wonderful little room. Brooms don't talk.

"You *blancos* always stick together," says Pablo's wife.

"You're a fine Christian woman. Help the stranger!"

An hour later Anna teeters back into the bar. An hour's sleep is an eternity. Seamen are standing at the counter. They stare at her. Is she crazy? Pablo's wife takes her roughly by the arm and shoves her back to the brooms. "I'm in my sixth month," Anna mumbles.

"And I'm in my fourth. Do you want to go or stay here?"

"No, no!"

"You can stay. I don't mind. You can scrub the floors."

Scrubwoman for a half-caste? Anna still has her money in a small purse on her breast, under her dress. "Thank you for your kindness, señora, but I'm afraid I must go. An important appointment."

She is sick, thinks Pablo's wife. "I'll bring you a plate of soup. You can leave tomorrow if you want to. So lie down again, Señora."

"No thank you. I have a pressing appointment. Adios, señora. What is your name?"

"Gabriela."

"That's the name of Camilo's new wife. Then you must be in your sixth month. I'd like to go out the back door. The noise in the bar . . . Or is it the sea? Give my love to your baby. Only three months more, Gabriela. I never had a child. Not even a bridal veil. *No importa.*"

She walks down the street and around a corner. The puddles cast little glittering lights in her way. The damp, warm air lies like a sack on her lungs. She longs like a child for warmth, security, attention. She should have accepted Gabriela's soup. Hot, hot soup. A spoonful for Papa, a spoonful for Mama, a spoonful for Fräulein Stein . . . mei . . . mei . . . She must pull herself together. She could go to a hotel where she could be a paying guest, not a scrubwoman. A hotel guest could do things slowly. That was the advantage of being a paying guest. No broom closet. A proper bed. Not a bench with straw sacks like the El Dorado gypsies.

Anna was so exhausted she would have slipped and fallen if she hadn't clung to the sailor. No, she didn't want anything from him, just to hang onto him. "Are you sick, señora?" Stupid question! Too sick to live, too healthy to die. "I have to hang onto something," she mumbled. "Not to me," he said. "I'm not a lamppost." Anna apologized with a certain dignity. "My mistake, señor. I'll be on my way in a minute. A pressing appointment." He freed himself cautiously. After all, you can't push a drunken woman into a puddle. Anna moved on. First to a cheap hotel, then on into no man's land.

For the first time in a thousand years she was free. She could go anywhere she liked. If only she knew where...

At five o'clock in the afternoon, Brother Fernando was drinking good strong coffee with Father Alonzo in the mission near Puerto Ayacucho. He had just finished his rounds in the villages along the Orinoco, and on the way back had visited the old protegé of Señor Sánchez. *El capitán* had been excited and irritable. Brother Fernando sounded worried.

"More excited than usual? Do you know of any reason for it, Fernando?"

There was a reason. Ever since the old man had met the young blond woman from Berlin, he had been difficult. Otherwise he would have greeted Brother Fernando with as much joy as he was capable of. This time he had only nodded, and then, in Spanish of his own invention, had whispered with Tucu and grumbled. Then suddenly he had done something that Brother Fernando could only see as an act of violence.

Fernando had been a carpenter before he had become a lay brother, and he had made a small table for the old man. *El capitán* had been delighted. Nobody else had ever given him anything. No one ever thought of his needs. But Fernando had. This time, in a fit of rage, *el capitán* had sawed the table up into little pieces (secretly, during the siesta hour) and had thrown them into the Orinoco. Then he had spat into the river. Fernando had watched him from behind the palm trees. Nobody knew why the old man had behaved like this toward a friend. Just the same, Brother Fernando intended to make him a new table.

Father Alonzo looked at the young lay brother silently. "You will not make another table for him, Fernando. We cannot encourage the madness of this old fool. There are too many of them around."

"But I feel so sorry for him, Reverend Father. He doesn't know what he's doing."

"Then he must learn."

Brother Fernando was silent. The afternoon sun was hiding

behind clouds. He could not help but feel sorry for the lonely old man.

"*El capitán* is sometimes a child," said Father Alonzo. "A bad child. If you give in to him on everything, he will become worse. I know, I know—the Lord pities men such as he. We are working in His name. But that doesn't mean we should grow sentimental about it, Fernando. On the contrary—our thinking capacities and our powers of judgment are sacred gifts too. They must regulate our compassion. We must remain hard even as we pity fools and sinners. To spoil a bad child instead of punishing him is not love. Mercy remains the gentle rain from heaven. Do you think I have forgotten it?"

"I won't make him another table," said Brother Fernando. "But I am very unhappy about it."

"That doesn't matter." Father Alonzo smiled. He rarely smiled. "It takes courage to say no, my son. I shall pray for your courage and mine."

*El viejo* spoke constantly about the girl from Berlin. Sometimes he called her Christina. Brother Fernando asked if the old man came from Berlin.

Father Alonzo didn't answer the question. "Don't talk about it, my son," he said.

"Nobody in the house knows that *el capitán* sawed up the table," said Brother Fernando.

"I don't mean the table," Father Alonzo said drily. He thanked the young man for his report and went to his study. There he wrote a letter to Carlos Sánchez in Caracas. It was a long letter, and the señor was not going to be happy about it.

"Did you get bad news, Carlos?"

"Nothing important." Sánchez tucked Father Alonzo's letter in a file with some business reports. He was frowning.

"What's the matter, Carlos? Something unexpected? You look upset."

"Not at all, my dear. I always expect the worst and am therefore never disappointed."

He rose abruptly and walked out to his acacia with its vaulted roof of feather-light red blossoms. The tree had been witness to many things: his engagement to Teresa, his quarrels with her, Carla Moll in a white dress on her first and last evening in Altamira, the mourners after Teresa's death.

He thought of the weekend in the Urbanización Palma Sola and Carla Moll in her snow-white dress. "You are beautiful, Carla!" "The evening is my element, Carlos." She had lied as usual. Betrayal was her element. Father Alonzo's letter had only corroborated his premonitions. In the meantime he had taken Carla Moll with him to Palma Sola. All's fair in love and war. Love? He knew what Carla needed, and how she needed it. He had arranged this night of love with cold calculation. Two passions, independent of each other. In the middle of the night he had searched her suitcase. She was so untidy, but—nothing. In the meantime she had slept the sleep of the innocent.

The second night each had spent thinking his and her own thoughts. During the day she had seemed embarrassed. She couldn't look him in the eye. Had she been Bonnhoff in the fisherman's paradise or not? Once she made a movement as if to shut her ears. Whenever he had brought up the topic of Samariapo, she had changed the subject. But he knew what he would do. He would study the *Comet*. The German wife of his friend Ruiz in La Guaira read the paper. And if the series "Where are they now? What are they doing?" happened to contain the story of Bonnhoff one day, then he would settle things with Carla Moll in his own way. He would destroy her. Quietly. There were ways and means. He would give it some thought. But there was time.

The afternoon sun set the acacia blooms afire. Until now the house on the Orinoco had been an ideal hiding place for Bonnhoff. A crazy coincidence had brought Carla Moll there. Sánchez had always looked upon coincidences skeptically. Now they took their revenge. But coincidence could just as easily punish the journalist Moll. All one had to do was help things along a little. He had to protect his father, a helpless old man, no matter what he had done in his 'best years.' He would protect Bonnhoff. The tree was his witness.

Pilar with fresh coffee. For a moment he stared at her as if she had been a stranger. She knew nothing about Palma Sola. He could see Bonnhoff in the garden with its high walls, could see him fishing, discontented, homesick, but safe. Of course it wasn't a normal life; that was an impossibility wherever Bonnhoff lived out his private mythology. A monstrous father...

"Has this woman from Berlin finally left?" asked Pilar.

"I have asked Señor Bendix to take her to the ship. Then at least I'll know that she's left Venezuela."

"What was she doing such a long time on the Orinoco?"

"I don't know, my dear Pilar. Why don't you ask her? In two or three months she'll be back in Berlin. She is a..."

"She is a whore," Pilar said angrily.

"Worse than that. She is a journalist. They are witches without broomsticks."

"Has something happened, Carlos?"

"Right now something is happening. Why do you ask?"

"Could you visit Bonnhoff soon? It would please him."

"You know that isn't true, Pilar. I think he should be moved somewhere else."

"Where?"

"If I knew that, there'd be no problem," Sánchez said drily.

"I thought the house on the Orinoco was the solution. What's happened?"

"Nothing. I'm just wondering..."

"That's not like you, Carlos. You never hesitate when it comes to making a decision."

"I haven't come to a decision yet. Why are you looking at me so strangely?"

"You're hiding something from me. Don't you trust me anymore?"

"You are the only woman I trust, Pilar."

"I'd do anything for you, Carlos. Don't forget it."

"I don't forget it. You're already doing much too much

for me. And for the old man. What sort of a life is this for you?"

"I'm going into the house. It looks like rain."

Sánchez watched her go, but his mind was already on the Orinoco. Bonnhoff's shadow darkened river, woods, shore.

"Here we are," said Carla Moll, when they arrived at the harbor of Puerto Cabello.

"Yes," said Bendix. "You'll call my parents in Berlin, won't you? When you can find time for it."

"I'll find time, Wally. Any special message?"

"No, no. Just that I'm all right." He sounded depressed.

"Shall I say something about the wedding?"

"No. That didn't work out. Señorita Martínez couldn't make up her mind to live on the Orinoco." He blushed a fiery red, but Fräulein Moll was looking at the gas tanks. She had thought so all along. She hadn't believed a word of his chivalrous version. Rosa Martínez was the last person to let a young man with a good business future go. She looked at him sideways. He looked taller, thinner, and very vulnerable. Honest to the core, as he always had been, but the spark of naive enthusiasm that had made him seem so young was snuffed out. He looked as if he didn't get enough sleep. "When you're on vacation in Berlin, you must call me right away," she said impulsively.

"Oh, Carla, you won't remember who I am!"

"Nonsense! I have a cast-iron memory."

"Señor Sánchez sends farewell greetings."

"Give him mine, too."

"Where will your next trip take you, Carla?"

"First I want to live outside my suitcases for a while. All this moving around in Venezuela has unnerved me."

"Is that the famous journalist speaking?"

"I don't see any famous journalist. You know what I need most? A change of climate, rest."

"That's logical for someone who keeps moving around the way you do. Do you remember the fisherman's paradise?

That was our only expedition together. I often think of it, Carla."

"I do too."

"That was really untouched nature down there," Wally said dreamily.

"Except for the Coca-Cola ads."

"We didn't see a soul while fishing. Odd, wasn't it?"

"Very odd."

"I'm going on board now."

"Shall I come with you?"

"No. I'd rather you didn't. I hate farewells. So let's make it short. You have my address in Berlin? I'm only asking because I've mislaid yours on the Orinoco."

"I wrote it down again. Here you are. I'll be writing to you anyway about all your harbor agents. I've typed them off for you."

"Thanks a lot. They may come in handy."

"I wish I could take other little nuisance jobs like that off your hands. You have more important things to attend to."

"You could be my secretary."

"Great! As soon as Señor Sánchez fires me. I have the feeling that can happen fast with him. By the way, a little farewell present, Carla."

"May I open it? When it comes to farewell presents, I'm a four-year-old . . . But how beautiful, Wally! You're dreadfully extravagant. Did you win in the lottery?" She was looking at a little brooch of Margarita pearls.

"It's nothing really, Carla. Pure egoism. So that you'll remember me longer. And here's something else from your secretary. I almost left it in the hotel. A sketch of the fisherman's paradise. You wanted one, didn't you?"

"How nice of you to remember, Wally!"

"Maps are not my forte. But I tried to get it all on. The circle here—that's Samariapo. And that's the harbor. And back there where I've circled it in ink is the Hotel Amazonas."

"With Cooper and Frau Padilla."

"Here's the route from Puerto Ayacucho to Samariapo. And here's the dock for the motorboats and canoes."

"Now I can find my way to the fisherman's paradise in my sleep! That's terrific, Wally. Thank you. Tell me, where was it that Zongo fished with me."

"About here, where I've drawn a few little fish. And way in back of it there was a white house, behind bushes and palm trees. There. I marked it with a little square. And this is where I fished. You can see the winding of the river."

"Marvelous! Have you shown this little work of art to anybody?"

"Of course not. It's a strictly personal souvenir!"

"I'm raising your salary!"

He had done her good. A younger brother. For a moment the world seemed to stand still for her. The final farewell. She felt a hand on her throat, not Sánchez's but her own. Even tears couldn't wash away the two nights in Palma Sola. On the second night she had pretended to have a headache, and Sánchez had taken her at her word. Of course. There was nothing left to seek or find. But she would never forgive his tactful reserve. Never! She thought of Bonnhoff. Eerie that a man as good as dead could spoil everything for the living. Without ever knowing it, Bonnhoff had effectively stepped between Carlos and herself. Perhaps with time and with the help of a change of climate, Sánchez would become a shadow and dissolve in the endless woods, mountains, harbors, the vast llanos, and the rivers. She didn't know what was waiting for her in Berlin. She had heard nothing from Wendt since she had left the Hotel Amazonas. Perhaps it was best that she didn't know.

"Good-bye, Wally. Do your best."

"Bon voyage. And give Berlin my love." His voice was hoarse. They shook hands and she was gone.

# 16

# Wilted Laurels for Sale!

Carla Moll:

I arrived in Tempelhof a day before Locker's wedding, and there was Mother with a crushed bouquet of roses and a rather shabby summer hat. It's a funny thing, but I can always tell when a hat has been marked down. Every season Mother gets a check from me to buy herself a fine new hat, which then lies in the closet because she prefers to wear a beat-up old one. A poisonous green one this time. I hadn't seen Mother for months and was a little startled. She looked old and frail, and her hair was much grayer. She looked shabbier than her hat.

"Don't you feel well, Mother?"

"I never feel well. You know that. Why are you so late? I'm exhausted from waiting."

"I wrote to you that you should wait for me at home. Didn't you get my letter from Panama?"

"I wanted to see you right away. But of course you can't understand that."

The change of climate was complete.

I was to spend the first night at Mother's so that we could drive to Locker's wedding together.

"You're going to be upset, Mother."

"Why?"

"Because it isn't my wedding."

"You can get a man like Locker any day. He's a bore. I feel sorry for his wife."

"You look so tired, Mother. Call them up and tell them I'm not getting back until the day after tomorrow."

"I wouldn't dream of it! I need a change every now and then too. Don't get me all upset, Carla. Everybody's dying to see you. We're going."

Locker's reception was lavish. All sorts of important people were there and the liquor flowed. Locker beamed at his Lisbeth, and she beamed at him. He never mentioned his gall bladder, which he had talked about pretty constantly with Hanns König and me on the Orinoco. I was in a daze. Sánchez and mother's cheesecake were probably weighing heavily upon me. I was wearing Bendix's brooch. The good fellow. I even felt a slight longing for Cooper. He hadn't really been that bad. But that's what I always say.

I felt lost in the elegant hotel, especially since my friends Lotte and Kurt Sommer hadn't arrived yet. Kurt was late everywhere because he hated to leave his files. Mother always came too early so she wouldn't miss anything.

I liked Lisbeth Wendt right away. She was a very composed girl, and I was sure she was a good doctor. Patients kept going up to her to congratulate her. "Are you going to give up your practice, Fräulein Doktor?"

"Oh no! I couldn't let my colleagues down, could I?" said Lisbeth. Dr. Hilda Probst was her partner, and if she felt Locker might be a disturbing element, she did her best not to show it for Lisbeth's sake.

"Cheers, Hilda!" Lisbeth said just then. "You're still my best friend!" Dr. Probst smiled for the first time. I didn't feel like smiling. I was still so shocked that Wendt had left Comet, that I didn't really grasp yet what his loss would mean to me. I had received the news in Panama City.

"Carla!" My friend Lotte came rushing up to me. We kissed and hugged like schoolgirls after vacation. Finally Kurt said, "It's my turn now, Lotte! Carla, you're more beautiful than ever! How do you like being back in Berlin after all your

adventures?" He gave me his searching judge's look and I,
stupidly, reddened.

"She's blushing!" Kurt declared, satisfied. "So there's a
new man!"

"You've got to tell me all about it, Carlchen," said Lotte.
"When my horrid husband is at the office and little Robert
is asleep."

"Robert never sleeps!" said Kurt Sommer.

Carlchen! I hadn't heard it for such a long time.

It was great to be with the Sommers again, but unfortunately, at Lisbeth's request, they had brought their four-year-
old son Robert along. The boy was as pretty and pudgy as
Lotte and was going to end up just as smart and sly as Kurt.
Right now he was bellowing his head off because he wanted
to drink his father's champagne. He poured his lemonade into
a flower pot. That's what his father did when he didn't like
his drink.

"Yes, he's a real brat," Kurt Sommer said proudly. "Gor-
geous dress, Carla! Here comes Dr. Hartlieb. A client of mine
is in his clinic. Stop screaming Robert, or you'll be sorry."

Dr. von Hartlieb? When and where had I heard the name
before? Oh yes, head nurse Christina Ullmann worked in his
clinic in Wilmersdorf.

Here in Berlin it was easier to understand why Bonnhoff
had mistaken me for her on the Orinoco. At that moment I
could see her clearly: a pale, gray-haired woman in her middle
fifties in a severe uniform and strong, ugly shoes. A strange
visitor to the editorial offices of *Comet*. Her soft hesitant
voice, "Shortly before the war I met a young Venezuelan.
He went back to Caracas in '38. His father's name was Carl
Friedrich Bonnhoff. He was a Berliner. Did you by any chance
hear the name Carlos Bonnhoff mentioned in Caracas, Fräulein Moll?" Did I? By chance? In 1938 head nurse Ullmann
had been young, Bonnhoff had been in the prime of life, and
Carlos still a green young man. Christina! Tina! At the time
she had been much younger than I was today at Locker's
wedding.

Kurt Sommer asked, "Everything all right?" I nodded. "I

don't know . . . there's something wrong, Carla. Is is because of Wendt?"

I was silent. I took a deep breath. "Now all you have to say is don't take it too hard."

"Have I said anything?"

Dr. von Hartlieb had an interesting face. It was rumored that he had offered resistance in Nazi Berlin. He was talking to a famous actor who in SS disguise had once protected many persecuted people and saved their lives. You had to be damned courageous to do that. He had given Wendt an interview to start the series, "Where are they now? What are they doing today?" The interview had been a sensation in postwar Berlin. His pseudonym had been Engelbert Schmidt. He was the son of a very popular writer in the Third Reich who had been a close friend of Goebbels. Today Ernst Hardenberg was the star of our Schiller Theater in Charlottenburg. Macbeth. Faust. King Lear. There really were a lot of prominent people at Locker's reception. Kurt, who knew everybody, had introduced me to both men. He had loved it. Dr. von Hartlieb didn't say anything and looked at me without smiling. Christina Ullmann must have told him about our meeting in my office. I had the feeling that Hartlieb didn't like me.

Hartlieb and the actor were the first resistance fighters of the Hitler era I had ever met. We were a new generation: Kurt, Lotte, Wendt, and all the rest. Wendt had written a foreword to the "Engelbert Schmidt" interview. Hardenberg and Hartlieb and many others had been the first champions of a secret revolution—like men and women in every country where bloody politics are being practiced who help, heal, save; and without whom our civilization would have disappeared from the face of the earth long ago.

Somebody came up to me with a man who looked familiar, although I had never seen him. "Dr. Wendrix would like to meet you, Fräulein Moll. His son is in Venezuela." I could sense what was coming. "My name is Bendix, and my youngest boy is Wally Bendix." He looked at me astonished. "I had pictured you much older and more dignified." We laughed.

We liked each other at once and still do. I got to know them all. The Bendixes are a real family. I reassured Wally's father, who had suspected that something was wrong. No, Wally was doing very well. Not a word about marriage. "You must come and see us, Fräulein Moll." And I wanted to. A miracle for me. I never visited families.

An emaciated woman came up to me and asked if I was a lesbian. I said no, I was a journalist, and Sappho withdrew, hurt. Time passed. Somebody asked me how I felt about Wendt's leaving. I said nothing. Two readers of *Comet* were talking about the new editor-in-chief. "I think the first number is excellent. Of course he's much younger than Wendt. Just thirty. I think Wendt was nearer forty."

"A change is a good thing," said the first man. "Fresh blood. To be honest with you—I was sick of Wendt's anti-Nazi fixation. Who wants to read that sort of thing anymore? It wasn't all that bad anyway. But you daren't say that."

Lotte dragged me away from the two men, who went on casting stones at Wendt from their private glass houses. "They're idiots! Don't let them upset you, Carlchen."

"Who's upset?" I said. My voice sounded hoarse. I was trembling. So things hadn't been all that bad, and Fritz Bonn-hoff had been nothing but a cheerful beer drinker in a smart uniform. And for *that* Hartlieb and Hardenberg and thousands of others had risked their lives daily? Smuggling persecuted people out of the country or hiding them in cellars?

And who entered the scene now? Head nurse Ullmann, naturally! This time not as a specter on the Orinoco, but in the flesh; with a dietician and surgical nurse on either side. Lisbeth wouldn't dream of getting married without this trio. They walked around sedately and silently, like the Salvation Army, only not singing. I stared at head nurse Ullmann. She was chatting with Lisbeth, lively and friendly. She didn't look at me, and I had no intention of sending greetings from Sturmbannführer Bonnhoff in Venezuela. She and Hartlieb were obviously good friends. They were talking animatedly. What had Ullmann been up to in the Third Reich? Nothing? Something evil? Something heroic? It was none of my business. But Bonnhoff knew her. Carlos did, too. I would ask her for an interview in my office one day. All I knew was where she was now and what she was doing today . . . I was glad that my generation didn't have to live in a dictatorship as those resisters had, when you had to creep around the Victory Column with a muzzle on, or think about freedom of speech in a concentration camp. I'm not made of heroic stuff. I'm in no hurry to get to the slaughterhouse. I left and got into a taxi in front of the hotel. Mother came home much later. I was already in bed. She brought me hot milk and was happy that she could look after me. She had heard that Hanns König, the cameraman, had gone back to Venezuela. Was he going to the Indians or to the guerrillas? Mother confuses them with "gorillas," and asked if I'd seen a lot of monkeys on the Orinoco. She had had a wonderful time at Locker's wedding, seeing the many friends and acquaintances whom she saw seven days a week. Dr. Schneider had finally dragged her home. Gently. She would have liked to stay. Lately he spoiled all her fun . . .

At last I was alone. At Locker's wedding everybody had acted as if Wendt had died, even though he'd only moved to Munich. Since we work nights at the office, I called his private secretary. It was only ten o'clock in the evening, a time when Frau Hannemann came to life. Like Wendt, I had never had any private intercourse with Edith Hannemann because we didn't really like each other. But now I had to talk to her. I had to hear all about the new man who sat at Wendt's desk.

Frau Hannemann wanted to meet for coffee. "All right then. Tomorrow, Moll. I have things to tell you about the office . . . not over the phone though, you understand?"

"How do you like the new man, Hannemann?"

"I've laughed louder in my life. So, tomorrow, five o'clock. The invitation's on me."

"You're kidding!"

"No. I insist!"

*  *  *

"His name is Oscar," private secretary Hannemann said in a sinister voice.

"And why shouldn't his name be Oscar?"

"I've always had bad experiences with Oscars."

In spite of the summery weather, which would still have been considered cold in Venezuela, Edith Hannemann had on the gray-brown suit which had given her the nickname "Partridge." She had a red beak to go with it, and she was a nestling. Wherever she was, there she stayed. I wondered if Oscar had found that out yet. She was forty-seven, and her birth certificate wasn't lying. She had shaken my hand like a fellow-sufferer. If there had ever been an office widow, it was Edith Hannemann. Only the widow's veil was lacking. She spoke in a subdued voice, and I wanted to laugh. "Wendt isn't dead, Hannemann."

"For me he is." Edith Hannemann ordered a liqueur. "Would you like one too?" she asked hesitantly. "Of course Oscar hopes he can fire me soon, but he's going to find that difficult. I guess his doll from Frankfurt is to take my place."

How did Frau Hannemann know what Dr. Ribbeck was hoping? I asked if the "doll" was in Berlin yet.

"Not yet. But I happened to see a letter from her." Frau Hannemann just happened to see everything. In the letter the doll had asked when she was to put in an appearance in Berlin. I asked if Frau Hannemann had happened to see Oscar's reply, but he seemed to attend to his private mail at home. I asked what he looked like.

"A bean pole. A bald head with a few blond hairs left. Ice-cold eyes. Definitely unsympathetic. You'll enjoy meeting him on Monday, Moll."

For a moment I saw Herbert Wendt at his desk—his intelligent face; his dark, unruly hair, his eyes that sparkled with every new idea, and his beautiful sensitive mouth. I also saw the chaos on his desk. There was always the cup of coffee that Frau Hannemann kept filled. Cigarette ashes everywhere. But Wendt was Wendt. You could go to him with anything. He had so much patience, and he had the right balance of seriousness and levity.

"Of course I make things as hard as I can for Oscar," said Edith Hannemann. "I owe that to Wendt. What can Oscar do about passive resistance? Nothing. He doesn't know his way around, and I've been here for years. You're practically a newcomer by comparison. By the way, Oscar gave me a raise."

"Well, that's certainly nice of him, Hannemann."

"A straight case of bribery. He wants to get on the good side of me. He thinks in three months he'll know it all, and then he can fire me. He's already fired three of my colleagues. And Fräulein Schröder. But she was really ready for it. Wendt only kept her on because of her sick mother."

"What did Ribbeck do in Frankfurt?"

"Political editor on a big paper. But he wasn't editor-in-chief."

"And now with us he does everything?"

"Mostly. You'll see at your first staff meeting. Do you think he accepts any suggestions from us? He knows everything better."

"How far had Wendt got with his book?"

"Right in the middle of it. *Berlin Fin de Siècle*. It's going to be wonderful. But who's going to type it for him now?"

Surely there'd be a typist in Munich, I thought, but I didn't say anything. I asked if Ribbeck was married.

"A fanatic bachelor. That's always suspicious. One never knows why people like that aren't married. He's turned everything upside down, Moll. God forbid that anyone should think that Wendt occasionally did things right! Oscar is reorganizing day and night."

"With whom at night?"

"I don't know. Not with Schmidt, yet. She has her eyes trained on Oscar."

Frau Hannemann ordered a third schnapps and went on reciting Oscar's misdeeds. He seemed to be a fast worker in every respect. She really didn't leave a good hair on his head, and evidently he had only a few. She spoke loudly, and the people at the next table were listening. "Pipe down, Hannemann! Pipe down! Oscar's best friend may be listening."

"He doesn't have any friends. All he knows is subscribers, patrons, fashionable hostesses, people with connections, politicians, and more subscribers."

I asked how he happened to know all these people, since he came from Frankfurt.

"But he's a Berliner, Moll! Like you and me."

"And Wendt?"

Frau Hannemann was silent, and at last I could ask her why Wendt had lost his highly paid job with *Comet*. All he had written to me was that he was moving to Munich on his fortieth birthday, with his wife and children. The letter had reached me in Miami Beach where I was spending a week trying to recover from Sánchez. To my annoyance I was discovering that I could recover neither from him nor from myself. The news of Wendt's dismissal was the final blow. I hate surprises. Wendt signed off as usual with "Detailed letter follows." That letter had yet to follow. I asked Frau Hannemann when Oscar had taken over.

"The day after Wendt's farewell celebration. Some celebration! How I suffered! Indescribable." Frau Hannemann always suffered indescribably. Wendt's case was typical. *Comet* had been bought by a big corporation which brought in its own people. Ribbeck, thirty-four years old, was a close friend of the head of the corporation. Moreover, subscriptions had been dropping lately.

I asked what Wendt was doing in Munich. He had a job with an art magazine. Art? He was a political man with a passion for week-to-week reporting. By inclination a historian, he was a critic of the times. Depressed, I asked what *he* knew about art?

"As if anything depends on that! I had a long letter from him yesterday. He wants to do a series on political art."

"And what do his new employers think of that?"

"I don't know yet. But I'll keep you informed, Moll."

Frau Hannemann assured herself through a cloud of smoke that I'd grasped the hint that she received letters from Wendt. I asked what Trude Wendt was doing.

"She took a job as a secretary because he isn't making

enough. Of course he's spent his severance pay. Well, you know him, Moll."

"Couldn't he find anything in Berlin?"

Edith Hannemann looked at me, speechless. As if Wendt would have stayed on in Berlin after this debacle! Frau Hannemann was looking at the ruin of the Gedächtniskirche. Then she said, "The whole thing is a disgrace. Wendt was right. But Ribbeck goes in for popular series: astronauts, things like that. That's when I think of Wendt's wonderful series, 'Where are they now? What are they doing today?' But one shouldn't think. Would you like to look at the new numbers? I can send them around to you for the weekend."

"No thank you. Or rather, yes."

"Oscar's going to make a play for you. After all, *Caracas for Beginners* was a huge success for the paper. Didn't Wendt send you over there at the time to look for an old Nazi?"

"What would you say if I'd brought the old Nazi with me this time?"

"I'd say that I'd heard you tell better jokes, Moll."

"So would I. Thanks for the coffee, Hannemann."

"My pleasure. So, until Monday, Moll. Perhaps you'll like Oscar. You always had funny taste. But that would surprise me."

"Me too. So—until Monday."

I drove to Lotte and Kurt. I simply couldn't stay home, answering Mother's questions. I called her up and she said that she knew I was bored with her. I should come home early. It was my last evening in her apartment. I had to get ready to move to my place. Oscar and Mother were just too much.

"I have a client who knows Ribbeck very well," said Kurt.

"How well?"

"He was engaged twice and never married."

"Your client?"

"No. Ribbeck."

"All things comes in threes," said Lotte. "Perhaps he'll get engaged to you."

"I'll bet! The pig's feet are wonderful, Lotte."

"My client says Ribbeck is to be approached with caution."

"In what respect?"

"In every respect."

"I'm not rash," I said. "Would you object if we changed the subject, Kurt?"

"I'd just like to know why Oscar was engaged twice and never married," said Lotte.

"Be patient until Monday. It's the first thing I'll ask him."

# 17

# A Change of Climate

Carla Moll:

My first Monday in the office was a total disaster. The weather was awful, so I couldn't wear my white suit. Not that I wanted to make any sort of impression on Ribbeck, but white suits me best, and it wouldn't have hurt if the new man had noticed it. So I had to wear my gray suit, which went very well with the gray day. With my red pullover, it looks smart, but if Oscar Ribbeck was a bull, I didn't want to risk enraging him. On that morning I had no idea what effect I was going to have on him, so I wore an innocent white blouse. He didn't express any rage; instead he made me intensely aware of the change of climate. It was ice-cold in the room. The air conditioning in the Hotel Amazonas couldn't compare with it. In a friendly conversation with Herr Ribbeck one risks freezing to death. A fur coat would have been the right thing to wear, but mine was in storage. After all, it was July, the trees were blossoming, and I suspect the birds were singing.

Oscar was expecting me at nine A.M. for our preliminary talk. Unfortunately, I turned up at Budapesterstrasse at 9:45. I had set my alarm for seven o'clock, but had forgotten to wind it. Without a bath and breakfast I might have made it by 9:30, but such a sacrifice was unthinkable for the sake of someone I didn't even know.

"Are you crazy, Moll?" Edith Hannemann was more nervous than I had ever seen her. "Your conference with the boss was for nine o'clock."

"My alarm misbehaved. And I had to take a bath and have breakfast."

Frau Hannemann informed me that Dr. Ribbeck never waited for anyone longer than ten minutes. He couldn't see me now until three and until then I might as well behave as if I were still in Venezuela.

"Did *he* say that about Venezuela?"

"*I'm* saying that. I can read thoughts, Moll."

"May I ask what else you read?"

"I'll tell you that at our lunch break. What do you intend to do until three?"

"Fly to Venezuela and back, of course."

Frau Hannemann said nothing.

"Please go in and tell him I'm here."

"Impossible. He's in conference."

"When Wendt was in conference he was glad whenever anybody interrupted him."

"Wendt!" said the office widow, melodramatically enough to qualify for the Renaissance Theater.

"A sharp wind seems to be blowing here," I said.

"Sh! Here comes Brunner," said Frau Hannemann.

Alfred Brunner, who had taken my place in the Foreign Lands department, greeted me coldly. As far as he was concerned, I could have stayed on the Orinoco for years! He had wanted to accompany Locker and König, and had done his best to get Wendt to give him the assignment. Frau Hannemann, moreover, had told me that Brunner saw Wendt's sudden downfall as God's justice. Wendt really had collected a lot of lame ducks in the Budapesterstrasse, but his editorials had always been right on target. At times they thundered and lightninged, but they could be convincing even in a gentler tone. All of us felt there was a touch of genius in him, and I think we were right. What made him unique in our eyes was his talent to allow everyone his own opinion and viewpoint, whether it was the messenger boy or Locker from the

Free University. Even I who had cost him so much money, was granted my blank periods. I had the feeling that Oscar Ribbeck would respond to them by firing me.

"Does Brunner get along with Ribbeck?" I asked uneasily.

"First rate!" Edith Hannemann looked even sourer than usual. "What do you expect in times like these, Moll? *Le roi est mort, vive le roi!*"

"French? My, but you've become intellectual!"

"Oscar swears by education rather than intuition. He's absolutely heartless!"

I don't know why I thought of Sánchez when she said this. He, too, was hard when he was angry. Icy. But as a lover he had fire. With his predecessors I had had no clothes on; with him I had been naked. That is perhaps the true difference between right and wrong lovers.

"What are you thinking of?" Frau Hannemann asked, her tone sharp.

I disliked waiting just as much as Oscar. Time, the moody beast, crept and stalled and dragged me through five unnerving hours. I drank so much coffee with my colleagues and smoked so many cigarettes that I waited for the interview slightly benumbed. I had seen Ribbeck fleetingly through the door of Frau Hannemann's office. His door had closed immediately behind his visitor. Dr. Ribbeck had a lot more hair than Hannemann had given him credit for. She has a tendency to exaggerate. Nobody would have called him bald. But he was a beanpole, very straight and thin. The old, carved wooden door to Wendt's office had been replaced by a modern milk glass one, and I could see Ribbeck's long, thin shadow behind it. He could probably see my shadow too, but until three o'clock in the afternoon I didn't exist for him.

During my walk through the offices I noticed that many of the rooms were empty. Ribbeck's employees evidently came and went as quickly as South American dictators. I nodded at the new faces; they didn't nod back. Wendt's old guard greeted me enthusiastically, with the noisy heartiness and the sort of talk that in Berlin hides depression, disgust, and grief. We sat in Dornbach's empty office; the man replacing him was to start next day. Dornbach had been in charge of interior politics; Oscar's man came from Frankfurt. Frau Hannemann's days seemed numbered. How long did Oscar's 'doll' intend to remain in the wings? But Hannemann had made plans. She would look for a job in Munich and in the evening type Wendt's book. "I've got my savings," she said angrily when I gave her a look. For the first time I had to take my hat off to her. "He can pay me when the book's a success."

"Ribbeck won't give you the runaround he gave Dornbach, Moll," said one of the photographers.

"He's already done that. He's let me wait until three because I was ten minutes late."

"It must have been more than that," said Renate Schaper from Fashions. "He always waits ten. But then he likes to see you in a state of contrition."

"He doesn't want 'What the stars say' any more either." Andreas pointed at his column. He also sold personal horoscopes to those who requested them. I was constantly surprised by how many readers believed that the stars didn't lie. At any rate they didn't lie nearly as much as Andreas. His column had brought us a lot of readers. But Oscar preferred "Everyday Psychology." The stars hadn't even foretold that Andreas would be fired at the end of the month. But he had lots of offers already, and his own private practice. He always landed on his feet. Should all of us move to Munich? Faber was already corresponding with Wendt about it. (Faber was in charge of the arts page.) I asked what Wendt's answer had been. He had written that there were too few Berliners in Munich.

"That's all nonsense!" I said.

Everybody was silent and looked miserable. Nobody had asked me a single question about what I'd done on the Orinoco. It was two minutes to three when Edith Hannemann appeared in the doorway. "Fräulein Moll? Herr Ribbeck is ready to see you," she said, as formal as the receptionist of an atomic commission. I powdered my nose and used Renate's lipstick. "Come on, Moll. You're pretty enough."

"He isn't going to look at you anyway," said Annemarie Schmidt. ("Advice to the Lovelorn: Dear Annemarie.") The page would be a must-out for Oscar.

"He is ready to see you," the office-widow repeated so loudly all of us jumped.

During this first conversation with Ribbeck I found him more courteous than I had expected, although he seemed completely impervious to female charm. He still had all his hair, but one could see where he would start balding ten years from now. He seemed somehow suspicious that someone might use him, deceive him, or make a fool of him. One shouldn't try to put anything over on him. This was his favorite expression. He could see through all maneuvers astonishingly quickly. "Maneuvers" was one of his pet words. "Such maneuvers won't get you anywhere with me," Herr, Frau, or Fräulein. But Oscar had a quite formidable array of maneuvers himself. He could twist your words until they lost their original meaning. "That's what you really wanted to say, Fräulein Moll. Why are you trying to put something over on me?"

"A misunderstanding, I assure you, Herr Ribbeck."

Then he would be silent and wipe his glasses. Soon I grew to hate his silences. They weren't pauses between speech and answer, they were an independent event, a negative transaction, a conversational murder—in short, a maneuver. But that wasn't all. Ribbeck could make us aware of our weaknesses in surprisingly virtuoso fashion. I shall never know how he managed to do that to me in the first five minutes. Was it his politesse, soaked in vitriol? His cold, keen eyes? His thin, sarcastic smile? I asked myself: "What do I do now? Where am I today?" Wendt, in Munich, was probably asking himself the same thing. That Ribbeck was loaded with talent, factual knowledge, and enthusiasm for organization, and that his intelligence was of the highly critical variety, was just as obvious as his spontaneous dislike of me. Wendt's old guard was evidently not his cup of tea, and you couldn't quarrel about taste. Only be silent. And Oscar was silent.

As he opened the door of his office for me and bowed slightly, he looked me up and down like the buyer of a well-constructed table or chair. Were there perhaps worms in the wood? Was the piece of furniture worth the money? I apologized at once for my unreliable alarm clock, and Oscar apologized for having made me wait until three o'clock. With a thin smile he said that punctuality in the office was very important to him because punctual employees were usually more reliable than geniuses with faulty alarm clocks.

"Do you consider me a genius?"

He looked me up and down again and said that for the present he considered me unpunctual. My little joke had fallen on stony ground. I had the feeling that he disapproved of geniuses. As for punctuality, Wendt had been a terrible example. He had come and gone as he pleased, but then had done his work fast and marvelously well.

I was glad that I hadn't put on my expensive white suit for Ribbeck. He had no eye for what a woman wore or how she wore it. He could have learned a thing or two from Sánchez in this respect. Carlos enfolded me with his eyes, or undressed me. I couldn't for the life of me imagine Oscar Ribbeck disrobing a woman with his eyes or otherwise. And he was only thirty-four years old!

He was as sober as a judge. He was a disenchanter, just as Sánchez and Wendt, each in his own way, had been transformers. Transformers of raw material, of gravity, of time and place, and of women. Suddenly I thought more kindly of Sánchez. He had died as far as I was concerned. Now I laid flowers on his grave.

"Are you listening to me, Fräulein Moll?"

"Of course I am. Why?"

"I got the impression that your thoughts were elsewhere."

"My thoughts were entirely with you, Herr Doktor Ribbeck."

He chose to ignore this bit of flattery. He was standing at the window, tall and straight as a ramrod, and the sun was shining on his thin, blond hair and the nasty little mustache over his upper lip. I wished I were far away; even with Sturmbannführer Bonnhoff on the Orinoco things would have been pleasanter. I had only been with Ribbeck five minutes, and they seemed like five years in a labor camp, in spite of the fact that he was most attentive. He offered me cigarettes (he himself didn't smoke) and ordered coffee for us. Hannemann set the tray down on a small table without uttering a word, most unusual for her. Ribbeck drank his coffee down in one gulp, standing—something I detested. I had dismal presentiments of what would fall down on my poor head during this interview, but Ribbeck took his time. He let me drink three cups of coffee while he talked about Mexico.

Mexico! Pictures cut out of a magazine were stuck on the wall over a white enamel medicine chest (Oscar was either a hypochondriac or he kept poison for his employees in it). But they were cut-outs from a Spanish magazine, or rather a South American one. Ribbeck had had the pictures mounted and attached to the wall with drawing pins. From Mexico he could easily have moved the conversation on to Venezuela, but he didn't. He was silent. An explosive silence. Then he explained the horrifying, rather demonic pictures of the Huichol Indians from the Mexican Sierra Madre to me. He forced me, for reasons best known to himself, to look at them and to listen to him. "This painting is called *The Fig Tree*. Are you listening to me, Fräulein Moll? The Indians believe that the soul, on its day's journey into the Land of Death, drags all the burdens of its sexual life with it. And they *are* burdens! I am in complete agreement with the Huichol Indians. As you can see, the woman carries the male organ to the fig tree; the male carries the woman's. The male soul hurls the woman's organ against the tree, then she dances with the departed male around three circles of fire. Grandiose, don't you think?"

"I can't see anything in it."

"That's what I thought, Fräulein Moll. And that's why I'm sending Herr Brunner to Mexico. I found these sketches in

South America. Herr Brunner was able to read a great deal into them."

"*You* were in South America?"

"Do you think that besides you, Professor Locker, and Hanns König no one has been there?" He didn't say when he had been there, and I didn't ask. I could hear Indians whispering on the Orinoco. The colors of the Mexican sketches faded . . .

" . . . annoying mules," said Ribbeck. He meant either Wendt's old guard or five black mules that were trampling on the soul of a dead man to punish him for his sexual sins. Ribbeck assured me that the procedure was only a passing punishment.

"As long as it lasts, it can't be much fun."

Ribbeck said nothing. Who had been talking of fun? He had maneuvered me into an impossible position.

"I have read your notes on your second trip to Venezuela, Fräulein Moll," he said, staring at me like a chameleon. It was a strange look, almost as eerie as the red-rimmed milk-glass eyes of the mules.

"I'm afraid I have to tell you that I've never received such a meager harvest from such a long, expensive trip. What did you do on the Orinoco?"

I said nothing. When it came to stubbornness, I could match Ribbeck's mules any day.

My silence seemed to annoy him more than anything I might have had to say. He was waiting for an answer. What had I done on the Orinoco? My mouth felt dry. I wanted a whiskey or a beer. The palms of my hands were wet, but-terflies fluttered in my stomach, and my heart was beating fast. Nobody had ever treated me like this.

Ribbeck stood in front of me and, in every sense of the word, looked down on me. "I do want to stress the fact that I am looking at the case absolutely objectively and nothing personal is implied. I want you to believe that."

I believed him. He was being as impersonal as the Berlin Hilton. He went on to say that he wasn't in the least interested in what I had done on the Orinoco or anywhere else as long as it hadn't been done at business expense. He said it courteously and was in no way hostile, but that was the gist of his short speech. However *I* felt hostile and greatly irritated because I had lost a man I either hated or loved. I could see very well how ridiculous and unjust it was to blame Herr Ribbeck (who thought more of the paper than of me) for the weekend in Palma Sola. But it has never helped me to realize how ridiculous I am. I definitely do not belong among those who profit by their mistakes.

It was over. Ribbeck intended to publish Hanns König's series from the Orinoco and part of his material from Brazil, with Locker's commentary. And from me he wanted, if anything, an article about Puerto Cabello and the new residential development there. What was it called? *Urbanización Palma Sola.*

"That has life, and you experienced it," he said, and had no idea how right he was!

"If you have no other plans," he went on, "I suggest you take over the editorial section, Foreign Lands, again. I mean on the old terms, and so on." He meant diligence, punctuality, and anything else one could do with the foreign lands to which people traveled.

"Herr Dr. Wendt was going to arrange radio interviews for me, and lectures. My material could be used that way."

"I was just coming to that, Fräulein Moll. Herr Doktor Wendt mentioned it to me. However, I have changed this plan somewhat." He changed everything, I knew that.

"I have arranged for television interviews. This would mean better publicity for the paper because you are decorative. You also seem to be fairly young, and with the right makeup could pass easily for twenty."

It wasn't a compliment. It was a stated fact. When it came to using material, Ribbeck could take a closer look at a woman.

"Thank you very much. I hope I won't make too bad an impression."

"In that case we would stop after the first program. But I don't think there's any danger of that. You can give your impressions of the Orinoco area, the port cities, the people you met..."

"Men too?"

He smiled for the first time. "Aren't men people?"

"Do you want to keep me on after the television appearances?" My voice sounded strange and far away.

"I said nothing about giving notice, Fräulein Moll."

"You said that to begin with I should take over Foreign Lands. You asked if I had other plans."

"And is that something one mustn't ask? I said 'to begin with' because I may have other assignments for you later. But for that I have to get to know your working methods. That your second trip to Venezuela was a great disappointment to all of us—in this respect I agree with Dr. Wendt—is unfortunately a fact, especially since *Caracas for Beginners* was so brilliantly written. A little superficial, but brilliant."

"I'm glad that you at least liked the book."

"Try to be reasonable, Fräulein Moll. Since the only thing I have seen is an article on Puerto Cabello and Palma Sola, and everything else is still in your notes, I can hardly consider you a nominee for the Nobel Prize. I think first of all you're going to have to breathe some Berlin air. I get the impression that the change of climate is causing you some difficulty. I am therefore giving you a week to get acclimatized. You can work at home. Here are a few statistics and a historical study of Panama and the canal. You could do something with it, if you're prepared to work. That you wasted precious days on the beaches of Miami was a further unpleasant surprise for *Comet. My* correspondents receive a set travel program. I'm afraid Herr Doktor Wendt was too generous."

"That's possible."

"I'm sure he was. He had a touch of genius..."

I already knew what Herr Ribbeck thought of genius. After a pause he said he had canceled the rest of Wendt's articles on escaped National Socialists. He was planning a series on the guerrillas in South America. I had met a guerrilla on the Orinoco, but only found out about it later, when Wally Bendix sent me a newspaper clipping. Camilo de Padilla at the Hotel

Amazonas. I had drunk a lot of coffee with his peculiar wife. Ribbeck was right. I was far from being perceptive.

Ribbeck spoke cautiously but without a spark of enthusiasm about Wendt's series, which had lost *Comet* a lot of subscribers. "I find these exhumations, however well intended, superfluous and embarrassing," he said finally.

The blood rushed to my head. "Do you find justice embarrassing, too?" I asked.

For a moment he was speechless, and I held my breath. Was I completely mad? Did I want him to throw me out? What would Mother do? And how would I pay for my luxurious stable in the Hansa quarter? Ribbeck's silence was gruesome. I felt as cold as I had with Sturmbannführer Bonnhoff on the Orinoco, whom I had found too late.

"The paper must deal more strongly than ever with the problems of the present and future," Ribbeck said icily. "Campaigns against old men, who decades after their misdeeds probably can't remember anymore what they were, are *not* on my program. Good day, Fräulein Moll."

"I . . . I'm sorry. I expressed myself badly."

"Good day." He opened the door and I was outside.

# 18

# Flow, Flow, Murky River

Carla Moll to Dr. Oscar Ribbeck (*Comet*, Berlin)

Dear Herr Doktor Ribbeck,

Unfortunately I still feel rather shaky after the flu, and my doctor says I should be careful about going out. And just now the TV interviews are supposed to start. There's not much you can do about bad luck.

I was not able to write the articles about Panama City and the Canal Zone. I have had a splitting headache more or less constantly. Do you still want them? After all, the Panama Canal is just about as famous as our Landwehr Canal. If I had been there for carnival, I could have made something of it, but of course when I was there, it rained. What I did like in Panama City was the tropical patio in the president's palace. The palms were really palms. The architecture is pseudo-Moorish. If you want the president's palace, I can let you have it stone by stone.

I take it you have lost patience with me. I feel the same way. I am sure the man taking my place is punctual, healthy, and works hard. Unfortunately I happen to be very fond of my office at *Comet*. I was waiting for Professor Locker's notes, which I was to work up, when Dr. Wendt deported me to the harbor cities. Perhaps nobody told you about it. On top of that I had one of my blank periods. Believe it or not, the Orinoco is a very murky river, and the Indians were no inspiration. Stone Age creatures. Tiresome material. They are like riddles no one wants to solve. Their Mongolian-shaped eyes mirror the river and the clouds. I was never really able to relate to them. Zongo was either indifferent and didn't trust me or he slipped away in front of my very eyes to same cosmic void or other. I didn't feel like treating my readers to my mistaken ideas of the Orinoco Indians.

Zongo never laughed. He didn't even smile. I can't establish any contact with people who always show me the same, serious face. On the Orinoco I felt exposed yet invisible. Perhaps Zongo was laughing to himself, and I was just too dumb to notice it. If he was, it was certainly over us Europeans. Over the Yanquis too. But above all, I am sure Zongo laughed (if he did at all) over my colleagues Locker and König, and over Mr. Cooper and me. Elliot Cooper is a well-meaning man from Chicago. At the fisherman's paradise a poisoned arrow was shot in his direction. Anyway, the atmosphere was so depressing, I simply couldn't write. But sometimes the Orinoco was beautiful, when it gleamed red-gold, like autumn leaves in the setting sun. But for the most part it was rusty, and in its depths stone-gray like liquid lead. Here in Berlin I can see the Orinoco so clearly, I must have noticed a lot subconsciously. If only Zongo had smiled at me, just once! His only contribution to our conversation was "your hat" and "sunstroke."

Forgive me for boring you at the last minute with my non-report on the Orinoco. I am only trying to explain why I have failed you so completely. Perhaps

I would have needed more incubation time, but that would have cost *Comet* even more, and the results would have been doubtful.

Since you have not answered my other two letters, I take it that you have written me off. But since I never seem to know which way the wind is blowing, I would appreciate it if you would let me know if I should look for another job.

Yours,<br>Carla Moll

Dr. Oscar Ribbeck (*Comet*) to Carla Moll

Dear Fräulein Moll,

I have received your three letters. Thank you. I regret that I was unable to answer before this, but I am still busy reorganizing the office.

At my request, Frau Hannemann called your doctor, and he seemed to think you could start working again in a few days. I therefore expect to see you for a talk next Monday at 9 A.M.

Herr Brunner has sent us some informative reports from Mexico which still need improving stylistically. I hope this work won't take too much of your time. By the way, if I may say so, I'd drop the 'give notice' innuendos. You're giving me ideas!

Your last letter made me think that your personal impressions of the Orinoco area are more real than anything else you hurriedly put together for *Comet*. Your other descriptions seem poorer in comparison. Whom did you want to fool with those conventional reports? Our readers, me, or yourself?

I suggest that you use your confrontation with the Orinoco Indians as a theme for your television interview. I would also be pleased if you would write your report on Panama City, still owed us, with care and élan. You can do it, Fräulein Moll. But talent without diligence is totally ineffective.

Your first television appearance is scheduled for the end of November. I hope you won't catch another cold between now and then. Take vitamins and avoid the night air.

Sincerely,
O. Ribbeck

Dr. Herbert Wendt (Munich) to Dr. Oscar Ribbeck
(*Comet*, Berlin)

Dear Ribbeck,

Your letter brought great joy to us here on the Isar. Many thanks from the bottom of my heart that you want to publish *Berlin Fin de Siècle* as a serial in *Comet*. That you have also found a publisher for a hardcover edition is simply stupendous! I hadn't dared hope for anything like that.

How I would like to do something nice for you! Unfortunately all I can do is tell you that I could do with an advance! My wife desperately needs a vacation because after she finishes at the office she spends the evening writing for me. And the two boys of course also make demands on their mother. But we celebrated in a big way just the same. Your ears must have been ringing.

I received a jubilant letter from Frau Hannemann. Not a word from Carla Moll. What's wrong with the girl? I hope she isn't giving you trouble. She has a natural talent for that. I had so much patience with her because she occasionally mixes brilliant observation with profound insight. That's her forte, when she feels up to it. But her 'blank' periods are truly a cross to bear. Perhaps you'll allow her her eccentricities, only don't let her take advantage or she gets out of hand!

One more thing. That you want to send Frau
Hannemann to me to type the manuscript—I don't
know how to thank you for it. With her help I'll
have the book done in two months. Perhaps as a
reaction to my dismal *Fin de Siècle*, a young Goethe
will one day again be sitting at every table in the
Café Kranzler. *That* I'd like to live to see!

> Ever yours,
> Wendt


Richard Cooper (Chicago) to Elliot Cooper (Hotel
   Plaza, Buenos Aires) Please forward.


Dear Elliot,

   My long letter to you from Zürich to Bogotá,
which I sent off at least two months ago, doesn't
seem to have reached you. Otherwise I can't explain
why you haven't answered it. After all, it concerns
your wife, not mine!

   At present I am with your mother. Somebody's
got to see to her! She is all alone now. Maudie chose
to go to Europe right after the catastrophe with Naomi. Incredible! Except for my wife, all the women
in our family seem to have gone crazy.

   Before I could ship her off to Chicago, Naomi
disappeared from Zürich without leaving a trace.
Didn't you get my telegram either? But Naomi was
always a law unto herself. Your mother promptly
got the heart attack she has threatened us with for
such a long time. She's all right again now. She says
to tell you you should file for divorce on the count
of desertion. I told her that before you could do
anything like that, you'd have to find your wife. I
presume she has not committed suicide. There wasn't
the trace of a corpse anywhere in the Sanatorium
Edelweiss. Dr. Sprüngli had to take a sedative. I

treated him to baked squab and a marvelous red wine, at *your* expense. It's *your* wife!

After a second bottle of wine, Dr. Sprüngli decided Naomi had to be in Berlin. I tend to agree with him. She was supposed to be cured of her memories in Switzerland. If she ever turns up again and you banish her once more, be so good as to go and fetch her yourself. She was a nice little girl. I'd never have thought she was so sly. But all of us change, and rarely for the better.

I have the feeling that Maudie knows more than any of us. She always did stick with Naomi. But her sympathy for your wife may have been mainly a protest against your mother. Your mother and you. She went to New York before her trip to Europe and took part in one of those women's protest marches against male chauvinism. If I am not mistaken, she burnt her bra before she left, which in some circles in construed as an act of heroism. In Maudie's case, no problem. Where she is wearing her brooch is front! She has not yet written to your mother. Right now I think she must be in Venice or Paris, adding to the oh so popular American tourist crowd.

How do you like Buenos Aires? Is there a lot going on? Don't tell me that you're also a business advisor at night. Well, after Naomi, you have every right to some fun, my boy.

Best,<br>Richard

Carl Friedrich Bonnhoff:

High time that I wrote my letters to Europe. I haven't written to my sister in at least twenty-five years. Not that Hilda wants to hear anything from me. As if it was my fault that the SS did Hilda's man in by mistake. I didn't interrogate Rammberg.

After Rammberg's death my sister turned into a fury, and her friend, Erna von Strelitz, encouraged her. I couldn't stand

Erna when she was a child. What a brat! I could have had both of them arrested, they way they blasted the Führer.

I remember how my family and Erna von Strelitz insulted me, especially Erna. The bitch had no consideration. Told me straight to my face what she thought of me. Did it when she was still young, in Potsdam. I must ask my sister whatever she saw in Erna. Thin, pale, no breasts, and sixteen already! And fresh! Called me Carl the Fat until I beat her up. She should see me now, with my stomach.

*Dear Hilda*, I'll write. We haven't heard from one another for a long time. Nonsense! That's no way to begin. Erna will say, "You've been lucky, Hildchen, that you haven't heard from the old bastard in twenty-five years." *Dear Hilda*, I'll write. I hope you are well and that your house in Zehlendorf hasn't been bombed. One gets fond of one's own shack. Both of us are old now, I'll write, and your husband's been dead and forgotten for thirty-seven years. I'm about as well as I could be, considering conditions. I am totally dependent on my son, Carlos, who since his visit to Berlin in '38 calls himself Sánchez, after his Venezuelan grandfather on his mother's side. My wife, Fidelia Sánchez, has been dead a long time too. Jesus . . . I can't send Hilda a list of my dead! And that mention of Carlos . . . I'd do better to leave that out too. Erna von Strelitz would laugh herself sick if she read it. Besides, they know all about it anyway. In spite of the fact that I've told him not to, Carlos still communicates with Hilda. Only not with me. But I'm only his father. I'd like to ask Hilda if she couldn't visit me here some day. Yes. But I must write that my sister should leave Erna in Berlin. Don't want her here. I haven't a soul to talk to here, I'll write to Hilda. I can write that to my own sister. Doesn't give anything away. And if Hilda insists on bringing Erna with her, she can, for all I care.

*Dear Hilda*, I'll write. Do you ever think of Mother, and Potsdam between the two wars? And our garden? Well yes, all things pass. But I can see Mother before me as if she were here. When I think of her, I smell lavender. Do you remember? She loved lavender. She used to collect beechnuts with us. Once I picked cuckoo flowers with her, and whatever else I could find. Cowslips. She loved wild flowers. When our pear tree was in bloom and Mother sat there in the middle of all that white glory, do you remember, Hilda? And when Father gave her the ostrich feather fan, and Mother never let him know that she found it too fancy. She never used it very much. She liked simple things. I guess a fan like that was fashionable. Father was lucky with women. After her death I never felt at home anymore. God, how noisy the Orinoco is again! It'll scare my fish away. I prefer it quieter, like the rain dropping on our ivy in autumn. Tucu is asleep. Those Indians can sleep. I'd like to be able to sleep like that. Whenever I think back like this, why everything went wrong for me . . . I had a lot of nothing in my life. But in the Third Reich, I was somebody. And then Hitler had to go and start his war. Conquer everything, lose everything. I had to wander off to South America in shabby civilian clothes with two SS brothers and forged papers. Pure luck that I wasn't strung up on a lamppost in Steglitz with other Berliners in '45.

Sometimes, when I'm fishing, I ask myself why I couldn't have been a nice, proper family man. Idiot! Fritz Bonnhoff with his sons and grandchildren. A man in the right party, if there ever was such a thing. Liked by all Prussians and Pots-damers, even Erna von Strelitz. My old man and Werner's old man were in the same regiment. What *was* the name of Werner von Strelitz's daughter? Naomi? No, Herta! Visited me in my days of glory in my house on the Tiergarten. Had been the house of banker Mandelbaum. Werner had funny sisters. There was Erna, and the other one, Margaret—a beauty before she married, and a splendid rider. And she went and married Lothar Singer, from the Weltbühne, a journalist. Radical magazine. "I have nothing against Jews," Werner von Strelitz said, "but one doesn't have to marry them." He laughed. The ass! Well, the Singer daughter, Naomi, looked exactly like her cousin Herta. I think to this day that it was Naomi who came to see me. Mandelbaum was her uncle. At the time of her visit he was in jail. *Somebody* had to move into his villa. I don't know why Erna took on so about it. I enjoyed the original Liebermann, and I gave Naomi—or was it Herta?—the old penguin on the mantel. She was still just a kid. Seventeen. Looked like fifteen. Margaret Strelitz read Nietzsche and Schopenhauer when she wasn't sitting on a horse. No wonder she married an intellectual. I wouldn't like to know what Lothar Singer read. Or Goebbels. Don't know how that bookworm ever got into the party. I must say that Dr. Lothar Singer expressed himself much more simply during the interrogation than Herr Socrates Goebbels. He had courage. I mean Singer did. Told me straight out what he thought was wrong with Hitler. *After* the party came to power.

*Dear Hilda*, I'll write. You can visit me on the Orinoco any time. You must have enough money, since Father disinherited me when I joined the SS. Not that I give a damn! Honor and recognition always meant more to me than money. I believed in the new Germany. I was dumb enough for that. No, I won't write that. It's none of my sister's business what I believed. I'll write: we can talk about old times—Potsdam and the beechwoods where we picked cowslips, not the Buchenwald concentration camp. One should be able to write about cowslips, for God's sake! They have nothing to do with the concentration camp. You can bring Erna along, if you want to. I don't care. But come soon. No, that's not right. Sounds as if I was crazy for them to come, when it's just the same to me. Let them stay home!

I feel like Jonah in the whale. Who knows—it might have been quite cozy there. Jonah didn't deserve his punishment any more than I did. He obeyed orders. Just another camp follower among the prophets. Like me. I think of him often. What did I have against banker Mandelbaum? Or bookworm Lothar Singer? I didn't even know them!

I must make my will. Tina Ullmann gets nothing, because on this very shore she tried to tell me her name was Carla Toll. What impertinence! And what should Hilda get? My old Rilke volume? Leafed through, dog-eared, with grease spots . . . Packed it next to my hair oil when I fled. Things like that happen. He who has no house now won't build one;

he who is alone now will remain alone and will lie awake, read, write long letters. There you are!

*Dear Hilda*, this letter is twenty-five years overdue, but something always seemed to prevent my writing it. How would it be if you and Erna...

Erna von Strelitz (West Berlin) to Carlos Sánchez (Caracas)

Dear Señor Sánchez,

I am sorry to inform you that your Aunt Hilda von Rammberg died after a long illness in her old house in Dahlem. I was with her to the end. We were together since childhood. We shared good and bad times together. Hilda always regretted that she was in Berlin only once in her life, when she was very young, but she was always touched that you wrote to her from Venezuela from time to time.

With the same mail you will be receiving a letter from the Rammberg's lawyer. Hilda has left you the old house and all family memorabilia, among which there is an old coffee set (Royal Berlin porcelain) that survived the bombings. Should you be able to dispose of the inheritance personally in Berlin, I hope, as the oldest friend of your German family, that you will come to see me. I live very near to the Rammberg house. To the end Hilda spoke about you and your letters after the war, to say nothing of your generous help in practical matters.

Permit me to express my sincerest sympathy.

Yours,
Erna von Strelitz

# 19

# Sánchez in Berlin

Sánchez arrived in Berlin on November ninth. Thirty-two years had passed since that date was entered into the history of Berlin as "the Crystal Night," when Hitler's men smashed the windows of the Jewish shops and strewed the elegant shopping streets with broken glass. At the same time they set fire to the Berlin synagogues and dragged thousands of Jews off to concentration camps. Sturmbannführer Bonnhoff had celebrated the Crystal Night with wine, women, and song. Only young Carlos had not joined in the celebration. He had remained upstairs in his dark room and listened to the noise. He didn't know what they were celebrating downstairs. Next morning Christina Ullmann enlightened him. He didn't say a word, and left the house. In Fasanenstrasse the eighteen-year-old boy saw the temple of God still burning, hordes of distraught observers, and soldiers whom they silently avoided.

When Sánchez arrived at Tempelhof airport on November 9, 1970, the date meant nothing to him. The city was gray and it was raining, which didn't bother him. He hadn't come to experience a poetic autumn. He didn't want to experience anything in Berlin; he wanted to ignore the city. Here Bonnhoff had had Christina Ullmann arrested, and here, shortly before the end of the war, Bonnhoff had boarded a plane for South America. At the time Carlos had been in Caracas for years, and his name was Sánchez. He was a good hater, and right now he hated Berlin. For him there was a stench of corpses in the November rain of 1970.

In Venezuela he could forget his father for months on end because there he was merely an impotent old man. But in Berlin, Sturmbannführer Bonnhoff again held demonic power over his estranged son. Carlos could see him in his black uniform, with his SS friends, Engelbert Schmidt and Ludwig von Hartlieb. He could see the music room in banker Mandelbaum's Tiergarten villa, which Bonnhoff had requisitioned, and where he had played Mendelssohn and Chopin when he was alone. Sánchez even saw, through a veil of nostalgia, Christina: young, blond, not very smart. He didn't want to see the journalist Moll. But he saw her on his first evening in Berlin. Everything he had decided to do in Berlin turned out differently; he had intended to stay three days and he stayed three weeks.

He walked into the Hilton with a stony expression. The Hilton could be anywhere in the world. That was why he had chosen it. From his window he looked for a long time at the Budapesterstrasse. This was the street of the Berlin Hilton with its exemplary service, and of the offices of *Comet*, with Fräulein Moll. As darkness fell, Sánchez went for a walk on the Kurfürstendamm. He needed fresh air. Although he had spent almost a year at the Technological Institute and had spoken German flawlessly, he felt more of a stranger in the New Berlin than anywhere else in the world. He walked into a restaurant and ordered dinner. Over coffee he realized suddenly that he had lived with Bonnhoff and Christina as if on a lonely island. So much had happened in Europe in 1938, that last year of a peace in which Hitler's Germany had not participated: Sigmund Freud had found sanctuary and a following in London; Shaw's *Pygmalion* was filmed; the *Queen Elizabeth*, the largest and most elegant ocean liner ever built, was launched; Pearl Buck, author of *The Good Earth*, won the Nobel Prize. And what had young Sánchez experienced in Germany? Hitler's demands for the Sudetenland had grown persistent and his troops had stood on the border of Czechoslovakia. The concentration camps had filled up. Bonnhoff had become increasingly power hungry and music-loving, and shortly before Christmas, Sánchez had flown back to Caracas without saying good-bye to his father. And now he was wondering how to spend his time in Berlin. He wanted to call on Fräulein von Strelitz early the following morning. He leafed through the evening paper disinterestedly. Suddenly a picture of Carla Moll caught his eye. She was to appear on television in an hour. An interview about her experiences on the Orinoco. In the picture her hair was done up high; she looked cool and arrogant. Sánchez looked at her with intense revulsion. He paid, threw the paper on the table, and went back to the hotel. He had to know what Carla Moll would have to say about the Orinoco.

Fräulein Moll on the screen was not the same as in Venezuela. She was serious, reserved, and, to all appearances, invulnerable. Sánchez had known her privately, loved and hated her, and could not find his Carlita in Fräulein Moll's television personality. She evidently knew what would be expected of the author of *Caracas for Beginners*, or a good director had told her. Anyway, she was polished, had an elegant hairdo, and there was no evidence of her irritating personality. She had never eaten her bread and butter in tears, she had never got drunk, she had never made love to Carlos Sánchez. Under the moon of Margarita Island, she had been expressive and beautiful. Now she was matter-of-fact, a career hyena.

Fräulein Moll, smiling a little ironically, answered the questions of a well-known journalist with anecdotes about Venezuela, all of which somehow concerned her. Fräulein Moll gave the impression that she had been the most interesting item in Venezuela. Professor Locker had come up with specific knowledge and facts on the Orinoco, and all he had got for it was a nod. Moll's approach was quite different. She must have left her inferiority complex in Sánchez's weekend house in Palma Sola. She knew how to handle television audience. If you weren't amusing and could not put on a good act, people switched to a crime show. Fräulein Moll parried all questions and in a charming and intriguing way disparaged the interviewer, who had himself written two books on South America. Sánchez was astonished. What a pity she hadn't exhibited talents like this at Cooper's dinner. She wore a white woolen dress, fashionably short, and closed up to the neck. Every now and then she would let it slip up to expose her beautiful legs. When Fräulein Moll was thinking things over, she lowered her eyes. She did that very nicely. After the third pause she said that one should civilize the Indian tribes on the Orinoco as little as possible.

"Why, Fräulein Moll?"

She opened her eyes wide and gave the impression that she had never heard such a simplistic question. Then she said thoughtfully, "Until now these people have had no desire for property or prestige. If a man catches fifteen fish and his tribal brother catches, let's say, thirty; it doesn't bother the man who caught only fifteen. He isn't competitive. He wants neither fame nor admiration. At best he would like a new canoe when his old one falls apart and medicine from the nearest mission—that is all. Sometimes he even takes the medicine."

The interviewer found this fascinating. The morals of primitive people were interesting as long as one didn't dwell on them. "Did you make any friends among the Indians, Fräulein Moll?"

"I make friends everywhere, even in exotic surroundings, as soon as I have overcome the cultural shock."

"Does that take long?"

"On the Orinoco it took me a long time."

It was the first true word she had spoken. She lowered her lids in an effort to shut Berlin out of her thoughts, then she said, "If by 'friendship with the Indians' one means that one does not get hit by a poisoned arrow, then I was quite friendly with an Indian called Zongo. Of course I could never read his thoughts, but then I can't do that with my Berlin friends either." The interviewer laughed heartily, but his eyes weren't laughing. In the end he asked her if one might expect another book about Venezuela. Fräulein Moll said one might.

"Thank you very much, Fräulein Moll. It has been very interesting."

Fräulein Moll had said nothing about Carl Friedrich Bonnhoff. To the very end she had managed to smile the interviewer into the background. And he had not been able to catch her up on anything. She was much more intelligent than she had been in Venezuela, Sánchez decided. Could it be the change of climate? And she obviously had her wild impulses under control. This should have pleased Sánchez, but it didn't. Because once she had set him on fire, and in some corner of his consciousness he still looked upon her as his property, whether he had abandoned her or not. It was the sexual credo in Latin America, and nothing could shake this old-fashioned viewpoint. Whether the women were housewives or mothers, whether they were inventors or doctors, whether they achieved prestige and prizes—they remained the property of the man whose bed they had shared. Career women so often lost their simplicity and naturalness, which Sánchez considered their most priceless assets. Fräulein Moll had smiled on the screen like a courtesan on duty: cold, mechanical, calculating. Sánchez never wanted to see her again.

"How was I?" Carla Moll asked her boss next morning.

"Not bad." Ribbeck drank his coffee standing. He did it to demonstrate how little time he had.

"Did you think it was going to be worse?"

"I didn't think anything, Fräulein Moll. I wanted to be surprised. I admired you."

"Well, that's a surprise!"

"With a pinch of salt, Fräulein Moll. I mean, you talked all the time but said very little. *Volat avis sine meta* . . . the bird flies without a goal."

"I know Horace."

"But evidently not Ovid."

"I always get those old Romans mixed up."

Ribbeck put his empty cup down on the coffee table. "There's no opportunity for a good, quiet talk here at the office. Could we have dinner together somewhere tomorrow evening?"

"Thank you. But I have a previous engagement."

For a moment there was silence. Carla's previous engagement was with herself, as usual, but she didn't want to talk about the ancient Romans with Ribbeck that evening. Did he sense it? She shouldn't have turned down his first invitation, whether he had caught her on Ovid or not. She had to be crazy! At any rate, overly irritated. Ribbeck was pale, but for her he was the red rag to the bull. His displeasure trickled slowly down on her head.

Ribbeck changed the subject to South America and asked if Fräulein Moll was working on the article about Bolivia. "Are you in a hurry for it, Herr Doktor?"

"Do you intend to wait until the next revolution breaks out?" Ribbeck picked up the house phone. "Herr Doktor Lindner may come in, Frau Hannemann. I am finished with Fräulein Moll."

"He's finished with Fräulein Moll," said Frau Hannemann in the next room.

"There's nothing new about that," said Lindner (Everyday Psychology) and walked into Ribbeck's office, pleased with himself.

"He won't grow old here," Frau Hannemann told Fräulein Moll. Hannemann was always the first one to know when somebody's number was up. Fräulein Moll, who never knew, looked down at the Budapesterstrasse, just as a conspicuous man in a camel's hair coat walked by. The white streaks in his black hair made him look like a brigand. That's impossible! she thought. But it was Sánchez.

"You're white as a sheet, Moll. Have you seen a ghost?"

"Yes."

"In broad daylight?"

"Yes."

"Would you like an aspirin? Guaranteed to help."

Fräulein Moll didn't want an aspirin.

\* \* \*

Sánchez was lonely. Later, after his return to Venezuela, he wondered how he had survived that first week of devastating memories and a bad cold. It rained in November in Venezuela too but the showers were short, and when they were over, bushes and flowers glistened in a dreamy glow. He went to the aquarium in the Budapesterstrasse daily and conversed grimly and at length with the crocodiles in their tropical setting. On the fifth day the crocodiles and the trees reminded him of Bonnhoff on the Orinoco. He stopped going to the aquarium. He spoke to no one except the lawyer of his aunt, Hilda von Rammberg, née Bonnhoff. The lawyer, Dr. Arnold, was a Berliner who saw things as they were. He had a precise answer for everything and distrusted both introspection and enthusiasm. Sánchez liked him, but whether the lawyer liked the gloomy Venezuelan remained open to question. After office hours Dr. Arnold was sociable; Señor Sánchez seemed to be an enemy of the people. Dr. Arnold wondered if he should ask Sánchez to the house for a drink, but decided against it. He didn't like to be turned down.

Sometimes Sánchez found it unbearable to recall the people he never wanted to see or speak to again. Christina Ullmann, SS man Engelbert Schmidt, SS man Ludwig von Hartlieb, and other friends of his father's. Probably they had perished during the war in Berlin's fires, like Christina in the cellars of the Gestapo. He remembered the Tiergarten villa in Berlin with agonizing precision: banker Mandelbaum's Liebermann, his collection of Venetian glass in the dining room, and the ridiculous stuffed penguin on the mantel in the library. The penguin went with neither Mandelbaum's etchings of Old Berlin nor with Bonnhoff's picture of the Führer over the desk.

Sánchez didn't want to go near the Tiergarten. The villa had probably been bombed. Once a pale little girl had visited his father in the library. Sánchez probably remembered it because there had been so few female visitors at the villa. He had only seen the pale little girl for a moment because he had been on his way to ride with Christina. In the evening the stuffed penguin was gone. Had the young girl taken it?

His father had said she was "a little Strelitz." Was she a relative of Erna von Strelitz? He still hadn't called up his dead aunt's best friend. Sometimes he felt like Rip van Winkle, that legendary Dutch settler, who after sleeping for two decades could no longer find his way around in his home town. The bold new architecture had turned Berlin into a strange city: the Congress Hall, the Free University, the Europa Center, the Academy of Arts, the extraordinary design of Philharmonic Hall . . . Had the Berliners changed as much as their architecture?

Sánchez was wondering about it as he walked through the Hansa quarter. This old section of the city, between Tiergarten and Bellevue, had been totally destroyed by bombs, and architects from twenty-two countries had helped to rebuild it in 1957. An architect from South America had been among them. Sánchez smiled for the first time as he wondered if Carla Moll lived here. The Hansa quarter went well with the woman he had seen on the television screen. In their cool, functional elegance these residential blocks gave the same impression of slick perfection. Sánchez could not imagine dust in these apartments or roomy old-fashioned kitchens or really comfortable chairs. The journalist Moll probably lived in the Hansa quarter. She had always been on the lookout for a cage. Women never rested until they had themselves, and if possible a man, behind bars.

One morning Sánchez drove to Peacock Island, where on a radiant summer's day his love story with Christina Ullmann had begun. Here they had sought refuge from Bonnhoff's nightmare world. Now, in November, the castle was closed, but Sánchez had had no intention of visiting it. He had been in it with Christina, and in every room they had kissed. Friedrich Wilhelm II had had the castle built for Countess Lichtenau. The little island was a place for lovers. But in November the lovers met elsewhere. There were very few people walking between the oaks, the high pines, the greenhouses. Sánchez saw only one lonely female near the Cavalier House. She seemed to sway under the gray sky. Was she ill or drugged? She was thin and narrow shouldered, like a child.

She was wearing shabby plaid slacks, a gray pullover, a gray jacket, and her blond-gray hair showed under the scarf she was wearing on her head. Everything on her seemed to sag. A button was missing on her jacket. Her complexion was gray too. She would dissolve into the gray air any minute. She stared at him out of dim, light blue eyes. "I have lost my parasol," she murmured. "I lose everything, one thing at a time. Did you happen to see it anywhere?" Sánchez regretted, but he had not. "It isn't important," the woman said softly. "What's so important about a parasol when so much . . . perhaps I forgot it here in September. Many years ago." She was trembling a little. Sánchez had never seen such a melancholy face. The frail creature looked lost in the Whistler ambience of the island.

"May I take you somewhere? It looks like rain. My car is outside."

"That's very kind of you. But I don't live anywhere. Before the war I had an address like everybody else. Do you think that's funny? Why are you laughing?"

"I don't think it's funny and I am not laughing."

"Thank you. When I was a child I was afraid of peacocks. Silly, isn't it?"

"There! Didn't I say it would? It's raining."

"Well, my parasol wouldn't have been much use to me, would it?"

"Please come with me. You'll catch cold. Should I take you to a hotel? Or a doctor?"

"I like to stand in the rain. I don't need a doctor. Are you a doctor?"

"No."

"Please go," she begged suddenly. "I can't stand it when someone wants to look after me." She turned her back on him. She needed help, and he would have liked to help her. Who was this strange woman? A piece of gray Berlin . . .

Back at his hotel Sánchez looked at the weekly program of events, *A Guest In Berlin*, and decided to go to the Schiller Theater. They were playing *Macbeth*, with Ernst Hardenberg. Sánchez stared at the picture of the famous actor. Was he seeing a ghost? He knew this Macbeth. Hardenberg was Engelbert Schmidt, the brutal, cynical SS officer who, on Bonnhoff's orders, had arrested Christina Ullmann in 1938 in the Tiergarten villa and probably murdered her. He looked older, broader. Sánchez was stunned. He never forgot a face. He didn't hear Shakespearean verses; he heard Engelbert Schmidt saying, "Get going, Ullmann. Pack your things. You may take *one* suitcase. Shut up, young man! Get along with it, Ullmann. Start packing!" Engelbert Schmidt—in the black SS uniform, with the death's head on his cap. The program said that the actor, Hardenberg, had recently triumphed in London. Sánchez crushed the brochure in his hands. Schmidt was as guilty as Bonnhoff!

That night Sánchez couldn't sleep. Next morning he rang Erna von Strelitz and asked if he could come to see her. After that he intended to fly straight back to Caracas.

Sánchez was restless. His hatred for "the children of disobedience" (as the Franciscan friars on the Orinoco had called the Nazis) had flared up again dangerously after his evening at the Schiller Theater. He had waged an honest struggle against this hatred. He had looked for excuses for Bonnhoff when there were none and had protected his father from the German authorities for years now. He would go on protecting him, but more angrily and more reluctantly than ever. His sternness, his passion for justice, the indignation over the behavior of the Nazis, burned like badly healed wounds while he bought presents for Pilar and Rosa Martínez. After the break with Bendix, he knew that Rosa would remain his secretary to the end of her days. What a life! It was really not pleasant to have to put up with someone like him. As he bought a leather handbag for Rosa, he came close to hating himself.

He had nothing more to do in Berlin except visit Erna von Strelitz. His aunt's house was to be sold. The legendary Royal Berlin porcelain coffee set was to be given to Erna after his departure, together with old family pictures of the Bonnhoffs in Potsdam.

* * *

Erna von Strelitz was very old, very lively, and highly unsentimental. She greeted Sánchez with curiosity, like an old friend. He was Hilda's nephew, that was enough. Sánchez felt almost at home in the old house in Dahlem. They were alone, sitting peacefully at a round table in an alcove. Fräulein von Strelitz had a guest from London staying with her, but she happened to be out. Actually she had asked her guest to leave her alone with Sánchez for a while. He had come such a long way, from Venezuela!

To meet again after so many years is often a shock, because, unreasonably, one still has a vision of the other person in his youth. Erna von Strelitz had seen Sánchez, age eighteen, when he had visited the house in Dahlem. He used to visit his Aunt Hilda without his father's permission or knowledge. Now, instead of the touching, fiery young man, a tall, very elegant, poised gentleman was standing in front of her. She hadn't imagined that Bonnhoff's son would be quite so assured and impressive. He recognized "Ernchen" at once. Her face had narrowed, her nose grown longer and more prominent, her mouth tight lipped. But the old fighting spirit was still in her sharp, blue, Strelitz eyes, the same Berlin irony, the old loyalty and reliability. Her white hair was as thin as her smile, her parchment-like skin as dry as her humor. She sat upright in an armchair and had spread a coverlet over her swollen legs. "Don't try to count my wrinkles, Herr Sánchez," she said. "You'd never get done." Like Sánchez, she was thinking of Bonnhoff. Gently, she asked if he was still alive.

"He can't die," said Sánchez.

"He didn't know how to live either," she said. "Carl Friedrich always took the wrong boat. There are people like that."

"My father is in a deplorable state," Sánchez told her. "Reality has become a nightmare for him. He has a persecution complex, dreadful fits of rage. He is afraid."

"Your father was never a hero. Forgive me for saying so."

"You may say anything."

"How do you like the crumb cake?"

He nodded. "Excellent!"

For a moment it was very quiet in the big room with the old family furniture. A certain Prussian sobriety and a lack of symbolism ruled here. It did Sánchez good. "I brought you a picture," he said, and handed her the photograph of an old, stern Venezuelan. "My grandfather Sánchez. He brought me up."

"You look a lot like him."

"I hope so." Sánchez smiled for the first time.

"May I keep the picture?"

"That would make me very happy. Emilio Domingo Sánchez was the freedom fighter of Margarita Island."

"That must have been heroic," said Erna von Strelitz. "And while we're on the subject of heroism, did you see Ernst Hardenberg as Macbeth?"

"I went to the Schiller Theater last night."

"A great actor, and a good friend of ours."

Sánchez couldn't believe his ears! His eyes glowed dangerously. If it hadn't been for his Venezuelan courtesy he would have jumped to his feet and left the house.

"I see you don't understand," Erna von Strelitz said gently, and in a few words she gave Sánchez a brief biography of this son of a Berlin actor who had been a close friend of Goebbels. As Engelbert Schmidt, SS officer and Bonnhoff's friend, he had seen the lists of those to be arrested by the Gestapo, and with the cooperation of Berlin resistance groups had worked tirelessly, warning people, saving lives, procuring false passports, and had helped to hide men, women and children—"submarines" they had been called—with people who felt as he did, until the day they dared to leave. Yes, one evening Hardenberg had pretended to arrest Christina Ullmann and brought her to Erna von Strelitz in Zehlendorf. Today she was head nurse in Dr. von Hartlieb's clinic. Hartlieb had also been a resistance fighter. He had copied Gestapo lists for Hardenberg in Bonnhoff's Tiergarten villa. All of them had risked their lives daily.

Sánchez was silent. At best it had always been easy to make a fool of Bonnhoff. Always on the wrong boat . . .

"Christina had to put on an act in front of you too," the old lady went on. "It was much too dangerous to tell the truth. The lives of so many people were at stake. Please don't tell your father anything about it."

"He wouldn't understand it anyway. He would think I was trying to humiliate him."

"He was so proud of you. He loved you almost too much. Hardenberg found it tragic."

"For whom?"

"For Carl Friedrich, of course. You were so very young. Venezuela lay open to you. He had nothing but you."

"And that wasn't much."

"That's what I thought," Erna von Strelitz said drily. It was so forthright and somehow funny that Sánchez had to laugh. He stretched his long legs and felt more at home every minute. He would not look up head nurse Ullmann, even if he decided to stay a few days longer in Berlin. She had to be over fifty now, and he probably wouldn't even recognize her. Not the Christina he had known.

"When are you going back to Caracas?"

"In a few days. I'm not sure yet. May I come to see you again?"

"That would be nice." It sounded reserved, but she was smiling. "But won't you be bored with such a dull old lady?"

"Dull old ladies are usually very interesting, señora." He laughed. Suddenly he was in high spirits. "When do women stop fishing for compliments?"

"In their graves, señor." She was looking at him surreptitiously. His teeth gleamed white. The white streaks in his hair gave him the appearance of a buccaneer. Was he a woman chaser? No, she decided. No need for that. It had to be his Spanish blood. Bonnhoff had never had any luck with women. This man could be dangerous where women were concerned, if he wanted to.

"I don't know where Ellen is. I'd like you to meet her."

"Ellen?"

"My young friend from London. A very good doctor."

So, again, a career woman like Carla Moll. In South America most women still let their men work for them; their main concern was that they were pleasant to look at. Sánchez approved of this.

"Here she is," said the old lady.

Sánchez hadn't heard the doorbell ring; Ellen apparently had a key. "Here I am," somebody said softly behind him.

Sánchez jumped up and stared at the visitor. *That* was Ellen? A very good doctor? In front of him stood the gray creature he had met on Peacock Island. She was wearing the same gray slacks and pullover, and there were still buttons missing on her jacket. "My niece, Naomi," said Fräulein von Strelitz. "The daughter of my sister, Margaret Singer. This is Herr Sánchez from Venezuela."

"We have already met. On Peacock Island. Did you find your parasol?"

"Unfortunately not. Where is Ellen, Tante Ernchen?"

"She should be here any minute."

"This must be some party," Naomi murmured. She sounded annoyed. "Hadn't I better leave?"

"Sit down and have a cup of coffee, Naomi."

"Shouldn't I leave? My husband says I have no social graces."

Was she a widow? Sánchez found her much brighter than on Peacock Island, almost too bright. A strange bird.

"I am Mrs. Elliot Cooper from Chicago. Anyway, that's the general opinion in Chicago."

Cooper? Sánchez couldn't believe his ears. There couldn't possibly be a second Elliot Cooper. He said slowly that he believed he had met Mrs. Cooper's husband in Venezuela.

"I'm sure you did," said Naomi. There were two red spots on the cheeks of her narrow face with its deep shadows under the eyes. "The world is hideously small, Herr Sánchez. There ... you see, Tante Ernchen, nobody can escape Elliot Cooper in the long run. Only I can. He is an industrial passenger pigeon, did you know?"

"Don't let your coffee get cold, Naomi. And please don't fix your hair when we're having coffee."

"I was doing it in honor of Herr Sánchez. It won't happen again. How is our Elliot?"

Sánchez said cheerfully, "I have no idea. We lost track of each other."

"So did we. We correspond only through our lawyers. A case of willful desertion. They are still trying to decide who deserted whom."

"That doesn't interest Herr Sánchez, Naomi."

"That's where you're wrong, Tante. Broken marriages interest everyone. The crumb cake is wonderful. Who baked it?"

"Ellen."

"She certainly can bake." Naomi was now addressing the canary in its cage in the corner. "Admit it, you old creep! Why is Hansi so quarrelsome, Tante Ernchen?"

"Did you take your pills?"

"Ellen's pills are not as good as her crumb cake. Maybe they tranquilize the English, but not me. They excite me. Uncle Werner says the same thing."

"Naomi is staying with my brother," said Fräulein von Strelitz. "Is he coming over today?"

"No. Right now he's playing solitaire. He finds it soothing," said Naomi. "This is my first meal today. May I have a piece of apple cake now, Tante Ernchen? That's from a bakery. You can tell right away."

She spoke like a child, with fearful impudence. "If I could bake as well as Ellen, would you like me?"

"I like you—you know that. There are a lot of things you could do if only you wanted to."

"But I don't want to. Did the glass cupboard behind you just move? It seemed to. It would be awful if the old cupboard were to attack me. I always say a person must be cautious, however dumb he may be. What do you think, Herr Sánchez?"

"I think you're very wise."

"Thank you very much. Nobody has said anything nice to me for ages. It doesn't have to be true. I find Herr Sánchez charming, Tante Ernchen!"

"That's good."

"Excuse me, Herr Sánchez, but should I have said that behind your back?"

"I like to hear nice things said about me, Mrs. Cooper."

"Elliot says everything about people behind their backs, but nothing nice. Just the same, he thinks he's a friend of mankind. Didn't you notice that, Herr Sánchez? It is of course easier to love mankind than to be nice to one's wife."

"I agree with you, Mrs. Cooper."

"Am I talking too much, Tante Ernchen? It's dreadful, Herr Sánchez—either I keep my mouth shut or I talk a blue streak with no commas or periods. I guess I have no social graces. Cooper is right. Dreadful, isn't it?" She was silent.

"Here comes Ellen," said Naomi's aunt, sounding immensely relieved.

"Well, there you are!" said Naomi. "Here comes Ellen! *Jubilate! Jubilate!*"

Dr. Ellen Driscoll was wearing a dark green dress that reminded Sánchez of damp grass. She looked cool, pure, and smelled of fresh air. The English declared that their rainy weather gave their women the most beautiful complexions in the world. The lady doctor must have run around in the rain a lot. Her skin was alabaster. Her dark eyes looked questioningly from Sánchez to Naomi. "Did you take your pills, Naomi?"

"Leave me alone! They don't agree with me, and they don't help me either!"

"Maybe not right away," her doctor said quietly. "You must be patient, darling." She stroked Naomi's gray-blond hair off her forehead. She had to be much younger than Naomi Cooper, but she was more mature and deliberate. Sánchez watched with interest how she led Erna von Strelitz into the next room. "Not so fast, Tante Ernchen. We don't want it to hurt, do we? . . . There. I'll come back and get you."

"Nonsense! I can walk alone."

"I know you can. But let's take it easy just the same. I'll make some fresh coffee."

"Oh, let me!" Naomi said eagerly, as Ellen Driscoll came back. "I want to do something, too!"

"Fine. I really am dead tired. And please bring some more crumb cake, Naomi."

Naomi took a squashed, greasy little package out of her handbag. "I baked a cake for you, Ellen, but I don't think it's any good."

Dr. Ellen bit into the damp, soft cake heroically. "It's very good. That was sweet of you, Naomi."

"I'll get the coffee now," said Naomi. "Then it'll go down better," and she ran quickly out of the room. Sánchez watched her go. One could no more be angry with her than with a helpless child.

"Naomi has been very ill," said Ellen Driscoll. "But she is getting better. She had withdrawn completely from reality."

"She gives that impression," said Sánchez.

"People with a great deal of imagination often lose contact with reality." Dr. Driscoll was silent for a moment, then she said, "Fortunately I have no imagination, so I am spared a lot."

"But don't you also miss a lot of beautiful things?"

"I don't have any time for that. My day in London is filled from early morning to late at night." It sounded a little short. But then she said, "Would you do me a favor, Herr Sánchez? I mean, if you intend to stay in Berlin a few more days?"

"I would be happy to."

Ellen Driscoll smiled. "I'm not sure, but I think it would do Naomi good if you went for a walk with her. She seems to trust you, and that doesn't happen often."

"I'll be glad to. We already met once, on Peacock Island."

"Well then, that's fine. Thanks a lot. Naomi lives with her uncle, just around the corner. The baron is very good to her, but impatient, like all the Strelitzes. But they are the salt of the earth."

"And when do I see *you* again?" Sánchez asked. He had to see her again. Her gentle vitality and her beautiful, serene face enchanted him. She seemed to fill the room with a green, shadowy light. Probably a man was waiting for her in London.

"I'll be staying in Berlin a few weeks more," he said, when he heard Naomi coming back. "Would you have dinner with me next Saturday night? It would make me very happy."

"Here is your coffee, Ellen. I'm afraid it's lukewarm. I can't seem to manage Tante Ernchen's stove."

"What do you want? The coffee's hot. Wouldn't you like another cup, Herr Sánchez?"

Sánchez heroically drank the cold coffee which in South America he would simply have poured down the drain. He didn't know if Ellen Driscoll had accepted his invitation or not.

# 20

# Ribbeck's Dinner

**Carla Moll:**

He called and invited me to appear punctually at seven o'clock on Saturday evening at a restaurant. He declared he couldn't talk in peace at the office. So he was shifting an hour at the office to a restaurant. Apparently, that was all. This time I said 'yes' at once. Ever since I had turned him down, Ribbeck had exuded his glacial air whenever he had to see me. Each day he seemed to grow taller and more disagreeable.

At this point nobody could pretend that Wendt would come back and the magical, old, easy-going way of life would start all over again. Wendt seemed to have written a book that might make him famous. He had become inaccessible. *Tempora mutantur* said Ribbeck when he fired Annemarie Schmidt of the sob-sister column, "Dear Annemarie," and introduced instead "Everyday Psychology." He is hideously treacherous. Annemarie doesn't understand a word of Latin, and Ribbeck had to translate it before she grasped that her days with *Comet* were numbered. Not even Edith Hannemann, who got invited to coffee by all our fallen heroes and heroines, had any idea what had become of Annemarie. She disappeared without leaving a trace, just like all the fun we had had under Wendt. None of us begrudged Wendt his success or possible fame, but when he visited Berlin he was a changed man. He was friendly as ever, but he had no time for us; only for his publisher and Ribbeck. He and Ribbeck seemed to be good friends, and that was astonishing.

When Mother heard that my boss had invited me to dinner, she was only too happy to relinquish me over the weekend. Her hopes that Ribbeck might turn out to be the man in my life grew to the same extent that my spirits sank.

The day before I had seen Sánchez at the Hilton. He could have invited me to a meal. I would have refused, of course, but he could have invited me, the bastard! The various interludes I had with him had at least brought some excitement into my life.

I arrived twenty minutes late on purpose, just to demonstrate to Ribbeck that this was *not* the office. If my lack of punctuality annoyed him, he didn't show it. He was more formal and cooler than ever. I was wearing a high Spanish comb in my hair and my lilac dress. Sánchez had given me the comb on Margarita Island and stuck it in my hair. It was black and gold and set with Margarita pearls. Startling, like Sánchez. Ribbeck did not appear to notice it.

"Would you like an appetizer or soup?" he asked. But my feelings were hurt, and Ribbeck did nothing to raise my spirits. Of course I had dressed with great care for nothing. I might as well have worn my gray suit and Frau Hannemann's felt hat.

He ate heartily, and I thought, thank God, he's at least enjoying his food! Whatever was left of my good humor he killed off with his extreme politeness. His good manners irritated me. I was being unjust and knew it. I couldn't forgive him for my not making an impression on him as a woman.

If Ribbeck were not such a bastard, I might have enjoyed the evening in the restaurant. I so seldom meet men who are taller than I. Ribbeck was as tall as Sánchez, but with that all resemblance ended. Even in this gourmet restaurant, Ribbeck was as sober as a judge, although he had good taste when it came to the drinks. I couldn't imagine him as a child or a schoolboy; he must have been thirty in his crib! Frau

Hannemann had managed to ferret out that he was thirty-six, not thirty-four.

Suddenly I was furious with myself that here, in this restaurant on the Kurfürstendamm, I was comparing him with Sánchez! Comparisons are neurotic, says Lotte.

Oscar Ribbeck was a cold fish by nature. Once I thought he was looking at my cleavage, but he was only reaching for the wine list. "Have you lost your tongue, Fräulein Moll?"

"I beg your pardon."

"Why are you so silent? Don't you like the trout?"

"Oh yes. Much better than red snapper."

"What did you say?"

"Red snapper. A Caribbean fish. Nothing spectacular. But on Margarita Island they cook it in a very special way. Piquant."

"Just like your travelogue, Fräulein Moll. Your health!"

"Your health!"

"Why didn't you describe Margarita Island? Were there any other specialties there beside red snapper?"

"The pearls on my comb are Margarita pearls. Otherwise there's nothing to report, really, except the sea . . . rocks . . . fish."

"And fishermen?"

"Of course. Somebody's got to catch the fish."

After this bit of information, Ribbeck lapsed again into his characteristic silence. He drank a third glass of Mosel wine, probably to recover from my scintillating conversation. I don't know why he likes to denigrate me, why I behave like an idiot, and why I want constantly to justify myself when I'm with him. He'll fire me one of these days, no doubt about it.

"But now, to change the subject, Fräulein Moll—this has been on my mind for some time."

I downed the excellent Mosel as if it had been Coca-Cola. Ribbeck looked as if he regretted not having ordered lemonade for me. I said, "When I see anything liquid, I get hellishly thirsty right away." Here I was, apologizing again!

"Unfortunately I'm not a climbing fish. They can live for a long time on air."

"Why would you like to be a climbing fish? You are a very pretty young lady."

I was so surprised I swallowed the wrong way and spilled some Mosel on Ribbeck's dark suit. He didn't like it, but chose to ignore the incident. Looking slightly disgusted, he wiped his trousers with a fine linen handkerchief. Then he said that with beauty alone I wasn't going to go far with him. He didn't express it quite so broadly, but that was the gist of it. He wanted to see results. And you couldn't put anything over on him. "A little more wine, Fräulein Moll?" He took off his glasses and wiped them. Without them he looked younger and more human.

"What you lack, Fräulein Moll is method. And to reach one's goals without method, well, for that I guess you have to be a genius."

"Are you looking for geniuses, Herr Doktor?"

"Hardly," he replied icily. "A genius would be hopelessly out of place on an illustrated paper. May I extrapolate for a moment on what I consider a methodical approach to one's work?"

Concisely and with a somewhat threatening overtone, Ribbeck began his lecture. There should be: a) preparation of one's material, with three choices for a title; b) a synopsis of all viewpoints, circa a thousand words ("Would you like red wine with the venison, Fräulein Moll?"); c) introduction of the report or series: why just this theme?; d) the historic basis of a topical theme. Example: the guerrillas in South America, student unrest in the world, black power, the Berlin Wall— a journalist must conquer the times, not vice versa ("It is always later than you think, Fräulien Moll."); and the summation: e) if the summing up is to be correct, it must present the logical ending of the text. "Are you listening, Fräulein Moll? Closing the typewriter is by no means an ending. Needless to say, a clear style is desirable. Never three words where one suffices. Flaubert's principle. Read Flaubert, Fräulein Moll. Nearly all journalists use too many words for what they have to say. But that doesn't appeal to the demanding reader. This also holds true for the novelist." Ribbeck cleared his throat. "And that brings me to what I want to say, Fräulein Moll. You should try . . ."

At this moment Sánchez entered the restaurant with a young woman I didn't know.

"What *are* you staring at?" Ribbeck sounded annoyed. He had been annoyed for quite some time now because I was obviously not paying enough attention to him.

"There's nothing to stare at."

"Of course there isn't. Well, where's the red wine? Thank you, Herr Ober. Very good."

"It's the same vintage you had last time, Herr Doktor."

"That's right. I'm a creature of habit. Drink a lot of it, Fräulein Moll. You're suddenly quite pale. The venison looks good, doesn't it?"

I thought: thank God he's at least enjoying his food!

Whatever had taken place between Sánchez and me in Caracas—at Cooper's dinner and in his house at Palma Sola—had been of a strictly private nature. Now for the first time I saw him with another woman who, at least outwardly, was the exact opposite of me. A slim, modest flower, one might say, blooming all by itself, not making any effort to attract the attention of the gardener. But she was a woman! Teresa Sánchez had been a fury, Pilar Álvarez an unrivaled goddess of darkness, and Rosa Martínez had definitely not been his type. This unknown creature belonged to a category that was almost extinct: she was a lady.

Her skin was very white, her dark hair was parted in the middle—a Madonna. She was modestly dressed, like a conservative English woman, whose severe, expensive suits outlive all styles. She looked serious, but not dark like Pilar; lively, but not hectic like Carla Moll. Wendt would have called her "a quiet light." I would never have thought that Carlos would have . . . He called the waiter over and in doing so turned to face me, but he didn't see me. I had never seen his face quite like this—not even in our most intimate hours.

Sánchez was aglow. Usually he was a brigand, who fairly quickly offered his bed to a woman he liked, but for this woman he was building a cathedral with a high altar! In the middle of a restaurant! Never had he seemed so Spanish. Don Quixote? Don Juan? *Caballero cristiano?* Was *this* his true face? He seemed to be experiencing a complete moral turnabout. Things that had been important to him were taking a back seat. His subconscious had become conscious, and ideal love had triumphed over the naked Venus. He was more of a stranger to me than Ribbeck. The funny part of it was that no one was laughing. Neither Sánchez nor his quiet light; neither Ribbeck, who didn't know what was going on, nor even I, who knew too much—at any rate, more than was good for me. The way he leaned toward her, the way he laid her scarf around her shoulders . . . I didn't want to see any more. After all, I had come to terms with the whole thing quite nicely, but now I was degraded to the role of onlooker. I watched Carlos give this woman things he had never given to me: adoration, sympathy, intense interest in anything she had to say. I had no idea he could listen like that.

Was I mistaken? Was I drunk again? No. I was not mistaken. Sánchez's gestures, the way he moved, had the convincing power of a master of pantomime. I didn't need to see his face. What in God's name did this woman have that I lacked?

"What is occupying your thoughts so completely, Fräulein Moll?" Ribbeck was looking at me sharply.

"You . . . you mean me?"

"Who could I possibly mean but you? Are you cold? You shouldn't be wearing such a low cut dress after the flu. After all, it's November."

"That's right."

Ribbeck was staring at me. In his eyes there was an undefinable expression. Scorn? Distaste? Boredom? Or perhaps a shadow of disappointment that I was drinking his red wine and offering no companionship?

"I'll get your fur stole, or you'll be flat on your back

again." That was all he needed, that my work be neglected again.

"What would an Indian from the Orinoco say about this place?"

"What would a deaf man say about Beethoven's Ninth?"

"Sometimes I ask myself, Fräulein Moll, what it must look like in your head."

"I can tell you that exactly: chaotic."

"May I give you some advice?"

"Please—no. That's been taken care of by my friends, enough to see me through decades."

"But I am one of your friends, Fräulein Moll. Does that surprise you? If I didn't have the patience of a friend where you are concerned . . ." He cleared his throat. "What I wanted to advise you in is this: in your profession don't show a man quite so clearly that you can't stand him."

I could feel myself turning a fiery red. "You're imagining things, Dr. Ribbeck."

"I was speaking of Herr Bräutigam." Ribbeck smiled maliciously. He had made a fool of me again. "Herr Bräutigam has complained to me about your rudeness. A little more red wine, Fräulein Moll? Lately I've been thinking quite a lot about you."

When Ribbeck thought quite a lot about someone, nothing good came of it. I asked him why he had been thinking about me. "After all, I have the pleasure of seeing you daily in the office," he said.

"That can't be a great pleasure."

"Who said it was a great pleasure? It would be nice if you would stop interrupting me constantly. I wanted to say that I don't think you are a hundred percent suited for journalism."

"You . . . you mean I'm not good enough?"

"You could do more in other fields."

"Are you finally firing me?"

"What I am saying is meant to help you in your development, Fräulein Moll. It has nothing whatsoever to do with your routine work in the office. But there's never a chance there for a quiet talk. You see, reporting today, when dealing with foreign countries, is concerned mainly with political, economic structures and changes. Society, the group—all sociological phenomena. Our series "The Guerrillas of South America" is an example. By the way, our subscriptions have increased by five percent."

"I know." I began to feel queasier and queasier.

"*Your* best work, however, consists of quite different, highly individual elements: fantasy oriented toward reality, interest in a specific case and the generation of suspense and drama. In short, you have the skills of a novelist."

"I'm much too indolent for anything like that. Besides, the novel is dead."

"Has been proclaimed dead. That's not the same thing. The novel, like Lazarus, comes to life again and again. Are you listening?"

I tore my eyes away from Sánchez's back. He was drinking a toast to the woman. He had raised his wine glass to her like a monstrance. The young lady with the Madonna parting raised her glass without touching his. She was smiling, but somehow didn't seem to be involved. She was perfect!

"Of course I'm listening," I said hastily.

Much later I realized that I should have listened to Ribbeck. My reactions often come too late. I can be distracted easily. He was explaining that today's novel was developing away from the pure action type story for primitive readers and was seeking its potential in manifold ways: analysis, differentiation, motivation. "Read Nathalie Sarraute. The baring of the subconscious . . . But as far as I'm concerned, it's too much of a textbook. If you could invest your temperament and humor . . ." He stopped short and shrugged.

"I'm afraid you're casting pearls before the swine, Herr Doktor." Since he had nothing to say to that, I decided that he agreed with me. Then he said in his most disagreeable tone, "I was trying to help you, Fräulein Moll, to develop your talents. That is my duty as your editor-in-chief. But if you don't want to develop your talents . . . it's your life."

"Are you angry?"

"Not at all. I think the best thing you could do is find a

man who is willing to spend his life working for you. Or are
you also too indolent for that?"

"You may be right." My smile was just right, too.

"Fortunately that is none of my business," he said. "First
I want to build up your television career. It's off to a good
start. That is due in part to your appearance. You *are* decorative. But I would like to bring a certain danger to your
attention..."

I never found out what was threatening me. A voice I
knew only too well said, "We'll never have a chance like this
again! May I join you?"

"But of course," said Ribbeck. "A glass of red wine?"

"I hope I'm not intruding." It was Annemarie Schmidt
from the column "Dear Annemarie," deceased.

"Good heavens, no!" said Ribbeck. "It's my pleasure."


With my numerous faults, I have one small asset: my
intuition is infallible. Unfortunately only where others are
concerned. I never know when the bell has tolled for me!
Just as I could sense the mood at Sánchez's table, I could
feel even more strongly the tension between Ribbeck and
"Dear Annemarie." Except for the look of cold fury with
which he had appraised her, Ribbeck had turned to stone.
Schmidt, on the other hand, was devastatingly lively, a dis-
jointed Rubens figure suffering from high blood pressure. At
first she ignored Ribbeck.

"That's how he does it, Moll! I'm warning you! He invites
you out, then he fires you. Why? Because he wants to sleep
with you! And he doesn't want any gossip in the office. That's
what he did to me. Watch it! Won't be long now and he'll
be sleeping with you."

"Don't you think it takes two for that?"

"I agree with Fräulein Moll." Ribbeck had come to. His
face was red. It was the worst thing that could have happened
to him in front of me, that could happen to any man in the
presence of a strange woman.

"Be quiet, Ossie!" She called him "Ossie." And to me

again, "When he needs it, he'll come. You'll get the hang of it, Moll."

"Try to act like a lady, Schmidt," I told her. "Even if it's hard for you."

"You just keep quiet, Moll. I may not come from such a fine stable..."

"May not?" Ribbeck's features were distorted. I couldn't bear to look at him. Even if he wasn't the pleasantest person in the world, this he didn't deserve. I couldn't help it—I imagined the two in bed. Why on earth had he fallen for Schmidt? A mountain of flesh, and in her rage it wobbled like jelly. But she had that phony motherly smile when she went after a man. She was forty-two and had been divorced twice. How could Ribbeck stand her? What a dumb question ...if that was what he needed.

"You never took me here, Ossie," Schmidt said reproachfully.

"Listen, Annemarie." His voice was hoarse. "I am in the middle of a professional discussion with Fräulein Moll."

"I can believe that. I want a piece of chocolate cake."

Ribbeck ordered it. He was big and strong, but it would have taken two bouncers to remove this colossus of a woman. He'd probably fire his housekeeper for telling Annemarie where she could find him. Schmidt was dangerous because she had none of the inhibitions of a woman of breeding. But all of us at *Comet* knew how she got away with it. She was so good-natured, so helpful, so generous, as if she kept a horn of plenty in her big patent-leather bag, as if she were ready to give with both hands. What she really did though was take with both hands. I was sure Ribbeck had recognized all this long ago, but like any man, especially a man in the public eye, he didn't want a scandal. I decided to talk to Frau Hannemann about it discreetly. Schmidt was afraid of Hannemann, as all of us were. Hannemann had already threatened Annemarie once when she had accused a young man, who had turned to "Dear Annemarie" for advice, of a phony pregnancy after a few evenings on the town. She had tried to get some money out of the poor guy. Did Ribbeck know about it? It didn't concern me. "Dear Annemarie" was his private funeral.

But in the elegant restaurant she was not exactly in her element, and under Ribbeck's icy glare she was whispering. Usually she yelled. She had let herself down on a third chair, breathing heavily. She looked grotesque seated because she still rammed herself into a tight girdle and bra. But she had the lovely pink skin of corpulent women in their second best years. I imagined she looked better with her clothes off. She never stopped eating the little cakes that were served with the coffee. "My favorites," she murmured. "Don't be angry, Ossie. I shouldn't have come, should I?"

"Don't eat so much nougat. It's not good for you." She stretched out her hand for a second piece. "Did you hear what I said?"

Ribbeck's voice was soft, but for anyone with a sense for vibrations there was a frightening undertone. She had only been at our table for about three minutes. Should I get up and leave? Should I stay? I was Ribbeck's guest. I sat rooted to the spot. Annemarie was on the point of exploding. "Ossie" would probably choke her to death if she started to make a scene. This was something I could do without. And I didn't have to do with it, because just as Ribbeck took the petit-four out of his Dulcinea's hand I was called to the phone.

I have the stupid habit of running around with my bag open. I wanted to blow my nose as I ran down the long, dimly lit passage and down some stairs to the phone booth (why are phone booths always at the other end of the world?) when someone came running after me.

"You lost your handkerchief, as usual," said Sánchez.

As a little girl I had hated blind man's bluff because I was afraid all the children would have disappeared when I opened my eyes. Now, when I heard Sánchez's voice, I closed my eyes for a moment, and didn't really want to open them again. But then I did, and stared at him, and he laughed. His teeth and the gray streaks in his glossy black hair gleamed white. He was in high spirits. He looked rested.

"You lack method, Fräulein Moll." Nobody had ever spoken a truer word over a glass of wine. Like a drowning man I could see all the scenes in Venezuela—my defeats and his misdeeds—from coincidence to coincidence, from catastrophe to catastrophe, from failure to failure. Perhaps the strange lady at his table was really cool, perhaps she would make him suffer, torture him with a smile as he had tortured me, only because I had had the misfortune to love him in the only way I knew how. And in the end, after Bonnhoff had stepped bodily between us, I had been the journalist Moll, the snake in the grass from the press, who had to be annihilated. But he was smiling at me.

"How are you?"

"Fine. And you?"

"Fine too," he said.

"Who . . . who is the lady at your table?"

I knew it was wrong to ask, but I couldn't help myself. His eyes expressed his disapproval, but he was still smiling, smoothly now, with a trace of impatience. He said the lady at his table was a doctor from London. Would I like to meet her? It was pure sarcasm, and since he received no reply to his offer, he half turned to leave.

"Just a minute, Carlos." I sounded breathless. I was in the magic cage again. I only had to see him, and it happened. He was my narcotic, my LSD . . . "Carlos," I said. "Listen to me for a moment." I spoke my own peculiar Spanish. "One must be able to forget and forgive."

Since Sánchez was capable of neither, he said nothing. "You consider yourself a good Christian, don't you?"

"Whoever considers himself a good Christian is a miserable one, my dear. And now will you please excuse me?"

"Right away. But I think we could be friends, Carlos. Now that you're in Berlin. I mean, there can be worse misunderstandings between two people, and they can still drink a cup of coffee together. Like civilized people?"

"You talk too much. Good evening."

When I came back from the phone, Ribbeck was alone. I didn't know whether he had removed Annemarie with psychology or force. He was sitting there, very straight as usual, and his pale, stern face betrayed nothing. He looked very lonely. A man without a woman is a beggar in the night, the Spaniards on the Orinoco say. But he was wearing his mask, he was aloof again, as in the office. He gave me a sharp look. "Is anything wrong, Fräulein Moll?"

"My mother. She's had another heart attack. I must leave at once."

"Is she at home? I'll drive you there."

"She's in the hospital. Wilmersdorf. Dr. von Hartlieb. Dr. Schneider said I should come right away."

Ribbeck had put my fur stole around my shoulders. "Wait here. I'll get my car."

"I . . . I have my little Opel . . ."

"You can't drive. Not now."

It all happened so fast. Ribbeck drove me to the hospital. We didn't speak. He took the key to my car. The garage would fetch it from the restaurant. He would attend to everything.

"If she dies now," I said, before we stopped. And then, "I must do more for her."

"Good night, Fräulein Moll."

As usual I forgot to say thank you. The car had turned into a side street before I thought of it. The night nurse came to meet me. "Fräulein Moll? Dr. Schneider is waiting for you. No, right now you can't see your mother. Dr. von Hartlieb and a nurse are giving her oxygen."

"Is . . . is it that bad?"

"Please wait here for a moment. The head nurse knows all about it. I'll get you a strong cup of coffee. No, no, you must sit down. And try to calm down. Here are some magazines."

I sat in a small waiting room, the kind there are all over the world: clean, smelling of medicine and sorrow. For the first time in my life I waited for Mother, not vice versa.

# 21

# A Very Ordinary Cup of Sorrow

Carla Moll:

I waited. Minutes? Hours? Years? Every now and then a doctor or a nurse looked into the waiting room and disappeared again. Dr. Schneider didn't come, although I had been told to come "right away." Head nurse Ullmann looked into the room for a second. I saw her for the third time in my life, and here in the hospital she was in her element: not hesitant and unsure as she had been that time in the office, not gay as she had been at Locker's wedding. She was someone to cling to—firm but compassionate. "You can see her soon, Fräulein Moll. Sister Theresa will bring you some fresh coffee. And here is a little pill, and a glass of water. For you, child. Please take it right away. It will make you feel better."

"How is my mother?"

"We mustn't give up hope, Fräulein Moll. Dr. Schneider will come soon and take you to her. It was a bad attack."

"Has she been asking for me?"

"Constantly. But now she's asleep."

"That's good, isn't it?" I said, relieved.

"Here is your coffee, Fräulein Moll. Oh, Sister Theresa, please see to it that Fräulein Moll drinks it hot. Why don't

you take off your stole, Fräulein Moll? It's very hot in here.
You'll catch cold when you go outside."

"But my teeth are chattering, nurse."

"That'll be better after the coffee. I'll see you later." She
exuded so much authority that I drank the coffee hot and took
off my fur stole. My low cut dress wasn't suitable. Nothing
was suitable! Mother had said I should wear my white woolen
dress to Ribbeck's dinner. High neck. But I hadn't listened
to her. I never did her any favors. That would have to change.
The time ticked away and not a second would ever return.
There! Dr. Schneider at last!

"I'm really going to look after Mother. Word of honor,
Uncle Schneider. As soon as she can go home, I'll go away
with her. For at least three weeks. Certainly for two. I promise
you . . ."

Our old family doctor stared at me. In his eyes there was
a look that prevented me from saying anything more. "You've
got to be brave now, girl," he said. "No tears. Not now. She
wants to see you. Come on. Cheer up! That's right."

He drew me by the hand into the dimly lit passage. I went
with him, like the little girl after Father's death. Uncle Schneider—no relative—is always there when something goes
wrong in the Moll family.

He pushed me gently into the sick room. Was Mother
unconscious? Her eyes were closed. Pastor Wernicke was
sitting in a corner, old, humble, silent. He also came to see
Mother whenever anything went wrong in the Moll family.
Dr. von Hartlieb was standing beside the bed, nodding. Head
nurse Ullmann was busy with a frightening looking apparatus,
but she was very quiet about it. Dr. Schneider stepped up
close to the bed and leaned over Mother. She was white, her
face strangely sharp, unfamiliar, her mouth half-open. They
had removed her dentures. She would be angry when she
found that out. Dr. Schneider whispered, "She is here. Do
you hear me, Katharina? Carlchen is here."

For a moment Mother opened her eyes. I think she recognized me.

I have to believe she recognized me.

* * *

The first week after Mother's death I hardly felt anything. I was in a state of shock. My friend Lotte explained what had happened. Mother had actually wanted to play bridge that evening, and Herr von Halm had come to pick her up. He found her lying on the floor, unconscious. Dr. Schneider came over fast and called me at the restaurant. In the week after the funeral I thought often of Locker's wedding and how Dr. Schneider had advised me to spend weekends with Mother whenever I could. It would make her happy. Unfortunately I couldn't sacrifice any of my precious time to make my mother happy.

I wasn't actually present, but my guilt feelings were, and I couldn't shake them off. They hummed around me like wasps and stung me, and robbed me of any courage I might have had. Guilt feelings are so senseless because no one loves enough. If only she could come back! If . . . would I be irritated again, distracted, self-centered? I remain the same horrible mixture of sensitivity, egoism, and hope, and I have the fairly well-developed talent for being able to bear the sufferings of others calmly. I'm only human, I told myself.

The funeral passed me by, shadowy. That wasn't Mother under wreaths of evergreen. Pastor Wernicke kept things short and to the point. For a few minutes, Mother lived again. I stood beside the Schneiders and the Sommers. All the Hahns were there too. They looked at me with hostility. They had never liked me. I was a bad daughter. It was written all over Frau Hahn's face. Frau Hannemann was there, of course, straight from the station to the church. She was crazy about funerals. She went to funerals even when they were no concern of hers. But to Mother's she came for my sake, all in black, with a hat that looked like a veiled cheese bell. Ribbeck sent a wreath in the name of the publishing house and a handwritten note that was so conventional, the paper was smiling . . .

In the first week after Mother's death, which I spent with Kurt and Lotte, I thought sometimes of head nurse Ullmann, and found myself envying this faded, tired, gray-haired

woman. So many people needed her, and I was so expendable.
Whatever had taken place years ago between her and Bonnhoff and Sánchez, she had shaken off the past, changed her
image, and become an excellent nurse. Should one change
one's image from time to time? Perhaps that was what Ribbeck had been driving at when he had offered to help me in
my development. I was too upset to think it through.

Mother had few friends but many acquaintances, who all
came to see me now. Frau Frosch thought this was wonderful.
She had always found my life-style much too quiet. When
you paid such a high rent, you should at least use the apartment! The Hahn family appeared, with children, grandchildren, and daughter-in-law. I found the latter the only
attractive member of the family, and young Hahn had been
quite right not to marry me, much to Mother's disgust.

I didn't see the Hahns or any of the others again. Mother's
death erected a barrier between her generation and me. I no
longer felt it was my duty to meet with narrow-minded and
opinionated people who liked to talk about sickness and death,
and try to lift their spirits. Actually, during this time of never-
again, the only people I could stand were Lotte, Kurt, and
Dr. Schneider. Sometimes I drank coffee with Frau Hannemann, not to please her, but because she was never boring.
What I really needed was a change of scene, but Ribbeck
didn't send me away to any foreign lands.

A few weeks after Mother's death I was lying on the couch
one afternoon, and suddenly I thought of Sánchez. Everything
came back to me like a rejected manuscript: Annemarie turning up at the restaurant, too, and Ribbeck's face. I wondered
what had happened after that—to Sánchez and his London
doctor, and to Ribbeck and his fat mistress. Everything had
probably gone on as usual, only without me. Life creeps or
races on, whether one is participating, watching, or ignoring
the circus. The front door bell rang and I jumped up. I hated
unexpected callers, especially condolers. I buttoned my long
housecoat quickly. It was Ribbeck!

"You?" I said.

Ribbeck didn't answer stupid questions. He watched me brush back my long hair. Mother had told me so often I should do my hair even when I was at home alone. You never knew ... How true! Since I didn't ask him to come in, Ribbeck asked if he might. No, he didn't want a cup of coffee; he didn't have much time.

As usual, his presence confused me utterly. I felt paralyzed. He asked in a low voice whether I had got over the shock. After a pause he expressed his regret that our pleasant evening in the restaurant had ended so sadly. That was how he described our trio, without batting an eyelash! I said nothing because Carlos had said I talked too much. Finally, sounding a little irritated now, Ribbeck said that everyone suffered a loss from time to time, that all of us regret things we can't change, and that work was the best medicine. That everyone couldn't be healed by the same medicine evidently didn't occur to him.

After that he was silent. I offered him a whiskey and he didn't refuse. He asked me how I had liked the fruit punch in Venezuela. Then he asked if I happened to remember a foreigner who had been in the restaurant with a lady when we had been there. A Venezuelan. I could feel myself blushing. Then I said no, I couldn't remember.

"You don't lie very well, Fräulein Moll. That has to be learned too." Of what concern could Carlos possibly be to Ribbeck? I wondered. I had forgotten that he knew everybody. What should I say now? With Ribbeck the right thing was usually wrong. Should I say: Don't stare at me like that, Herr Ribbeck. Yes, yes, yes, I know the *cabellero*, in and out of bed. We slept together, yes, but we were never intimate. You must know that for these South Americans all nature is a double bed. They need sex all the time, not only occasionally, like you! Should I say that?

"The man is Carlos Domingo Sánchez, an extremely important entrepreneur from Caracas. I met him the other day at a reception."

I said nothing. So Ribbeck had met my buccaneer socially. Great! Ribbeck and his maneuvers!

"By the way, I have asked Señor Sánchez for an interview for our guerrilla series. He's staying at the Hilton."

"I'm sure he won't give you the interview."

"What makes you think that, Fräulein Moll? We'll get it on Monday, at the Hilton. I have already told him to expect you."

"I don't want to do it."

"I have told Señor Sánchez that we are sending over the author of *Caracas for Beginners*."

"And what did he say?"

"That he is not afraid of lady writers. He was charming. Most agreeable and modest."

I didn't know whom Ribbeck was talking about, certainly not Carlos.

"I am taking your nervous condition into consideration, Fräulein Moll, but please don't make any difficulties for me now. As I have already said: work is the best medicine. A nice place you have here. Unfortunately I have to go. Thanks for the whiskey. So . . . until Monday."

What was going on here? Sánchez had every reason to keep his visit strictly private. Our interview would probably begin with the guerrillas but would doubtlessly end with Sturmbannführer Bonnhoff's lousy fish. Had he really agreed to the interview or was he only leading Ribbeck on? On Monday I would find out.

# 22

# The Great Unknown

The interview with Sánchez was to take place on Monday afternoon. On Monday morning Ribbeck received a letter from the Hilton. Sánchez regretted that he could not give an interview to the author of *Caracas for Beginners* because in an hour he had to fly to London. He thanked Ribbeck for the stimulating conversation at the reception which a well-known architect had held in Reinickendorf. The residential development on exhibition had made a great impression on Sánchez. The lustrous colors of the concrete edifices had reminded him of his tropical homeland. Álvarez and Sánchez were working on a similar project in Puerto Cabello. A polite, formal letter. At the end he thanked Ribbeck for the interest *Comet* had shown in Venezuela.

Ribbeck folded the letter and frowned. Had Sánchez wanted to give the interview or not? Ribbeck didn't know and would never know. Too bad! The Venezuelan was an impressive personality. Ribbeck had made inquiries about Álvarez & Sánchez. The firm was building all over Venezuela, also in the Orinoco industrial area where there was iron ore, and where there were guerrillas who could make a good story for a journalist. In this area Fräulein Moll had caught mosquitoes on her expense account. Ribbeck's face darkened. He didn't know that Carla Moll had met an honest-to-God guerrilla in the Hotel Amazonas, Camilo de Padilla. On that Monday morning, even Fräulein Moll didn't know it.

Ribbeck told Frau Hannemann over the intercom that she should send Fräulein Moll to him at once. "She isn't here yet, Herr Doktor."

"I beg your pardon, Frau Hannemann. It's ten thirty!"

"I hope nothing's happened to her. She drives so fast."

"Send her in the moment she arrives!" Ribbeck said harshly. Moll had probably washed her hair and done it up in some crazy fashion for the interview. Shameless person! She didn't deserve such glorious hair. It had glittered like gold over her housecoat. It was pouring cats and dogs outside. It would serve her right if she arrived at the office soaked through! He'd give her hell, he thought, as he drummed a little Beethoven on top of the desk. In time. He was very musical and played the violin quite well, but only he and his closest friends knew that. Annemarie was allowed to play the rock music she loved and sing like an asthmatic cat in the apartment he had furnished, before and after his visits. Horrible that he needed her every now and then.

Sex was the disturbing element in his oh-so-orderly life. He had matured early. Actually he had needed a girl at age thirteen. But then there had been the fear of his father, of the giggling, incomprehensible girls, and the fear of himself. Today, twenty-three years later, he could recall the tension that had torn him apart at the time, his bad report cards, his desperate attempts to shake off the mysterious restlessness and confusion. In his father's house it was called "the secret sin." It had taken a long time before he had been able to take what he wanted when he wanted it, without scruples. And how he wanted it! Forget it . . . Two broken engagements lay behind him. He had known the first girl too little, the second one too well. A quarter to eleven! Had Fräulein Moll really driven into another car? Or into a lamp post?

At his best, Ribbeck was not a patient executive, but if kept waiting, he became dangerous. Then he automatically remembered all the failures of his colleagues and staff. He was one of those people who can discover a flaw in the purest

diamond. And in her profession Carla Moll was no gem!
Since his arrival, the woman had served him one failure after
the other. Fresh answers. Incorrigible lethargy. Absent-mind-
edness. Surreptitious flirtation (something he hated). On top
of that, ingratitude all along the line. Ingratitude for his efforts
to activate her talents. Ingratitude for his many attentions;
the fine dinner at the restaurant, his visit of condolence on
his free day, a day on which he could have done many better
things. All pearls before the swine. She had said so herself.
She was not stupid. She was degenerate. More so every day.
No energy, no powers of concentration, nothing but vanity
and arrogance. He had not forgiven her for her indifference
in the restaurant. Unfortunately he bore grudges. What was
he supposed to be anyway? A saint? Godamnit! He was an
editor-in-chief, waiting for Fräulein Moll. In the restaurant
she had devoured Señor Sánchez with her eyes. Then he had
followed her to the telephone. Ribbeck was positive that they
knew each other. When she had come back to the table, she
had been white as a sheet. But that may have been the result
of the message about her mother. She couldn't possibly have
been a good daughter. Had probably neglected the old woman.
And who looked after Fräulein Moll? Ribbeck had the answer
ready: she looked after herself!

There she was at last. Breathless. The raindrops dripped
from her coat onto Ribbeck's fine carpet. Fräulein Moll's
excuses cried out to heaven! The car had broken down. No
possibility of getting it fixed on Friday. No taxis in the rain.
She had walked. Ribbeck asked if her telephone had broken
down too. She probably hadn't thought of anything as practical as phoning. Or leaving the house earlier. Never heard
of getting up half an hour earlier . . . Oh, the hell with it!

"I don't want to hear any more. I was patient with you,
Fräulein Moll, because you were sick and have suffered a
great loss recently. But now I'm telling you, if you come late
once more, once more, I say, and then bore me to death with
idiotic excuses, we'll have come to a parting of the ways. Is
that clear?"

"I said I was sorry." She turned to go.

"Just a minute, Fräulein Moll. Your interview with Señor Sánchez has been cancelled."

"Are you sending someone else?"

"Señor Sánchez flew to London this morning."

Carla Moll stared at Ribbeck. For a moment she was speechless. Sánchez had gone to see the lady doctor in London, no doubt about that. Then she shrugged. "So what! These South Americans are unreliable. A lot of meaningless small talk."

"You think so?" Ribbeck was drinking his coffee standing. For the first time he didn't offer her a cup. She had never seen him so angry. Then he was talking to Frau Hannemann. "I'll be free in three minutes. Please ask Fräulein Doktor Wirth to wait."

Was this her successor? Carla held her breath. Was Ribbeck serious at last.

"I have arranged something on television for you, Fräulein Moll. Your reports on South America . . . if you ask me, a lot of meaningless small talk . . . You are to interview foreign visitors to West Berlin in an hour of your own. Every ten days. If you can manage to be punctual."

"I never did anything like that. What sort of questions do you ask?"

"That evolves out of the conversation itself."

"Thank you very much for getting the spot for me, Dr. Ribbeck. I'm broke. And I think I'll enjoy this."

"That's a relief! I am increasingly convinced that the mass media, like television, is the right place for you. It gives you a chance to try out a new hairdo every time and doesn't demand much serious thinking."

"You'll laugh, but sometimes I do think."

Ribbeck wasn't looking at her. Then he said in a strange tone of finality, "I had big plans for you, Fräulein Moll. Because you really can write. But you are so satisfied with the mediocre. You'll go on walking the path of least resistance, and that doesn't interest me very much."

"I do my best."

"Yes. So practice your platitudes on television. And do

your routine work here in the office as long as I have work for you to do."

"Why are you so angry with me? Because you overestimated me? What do you want from me anyway?"

"Nothing more, Fräulein Moll. Only that you appear at the office punctually, and if you find that impossible, to let me know. That is all."

He opened the door to let her out. As she walked through the waiting room to her office, a young woman rose. Carla Moll heard Ribbeck say, "Welcome, Fräulein Doktor. Sit down, please. A cup of coffee? Sugar? Cream?"

Was this Ribbeck? So friendly and cheerful. Was Fräulein Doktor Wirth a rising star? Carla didn't know. All she knew was that somehow or other Ribbeck had written her off.

Annemarie was complaining about Ribbeck, as usual. "The other day I called him up and said, 'It's me.' And do you know what he said? He said, 'Who is me?'"

"He knows thousands of people."

"You shouldn't call him at the office," said Frau Hannemann. "Can't you grasp that? He's much too busy for private conversations."

"Nonsense! I'm very busy too, but for Ossie I always have time. I make a lot more money now than I did in your stable."

"What are you doing anyway at *Your Home—Your World*?"

"Don't turn up your nose at it, Moll. I give 'Advice and Consolation' as I always did. Ossie got me the job after I gave up the work at *Comet*."

*She* gave up, thought Carla Moll. Schmidt was a riot! Still Carla didn't feel like laughing. Had Ribbeck got her the job on television to get rid of her? A parallel case?

"What's the new one going to do at your place?" Annemarie Schmidt asked.

"Your work," said Frau Hannemann, and ordered a third liqueur.

Carla suppressed the thought that Ribbeck was the only man she had ever known who had thought of her development intellectually. Sánchez had thought only of bed. She wondered how far he had gotten in the building of his cathedral in London. Was his "still water" more talkative in there? And did she, Carla Moll, have no bigger worries? Ribbeck was definitely planning her dismissal. He didn't want anything more from her, not even achievement. It gave her a curious feeling of guilt. As if he were her last chance.

"Wake up, Moll. What's the matter with you?"

Frau Hannemann found her changed. A real depression lurked behind her sauciness. It couldn't have anything to do with the office. To be in Ribbeck's bad books was something she was accustomed to. Grief for her mother? But she had always groaned when she had had to go to see her.

"Nothing," said Carla Moll. "And that's the truth." She couldn't explain to Hannemann that she felt guilty because she was as she was, and that since her mother's death she had been living in a no-man's land. "Who will look after you when I am gone?" Hannemann and the Sommers did what they could. They were good friends, but couldn't be expected to change their way of life for Carla Moll. There was nobody who could be expected to do that. And she was the last person to wear herself out for friends or acquaintances. You had to learn that in childhood.

"I didn't want to talk about it, but since we're sitting here together so pleasantly . . ." Annemarie cleared her throat. "Soon the birds will be singing it from the trees. I'm getting married again."

"For the third time?" Hannemann's eyebrows went up. "Have you considered it carefully, Schmidt?"

"Don't come to us later for advice and consolation," said Carla Moll.

"Don't worry, Moll. I'm not going to be a soccer widow. On Sundays he stays home."

"Who is the fortunate man?" Hannemann's tone was sour. "What does Ribbeck have to say about it?"

"He is the fortunate man. He slapped my face the other day, but made up for it with this gold bracelet. Doesn't look like much, but it's real gold. Ossie is satirical by nature, but he's a good man."

"You mean sadistic, Schmidt," said Carla Moll. "Ever heard of the Marquis de Sade?"

"But of course! Who was he by the way?"

"Ossie," said Fräulein Moll. "Congratulations, Schmidt."

Frau Hannemann was speechless, unusual for her. Schmidt was six years older than Ribbeck, divorced twice, had high blood pressure and no breeding whatsoever. Was it unbelievable? Of course it was believable. Men!

Ribbeck put down his bow. "You are a wonderful accompanist, Fräulein Wirth. But that's enough for today. I mustn't abuse your generosity."

Susanne Wirth laughed. "But I enjoy it! You play very well."

"If I had more time to practice, my playing might improve. But I'm still reorganizing things at the office." He thought of Carla Moll and his face darkened. Such a waste of talents he would have given his eye teeth to have. There was a profound need in him to admire someone who could do things that were beyond his capacities. He did not have the imagination of a novelist, but this woman, Moll . . .

Susanne Wirth was looking at him. There was a strange expression in her sharp, clever eyes. Sympathy for this difficult, self-assured man? That was absurd! Ribbeck was the last person likely to weep on her shoulder. Right now she was writing a series for Ribbeck on "The Miscarriages of Justice." It was going over extremely well; she showed the courts, with their enigmatic rites and ceremonies, as the modern substitute for the medieval morality plays. Ribbeck was already scouting around for a publisher of a hardcover edition. A great girl, Susanne Wirth. There were far too few of her kind around. Sensible, nice without being exciting, with a sense of duty and a shameless amount of know-how.

Dr. Wirth came to the office once a week and worked on a column, "The Law and You." She answered readers' questions on inheritance law, libel suits, rehabilitation problems after release from jail, residents' rights, insurance problems, and any other legal complications. Actually, what Dr. Wirth had to say was a lot more important than what the stars said. Ribbeck's employees knew it because he hadn't minced words about it. Doktor Wirth was his favorite. Even Frau Hannemann had to admit that.

Doktor Wirth found that Ribbeck didn't look well. His long, thin face seemed hollowed out. His sensitively flaring nostrils, his distrustful gaze—a mixture of greyhound and bloodhound—nervous, always on the go after something. But how he could play the violin! From what depths did these tones come? Clear, full of a swinging, disciplined passion, they rang out in the music room in his Grunewald villa. But as soon as he put the bow down he was again an enigma.

"Do you eat enough, Doktor Ribbeck?"

"I think so. I just don't show it. When can you and I dine together?"

She leafed through her date book. "How about next Tuesday?"

"I'll arrange it. Thank you very much," he said formally.

"I thank *you*." She rose. "By the way," she said, "I am going to be married soon."

"Congratulations! But I hope you'll continue to work for us."

"But of course. Fritz is a lawyer too. He is a close friend of Kurt Sommer's. We met Fräulein Moll there the other day."

"Berlin is a village, always was."

"I've read *Caracas for Beginners* in the meantime. Lotte Sommer gave it to me. You know, Carla Moll really can write."

"She gave it up long ago."

"What a pity!"

"Thank you again for the wonderful evening, Fräulein Wirth. May I hope that we will still play together after your marriage?"

"Fritz plays the cello. He's always wanted a trio."

"Wonderful!" said Ribbeck, almost warmly. "Please bring him along next Tuesday. It would be my pleasure. Are all jurists musical? Perhaps as compensation for the dryness of law?"

"I suppose music is always a compensation for something. One's career alone is never enough."

"Possibly. By the way, I've had some ideas for a book edition of 'Miscarriages of Justice.' From the perspective of the bystander. You can ignore them..."

"I'll do nothing of the sort. I'm *very* interested. Many thanks."

Ribbeck was silent for a moment. He didn't want thanks; all he wanted was the undivided attention of the person he was talking to. That gave him a modest feeling of happiness.

"Perhaps you could write about the origins of miscarriages of justice. And about trial by jury. If I were a jurist, I would cast as much light as possible on these problems."

"You mean that the lay man doesn't belong in the court-room?"

"I mean just that. I may be wrong, but I shall never reconcile myself to the fact that people who have to decide on life and death and long sentences are chosen by casting lots. Justice should have her blindfold removed!"

She looked at him, astonished. He was speaking as coolly and precisely as ever, but there were drops of sweat on his brow. Was he thinking of a specific case? Perhaps it was just intellectual passion that broke forth unexpectedly when he was faced with something that truly interested him. He seemed to be a lonely man, a lonely man who knew a lot of people.

"Let's imagine one of the jurors has a gallbladder problem and comes to court in pain. For that man every accused is guilty. Or a woman whose husband has recently left her, who has to decide on the guilt or innocence of an accused husband. She is biased, Fräulein Wirth. Not her fault, but she is biased. Her man left her, and here she has to judge a similar sinner. Make clear to your readers how very much private experiences and problems can influence a verdict. Not always, but certainly in more cases than we realize."

She was taking notes. Ribbeck watched her and thought: I'd like to see Carla Moll behaving like this. That she would listen, just once! He said slowly, "Trial by jury complicates the simplest facts. But no jurist will agree with me. Perhaps I am biased. My father was a public prosecutor."

"I know. I have read his writings."

"I haven't," Ribbeck said drily. "I draw the line when it comes to juristic German." He laughed, but behind his laughter a fine ear could have heard an old anger, perhaps even a little pain. It couldn't come from a harmonious parental home. But, thought Susanne Wirth, I don't think I would have liked to have him as a son...

She was trying to find the right words. How honest she was! Refreshing in his sphere of flatterers, strivers, and... Annemarie Schmidt.

"I mean," she said, with an enchanting smile, "you seem to have a passion for dissecting and recognition. You should read your father's works. You have it from him."

He laughed again. "Come on," he said. "The wine is waiting. Three cheers for 'The Miscarriages of Justice.' Yes, these cerebral dramas with a deadly outcome were not for me. My father was disappointed. I'm afraid a son's main role is to disappoint his father. Your father probably adored you. Daughters are better off." His eyes were restless, wintery. Susanne thought: he should marry. He needs a home. Ribbeck said softly that nobody really knew anybody else. Then he cleared his throat, embarrassed, and offered her some more wine.

"Thank you, Herr Ribbeck, but not another glass. I'm driving."

"I would have liked to drive you home, but I am expecting a visitor."

"It was a wonderful afternoon."

"Until next time, Fräulein Wirth. Yes, a week from Tuesday. My best to your fiancé." He spoke mechanically, like a stranger on a station platform, his expression lifeless. He didn't seem to be looking forward to his visitor.

He went back to the music room and finished the bottle of Mosel. He waited. Another hour. Too long for doing nothing, too short to plan anything. He turned off the ceiling light.

* * *

If Ribbeck had been able to, he would have reorganized time. But an hour had sixty dragging minutes, every minute had sixty treacherous seconds. He drank his wine, waited for his visitor and stared unblinkingly at the only oil painting in the living room: his mother, who had died in childbirth, his birth, in 1934. He had grown up in Grandmother Ribbeck's house. His father, a young, talented lawyer, hadn't minced words against the illegalities of Nazi law and as a consequence had spent some time in a concentration camp, after which he had lived in the family home on the Havel River, a bitter man. There had always been plenty of money in the house, but no contentment and little joy. And then the war had come. For Ribbeck's father, the war and imprisonment had been a change. And afterward had come the triumphant ascendency of the few rejected but courageous jurists in a divided Berlin. The Allies didn't like old Ribbeck either, but they trusted him. Public prosecutor Ribbeck—everybody knew who that was! A man always in the service of justice, but one who never forgave or forgot. Until his death he worked fanatically for the extermination of any remaining Nazis in law or life. To be sure, justice was entirely on his side, but he lacked a deeper understanding of human frailty.

As a schoolboy, Oscar Ribbeck had admired his father, or rather his father's legend, which acted as a bracer for the entire family. Alexander Ribbeck, political martyr. He was an honest man, but he lived in darkness. Prosecutor Ribbeck was unpopular. He laid low every victim under his jurisdiction, that was his job. However, prosecution became a passion with him.

At home he was taciturn. His family read about him and his achievements in the papers. His son respected him highly. He was even proud of his famous father, but one couldn't love Alexander Ribbeck any more than one could love the angel with the flaming sword. And the boy, who had matured early, needed warmth. That was not forthcoming in the Ribbeck household. There one lived cerebrally or vegetated like the aunts and cousins. All the men were brilliant in one way or another.

For Oscar things were difficult because he began to re-
semble his father more and more, not only in appearance but
also in personality: an intolerant moralist, suspicious, resentful, autocratic, and in constant need sexually. Like his
father he had a hearty sex drive, but couldn't stand the conversation of his ladies. It was a dilemma. Women to whom
he was attracted sexually, bored him intellectually. He was
really a man for men, but he had few male friends. In one
respect he was very different from his father; he had never
hunted down criminals. When he had stopped the series about
former Nazis "Where are they now? What are they doing
today?" he did it as a mature man. But still it was a protest
against his father. He could remember his conversation with
Fräulein Moll on the subject word for word. He should have
fired her then and there. But he had liked her writing style,
and her hair.

The estrangement between father and son became acute
when Oscar wanted to study philosophy and journalism. The
Ribbecks had been jurists for generations. Goddamned stu-
pidity of the boy! With the fine brain he'd inherited from his
father. Oscar's mother had possessed little of all this, but as
a woman she had been so right for him. Alexander Ribbeck
had never gotten over her death. When he needed sex, he
paid for it. It had never occurred to him to marry again. On
weekends he left the family house on the Havel. "Don't ask
so many questions, Oscar. Your father is going to visit friends.
He works hard all week so that you can have a happy life,"
said Grandmother Ribbeck. Oscar reddened with indignation.
He didn't have a happy life! He couldn't even invite any of
his schoolmates over because his father had meetings there
or was writing commentaries, and the house had to be quiet;
and because Grandmother invited her own friends, and they
didn't want any hungry, noisy little boys around. As a result,
Oscar was lonely. He met other boys only over sports, but
there was no opportunity for conversation then. He was good
at sports, but he didn't enjoy them. He wanted to take violin
lessons, but his father considered this superfluous. He should

enter the Rowing Club. Prosecutor Ribbeck was utterly unmusical.

Oscar told his grandmother that all this business about his happy life was a damned lie! He told it straight to her smooth, unpowdered Prussian face. He was trembling all over. He was only thirteen. But he said it and stoically accepted the slap in the face he got.

One evening he ran away. His father found him in the night, half frozen, on the banks of the Havel. In spite of Grandmother's plea, he had not notified the police. He would find his son himself. He carried the boy back to the house in his arms and wouldn't let his mother say a word. She was so astonished that she obeyed him. When Alexander Ribbeck came to see his son later, he was in bed, drinking hot milk. He didn't apologize for his behavior. "Why did you run away?" No reply. "Well, how long do I have to wait for an answer?" The boy heroically fought back childish tears. "Don't do it again," said his father in a gentler tone. "You're a bright boy, and a thing like that is stupid." He cleared his throat. "On Monday you can start violin lessons, but if your school work suffers because of it, you can forget it." "Thank you." Oscar's voice was hoarse. Old Ribbeck looked down at his son's blond head and fleetingly stroked his hair. A little boy like that needed a mother, goddamnit!

It was the first time his father had ever behaved like that with him. Oscar's heart flew out to him. But then everyday life started again and prosecutor Ribbeck was his old grim self. He never stroked Oscar's hair again. The boy sometimes wondered how mothers behaved to their sons. All his school friends had mothers, and they seemed desirable things to have. Slowly he came to the conclusion that mothers always loved their sons, but fathers did so only if their sons came up to their expectations.

At the age of twenty-five he became engaged for the first time. He had had enough of whores. He longed for a home of his own and a family. Marion was frail, pale, and shy. She came from a good, fairly poor, civil servant family. That was all right. She was a Madonna, and no sensible man could

expect a bank account from a Madonna. Besides, Ribbeck
had inherited his mother's considerable fortune. He called his
bride *ma petite vièrge*. She smiled and said nothing. She was
very reserved, and he found that attractive. It was also something new for him. He didn't realize for a long time that his
Madonna was a lesbian. She wanted a provider for herself
and her girlfriend. With Ribbeck she'd hit the jackpot. A
good family, a journalist with the best prospects, and he had
money. But Ribbeck became increasingly mystified by his
fiancée's behavior. Something was definitely wrong.. His experience told him that. But when Marion, shortly before the
wedding, actually shrank from him in obvious revulsion, he
saw the light. Even then he knew how to hide his suspicion
and bade her an exceptionally friendly farewell. On the next
day he followed her cautiously, like a hunter stalking his prey.
He saw the house of her friend in Zehlendorf, saw her get
into a car arm in arm with the woman, and knew, after one
look at Marion's excited little face, where he stood. During
their brief parting scene his little virgin became so insulting
that he struck her. That was ten years ago.

He didn't want to think of his second fiancée, but she had
not been a lesbian. Here too his mistrust had saved him from
a catastrophic marriage. Of course he had no intention of
marrying Annemarie Schmidt. He had heard in the office,
through Herr Bräutigam, that she was spreading rumors to
the effect. He had laughed so loudly that Herr Bräutigam had
stared at him, flabbergasted. No, that was not on his program.
Schmidt's wishful thinking didn't interest him, but he had
been mistrustful for some time now. He would have to give
it some thought.

He looked at his watch. Where was his visitor? There he
was! Ribbeck jumped up. An insignificant-looking man entered the room. The conversation lasted five minutes. The
visitor spoke and Ribbeck listened without interrupting. Then
he said, "So, until tomorrow, at five o'clock."

# 23

# Five O'Clock
# in the Afternoon

When Naomi Cooper wakes up she downs a good swig of whiskey. Then she breaks out in a sweat, reddens like a rose, and wishes it would get dark again! In November, night falls early, but not early enough for Naomi. Right now the morning sun streams into the room and Naomi draws the curtains fast. She turns on the desk lamp and writes a letter to Maudie Cooper in Paris, her only friend. In the letter she accuses Elliot Cooper of various crimes: of mental cruelty, of an uncontrollable attachment to his mother, of neglecting his faithful wife, and of treacherous silences. After a careful reading of her accusations, Naomi tears up the letter. Meanwhile it has become five o'clock in the afternoon because Naomi writes her letters in installments. In between she goes for walks, or visits Tante Ernchen or waits in vain for Sánchez, who had promised to go for a walk with her, or she converses with her penguin, August. In the afternoon her thoughts become as tangled as the woolen threads in the needlepoint she wants to give Tante Ernchen for Christmas. Baron von Strelitz doesn't want any presents. All he wants is to be left alone. That he can have. Naomi hides in her room. She'll write the letter to Maudie tomorrow morning. Should she fly to Paris to see her? Tante Ernchen says, "Pull yourself together, Naomi! It's simply dreadful! *Do* something!" She sounds like Elliot, and Naomi runs away.

One day at five o'clock in the afternoon she does something so dreadful that Ellen Driscoll leaves her practice in London and flies to the Strelitzes in Berlin. Whereupon Sánchez flies back to Caracas. He dreams of Ellen because man cannot live by oil and iron alone. He has to be patient with Ellen. He must wait for her promised visit to Caracas. Once he has her settled in the Villa Acacia, he will teach her how to dream. He intends to marry her.

Maud Cooper (Paris) to Elliot Cooper (Chicago)

late November, 1970

Dear Elliot,

Why haven't you answered my last letters? I began to wonder if you were ill, but your mother wrote that you were fine. You never get sick, unlike your wife. I take it Naomi is still your wife until this idiotic divorce goes through.

It's five o'clock in the afternoon, my time to write letters. In the morning we tear around in museums and churches and there always seems to be something to do in the evenings. Friend Betty sees to that. Do you remember Betty Chesser? In the days of her youth she wanted to marry you, but I talked her out of it.

I must say I am homesick for Chicago, but daren't tell Betty. She behaves as if she couldn't live without Paris. I'm sure the French are people just like everybody else, but you can't tell her that. And I don't think much of their famous food or their old buildings or their appalling plumbing!

But I'm sure none of this interests you. And I've really only been rambling on because I have something to tell you and I don't know how. This morning I received a letter from a London doctor: Dr. Ellen Driscoll. She flew to Berlin because Naomi tried to commit suicide at her uncle's house, a Baron von Strelitz. Dr. Driscoll found my Paris address in Naomi's address book. Naomi is out of danger now, but she has had a rough time. Dr. Driscoll writes that while Naomi was in a coma she called constantly for you. I thought you should know.

Love,
Maudie

Ribbeck had enjoyed the morning staff meeting. He had succeeded in squashing every argument and objection to his proposals smoothly, politely, and in his usual deadly fashion. "Ladies and gentlemen . . . You accuse me of thinking I know everything. I am not that presumptuous. Did you say something, Fräulein Moll? I only correct things when I am absolutely sure I am right." He smiled sarcastically. It was 9:30 A.M., and at five o'clock he would let himself into the apartment in Steglitz which he kept for Annemarie. She'd get the surprise of her life. The detective he had hired had observed that her lover visited her every Tuesday and Friday at six o'clock in his, Ribbeck's, love nest. Ribbeck had it all planned. At five o'clock he would wipe up the floor with Annemarie Schmidt. At six o'clock he would take on her lover. One after the other. Quietly. Annemarie would be seeking comfort with her aunt in Neukölln or she would have jumped into the Teltow Canal. No. Too fat for that. Fat rises. At any rate, things would be lively. What on earth made Annemarie think that he would spend only his weekends in an apartment he was paying for? A shameless and stupid woman. Had she taken a lover after Ribbeck had given her hell because of the rumors she had spread around that he intended to marry her? Before he'd marry Annemarie Schmidt he would have to be insane, senile, or deaf. He looked at his watch. He could still read a few pages of Descartes. "I doubt, therefore I think; I think therefore I am." Descartes had the effect of a tranquilizer on him. He only realized through this experience with Annemarie what happened when an intellectual let himself be ruled by sex. A blessing, actually, that he wouldn't have to listen to her babbling anymore.

On his way to Lichterfelde, Ribbeck went over all Anne-marie's shortcomings again to reassure himself that he wouldn't have any regrets. She was monotonous in bed. She was a glutton. She constantly expected jewelry and other material displays of affection. She had a grating voice and horrendous table manners. He had cured her of the worst, but she was by no means ready for a restaurant appropriate to someone like Carla Moll. He didn't want to see her eat lobster . . .

She hadn't always been a bore in bed. At first she had stimulated passion—the usual act. Or had she felt passion and he had killed it in her? Ribbeck frowned.

He would be very calm with Annemarie. Melodramatics were not for him. He was the accuser—logical, ice-cold, ironical, like Public Prosecutor Ribbeck. At this moment he bore a striking resemblance to his father. His lukewarm war with the accused, Schmidt, was over at last. This stupid woman had assumed she must be intimate with him, just because he slept with her over the weekends. She wanted to meet his friends! She called him at the office, although he had strictly forbidden her to do so. She drank coffee with his enemies. Besides, she snored. Why had he ever been attracted to her? But she had always been willing when he had wanted it. No complaints on that score. Had she worked off the apartment and his presents? This Brundhilde with the high blood pressure who received strange men in *his* love nest? He must not think about it. He had to concentrate on the road. He had almost cast a glance at the shop windows to get an idea of what he could give her for Christmas.

Ribbeck sat at the steering wheel, rigid as a statue. He drove slowly, as if he wanted to put off the moment of reck-oning as long as possible. He hated scenes. Of course she would be loud. The sweat under her arms would ruin her dress. When she was excited, her armpits sweated, in spite of all the deodorants she used. At times the smell excited him; incomprehensible since he was so fastidious. But it was more understandable than he liked to admit. His nursemaid had given off the same, acrid, animal odor. It had annoyed his grandmother, and she had often mentioned it, but his father had said, "Leave her alone. She's good to the poor child." They didn't let her go until he had started school.

He arrived, finally, and walked slowly up the stairs to the second floor. The apartment was in a renovated villa. Respectable people lived on the ground and first floor—downstairs a retired music director who liked to recall only pleasant things, and on the first floor a young couple who were still forging their memories. Ribbeck stood between both generations.

Should he knock on the bedroom door? Or did she receive the fellow in the living room? Would she call out, "Come in!"? Would she be dressed, half-dressed, or naked? While taking off her clothes, the disadvantages of her figure were obvious, but once she was naked, she became powerful. Her Rubens figure had its own, mysterious charm—damnit all! Sex was a grim business. It had been grim when most aspects of it had been forbidden. But today . . . One of *Comet*'s feature articles was entitled "The Indulgent Society." Unfortunately he didn't belong to this society. That was the trouble.

He was still standing in front of the door to the apartment, suppressing a nervous cough. It was ridiculous to be nervous, he told himself. It was his apartment door, his apartment, his whore! Everything here belonged to him . . . Nothing here belonged to him.

He closed the door behind him silently. He wanted to surprise her playing the pop music she usually played when she wasn't expecting him. He grasped his cane firmly, as if intending to beat her with it. His father had held his cane like that; Ribbeck had forgotten this. But Prosecutor Ribbeck had never beaten anyone with his cane; he had done his thrashing in a more subtle fashion.

Ribbeck walked into the apartment. There was no strange overcoat on the rack. Of course not. She didn't expect the fellow for another hour. It was very quiet. Was she asleep? Perhaps resting for the erotic encounter that lay ahead? After all, until four P.M. she gave "Advice and Consolation" in her new paper. That had to be tiring when one had nothing to say.

He tore open the bedroom door. The bed was empty. He cried out in his most threatening tone, "Where are you?" He wasn't worried, he'd find her. He ran into the living room, the small dining room, the bathroom, the kitchen. She must have seen his car from the window. He ran out into the hall and looked all around him crazily. Had she hidden in the attic? Had she hanged herself up there? He went back into the apartment. He had to think, coolly, calmly, collectedly. Then he saw the letter. It stood on the coffee table like a photograph, leaning against an old brass candlestick. A Ribbeck family heirloom.

The letter, addressed to him in Annemarie's big, shaky handwriting had been staring him in the face all the time. He picked it up. It was heavy. He sat down on the arm of a chair, wiped the sweat off his brow, and began to read. He took off his glasses, wiped them clumsily, like a pedantic old man, put them on again and closed his eyes for a moment. Then he shook himself. You couldn't read a letter with your eyes closed.

The pages were numbered with big, impressive numbers. As usual he counted them. He hated to be interrupted in the continuity of any reading matter by finding page six where page three should have been. Then he read.

By the time he had finished reading, it had grown dark. He turned on the light. He stuck the letter in his breast pocket; he would have to burn it when he got home. Nobody should read it. He took his old raincoat out of the closet in the foyer. It was pouring outside. He turned out the light and walked into the bedroom. It had been his intention to leave the snake pit as quickly as possible, so why was he . . . The bedroom was the emptiest room. A tall thin man, his features distorted, was walking toward him, his reflection in the mirror, his hair flopping across his forehead. He brushed it back, repulsed. His eyes were slightly bloodshot. What had she written? "Nobody could love you. You must know that. You exploit people, that's why you are exploited."

The dumb creature had married a traveling salesman the night before. She had had no idea that Ribbeck was having her watched. "When you come to the apartment this Saturday, I will have left long before. Arthur doesn't earn very much, but he is a human being, flesh and blood. I'll be working too. I never want to see you again. I'm taking the linen with me. I believe you gave it to me. And the new pots and pans. Moll won't cook for you. I told her that you were going to marry me, just to see her face. A snake in the grass, if I ever saw one! My Arthur has known me longer than you have, but first his wife had to die. I did try, Oscar. I wanted to be more than a piece of merchandise for you. That's what the girls in the office said I was behind my back. Somebody told me. *You never loved me*. Never. Not even when I spoke softly or wore dresses that you liked because they weren't showy, or when I tried not to disturb you, or listened to classical music with you without falling asleep. I did try, believe it or not. I'm taking the bedside lamps with me too because you didn't like them, although they have such pretty pink shades. I bought them, and whatever I bought you classified as junk. My Arthur is not as clever or dignified or witty as you, but he listens when I talk. You never did, Oscar. I am not going to thank you for what you did for me. I worked hard for it. When I looked at your respectable, ice-cold face, I sometimes felt wretched. I closed my eyes in bed. How could I possibly love you, or even like you? I'm taking the coffee cups with me. They're a little nicked, and you didn't want to drink from them. You're too elegant for that! My Arthur will drink from them. So will Tante Machowski. I'm taking the coffee pot too, because it matches the cups. I'm sure you won't object..." And on and on like that.

An artificial red rose lay in a corner of one cupboard. Ribbeck hated artificial flowers. When had she worn it? When Arthur visited her on Tuesdays and Fridays? He had probably liked it. Ribbeck took the flower out of the empty cupboard and crushed it under his foot. Then he stepped in front of the mirror and looked at himself again, this time with intense interest. Annemarie was right. Who could possibly love him?

His house in Grunewald was dark. Bender, his chauffeur, was on vacation, and his housekeeper went home to her husband and children when she had finished working for him. She got her husband's supper, put the children to bed, and left her husband alone happily with his beer, newspaper, and television. One day she had told Ribbeck about her daily routine. What a life! he had thought. Not very amusing or varied, but after all, a life. They expected her every evening at six o'clock, and greeted her joyfully. She had admitted it herself, a little embarrassed. "The children just can't wait till Mommy comes home, Herr Doktor. They're all over me like little monkeys." Of course children couldn't wait until Mommy came home. At age three, Ribbeck had waited in vain.

It was evening, and Ribbeck had no intention of wasting it. He could play the violin. That reminded him that Anne-marie had taken the record player with her, too. Because the record player went with the records, and he didn't like pop music. Thoughtful of her! He didn't touch his cold supper, although his housekeeper had prepared his favorite dishes: cold chicken and deviled eggs. He took off his wet clothes in his somber bedroom, took a hot shower, and put on a dark suit. Like his father, he always remained fully dressed until he went to bed. The Ribbecks didn't go in for robes. They didn't want to get that intimate, not even with themselves.

He burned Fräulein Schmidt's letter in an ashtray and began to work on some manuscripts. He worked doggedly for two hours. At last he felt hungry and ate everything. It tasted good. Perhaps he was repulsive after all, and his classical education, his music, his private collection of paintings and rare stones, were only a veneer of culture covering his sex drive and his sporadic brutality. He had been cruel to Fräulein Schmidt—often, in fact. And her big, fat childlike tears had bored him excruciatingly. His father had also treated boring people badly, but he had never slapped nor beaten anyone. Oscar had done that, as a schoolboy. He had studied boxing and had been able to use it to work off a lot of his pugnaciousness. From now on he would avoid women, above all Fräulein Moll. Perhaps Schmidt was right and she, Carla

Moll, was after him. If she were, she'd have to get up a lot earlier!

Just then her televised interview with the South American painter began. Ribbeck stared at her. She was changed. She was wearing a dark suit with a turtleneck pullover and . . . it was the way she'd done her hair. It was parted in the middle and gathered together in a knot at the nape of her neck. She looked as if she'd gone to school in a nunnery! She looked enchanting! It would have been hard to find a more exciting mixture of innocence and Berlin irony. The painter from Uruguay seemed to feel the same way. He was devouring her with his eyes and showering her with compliments. Her Spanish was excellent. Ribbeck hadn't known she could speak Spanish that well. The painter of course invited her to come to Montevideo.

Ribbeck smiled grimly. This was her specialty: maximum effect with minimum work. Suddenly he saw her again on that Saturday afternoon in her apartment, the door to her bedroom half open and the disgusting disorder on her vanity table—open cream jars, bottles with no caps—a slovenly person. He paid her too much. He had had an urge to walk into the bedroom and straighten out the mess of expensive cosmetics. But she had misunderstood him. He stared at her on the screen and abruptly turned the program off. His little convent pupil would certainly have dinner with the painter from Montevideo after the program, and she would arrive at the office late again tomorrow. This time he'd throw her out. Yet she had a good background. Her father had been a university professor and a prisoner of war in Russia. Years after his return to West Berlin, he had suddenly about-faced and moved to East Berlin. He had been shot on his flight back to West Berlin two years later. A Don Quixote of his day. Carla Moll probably had her unpredictable behavior from him. Her mother had been a Mark Brandenburg aristocrat, like Ribbeck's grandmother. Frau Moll had certainly put the lids on all her cream jars and closed all her bottles. But she had brought her daughter up badly. Perhaps she had been unmanageable. She should have been punished physically.

He, Ribbeck, would have seen to that if he had been her father. But when she was born, he had been six years old. He shook himself. He must not imagine embracing Carla Moll or beating her. He must have lost his composure completely, in the course of which he had almost forgotten Annemarie Schmidt.

He took out his rock collection. For him the stones had mysterious power. It could have been the mathematical precision of the crystals. Principles of order delighted him. Looking at his unfeeling stones, Ribbeck relaxed. He went to bed feeling calm, and in his dreams solved one or two mathematical equations.

He is changed, thought Pilar Álvarez. At last she again drank coffee with Sánchez after work. He was as friendly and brotherly as ever, but she could sense a strange tension in him, as she could sense everything that went on inside him. She loved him—silently and hopelessly. All she wanted was to sit with him on the terrace of the Villa Acacia at five o'clock in the afternoon, forever and ever, and feast her eyes on him without his noticing it; to listen to him and advise him when he asked for advice. In the many years that lay behind them this had happened occasionally, and had always made her happy. At moments like that she knew Sánchez needed her. After his return from Berlin she had had the feeling that he would never need her again. She sat there like a statue in black. Sánchez had told her practically nothing about Berlin. She had never been to Germany. Sánchez evidently found it tiring to talk about people and conditions about which she knew nothing. The only Berliner she knew was the journalist Moll, and she had been more than enough.

"We are going to have a visitor," he said.

"I hope not Señorita Moll."

He looked at her in such astonishment that she was embarrassed. No, he had invited a lady doctor from London, and she would be coming in March ... Before the rainy season? "Yes," said Sánchez, "before the rainy season. March

and April are cold and raw in London. I froze there in November."

This was the first Pilar had heard of his being in London.
She drew her thick eyebrows together, which gave her an
expression of gloomy dissatisfaction Sánchez hated. "What's
wrong?" he asked, irritated.

"I didn't know you were in London."

"Well now you know."

"Now I know."

"It was the best thing that ever happened to me."

"You always say one shouldn't be impulsive."

"I have given it a great deal of consideration."

"Are you going to marry her, Carlos?"

"If she'll have me."

Pilar's appearance worried Sánchez. The blood had drained
from her arrogant face. He should have prepared her for the
news. He had kept his feelings hidden. He could see Ellen's
mother-of-pearl skin, her clever eyes, her charm. He missed
her coolness, her gentle calm, her vitality, her compassion
for the sick children she nursed and comforted. That had been
the best thing of all, to see her in the children's clinic. Ellen
Driscoll had to have a fault, he had told himself so and
watched out for it. He hadn't discovered it. At most a little
too much practicality. A sober angel. She would give him
wonderful sons.

"I'll look for an apartment," said Pilar.

He awoke out of his daydream and asked her if she had
gone crazy.

"Three people under one roof is no good."

"We lived here with Teresa," he said.

"She didn't count."

Pilar was really being very nice about it, Sánchez thought,
and offered her a cigarette. She refused it. He shrugged and
lighted one for himself with the feeling that he was in trouble.
He hadn't expected this. Pilar would always look upon Ellen
as an intruder. He tried for a moment to imagine how Pilar
must be feeling. *Madre de Dios!* She lived only for him. For
her this was a disaster.

"You must always live here, Pilar." He rose. "This is your house, the house of your father. Here you are and here you stay."

"Never!"

"Then I'll go. I'll build another house."

He was capable of it. Pilar was trembling inside, but outwardly she maintained a stolid, uncompromising stance.

"First of all we stay here." Sánchez passed his hand gently across her coarse black hair. She turned her head aside brusquely. Carlos had assured her after Teresa's death that he would never marry again. She was sure that the London woman was much younger than he, and had no money, and . . . and . . . She walked into the house without another word. Sánchez stood as usual under his acacia tree and watched her go. He tried to be objective, but Pilar wearied him, and he longed for Ellen Driscoll. Pilar had talked a lot of nonsense, which was unusual for her. Still, he felt guilty. It saddened him, but it would not shake his determination. He hoped that the three of them would be able to live in the big old house, but without realizing it, in this one hour his relationship to Pilar had changed, imperceptibly, but definitely to Ellen's advantage. Perhaps love was cruel. Nothing in life remained the same; everything changed.

Pilar was his closest relative, the only family he had. Bonnhoff didn't count, just as Teresa hadn't counted. He had always been happy to know that Pilar Álvarez, his sister-in-law, was his confidante and partner in business. He didn't want to lose her. They had been young together. He had almost married her.

Was she truly related to him? For the first time he had the impression that families make it their business to obstruct the love life of their relatives, and if possible destroy it. Granted, they didn't do it consciously. Probably Pilar had been startled to see him in a state of enchantment. Sánchez could understand this. And yet the concept of a family seemed suddenly monstrous, ready at any moment to devour its children. To devour their happiness. To wind the chains of respectability, decorum, practicality, and solidarity around them, making it impossible for them to break away and move out into the world of Eros. What a yoke around one's neck! Pilar was suddenly a burden. Sánchez would soon escape to Margarita Island and choose the pearls for Ellen's necklace, one pearl at a time. He, the impatient one! And the mountains would watch him silently. Ellen and he would eat shellfish and rice with green peas, and he would show her his true home. He would be very patient. The eternal island sun would melt Ellen's coolness. He had not asked her to sleep with him. It had been very difficult, but he hadn't been sure; perhaps he would lose her if he expressed his passion too soon. She would share his bed for years to come. She would be his wife, the mother of the children he had longed for in vain from Teresa. Again he saw Ellen, surrounded by sick children, a little Madonna in the London fog. Suddenly he remembered that he had never called for Naomi Cooper to take her for a walk. He had forgotten everything because of Ellen.

The blossoms of the acacia were big, red drops of blood in the twilight. Soon night would fall. That happened quickly in Venezuela. The cool wind was refreshing. During the day the whole country lay like a dried out ox pelt in the blazing sun. He would begin to look around for some land, secretly, if Pilar didn't come to her senses. A simple house with a large garden. Ellen wouldn't like the ostentatious luxury of Caracas; she preferred unobtrusive beauty. For that London was the right place. It hurt him to realize this. But you couldn't weave lies around the truth. Anyway, Sánchez had never tried. Ellen wouldn't give up her profession. He could understand that in the case of a doctor of her reputation, although the Venezuelan wives liked to let their men work for them. He would build a children's clinic for Ellen. She had rebuilt the old Driscoll family home in Brighton for this purpose, partly with loans which she had gradually paid off. Sánchez had watched her radiant face as she had shown him the modest building. Dr. Ambrose Prior, a colleague and friend, ran it; she spent every weekend there. If the parents of the children could pay, they did;

but many enjoyed the sea air and the nourishing food for
nothing. Ellen chose the children from London's poor East
End. She was unsentimental in her choices. You couldn't
put anything over on her. She knew instinctively which
child was in greater need of care and better surroundings.
Sánchez was astounded. His first impression in Berlin had
not misled him. A sober angel.

Ellen was tireless, but he'd change that, cautiously, in
Caracas. The climate wasn't conducive to hard work anyway.
"I'll see what I can do, Carlos." Before he had flown back,
she had promised him to come. She had no idea of his plans
for marriage. He wasn't at all sure of himself, and he found
this almost unbearable. It had never happened to him before.
He was constantly racking his brains to figure out what he
could do for her. Yes, he could build a children's clinic for
her in Caracas. A good parcel of land. He wouldn't lose
money on it. The firm of Álvarez & Sánchez didn't approve
of losing money.

Suddenly he thought of his old friend in Puerto Ordaz. He
had written to Gilbert Preston from London, but received no
answer. Preston usually answered letters quickly. Sánchez had
seen the Prestons last at Cooper's dinner in Puerto Ayacucho.
Centuries ago. Yolanda had bored him; she talked too much.
Unlike Ellen, who perhaps spoke too little. For instance Sánchez would have liked to know how, born in Berlin, she had
ended up in London. Had she had English parents in Berlin?
She had arrived in Southampton as a child, shortly before the
war. That was all she had told him about it. She was extremely
reserved. Like him. But his discretion had a deeper reason.
Nobody should know about Bonnhoff's existence on the Orinoco. Not even Ellen. He was so happy. He felt the incom-
parable happiness that comes from anticipation.

The morning mail lay on his desk. He hadn't read it yet.
Among the letters, one from Puerto Ordaz. At last! It wasn't
from Gilbert Preston but from his brother, Vincent, the senator from Washington. Something had to be wrong. He had
never met Gilbert's brother.

Puerto Ordaz, December 1970

Dear Sir,

I do not know you, but my brother, Gilbert, has told me so much about you and your long friendship that I feel I must write to you at once. I arrived here yesterday evening from Washington to see what I could do to help my sister-in-law, Yolanda, and the children. Gilbert was kidnapped by guerrillas in the Orinoco area. I imagine that the kidnappers belong to one of the groups who have made it their aim to destroy the "Yanquis and imperialist exploiters of Venezuela." I find in my files frequent mention of a certain Camilo de Padilla, a former miner in Cerro Bolívar, who has threatened my brother and the mining company several times. The police are looking for him. We have not publicized any of this yet, in order to protect my brother, but we cannot keep silent any longer. Gilbert is lost. I brought the ransom money demanded, that is—I had it delivered to a harbor dive and watched from a distance to see that this really took place. Nothing has happened since then.

Yolanda tells me that another American, the business consultant Elliot Cooper, just managed to escape two attempts on his life here in the Orinoco area, and that Gilbert suspected this man, Padilla, at the time. I am told that Gilbert drank his coffee at the Hotel Amazonas carrying a loaded pistol. I begged him on his last visit to Washington to come home with his family. But he wanted to stay in Puerto Ordaz. And Yolanda, being Brazilian, didn't want to leave South America either. I imagine that was his main reason for staying. The poor woman is desperate. I'm afraid I'll have to return to Washington in a few days; my affairs can't be put off any longer. I wanted to take Yolanda and the children to her family in Río, but she refuses to leave Puerto Ordaz. She wants to wait here for Gilbert. I fear

she'll have to wait a long time. But we must not
give up hope. If my brother doesn't turn up soon,
though, there will be little chance that he will sur-
vive.

Could you come to Yolanda for a few days? She
needs help and sympathy. This is your country, señor.
Perhaps, with all your connections you could find
out where they have taken my brother. But I fear
that in a country this size that will hardly be possible.
I beg you—try to persuade Yolanda to go to her
family in Río. She should not stay in Puerto Ordaz
with the children, not the way things are. She has
always been stubborn, but Gilbert is her whole life.

Sincerely yours,

Vincent Preston

Sánchez went to find Pilar. She was sitting on the small
veranda. She didn't move. He said, "Preston is dead." He
knew it, although the papers only reported the news four days
later. He showed Pilar the letter and said he would have to
go to Yolanda in Puerto Ordaz. "One loses one friend after
the other, Pilar. Either they die of an illness or they find better
friends, or some fanatic finishes them off."

Pilar said nothing.

"Murderers are stupid," said Sánchez. "Some day their
enemies will die anyway, without their help. Why don't they
tell themselves that?"

Anna Carlovac, formerly Padilla, knew that she was the
lowliest of the low in Puerto Ordaz. She scrubbed floors in
a bordello and took breakfast to the exhausted prostitutes—
one of them actually looked like her former governess, Fräulein Steinmeister: German, blond, arrogant, and a trouble-
maker.

Five o'clock in the afternoon, when the bar was almost
empty, was Anna's big hour. She played cards with the bartender, a giant, good-natured mulatto, who was much nicer
than Padilla ever was, and for two glasses of schnapps, she

would read his palm. He listened fearfully. The white fortune-teller could have magical powers. Pedro brought her clients for a very small percentage: sailors, pimps, usurers, drug peddlers, thieves, barflies, even a future murderer. They, too, wanted to know what the next day would bring. Anna made a fair amount of money, but her position in this elegant "tourist home" was not worthy of her origin. In the evenings she brooded about Padilla, his new wife, and Mamacita. They should all burn in hell! "You will become a famous man, Pedro. With a stone house and many sons." "When?" asked the bartender, delighted. Anna wriggled out of that one subtly.

On this particular afternoon Anna Carlovac was reading the morning paper in the empty bar. She saw Preston's picture. Another Yanqui dead. Beside it a picture of Camilo, a high reward on his head. Anna was astounded that he could be worth so much. Anyone who saw Preston's presumed murderer should notify the police immediately. Anna smiled. The police could wait a long time, in spite of the reward. The police were not popular.

The bartender, Pedro, came in, dressed in a shirt and shorts, and took the paper away from Anna without saying a word. Then he disappeared again behind the beaded curtain. He looked a lot like Padilla, but Pedro couldn't hurt a mosquito. At least not in Anna's opinion. She turned around nervously. Was someone standing behind her? Padilla? He wouldn't dare. He couldn't expect any mercy from her. No help. Not a kind word. She wondered what Mamacita and Padilla's new wife were saying about this mess. Mamacita couldn't even read or write! In Yugoslavia they said the stupider the peasant the better his horse understands him. But this was Puerto Ordaz. Mamacita drove around in a motor car, and Anna, in spite of her fine German upbringing, cleaned the rooms of prostitutes.

The bar shook as if in an earthquake. Or did it only seem so to Anna? A huge shadow stood suddenly behind the beaded curtain. The dark head was threateningly like Padilla's. The curtain moved gently like palm leaves in the evening breeze. It was supposed to project an erotic illusion, but had failed to do so for years. The men came, paid for their pleasure, and left. Anna suppressed a scream because now the beaded curtain was moving wildly. Where was Pedro? She must be dreaming.

Padilla walked through the beaded curtain into the bar. He closed the shutters that opened out onto the street. Now the room was dark. There they were, two giant shadows and an abyss of fear and distrust between them. She wanted to ask him what he was doing here. She would call the police if he so much as touched her. Padilla, or his double, drew nearer. "Help me, Anna! You've got to help me!" At that moment Pedro walked into the bar and at once grasped what was going on. "It's you," he said softly.

"It is I," Padilla whispered softly.

Anna wanted to ask how the two happened to know each other, but couldn't utter a sound.

"I have lost my watch," said Padilla. "What is the time?"

"Five o'clock. Did anybody see you come in?"

"Only an old beggar at the front door. He has a guitar and a wooden leg."

"You can't stay here." Pedro closed the doors to the other rooms of the old house. There was a deadly silence in the bar. Then the three people heard a loud knocking. But it wasn't the police, it was the beggar who was beating with his wooden leg on the street outside. He had taken it off because of the heat and was pounding on the cobblestones in time with the daily street concert; the shrill cries of the street vendors, the sound of Coca-Cola bottles smashing, the tooting of cars, the hammering of the workshop, oaths and laughter from a thousand throats, a faraway rushing sound from the river delta where the Orinoco and the Caroní River joined forces. That's where they had found the naked, mutilated body of the Yanqui Gilbert Preston, in the underbrush along the banks of the river.

The beggar beat his wooden leg louder. Pedro listened. He understood the signal. Don Jaime must have seen something suspicious. "You can't stay here, *amigo*. They're on your heels," said Pedro. Anna looked from one to the other, speechless. Who was Pedro? She had known the gray-haired mulatto for years and hadn't known him! He was for Padilla. That meant he was against her! "Pedro! He is a murderer!" she screamed.

A huge hand shut her mouth. Padilla's hand. She struggled for breath. This was the end! The cards hadn't foretold this. But of course it wasn't the end. Pedro pushed the wall behind the bar to one side and opened a trapdoor to the cellar. He shoved Anna and Padilla down the stairs and followed them, after having pushed the wall with its shelves of bottles back into place. Now the police could come. The old Spanish house had a secret passage that led to the harbor.

Don Jaime strapped his wooden leg on again and played a song on his guitar. He had no troubles. The guerrillas took them off his hands. He was a free bird in the rain forests. Nobody paid any attention to beggars and invalids. Don Jaime was very pleased that he had finally reached the bottom rung of the ladder. Once upon a time he had had money and trouble. One dead man more or less? *No importa*.

# 24
# Fear

Anna Carlovac was afraid. Ever since Padilla's visit to the bar and his flight to Maracaibo, she trembled at every sound, every conversation, at every strange man entering the Casa Conchita. But above all she trembled when she read a magnificent future for Pedro every afternoon. Nothing had changed in the room with the ridiculous bead curtain. The beads were falling out like Anna's hair. Pedro drank sangría and smiled. The broader his smile, the more she feared him. She realized that she had never really known Pedro Angíl Eduardo Ríos at all. He was a terrorist, Padilla's comrade in arms. Anna knew more than was good for her. Since Padilla's flight, Pedro hadn't let her out of his sight. "Keep your mouth shut," he said threateningly. Once he had held his fat hand on her lips until she had scarcely been able to breathe.

On Saturday evening she always went to a nice restaurant in the harbor and ate paella. She hid her gray hair under a veil and wore a machine lace mantilla over her old dress. Señorita Carmen had given her the mantilla. She was young and pretty and wore real lace. She was popular in the Casa Conchita. She was so stupid that she thought her popularity would last, but Anna knew better ... The mantilla had two holes and most of the fringe was gone, but it had never occurred to Señorita Carmen to mend it. What a dreadful country, thought Anna. But she didn't mend the mantilla either.

The restaurant, La Terraza, was crowded with seamen, tourists, and natives. To her disgust Anna saw that two men were seated at "her" corner table. The man with his back turned to her was definitely a gentleman. His broad back in a silk shirt (no holes, no spots) looked familiar. She stood and stared. Not a table free anywhere. This was her day off. She was a lady in a mantilla, and that corner table was hers.

Just then the captain who had been sitting with the señor in the silk shirt got up, and Anna rushed over to the table. The señor rose politely. The captain was gone. The strange señor asked Anna to be seated. He was still drinking his rum. Anna sat down hesitantly. Suddenly she was afraid again. She brushed her hand nervously across her brow. The strange señor was staring at her. His dark, glittering eyes bored holes through her dim, pale blue ones. He knew this woman. He never forgot a face. As he was leaving the Hotel Amazonas in the gray light of dawn, this woman had been standing in front of Carla Moll's door. Hair in a gray and blond braid, naked flat feet, and a house coat held together with safety pins, like her poor black mantilla. An odor of vinegar, onions, and chili, the moldy smell of damp bushes, a general air of desolation . . . *Madre de Dios!* This Goya model was Padilla's wife! Where was Padilla? Sánchez had spent a week with Yolanda Preston in Puerto Ordaz, asked ship captains and air pilots for information, looked through police files, sought the help of influential friends—to no avail. Preston's murderer and his wife had disappeared from the face of the earth, and now, after fruitlessly questioning a captain he knew, Padilla's destroyed and confused wife was sitting in front of him. She was studying the menu. Her fingers, swollen and knobbed by arthritis, were trembling. Scrubbing floors didn't help them.

"I think we met once," Sánchez said, smiling, "in the Hotel Amazonas. No. Please sit down again. You're not bothering me at all." He didn't look as if he would ever let anybody bother him. "I can recommend the paella. It's the specialty of the house."

"I know, señor. I eat here every week."

"Alone?"

Anna's cigarette fell out of her hand. Preston's friend, who looked like a movie star, had to be working for the police. They were searching all the harbor dives, naturally. "Yes, señor," Anna said with a trace of irony. "Alone."

She had no intention of eating paella when someone else was paying for her dinner. Sánchez ordered broiled fish and the famous pineapple cantaloupe with liqueur and cream for dessert. The grated coconut lay on the tropical fruit like snow, reminding Anna of Belgrade in the winter, skating on the river, hot chocolate with cream in a Balkan café on the boulevard, gilt, plush, gypsy music. Belgrade—a lost paradise.

She spooned up the pineapple cream greedily. Sánchez had never seen anyone eat so fast and so fearfully as this señora. "In Belgrade I used to go to exhibitions and art galleries, señor, with my own governess. Today I think—what for?"

"How long have you been living in Venezuela?"

"Too long. Thank you for the meal, señor. When I came in and saw you I told myself: that man is a gentleman, and compassionate. He speaks very high-class Spanish. He knows how to behave to ladies in sackcloth and ashes."

Sánchez thought she's putting on an act for me. She knows where Padilla is.

"Money, pride, decorum—all down the drain, señor. Why are you looking at me like that? Do you like my mantilla? A few holes, but otherwise it's very pretty, isn't it?"

"What are you doing all alone in Puerto Ordaz, señora?"

"This and that. I camouflage myself. In Serbia they covered the frescoes and cloister walls with watercolors so that the Turks wouldn't destroy them. A useful lesson, don't you think?"

"I think you know where your husband is hiding. He is a threat. Gilbert Preston was only one of his imaginary enemies. You are an intelligent woman, señora. You think a lot, don't you?"

Anna didn't move. The señor's voice was honeyed. She was so hungry for friendliness and courtesy that she would have loved to do him a favor. A rope around her neck. She couldn't utter a sound.

"Please, my polite, sly señor, don't ask any more questions! We were chatting in a charming and civilized fashion. This happens to me only in my dreams, señor. It is better than all the art galleries. You are smiling?"

"Not at all."

"You just mentioned my husband, señor. Allow me to point out a mistake. I have no husband. Padilla left me for a younger woman."

"I'm sorry to hear that."

"No need to be sorry. I don't consort with murderers and rebels."

"Didn't I just say you are intelligent, señora?"

"And humorous. In my hotel I am recognized for my wit."

"Where do you live in Puerto Ordaz?"

"Sometimes here, sometimes there. I am greedy for change. Life becomes more and more boring as one grows older. Who looks at me to see whether I mend my mantilla or press my dress? No one! You won't escape this fate either, señor. Are you afraid of old age?"

"No. That would be senseless."

The señor's face clouded. He didn't seem to be very patient. Anna could hear the screeching of wild birds. She could smell the oil on Lake Maracaibo where the Yanquis were putting up oil rigs. That's where Padilla was working now. He was afraid of hell fire. That was his problem.

Sánchez leaned forward and asked, "Won't you tell me what's troubling you?"

"Nothing. I am in a very good, almost reckless mood. I would like another pineapple with rum, please."

Anna was enjoying the fruit and the señor's smiles; nonetheless she kept her mouth shut. For years she had dreamed of this chance for revenge.

"What happens to me if I betray Padilla?"

"To do your country a service is not betrayal."

"*Your* country, señor. I am an unwelcome guest here. But if I could be of service . . . I have to think it over. My brain has a few holes here and there . . . too many knocks on the head. I often lose the thread."

"All of us do that," said Sánchez.

Anna thought. If one can do a country a service one suddenly gains importance. To say nothing of reward money. She, degraded and downtrodden, would suddenly be somebody. A lady with a mantilla. Treated with respect wherever she went. There she is! She saved the country from the guerrillas! Anyway, from two: Padilla and Pedro. Joan of Arc in Puerto Ordaz. Anna's back itched, but she couldn't scratch herself. Not in front of the señor who was treating her with such respect. So tell him that Padilla is hiding in Maracaibo. Who are you anyway? The savior of Venezuela or a rabbit? Anna was trembling. Twenty years with Padilla, and so many insults. "To do your country a service is not betrayal, señora." Holy Mother of God, pray for us . . . sinners . . . now . . .

"I don't know where he is, señor."

"That's what I thought," Sánchez said amiably.

Sánchez let the night wind cool his temples. In the harbor ships come and go. Why wouldn't the woman speak out? She obviously loathed Padilla. He could come back and abuse her again. Or was she thinking of happier days? Or that today's fugitives might be tomorrow's conquerors?

Tomorrow Sánchez must return to Caracas. He must write to Cooper or go to see him in Chicago to reassure him about the safety of United States investments in Puerto Cabello. He has to think of Preston again. A friend. Soon he will be a grim anecdote in the political annals of the seventies. Preston, a wise Yanqui, but nonetheless unable to escape the violence of his adopted land. A land of power-mad presidents, cruel romanticists, unscrupulous demagogues, and known and unknown martyrs. For the last months of his life, in the year 1970, Preston had drunk the famous Venezuelan coffee with a loaded pistol in his pocket. It hadn't helped him.

Preston's senseless death pained and infuriated Sánchez,

but it was difficult, if not impossible, for him to find out anything about the guerrillas' hiding places. Padilla had been seen prowling around Preston's house the day before the kidnapping, but had disappeared since. Rebellions and acts of violence took place everywhere on this gigantic continent—in the petroleum areas, in both the festive old Spanish and Americanized cities, near Cerro Bolívar, on the vast llanos, in the silent forests and mountains, on the shores of the Orinoco and the Amazon. He sighed. He had been born in Venezuela, yet his knowledge of its landscape was fragmentary. Sánchez found Preston's death almost as incomprehensible as the two attempts on Elliot Cooper's life. The question was whether it was possible in these lawless times to plan and live sensibly at all! Had Preston been afraid in the end? Had he trembled when faced with eternity? Had he groaned, sworn, prayed? How would Bonnhoff die? . . . If he ever died.

"Preston is dead," Cooper told his mother over dinner.

"Gilbert or the senator?"

"My friend Gilbert in Puerto Ordaz. I don't know his brother."

"That's too bad. He's very influential." Mrs. Cooper cleared her throat. "How often do I have to tell you that I don't want to hear about sickness or death when I'm eating? You are becoming increasingly inconsiderate, Elliot. However, it doesn't surprise me. Gilbert was too fat."

"He was kidnapped and murdered by guerrillas."

"I don't believe it!"

Cooper repeated what he had just said, watching his mother steadily through his strong glasses. She was sitting rigidly upright. Not even a whirlwind could have disarranged her towering hair-do. Her bosom was a bastion. How had his father managed to storm it? Cooper pulled himself together. He was very tired. He had visited a prostitute the night before as he had in the days of his youth with Richard. The girl had had an agreeable, full-moon face. Only her dark eyes had had an unsure, fearful look. It had reminded him of Naomi.

When should he break the news to his mother? Now, or after dinner? Over coffee, or while they were playing cards in the library? He nearly always won. A cynical Frenchman had said that cuckolded husbands were lucky at cards. So were confused husbands.

He looked around the old accustomed dining room, everything highly polished, like his mother. Still he was sure that the dust of decades would billow out of the heavy drapes if he were to pound them with his fist. Decades? Centuries! But of course he didn't pound. He wasn't hysterical, like Naomi. He decided it would be best to tell his mother over coffee. He shouldn't spoil the rest of her meal.

"If he'd stayed home, this wouldn't have happened to Gilbert." Mrs. Cooper sounded annoyed. "That's what comes of racing around all over the world. Remember that, Elliot. You are all I have."

"Nowadays things like that happen everywhere. Even in Chicago. Nobody is safe from violence."

"I feel very safe in my own home," said Jane Cooper, sounding injured. "Do you want to ruin the little appetite I have left? By the way, when will your divorce be final?"

"Do you want to ruin the little appetite I have left, Mother? Naomi isn't in Berlin with her uncle anymore."

"Fortunately that no longer concerns us. Her attempted suicide was a dramatic act, like everything else she does."

"Naomi is in London, Mother."

"Did Baron von Strelitz throw her out?"

"She is recovering with a friend, a London doctor. Dr. Ellen Driscoll. She felt that Naomi needed a change of climate. She wrote me a very nice letter."

"Naomi doesn't write very nice letters."

"I mean Dr. Driscoll wrote to me. Of course, Naomi can't stay there forever."

"Don't you like the roast beef? You're fooling around with it as if it were leather. What's the matter with you, Elliot?"

"I'm tired."

"No wonder, when you stay out half the night."

"I think that's my business." His heart was beating wildly.

He had to tell her. No, not over the roast beef. A piece might get stuck in her throat. She'd turn blue, choke, jump up gasping, then fall like a felled tree and lie on the carpet, barring his way to freedom. But that's what she'd always done. He coughed. He felt guilty. He loved his mother in spite of the fact that she had driven Naomi out of the house.

The house was eerily empty and silent with Naomi and Maudie gone. Maudie hadn't written when she was coming home. Now his mother *really* had him. And soon that would be a thing of the past too. The old fear that he might displease his mother choked him. But there was no avoiding it, even if from now on she would be as displeased as she was in his worst dreams. The roast beef had been removed. Over the dessert: applesauce. Nothing much could happen over that.

"Mother, there's something I've got to tell you. But you must promise me not to get excited."

"I never get excited."

Since Cooper feared the worst, he smiled radiantly. "I'm glad to hear that," he said, and added, against his conviction, "I know how sensible you are." Pause. His mother didn't speak or move. Feeling extremely uncomfortable, Cooper mumbled, "A few years from now I'll be fifty."

Mrs. Cooper, sounding unfriendly, said, "I'm over seventy, and there's nothing much I can do about that. Do get to the point, Elliot."

"I shall get to the point," said Elliot, as smoothly as if he were addressing a group of industrialists. "I intend to move out."

"You're joking!"

"I've bought a house, not far from here. It's being renovated. It will be finished in three months."

"And I knew nothing about all this?"

"You do now. I didn't want to bother you with details. I decided to do this quite suddenly." Since his mother seemed frozen in a stony silence, he said hurriedly, "I hope you'll like the place. You must visit us often."

Mrs. Cooper chose to ignore this embarrassing invitation. She asked sharply who had helped Cooper to get the house, and when he mentioned Maudie, her lips tightened. "Maudie?" Her voice was shrill. "That snake in the grass whom I brought up like my own daughter! I suggest you back out of the deal, or you can consider it a capital investment. You'll find plenty of people who want to rent. I'll find a reliable agent for you through Roger Brown."

Now Cooper was silent, and his mother began to feel uncomfortable. For the first time she felt his determination, and that it conflicted with hers. "Be sensible, Elliot. You can't live anywhere as comfortably as at home. You always said so yourself. Why do you need a house of your own?"

"For my wife and me."

"Then I'd advise that you get along with your divorce. I take it you intend to marry Roger Brown's youngest sister."

"I'm married to Naomi, Mother. I have instructed Roger to stop divorce proceedings. Naomi can't live like this and neither can I."

There. It was out. And the strange part of it was that at that moment, with his mother glaring at him, he could feel his responsibility to Naomi, and that he wanted to bear it. In her delirium, after her suicide attempt, she had called out to him. Maudie had written to him about it, and Maudie was not the one to embellish or exaggerate. "I hope you understand, Mother. You are so sensible."

His mother seemed to have turned to stone. But she was not going to fall down on the carpet like a felled tree. She was stronger than the mightiest oak and her strength was deeply rooted in her silence, the silence of revulsion. Cooper wiped his glasses. He couldn't sit with this stony figure forever. He rose abruptly and said, "I intend to fly to London and see what I can do for Naomi."

The furious way she looked at him was more powerful than words. She was pale under her make-up. But a few minutes later she had recovered her poise. With a pained smile, still without saying a word, she walked ahead of him into the library where their coffee was served. They drank it every evening out of costly English china. She looked up at the ceiling and said, "Naomi broke two of these cups. She was always so careless." It sounded like an obituary. As if the conversation had never taken place. I have to leave her her pretenses, thought Cooper, feeling sorry for her, the sorrow one feels for children or confused teenagers. He was the adult, the head of the family who had to help the helpless and comfort those in need of comfort. She was taking it bravely and somehow she would master the situation in her own way.

"I'll write to you as soon as I get to London, Mother."

"That would be nice," she said, steadily.

She would get along very well without him. She knew it and Cooper knew it. She had cast-iron vitality, many interests, and friends. Naomi needed him. He had no idea what was awaiting him in London. He didn't even know whether Naomi, when she was conscious, would want to see him. He had written to Ellen Driscoll that he was coming. Would anybody be at the airport? Naomi? He expected nothing and no one. Without any expectations he could not be disappointed.

# 25

# Cooper Balances the Books

Cooper had never been in London and didn't know that the city paid no attention either to natives or to strangers. Londoners took everything in stride. Strawberries in Kent at the end of October astonished no one. Garbage collection and electricity strikes were met with the same equanimity. They wouldn't last forever, and after all, one was used to occasional black-outs from the war.

Cooper looked around Heathrow airport. Naomi, of course, hadn't come to meet him. There was no message for him at the arrivals desk. Normally a guest of international corporations, Cooper was used to a reception committee, but even though now his business was private, Ellen Driscoll, with whom Naomi was living, knew when he was arriving. After her nice letter to Chicago he had expected more.

He began to feel sorry that he had come. Was Naomi really worth the break in his relationship with his mother? Who did he think he was, anyway—Don Quixote? He had always prided himself on his healthy common sense. Cooper had flown to London the morning after his talk with his mother. A good thing, because he couldn't have stood her stony smile a moment longer. And it might have shaken him in his decision.

All around him Londoners were conversing in the Queen's English. They joked and laughed and he didn't know why.

He was sure of only one thing: this trip to London was a mistake. He couldn't find a taxi. If he ever got one he would drive straight to his hotel, eat, drink fruit juice, write to his mother, and think. Only then would he call Dr. Ellen Driscoll. In spite of her nice letter, he wasn't eager to meet her anymore or to consult her about Naomi. He felt uncomfortable and unwanted.

On the drive to the hotel, Cooper could have taken his first look at London, but he was too exhausted, so he closed his eyes. A business associate had recommended a hotel in Dover Street, an English family hotel with comfortable chairs, chintz, plain food, and quiet rooms, around the corner from Piccadilly. There he recovered his composure. A whole network of social groups and individuals with their own formula for living were spread out before him in London, but he was to experience scarcely any of this. The Londoner kept his private life to himself. Thus Cooper never found out that Ellen Driscoll and Naomi had met the Venezuelan, Carlos Sánchez, in Berlin. Ellen was a Londoner and Naomi had almost forgotten the incident.

He tried for a third time to reach Ellen Driscoll. The telephone rang, but nobody answered. Had something gone wrong? Had Naomi gone back to Berlin without informing her hostess, as she had left the sanatorium and flown to Berlin practically under Richard Cooper's nose? It would be like her.

Cooper slammed the receiver down on the hook. It was humiliating; he was trying to get through to these women simply to save face. He would not be shamed in front of his mother! Cooper got the impression that he counted for very little with Dr. Driscoll and Naomi, and this didn't raise his spirits. But he was angriest of all with Maudie, who had talked him into buying the house because Naomi had allegedly cried out for him in her semi-conscious state. He had been so hungry for a little sympathy and attention that he had taken off for London like a crazy fool! But this was the last time anyone was going to make an ass of him! Mother had been right after all. He tried the phone again. At last! A stern voice answered, "Dr. Driscoll's office." Odd, but after Ellen Driscoll's letter, he had expected her voice to be soft and feminine. He asked hesitantly whether he was speaking to Dr. Driscoll.

"Claxton speaking."

He learned that Mrs. Claxton was Ellen Driscoll's housekeeper, that Dr. Driscoll was taking a child to the children's hospital for a heart operation, and that it was the doctor's orders that Miss Naomi should receive no strangers.

"This is Mr. Cooper from Chicago. I have just arrived."

Silence. Cooper asked irritably if Mrs. Claxton was still on the wire. Of course she was still on the wire, but she had nothing to say, so she said nothing. Cooper, getting angrier all the time, explained that he was Naomi's husband, not exactly a stranger. "Oh," said Mrs. Claxton. She didn't sound pleased, and after a pause, "Well, yes . . ."

Cooper said he would be in Chelsea in an hour. He had to speak to his wife, and Dr. Driscoll knew all about it.

"Miss Naomi sleeps in the afternoon, sir, and must not be disturbed."

Cooper repeated, in a tone he reserved for irksome subordinates, that he would be there in an hour.

Mrs. Claxton called Ellen at the hospital. Mr. Cooper was determined to burst in on them in an hour. "Dear, dear," said Ellen Driscoll. "I must have got his arrival date mixed up with a patient's. I hope you were very nice to him, Claxton. Americans are so sensitive."

"I did my best," said Mrs. Claxton.


"We're getting a visitor." Mrs. Claxton spoke loudly, as if addressing a meeting, but at least Naomi opened her eyes.

"I'll stay upstairs, and I don't want tea."

"I'm afraid not, Miss Naomi. The visitor is for you."

"I'm afraid you're wrong, Mrs. Claxton. I never get visitors."

"Perhaps it isn't a visitor."

"And what do you mean by that, dear?"

"I've been told that it's your husband who's coming."

"Cooper? You mean Elliot?"

"The name is Cooper, and he'll be here in an hour. No, no, child, not your robe. Miss Ellen doesn't approve of that for tea. Nor does Dr. Prior." In Naomi's silence she could sense protest. Naomi didn't want to see Cooper. He could discuss the divorce with her lawyer. She would have to drink if he came. And when he left.

"Nonsense, Miss Naomi. You get along very well without the stuff. So . . . the gray suit. That looks nice and proper. Hold your head still. We'll make a nice neat knot . . ."

"You and your knots! Do you think it's easy to be married to the same man all the time?"

"Well now, we can't have fun all the time." Mrs. Claxton hadn't had an easy time of it with Mr. Claxton, deceased. But you got used to everything in this life. Keep a stiff upper lip, that was all!

Naomi sat on the little stool in front of the vanity table and stared at Mrs. Claxton. It was very quiet in the room with its mahogany furniture and chintz. Here old Mrs. Driscoll had died, and here sat this poor little lost bird from Berlin, gazing at her unflinchingly. Mrs. Claxton felt a rough kind of pity for Naomi, if only because she hadn't been born in England. A handicap. But nothing you could do about that. "You're telling me the truth, aren't you?" said Naomi. "I mean, Ambrose never tells me anything." Dr. Ambrose Prior was Ellen's partner and had cured Naomi of her alcoholism at the children's hospital in Brighton. Without psychiatry. With nothing but friendliness and firmness. Mrs. Claxton felt uneasy. She didn't like the way the child was looking at her. Miss Naomi wasn't going to do anything foolish again, as she had done at her uncle's house in Berlin? The poor little thing. Hard to believe that she was over forty. Helpless as a baby . . .

"What's to become of me, Mrs. Claxton?"

"And now what do you mean by that?"

"You know very well. When . . . when Ellen gets married, then . . . then I can't stay here anymore. Where am I to go?"

"We'll cross that bridge when we come to it." Mrs. Clax-

ton's tone was sharp. What really was to become of Miss
Naomi? Unfortunately she was not in a position to give this
Mr. Cooper a piece of her mind. It was a shame to abandon
a helpless woman like this. Divorce! Very convenient for the
man. Mrs. Claxton didn't think very much of the opposite
sex, with the exception of Dr. Ambrose Prior. At least not
the men who ran around King's Road today with long hair,
smoking "joints," and could be knocked over in a windstorm.
Mrs. Claxton was astonished when Mr. Cooper turned up in
Chelsea an hour later with a normal haircut, no cigarettes,
and an unobtrusively tailored suit of first-rate material. Television had taught her that all Americans were hippies.

Mrs. Claxton had not stocked up on candles and matches
for nothing. Just as Cooper's taxi stopped in front of the
beautiful, old Regency house, the lights went out.

Ellen Driscoll. She greeted Cooper with great charm because she was a charmer. Only she was too busy. She told
Cooper without any embarrassment that she got all dates and
birthdays mixed up. In this respect she was impossible, and
Cooper should please forgive her. She was friendly, unaf-
fected, and so relaxed that Cooper's heart went out to her.
But then the bell rang, and Mrs. Claxton called Ellen into
her office. So she also practiced at home. Did Cooper only
imagine that she hurried out of the room as if relieved? *And
he was left alone with Naomi.*

At first he had scarcely recognized her. The candles flickered in front of his tired eyes, and anyway he had expected
to see her in the slovenly robe he knew only too well, her
hair a mess—as she had looked at home. He had never seen
her in this gray suit that went well with her silver-blond hair.

"Is that a London suit?"

"Yes."

"Tailor-made?"

"Yes."

"How old are you, Naomi?"

"What are you doing here?"

For a moment Cooper was stunned. The blood rushed to

his head. What had he expected? Romance with candlelight? "They fell into each other's arms and wept tears of pain and joy..." Who had said that so ironically? Oh yes. Miss Moll. In the Hotel Amazonas. Centuries ago. But now he was sitting with Naomi in London. Served him right! Europeans liked to make fun of American sentimentality. It had always vexed Cooper, but what had driven him here to Chelsea if not sentimentality? Naomi seemed neither to need nor want him. He was used to the latter, but she had always needed him. He would have liked to know what she would do without his checks. Everything was so different from what he had imagined in Chicago. But Naomi had cried out for him. Dr. Driscoll must have heard wrong. Now, fully conscious, Naomi was monosyllabic and as hostile as ever.

"Can't you imagine why I am here, Naomi?"

"No."

"Then I'll tell you. I wanted to know how things stood with you regarding our divorce. You say one thing one day and something else the next."

"Leave me alone. I have a headache."

"But we've got to talk it over."

"Do you have a cold, Elliot? You sound hoarse."

"Of course I have a cold! In London you're in a draft all the time." Cooper got up and shut a window firmly. "Listen, Naomi, this is probably the last time we shall see each other. What do you intend to do after the divorce?"

"I don't know. Perhaps something with children."

"You're joking."

"No. That's what I'll do. If they want me."

"Who is 'they'? Ellen or your Ambrose."

"Unfortunately he's not mine," said Naomi.

"He's lucky," Cooper said drily.

"You're right. He's too good for me."

Naomi was two people. Now she was a disarmed child. Decades ago Cooper had wanted to protect this child. Her intellectual age lay anywhere between six and sixty. She wanted to work in a children's home if *they* wanted her? "That I would like to see," said Cooper.

"You're not being very helpful. I always thought: Elliot is not my ideal, but at least he's helpful." Then she fell silent, brooding, and Cooper found he had nothing to say. She looked young, thin, and lost in the candlelight. "Shall I tell you what your problem is, Naomi?"

"If it makes you happy."

"It doesn't make me happy," Cooper said angrily. "I am a man like any other man and I would like to have a reasonable wife. And a happy marriage. I suppose you find that very funny. You dream of failure the way others dream of success. And that is your problem."

"And you dream of success."

"Naturally."

"You are obsessed by success, like all Americans, and that is *your* problem." She jumped up to light another candle. "This is my duty. I mean, the candles. Ellen gives me a lot of little things to do so that I won't feel superfluous." The last words were whispered. Cooper would have liked to take her in his arms and console her, but that was a step he couldn't take.

"Everybody here likes you," he said, feeling ill at ease.

"That won't last long."

"And what do you mean by that?"

"Ellen is going to be married soon. She has put up the house for sale. Her friend doesn't want to wait any longer."

"I can't blame him. She is an enchanting young woman—clever, tactful, and with a lot of vitality."

"The exact opposite from me," Naomi said with her disarming, melancholy frankness. Cooper said she was very nice when she made the effort. And he was so pleased to see that she had finally stopped drinking. That was the first step . . .

"Where to? Do stop preaching, Elliot. Do you think I'm going to drink milk now with you and your mother?"

"I forbid you to speak about my mother!"

"Oh dear God in heaven! I forgot long ago that she existed. Give her my best regards."

Cooper rose to his feet so abruptly that his chair toppled over. In the dim light he couldn't see that Naomi was trembling. He had been prepared for a dialogue, but Naomi could drive a saint to distraction. He walked up to her slowly, and she stepped back. "If you lay a hand on me, I'll scream the house down!"

"Don't worry," he said. "I wouldn't touch you if you were the last woman on earth!"

"Here I am," said Ellen as she entered the room. "Please excuse me, Mr. Cooper. I was looking forward to talking to you so much, but I seem to be constantly on the go. Please sit down again. We'll be eating in half an hour. Dr. Prior may be joining us."

"Thank you very much, Dr. Driscoll, but I regret I won't be able to stay for dinner. I have an important engagement in my hotel."

"Too bad. Then may I expect you on Saturday for lunch? I would like to get to know you better. Do come."

She was so friendly that Cooper managed to calm down. He decided to accept the invitation, but only because Ellen Driscoll was apparently the only person in London who wanted to get to know him better, but he felt the need to justify himself in front of her. He had to explain to the doctor why he now intended to rid himself of Naomi. He couldn't see any other solution although he had flown to London counting on a reconciliation. He had even bought a house and shocked his mother. His instincts told him that Ellen Driscoll would beg him to think it over once more. It was a husband's duty to stand by his wife through sickness and health—Cooper had read the message on Ellen's face, and during tea she had talked about various "cases" where the husband had behaved just like that. Very subtle for such a prudent angel. How had he happened to think of this characterization? Oh yes—at his dinner in the Hotel Amazonas, Sánchez had used the expression and regretted that such women didn't exist. Cooper's thoughts wandered back to his own dilemma.

All the women he had known in his life had robbed him of strength. Vampires! He was staring at an antique vase with a Greek motif. Bacchantes consuming the flesh and blood of animals. Ellen Driscoll noticed what he was looking at. Noth-

ing escaped her, which made Cooper feel uncomfortable.
"Ambrose's father brought that vase from Greece," she said.
"He was an archeologist." She put the flashlight, with which
she had lit up the vase for Cooper, back on a corner table.
"Ambrose says that the old Greeks with their bloodthirsty
myths weren't much better than Jack the Ripper, only they
had a stronger sense of beauty."

Ambrose says . . . Ambrose says . . . Dr. Prior was being
constantly quoted in this house without ever appearing. Cooper
could hear a clock ticking. How much time had he spent
here? Twenty minutes? Twenty hours? A lifetime! He suspected that Ellen Driscoll wanted to tell him something he
didn't know about Naomi. Nothing pleasant, he was sure of
that.

At that moment the lights went on again. Naomi's face
was white, shockingly thin and innocent, with its parted trembling lips. Only her eyes were old, snuffed out. A tired, matte
blue. A blue without hope. What had life done to her that in
her best years she looked so hollowed out? What had he done
to her? Or his mother? Nonsense! His mother had done her
best to cope with Naomi for years. And who had tortured
whom? Cooper brushed these morbid thoughts aside. It was
*all* Naomi's fault, whatever might now descend upon her. It
didn't hurt him anymore, but he felt sorry for her.

Ellen Driscoll was watching him sharply, like a doctor,
not like a friend. She said softly, "I'm afraid you're not
sleeping well. Do you have anything to take for it? If not I'll
give you some pills." Cooper said he slept very well, thank
you. "The house could burn down and he wouldn't wake up,"
said Naomi.

"Is that so?" Cooper's voice was so hoarse, he could only
whisper.

"London is tiring," said Ellen Driscoll. "Try gargling with
salt water, Mr. Cooper. Does it hurt you to swallow? Maybe
I should take a look at your throat."

"It's nerves, Dr. Driscoll. It happens to me sometimes
after long conferences. Yes, London is tiring."

Naomi was tiring. He knew it, and Ellen Driscoll knew

it. Cooper hadn't seen his wife for a long time and he had forgotten that Naomi was either silent or talked incessantly. But on his second visit, for lunch, Naomi scarcely spoke to him or Ellen. She looked steadily at a photograph of Dr. Prior on horseback. Since the picture stood on an end table, Naomi kept her eyes fixed on the table the whole time. Every now and then she told a short biographical anecdote about Prior. "Ambrose is happiest on his horse, or on his boat. He says on his boat he can't be reached, and that is bliss."

"He doesn't seem to be very sociable," said Cooper. Gradually he was becoming impatient.

Naomi must have sensed it because she said, "Ambrose says patience brings roses and results."

He might have been right, but Cooper didn't want to hear anything more about Ambrose Prior as long as he lived! Was Naomi in love with the doctor? He took a look at the photo on the end table. Dr. Prior looked cool and sensible. So did his horse.

"Eat your fish," said Ellen.

"I can't eat."

"You must force yourself. I keep reminding you of that."

"Ellen wants to keep me alive by force," Naomi explained. "What for? Homeless people are better off in their graves."

"Oh my God!" murmured Ellen.

"Does Naomi take anything to stimulate her appetite?" Cooper asked, just for something to say. He could sense tension between the two women. He said gently that Naomi would soon be skin and bones if she went on like this. Naomi asked the Ambrose photo whether Ambrose had heard that . . .

Ellen said quickly, "I've put her on a new regime. She's going to get something to stimulate her appetite. Are you taking the new medication, Naomi?"

"Leave me alone," said Naomi, obviously irritated.

"Behave yourself, Naomi," said Cooper. "You should be grateful to Dr. Driscoll."

"I know."

She sat there, shoulders hunched, and didn't move. Her delicate face was gray-white, like a wall that needed painting.

Only her upper lip was bright red. She had forgotten to put lipstick on her lower lip, or perhaps given up the effort before finishing it. Naomi crushed her napkin, straightened it out, and crushed it again. At home she had tied strings in knots and untied them, endlessly. It had made Jane Cooper very nervous. Yes, yes, Naomi had weird habits. Ellen chose to ignore the business with the napkin.

"You really eat too little, Naomi," said Cooper. "You've got to think of your health."

"For your sake? Don't let him fool you, Ellen. When nothing else works he tries sweet talk." She behaved as if Cooper wasn't present. "Just try living with his mother, Ellen, and see how you like it."

"You shouldn't say that," said Ellen.

"Let her talk." Cooper's tone was icy. "I've been listening to it for years."

"What do you think of that, Ambrose?" Naomi asked the photo. "In Chicago nobody ever asked my opinion. Imagine it! As if I had no right to an opinion. Am I an idiot? Or illiterate? My father wrote books. But in the United States it's a stigma to be a foreigner. Funny . . . because everybody is a foreigner there, except the Indians. Depends on when you got there. Anyway, in the Cooper house I was poor white trash. Only Maudie was nice to me. Be quiet, Ellen. You don't like me anymore, and I can understand that. Do you think I like you?" She pushed up her sleeves, and the two thick red scars became visible, right next to her arteries. "Well, in London I'm a troublesome foreigner too."

"Personal value has nothing to do with nationality," Ellen said, barely able to hide her displeasure.

"You mean the Strelitz family?"

"Yes. Them too."

"Oh, Ellen! Last night I dreamed I was back in Berlin." Suddenly Naomi's eyes sparkled. "The Wannsee was so calm, and I was pushing a baby carriage, white, with a light blue top. But no child in it, only a head of cabbage. Bonnhoff was walking beside me, laughing his head off, so I woke up. Do you remember, Ellen? Sturmbannführer Bonnhoff? He visited Papa in the Oranienburg camp, the pig! I wanted to find him in Venezuela. Bonn is still looking for him. But Elliot thinks I dreamed the man up. But I went to see him because of August."

"Wake up, Naomi," said Ellen. "You're in London. Your August too. Everything is all right."

"Nothing is all right," said Naomi.

This time Elliot said, "Oh, my God!"

Ellen rose and took Naomi by the arm. "Come. Claxton will take you to bed. You must rest."

"Claxton is fun," Naomi murmured. "I would like to laugh again." She walked up to Cooper and said, with obvious difficulty, "I'm sorry, Elliot, I truly am. The expensive trip and all that. You're so red. Do you have a fever? Ellen will give you something. I . . . I wanted to be nice to you, I really did. I guess I've forgotten how. Funny, that one can forget something like that. Don't let it bother you . . ."

After Naomi had left, there was silence. Ellen didn't want to talk about Naomi; she had to have Cooper in a better mood before telling him what had to be told. Cooper could sense the tension in her, and her silence made him suspicious. He didn't like her nearly as much as on their first meeting, when he had found her warm and consoling. Now she seemed cold and frighteningly serious. Also evasive.

"Is there something about Naomi I should know?"

"Unfortunately I don't know what you know, Mr. Cooper. The long separation . . . only letters between South America and Berlin . . . Naomi is getting better, slowly but surely."

Cooper looked at Ellen critically, as if she had been a colleague at the conference table. It wasn't true that Naomi was better.

"Your letter to Chicago gave me the impression that my wife was well again."

"She is well. But we must count on little relapses. And she has just gone through a withdrawal cure. Possible neurotic upsets have to be taken into consideration. They'll come and go. Please don't get excited, Mr. Cooper. That doesn't do anybody any good and is bad for your circulation."

"I am not the least excited!" Cooper was furious. "I'm sorry to have to say this, but I find my wife's condition miserable."

"Dr. Prior has dismissed her, and he is a very conscientious doctor. That should suffice. *We* are satisfied with Naomi."

Cooper stared at the woman. She was smooth and cool as marble. He said slowly, "You can't be serious, Dr. Driscoll."

"I was speaking from a medical standpoint," Ellen said calmly, as she lit a cigarette. "My private impression of your wife, Mr. Cooper, has nothing to do with the medical picture."

"And what is your private impression?"

"Well, you must know your wife better than I do. I only met her shortly before her suicide attempt in Berlin. Baron von Strelitz and his sister are my dearest friends. It was for their sake that I took Naomi with me to London."

That was clearer than anything Ellen had told him until now. Naomi had to be a great burden, especially since the doctor was going to sell her house and be married soon.

"We have a club here," Ellen Driscoll was saying with a wan smile, "called the Club of Brilliant Failures. Only men. But Naomi would fit in well there. She told me that she would have studied philosophy if Hitler hadn't come to power."

"I know. I know everything about his period in her life."

"You do?"

"It's her favorite topic," Cooper said irritably.

"She has too much imagination," Ellen said. "People like that lose contact with reality. Don't look so desperate, Mr. Cooper. All Naomi needs now is a helping hand."

"I have done my best, and more. But Naomi's imagination goes far beyond what can be considered bearable. She must be put in an institution, before or after the divorce."

"I attribute this suggestion to the fact that you are upset, Mr. Cooper. Your hopes simply outstripped the facts. If all the people with anxieties and depression were to be institutionalized . . . There are other possibilities than London or an institution. I'm sure you realize that. We'll think about it together."

"She is mad, Dr. Driscoll! Did you hear her mention Sturmbannleiter..."

"Sturmbannführer," Ellen corrected him.

"A man called Bonnhoff. An absolute figment of her imagination. A phantom from her youth in Berlin. A nightmare figure of her sick mind."

"No, Mr. Cooper. The man exists and his name *is* Bonnhoff."

"I beg your pardon?"

"The Strelitz family knew him when all of them were young together. Shortly before the collapse of the Third Reich he fled to South America."

"And what... what has this man to do with my wife?"

"He tortured her father, a brilliant journalist, in the Oranienburg camp. And that was the last the world heard of Dr. Lothar Singer. Naomi was seventeen at the time. But didn't you just say you knew all about that?"

"Did you know the man?"

"I was five years old at the time." That was all she said. She had been six when they had brought her to London. Her father, a famous jurist, had struck an SA man, and been shot on the spot. Erna von Strelitz and a Berlin actor, who had called himself Engelbert Schmidt in the resistance movement, had brought her to England with the last children's transport before the Second World War. Ellen knew all about this period, the only thing she didn't know was that Sánchez was the son of Carl Friedrich Bonnhoff. This secret was buried with Werner and Erna von Strelitz. Ellen couldn't see any reason for telling her story to Elliot Cooper. Only Ambrose knew about it.

"Is this man still alive?" Cooper asked.

"Who knows? But the German authorities are still looking for him, presumably in Venezuela."

For the first time Cooper had some idea of what Naomi had suffered, and he could feel her dimmed eyes, overshadowed by ineradicable grief, looking at him through the wall.

"Dreadful things happen all the time," Ellen said somberly. "But one must shake off the past. It's more difficult for Naomi than for more robust people." Or for people who are loved, she thought. She had love. Naomi had had only Cooper and lost him.

"Perhaps you can see things differently now, Mr. Cooper."

The quiet statement startled him. Certainly he had been unjust to Naomi by considering her truth to be fiction or madness. The truth would have been unbearable even for someone who had always been secure. Only Maudie believed that Naomi had visited Bonnhoff. Was Maudie much cleverer than he. Not cleverer . . . kinder, rather? When it came to balancing the books, all the credit would be on Maudie's side.

"What should I do?" he asked. He couldn't pack Naomi in a trunk and ship her to Chicago. Dr. Driscoll had to realize that. Naomi had never been as hostile toward him as here in London. In the clinic, with the children and Dr. Prior, she seemed to have been happy. Yes, that would be the right thing.

"Dr. Prior seems to have had a good influence over Naomi," Cooper said hesitantly. "Couldn't she stay in Brighton until she is completely healed?"

"I'm afraid that's impossible."

Cooper said he would like to speak to Dr. Prior personally, to see him tomorrow or the next day. He realized he wasn't being very tactful, but he wasn't himself today.

If his request annoyed Ellen, she didn't show it. She said coolly, "Dr. Prior is in Canterbury, visiting an old friend. He is staying over the weekend, or longer. The Cathedral fascinates him."

"Isn't it possible for me to speak to Dr. Prior about my wife?"

Ellen looked so astonished that Cooper coughed, embarrassed. "I can't stop you from waiting for him," she said, "or going to Canterbury. The Cathedral is well worth a visit. But my colleague can't tell you anything different from what I have already told you. You'll just have to believe me, Mr. Cooper. Naomi can't go back to Brighton."

"Why not?"

"For various reasons." Ellen paused. "There's not much

point," she went on, "in talking about a matter that's closed. But if you insist..."

"Did Naomi do anything bad in Brighton?"

"If you mean did she set the house on fire or perpetrate any other act of violence, then I can reassure you—no. But you see there can be a certain unhealthy relationship between patient and doctor, an undesirable emotional involvement that damages the treatment and is embarrassing for the doctor. Naomi imagines that she is in love with Dr. Prior."

Oh, dear God! thought Cooper.

"In analytical medicine this is called 'transference.' It is really nothing out of the ordinary, but Naomi has such curious reactions that Dr. Prior brought her back here. I don't want to trouble you with details. Believe me, he went about this with his usual tact and humaneness. Moreover he wants to marry soon, and if for no other reason..."

"I understand."

Well, there was nothing to be done but take Naomi back to the Strelitz family in Berlin. They were her closest relatives. Ellen listened calmly to the suggestion, then she said that this wasn't possible either. Cooper managed to control the fury welling up in him. "You have done much for my wife," he said, "and nobody could be more grateful than I am. You must believe me. But don't you think Naomi should decide whether she wants to return to Berlin or not."

"She can't decide it."

"I don't understand." Cooper's voice was cold. "You just assured me that Naomi was healthy, and now you talk as if she weren't capable of making a decision. May I ask for an explanation?"

Now Ellen was looking at him with a certain compassion, which did not seem entirely medical. Cooper sensed that she knew something decisive and was about to reveal it to him.

"I had hoped that you would take Naomi back to Chicago with you," she said. "Then I wouldn't have to tell so many sad things. I haven't told Naomi yet. I didn't want to excite her unnecessarily, I mean concerning Berlin. I was going to write to her about it later."

"Has something happened in Berlin?"

"Two weeks ago her aunt died." Ellen said it calmly, but her lips were trembling. Tante Ernchen had been her friend, no—her mother. Ellen's mother had died in childbirth. Ellen herself hadn't yet quite grasped the fact that Erna von Strelitz wasn't waiting for her in Dahlem any more.

"But there's still the Baron," said Cooper. "Wasn't Naomi living with him anyway?"

"Yes. Werner von Strelitz is the salt of the earth, but he is not a patient man."

"Naomi will have to pull herself together."

"I'm afraid we're talking at cross-purposes, Mr. Cooper. The Baron is selling his house. He is going to move in with his daughter in Sweden. His only son was killed in the war. His wife died long ago. What else can he do?"

Ellen was silent. She had said all there was to say. Cooper rose and thanked her for her hospitality and patience. And he meant it. "So what do we do now?" he asked her.

"Perhaps we can persuade Naomi to go back with you."

"Perhaps," said Cooper. He felt very tired.


"Cooper speaking. May I speak to Dr. Driscoll?"

"The doctor isn't here."

"Good evening, Mrs. Claxton."

"Good evening, sir."

"When will Dr. Driscoll be back?"

"She has gone to the theater with Dr. Prior. Is it important? You can call Dr. Powell. His number is . . ."

"Thank you. This call is private."

"Oh."

"Is my wife at the theater too?"

"No."

"I would like to speak to her."

"She is asleep and must not be disturbed."

"Please wake her. I am flying back to Chicago tomorrow."

"Oh. Would you like supper?"

"Thank you. I have eaten."

"I'll prepare Miss Naomi for your visit."

"Is that necessary?"

"Well—yes, sir. Goodnight, sir."


Naomi received him in her faded housecoat. She looked more familiar than in the tailor-made suit. She had just washed her hair, and it gleamed silver-blond, like the wet feathers of a bird. Mrs. Claxton brought Cooper a glass of milk without saying a word.

Naomi was sober and pale. The sight of her face startled him. Her cheekbones were too prominent under her delicate, translucent skin. There were deep blue shadows under her eyes which Cooper hadn't noticed at lunch. Her eye were dimmer, too. Had she been crying? She tried to smile. The effort was heartbreaking, and Cooper actually did feel a stab in that region, although Naomi didn't deserve his pity.

Cooper cleared his throat. "I've thought a lot about you, Naomi, during these last days."

"Didn't you have anything better to do?"

"Apparently not." His tone was sharp. "I still feel a certain responsibility for you after all these years."

"Nice of you. But not necessary."

"I'll be the judge of that. Listen, Naomi, can't we talk like reasonable people for a change?"

"Of course we can. You're reasonable enough for both of us."

"What's going to become of you?"

"I don't know."

"But now you're going to have to look after yourself. Do you realize that?"

"What are you driving at, Elliot?"

"I want to know what's going to become of you." Cooper stuck stubbornly to his theme.

"Something will become of me. I'm not really interested."

"What are you going to live on?"

"Money is the least of my worries," said Naomi, with the ignorance of those who let others earn their money for them. "I don't want anything from you. Don't be afraid."

"I'm not afraid."

"Now you're angry again. Cheer up. I'm inheriting some money from my aunt."

"What aunt?"

"Erna von Strelitz died two weeks ago. I found a letter from my uncle in Ellen's desk."

"You shouldn't read other people's letters."

"She was *my* aunt. Ellen kept it from me."

"She probably didn't want to upset you. How do you know that you're going to inherit something?"

"Tante Ernchen told me. Ellen gets the old house in Dahlem and I get five thousand marks. I've never had that much money. Just imagine!"

Cooper said hesitantly that for a short time it would probably suffice.

"My August needs a little fur coat. He freezes so here."

"Stop that nonsense, Naomi! You only want to annoy me."

"For the last time. But as far as August is concerned, I know he's only a stuffed penguin, but he belonged to Grandfather Strelitz. That makes him a relic. Yes, yes," Naomi said bitterly, "if he had gold feathers and diamonds for eyes he'd be a collector's item in the United States. But you see, he comes from Mark Brandenburg, and they're not showy there. You should have seen grandfather's coat. His overseer had a better one. And August and I are shabby too."

Cooper said nothing. His mother wore mink. Naomi didn't have to wear this faded old housecoat and no makeup. And old slippers. He was still looking at her fine, ascetic face. She came from another world. She had a noble shabbiness.

"Why don't you say anything, Elliot? Are you angry with me?"

"No."

"I tried so often to please you, but I simply couldn't bring it off. I'm sorry. Are you glad to be rid of me at last?"

"We haven't reached that point yet."

"But we will soon. Aren't you the least bit sorry?"

"Oh, Naomi!" Cooper sighed. "You're such a child. When you want to be you can be charming and sensible, but you don't want to be. Why are you so different from other women?"

"Mrs. Claxton says I'm half-baked."

"You're alone too much. Why didn't you go to the theater with them?"

"Ellen forgot to get a ticket for me."

"One doesn't forget things like that!"

"Ellen does."

"How did she explain it?"

"In England people don't explain things. They let the facts speak for themselves. Ellen is much more English than Ambrose."

"Do you love Ambrose?"

"I don't know what love is. Ambrose is very friendly. And he listens. Just like Maudie. She is wonderful. I thought that perhaps she could help me."

"What could she do for you?"

"She knows such a lot of people. I'm such a recluse. That's what you always say. Perhaps she can get me a position as a babysitter."

"In Paris? Have you suggested it to her?"

"When you sound so unfriendly, I'm afraid again. I thought we were going to talk nicely and reasonably."

"That's what we're doing. So what do you expect Maudie to do?"

"Something in Chicago, of course, when she gets back. I could move in with her, but she doesn't want to leave your mother alone. Maudie is so considerate. All of you could learn from her. Especially Richard."

"We can discuss my family another time. Have you written to Maudie already?"

"I wanted to, but I had a headache. I'll write to her in a few days. But if I'd embarrass you in Chicago, I mean if I took a job as a babysitter . . . I mean . . ."

"Go on, Naomi."

"You wouldn't like that with all your connections and your millions and . . . and . . . your mother. But I was a servant in your house when I came to the States, so what's the difference?"

"That you're my wife—that's the difference," Cooper said grimly.

"Really, Elliot! You're funny. You want to get rid of me. I can understand that. You say I have to look after myself now, but when I tell you my plans, you're angry. Perhaps Chicago is the wrong place. I could try somewhere on the Mississippi. What would Roger Brown's sister say to that?"

"What has that dumb girl got to do with it?"

"You're going to marry her, aren't you? Perhaps I can be a babysitter for you then. Special price!"

"Stop all this idiotic nonsense!" Cooper was screaming as in the best days of their married life, and Naomi shrank away from him. But she said, trembling, "It's not nonsense. I've got to do something after the divorce. I know, Elliot. I'm no good. Nobody . . . nobody can use me . . ."

"Is that what you think?"

She closed her eyes, exhausted. Some of her hair had fallen across her face. He stroked it off her forehead. "Look at me, Naomi."

She opened her eyes wide when she heard the unusual gentleness in his voice. "Why do you think I came to London?"

There was an expression in his eyes she had never seen before, or perhaps only during the first weeks of their marriage. During the first weeks and months when they had been man and wife. When he had really saved her from the most unbearable situation. When he hadn't expected any gratitude, but *he* had been grateful. But oh, what had become of it!

He drew a photograph out of his pocket of a white house in a garden with old trees. The house was beautiful—not too big, not too small—and Naomi looked at it, astonished. "My house," he said. "I bought it through Maudie."

"But . . . but what will your mother say?"

"She knows about it. She'll get used to the idea that I want to live alone with my wife. The only question is: will you get used to the idea?"

Elliot couldn't possibly have asked that question! But he had. And now he was standing by the window wiping the sweat from his brow. Naomi stared at his back. It was incomprehensible! Elliot had come to her. And he had explained to his mother what *he* wanted. He wanted her, Naomi, who looked like nothing, could do nothing, didn't make anything of herself. Who had never been a success at anything, while success was so important to him.

Naomi walked up to him. She barely reached his shoulder. She stroked his arm shyly, the wonderful material that Mrs. Claxton had admired. "I can't agree to it," she whispered. "I've already ruined half your life, Elliot. You deserve something better. And . . . and . . ."

"And what else?"

"You know what. I'm a person who simply can't bear being pitied."

She couldn't go on, and there was a pause. Then he told her not to cry. It gave her a red nose, and he didn't like that. "It's going to be awful," he said, almost merrily, "but I don't seem to want anything better."

Cooper, balancing his accounts. Of course their temperaments would clash again, and there would be endless, futile discussions. Of course he would continue to pursue success and try to impress every pretty, amusing woman. And Naomi would continue to be a case in her own right. But it would all take place between them alone, and perhaps they would again discover what there was to love in each other. In his loneliness and bitterness, this was something he had forgotten. And gradually they had to learn to trust each other. Cooper would see the long, torturous period of their estrangement as something that had happened to another man. And perhaps it had . . .

"What shall I do?" Naomi asked. "All my stuff is in Berlin, and half of it I've lost or I don't know where it is."

He took her in his arms. He wanted her to let him love her, stay with him, and sometimes to laugh at him, as she had done during their earliest times together. That was what he wanted.

"What do you see in me, Elliot?"

"I don't know." And that was the truth. "And by the way, I'm going to—we're going to stay another week in London."

"I thought you were flying back to Chicago tomorrow?"

"I haven't paid for the ticket yet."

"You and your tricks!"

"Me and my tricks," Cooper said, pleased with himself. "Listen, Naomi, I haven't really seen anything yet. How about showing me London?"

# 26

# Calm Before the Storm

Elliot Cooper (Uruguay) to Carla Moll (West Berlin)

Montevideo, February 1971

Dear Miss Moll,

How are you? I've been meaning to write to you for some time, but so much important business came up in the last months. Did you receive my New Year's wishes? I almost came to Berlin in December, but ended up in London instead.

I hope you had a pleasant holiday. We celebrated ours with the family, and in January flew to Uruguay. I am happy to say that my wife is well again and is enjoying the sunshine, the beach, and the swimming in this charming little republic that they call the Riviera of South America. We are going to be here until the middle of May and then intend to vacation on the Atlantic coast, not far from the border of Brazil. The world famous fishing grounds in Uruguay tempt me. Do you remember the fisherman's paradise on the Orinoco? I persuaded you to go and see it with young Mr. Bendix. He is still in Venezuela and writes to me fairly regularly. My wife says that's German loyalty!

I often think of our little circle in the Hotel Amazonas. Do you remember Gilbert Preston, whom Señor Sánchez brought along to my farewell dinner? He was recently kidnapped by guerrillas in Puerto Ordaz and murdered. His wife has gone back to her family in Río, with the children. Señor Sánchez wrote me a very touching letter; Preston was one of his best friends. So you can see we are all in one way or another in touch with each other, and it would be nice to see you in Uruguay. Señor Sánchez is going to visit me in Chicago where we shall discuss further *rapprochements* between Venezuela and the United States. I am especially happy that he will be our first guest in our new house. My wife is looking forward to seeing him again too. She met him quite by chance in her aunt's house in Berlin. Small world!

The people here are so gentle and friendly. It does her good. Fortunately, she doesn't follow the political disturbances. I'm sure you read about them. The headlines of our times read more like obituaries every day. All we can do is hope that this phase of violence will soon give way to more peaceful development. No one wants to invest capital in troubled waters.

But enough of all this! My wife saw you on television, interviewing a painter from Montevideo—this was during her weeks in Berlin—and she would like very much to meet you. Perhaps a series on Uruguay would interest your paper? I would be happy to introduce you to government and business people. Give it some thought. I am sure your reports on life on the Orinoco were just as successful as *Caracas for Beginners*. When will the book appear?

To a meeting in Montevideo!

Sincerely yours,
Elliot Cooper

Best regards from
Naomi Cooper

Carla Moll:

I couldn't afford to waste Cooper's letter. Influential friends in foreign countries are worth their weight in gold. I was sure his letter would raise my shrinking credit with Ribbeck. Too bad that I couldn't cross out the bit about my successful series on the Orinoco, but Ribbeck reads everything anyway: what's crossed out, mirror writing, between the lines. Ribbeck will not be pleased to hear news of Sánchez. After all the señor refused to give *Comet* an interview in Berlin. Perhaps he was having a bit of fun at the time with Cooper's wife. I have the feeling she wants to meet me just about as much as vice versa. I have no luck with wives.

Over breakfast I was already looking forward to Ribbeck's expression. When he was annoyed, he reddened slightly—a negative sunrise so to speak. Ribbeck only talked with his new satellites: the jurist Wirth or Herr Bräutigam; if the coffee wasn't strong enough, with Frau Hannemann. I was never present. All I was there for was to translate the work of others into more stylish German. The others all write like Locker. Bräutigam would cover his "Thousand Words in Spanish" with his fat hand, as if he were afraid I was going to steal a dozen words. Idiot! He and Ribbeck conversed a lot in whispers. He couldn't forgive me my talk show with the painter from Montevideo, because Uruguay is *numero uno* on Ribbeck's list. At the last staff meeting he told us to get our own connections for the paper. After all, he couldn't do everything himself. Well, Moll would show him about making connections!

I was so punctual at the office, it startled me. Hannemann asked right away if I was feeling well. I asked her to tell Ribbeck I wanted to see him at once. He was in a conference, of course, and couldn't see me until three. Didn't seem to be exactly longing for me, and Hannemann agreed with me on that. Then she said, "Watch it! Things are popping."

"Again?"

"They never stop."

I asked Hannemann what our friend Bräutigam was constantly whispering about with Ribbeck. "When I walk by, they stop," she said. "Bräutigam was invited to dinner with Ribbeck the other night at his Grunewald villa. He asked me to phone and tell his wife. Big deal. Bräutigam was bursting at the seams with pride."

"If you happen to find out what's going on there, you'll tell me, won't you?"

"What I don't know doesn't bother me. Make a note of it, Moll. Comes under the heading of the art of living."

I got cold feet. Hannemann sensed or knew something that wasn't going to please me. Ribbeck had never invited me to his villa, and I wasn't under the impression that he was about to do so. I walked into my office and leafed through a report on Swedish socialism. Great for the Swedes, but these elegant homes for the aged in beautiful botanical surroundings didn't do me any good. To lift my morale I read Cooper's letter a second time. I crossed out the line about the Orinoco. I'd say that was a private affair. Could have been. I skimmed over Cooper's declaration that his wife would like to meet me. I thought she wanted to be alone with him.

When Ribbeck was finally free, my nerves were jangled. I could hear them! He knew that to be kept waiting finished me off. Herr Bräutigam left Ribbeck's office looking radiant. "Herr Doktor Ribbeck is free now, Fräulein Moll." Herr Bräutigam was a master at superfluous announcements.

If one hasn't seen a room for a long time, one expects changes, but Ribbeck's lair was unchanged; so was he. There were the sex games of Ribbeck's Indians, and he was the same old bastard. At best he seemed thinner, sterner, and more malicious, but that could have been an optical illusion.

"Is your report on Sweden ready to go to press?" If he had said hello or anything equivalent, it had escaped me. Of course by three o'clock he was a little shopworn, but at least he could have said that we hadn't seen each other in quite a while, and asked how I was. He was probably scared to death that he might be pleasant.

"I had to rewrite the article. It was too stilted."

"Herr Henker is extremely thorough. I hope you haven't

rewritten any facts. Why did you want to speak to me, Fräulein Moll?"

"I guess I wanted to see you again after such a long time."

"So you have seen me again," he said, in his nastiest tone. But I had Cooper's letter. Nervous or not, it was my turn at last. The international business consultant was apparently a prominent man in Latin America. Perhaps that was why everything he said in his letter about his work was so modest. He had to be top drawer if Sánchez visited him. And I was sure he had all the connections and influence Ribbeck could wish for. God bless Cooper! Ribbeck was standing at the window again.

"So what brings you to me, Fräulein Moll? Please make it short; I don't have much time."

He treated me like yesterday's newspaper in the wastepaper basket. He sat down behind his desk, coughed a little impatiently, and didn't offer me coffee. I handed him Cooper's letter. He wanted to know what it was, and I said it was a letter. Ribbeck's eyebrows went up over my fresh reply, which I felt I could risk with Cooper's backing. It gave him the appearance of a hostile, arrogant Brahmin. But he read my letter because he had to, and I saw—my heart beating fast— that he was making notes.

"This is very interesting, Fräulein Moll, and comes just at the right time." What more could I have asked for? Then Ribbeck asked what the crossed out part meant. "A private message. Mr. Cooper and I are good friends." Ribbeck digested the explanation, then he said, "A private message pertaining to the Orinoco and *Caracas for Beginners?* You must think I'm a novice, Fräulein Moll."

I reddened. I must have crossed the lines out too hastily. But Ribbeck was already miles ahead of me. He had made it clear that I couldn't put anything over on him, and that was that. Why the long pause when he didn't have much time? His silence was even more pregnant than usual. Odd. When would he finally say which plane I should take to Uruguay? I could feel the sweat breaking out on my forehead and upper lip. Ribbeck's second profession was sadism.

"An important letter, Fräulein Moll," he said finally. "Thank you for letting me see it." He handed the letter back to me and stood up abruptly. I rose too, and we stood facing each other like enemies.

"When may I fly to Montevideo? Of course I'll finish my work on the current article first. I suppose Herr Bräutigam can take my place while I'm gone."

"Herr Bräutigam has no time. What is it you wanted to know?"

"When I could fly to Montevideo." I stopped because my voice cracked like a record that is suddenly broken off in the middle.

"You're going to have to forget about that, Fräulein Moll."

It was pouring outside; there was a muted, thunderous rumble over the streets and office buildings. I was staring at Ribbeck, but it didn't seem to bother him. He turned away and walked back to the window. "Awful weather." I said nothing. He cleared his throat. Then he said, faster than he usually spoke, that he was truly sorry that I couldn't join the expedition. The high cost, etc. . . . What expedition? I couldn't utter a sound.

"The point is . . ." he began, and I had to admit that he had a point. It had been planned, conferred on, and organized for months. Ribbeck was sending a team to Uruguay, Paraguay, and Bolivia. Not to look for old Nazi war criminals, though. There was a possibility for such research in Bolivia, but the main purpose was to come up with local color. Like Wendt in the good old days, Ribbeck was sending out Locker, star photographer Hanns König (just returned or called back from Venezuela) and a journalist from *Comet* who was to edit Locker's notes and add his own impressions. Even before Ribbeck announced it, I knew that this literary nursemaid was going to be Bräutigam. Had Ribbeck been tutoring him in literary German?

I was not going to accept this defeat without a fight.

"You can't be serious, Herr Doktor Ribbeck."

"Unfortunately I don't have time for witticisms." Ribbeck shook his head sadly. "See things as they are, Fräulein Moll, not as you would like them to be. Herr Bräutigam is a very capable man."

"That's a matter of opinion."

"Everything is a matter of opinion, and in this office it is my opinion that counts, Fräulein Moll, not because I am a dictator but because I am responsible for the whole business."

"Of which I am a part."

"Quite right," Ribbeck said ironically. "I know your capabilities and your limitations. Don't be so hurt, Fräulein Moll. It is my duty to place my staff where they belong."

"You don't want to see women advancing. Everybody here knows that!"

"That's news to me. I just found a publisher for Dr. Susanne Wirth's new book. Perhaps because I don't want to see her get along?"

"But for me you have no understanding at all!"

"Too much, Fräulein Moll, and that is your misfortune."

I hadn't realized that beside my love-hate for Sánchez I could hate so wildly and so unbecomingly! This was a conspiracy against me, or at least I saw it that way. Cooper's letter had truly come at the right time. Locker had met him briefly in the Hotel Amazonas, but Cooper's importance in Montevideo was something this learned sleepy-head had missed. To please me, Cooper would read Ribbeck's letter of introduction and give Locker and Bräutigam information and introductions. And I could stay home and vegetate!

Sometimes one sees a situation only as it affects one's self. Anyway, I saw everything Ribbeck said as diabolical. I'm sure I wasn't fair to him in some respects, but he had outmaneuvered me. I would have liked to have seen the notes he made while reading Cooper's letter. I found his behavior treacherous. He evidently considered stealing information perfectly natural. He had often told us at his meetings that every publishing house was a family that had to help and promote other members in their work. Ribbeck's family in the Budapesterstrasse would have been hard to beat when it came to intrigue, envy, and bickering. Although the time left us could surely only have been seconds, he rang for coffee.

Frau Hannemann, with her computer face, put down the tray on a small table. Ribbeck looked like the Sphinx of Thebes after a successful day's work. The coffee slowly grew cold. "Drink your coffee, Fräulein Moll. It will do you good."

I drank my coffee, and it did me so much good that I asked for something stronger. Ribbeck produced it like a lamb, or rather like a wolf in sheep's clothing. Had he noticed how remarkable I thought his maneuvers were? I downed the expensive French cognac as if it had been water and got up.

"One moment more, please, Fräulein Moll."

"I think we've discussed everything."

"I would like to explain to you why . . ."

"There's nothing to explain."

"May I finish? You're very angry with me, aren't you? You think I'm behaving despicably. But please let me explain myself."

"Don't make fun of me, Herr Doktor."

"I am doing nothing of the sort. I worry about you to some extent. You are not reliable. You tend to impulsiveness."

"Do you mean that I'm likely to shoot you after the coffee?"

"You are doing serious damage to yourself, and I'd like to prevent that."

"Send me to Montevideo."

"Please don't be childish. I tried to explain my reasons to you. What I wanted to say was that in your profession one must constantly try to live up to expectations."

"Yours?"

"In your case—yes."

"With you I've had as much chance from the start as a virgin in a bordello."

Ribbeck turned on his desk lamp. It gave forth the kind of light that is so depressing in railway stations—cold, dim, official, and disconsolate. Ribbeck liked that sort of illumination. He said I was nervous, I said no I wasn't. I was laughing myself sick! He looked at his watch, then gave me the strangest look. Was it a plea for understanding, for my recognition that this paper was his bread and butter, his beloved and his whip?

"What are you thinking, Fräulein Moll?"

"Nothing."

"As usual."

Ribbeck had overcome his fit of humaneness. He was drinking his coffee standing again. A new tension hung in the air. Hannemann's "Caution" was requisite, but Moll remained Moll.

"Do you know why I am not sending you to South America again?"

"Because you don't want a best-seller."

"I would envy you your confidence if I weren't so sure that you are deceiving yourself."

"You're very kind."

"I don't run this paper to be kind. I'm not sending you to Uruguay because you are too weak in factual reporting. For a journalist the facts are of primary importance. I told you once over dinner that imagination and an understanding of the human being are the arms of the novelist. *If* you can learn to work."

"Why? I never follow through."

"If you would listen to me for a change, I would like to give you some advice."

I was silent, choking with fury and disappointment. I had set my heart on Montevideo. Ribbeck was standing at the window again, his back turned to me. His ramrod, merciless back should have warned me not to provoke him further. But no! I assured Ribbeck that I had had enough advice to last me for the next hundred years. Since he said nothing, I went on and on and each time became more careless. I said Herr Bräutigam was a mediocre man, and for that reason stupid. I said I wouldn't let myself be robbed like this of my connections in Uruguay. Ribbeck wheeled around and eyed me with an icy look.

Ribbeck pressed a button and asked Frau Hannemann to come in for a moment. Was she to drag me out?

"This is just a matter of procedure, Frau Hannemann.

Fräulein Moll is of the opinion that we get our information in an illegal manner."

"I didn't mean it like that!" I said hoarsely.

"Fräulein Moll gave me a private letter from Montevideo to read. She notified me through you that she wanted to see me. Not I, her," he added sarcastically. "Do you recall this, Frau Hannemann?"

"Yes, Herr Doktor."

I remembered too late that Ribbeck's father had been a public prosecutor.

"Since we are sending a team to Uruguay, I jotted down a few things that might be of interest to us as a matter of course. Fräulein Moll showed me Mr. Cooper's letter of her own free will. I could only surmise that she wanted to do the paper a small service for a change. Please, Fräulein Moll, corroborate in front of Frau Hannemann that I did *not* ask for permission to probe into your private correspondence."

"I corroborate it in front of Frau Hannemann." She looked away.

"Thank you. So now you get the picture, Frau Hannemann?"

"Yes, Herr Doktor."

"I am responsible for the reputation of this paper and will not tolerate any mendacious declarations of our working methods being spread around. Thank you, Frau Hannemann. I am relying on this unfortunate incident remaining between us."

"Certainly, Herr Doktor." Exit Hannemann.

"May I go home at once?"

"As you wish, Fräulein Moll. Your salary will be paid to the end of the month."

"Thank you. I guess that's all."

"I think it is."

"I must say, I'm pleased with the solution," I said boldly. "My work isn't appreciated and I'm wasting my time here."

"I'm glad that for once we are of the same opinion. Good luck to you, Fräulein Moll."

He bowed slightly and opened the door for me in a way that made an irrevocable event of an everyday gesture.

"Well, that finally did it, Hannemann!"

"You never know when to back off, do you?" Edith Hannemann wanted to say something else but decided not to. So she didn't say what a good thing it was that my mother hadn't lived to see this day. I gave her credit for that. Of course Hannemann was absolutely right in everything she said then and later, and also in what she left unsaid.

"Do try to straighten things out again," she begged imploringly. "It isn't half as bad as..."

"Hell can freeze over before I'll apologize to Ribbeck..."

"Think of the business with Brenner? That stank to high heaven, but he had it all smoothed out again the same day. *And* with a raise!"

"And with humiliation. I am not Brenner!"

"Too bad. And stop talking nonsense. I think you've said enough for today. You're hoarse as well. Here's a honey drop."

"Keep your advice and your honey drop, dear Frau Hannemann. It's all your fault anyway."

"I *beg* your pardon!" Hannemann was talking like Ribbeck. Somehow half the staff had caught his tone. Lately Bräutigam had been saying to his wife on the phone, "I *beg* your pardon!"

"You knew all about this expedition, Frau Hannemann, and what you didn't know, you snooped around and found out!"

"I never snoop!"

Something in the way Edith Hannemann was looking at me went right through me. She was horrified at what I had done, but she was on my side. Possibly until this afternoon, she had thought that Ribbeck would send me to Uruguay after all. I swallowed hard. Don't get sloppy about it, I told myself. I could see Ribbeck's merciless back. "You can say what you like, but it's no way to say good-bye."

"What did you expect? Hearts and flowers?"

I was silent. Perhaps it was no way to say good-bye, but it was the way Ribbeck did it. And I'd better go and get my stuff packed. I was attached to my little office and to the whole goddamn shebang. Montevideo was suddenly a matter of complete indifference to me, as if it had been erased from the map.

"He's still in his office, Moll. I'll call and see..."

"Don't you dare! I'm going to pack now. We'll see each other occasionally, won't we?"

"Some time. At Kranzler's. My treat."

Hannemann treated only at world's end...

It was so eerily quiet in my apartment that I called my friend, Lotte. "Listen, Lotte, it's all over."

"What's all over?"

"I've been fired. Three hours ago, to be exact."

*"What?"*

"A little difference of opinion with editor-in-chief Ribbeck."

"About what?"

"I don't want to talk about it, Lottchen."

"I thought that was why you were calling me."

"Oh, I was just wasting time in that stable. I'm enjoying the TV work more anyway."

"But Carlchen! Your job with *Comet* was security. And your whopping salary. Have you given it enough thought? Wait a minute. Kurt wants to talk to you."

I heard a brief dialogue between the two, then Kurt Sommer, asking me if I'd gone stark, raving mad! "Listen, Carlchen, you've got to set this thing right, right away! Shall I ask my colleague Wirth to speak to Ribbeck? She's often over at your place."

"Your chaste colleague Susanne Wirth is *out*! I'm through with Ribbeck."

"Or he's through with you?"

"Things like that are usually mutual. A divorce lawyer like you should know that."

"I never mind learning more. What in God's name are you

going to do now, girl? Television is an uncertain business,
and you're not on salary."

"I can write novels."

"You can *what*?"

"Forget it. A little joke."

"I think I'd better come over, Carlchen."

"Sweet of you, but no. I want to think this thing through
by myself."

"For heaven's sake . . . look here . . . the thing is . . . Leave
me alone, Lottchen. I'm trying to talk some sense into your
friend." Lottchen tore the receiver out of his hand and told
me I shouldn't act up.

"I *beg* your pardon!"

"Act up!" Lotte repeated. "You know you're not reliable.
I'm worried about you. I'm coming over."

"No you're not. You're expecting another baby and according to your father, are not supposed to get excited."

"I won't stay long. Robert isn't screaming at the moment,
and Kurt's going out later anyway."

"No, Lottchen. I'm coming tomorrow evening."

"And be punctual. We're having potato pancakes. Do you
want cranberries or applesauce?"

"Both!"

Later, when the doorbell rang, I started. I didn't want to
open the door, but at the third ring I did. Ribbeck couldn't
do more than kill me, and that I wouldn't have minded. It
was Kurt Sommer.

"What do you want, Kurt?"

"Beer."

"What do you want?"

"I want to know what happened."

He was serious, every inch the successful divorce lawyer,
and said he wanted to get right to the point. "I didn't tell
Lotte that I was coming to see you. And please, for once in
your life, keep this to yourself."

When Kurt Sommer wants to know something, it isn't
easy to keep it to yourself, so I told all. My report didn't
seem to please him. "Well, then there's nothing more to be

done," he said finally. "Don't talk to anyone about it, promise me."

"Why not?"

"Or we'll have a lawsuit from Ribbeck accusing you of malicious libel."

"We?"

"In which case I'll unfortunately have to defend you." But Kurt was smiling, and I had to think again what a great guy he was. He told me to keep my mouth shut. I told him he'd said that once already.

"You know," he said, "you're a smart girl, and you can write. How could you be such an idiot? I met Ribbeck the other day at Wirth's house, and he made a first-rate impression on me. Extremely intelligent and courteous."

"You don't know him at the office. As far as Ribbeck is concerned, I've had it!"

"Well, all I can say is that sometimes you're six years old. My son Robert is smarter when it comes to getting something he wants."

"He takes after you."

"I hope so. You and Lotte don't exactly set a good example for Robert. You talk first and then you think it over, and then it takes a long time before you realize what you've said. I happen to like it."

"But Ribbeck doesn't." I gave Kurt a kiss, and he patted me on the shoulder. "All right, little one. Have a good cry, and tomorrow we'll talk some more about it."

"Thank you, Kurt. I feel better already."

"If you keep your mouth shut, you'll keep feeling better. Maybe you'll talk your next heroic action over with me." I promised I would. That evening we couldn't know how soon I would break that promise. It came about because I read the evening paper. They were looking for prominent Nazis again, offering high rewards. Not Bonnhoff, but it made me think of him. "Where are they now? What are they doing today?"

I knew where Sturmbannführer Bonnhoff was and what he was doing today: catching fish in the Orinoco. And over his poor old head was a flaming arch spanning from Venezuela to Berlin. Was it my fault that I knew where he was?

# 27

# Headlines

Carla Moll:

In the Hotel Amazonas I had often felt alone, in spite of the fact that I had Cooper; funny, sloppy Señora Padilla; Wally Bendix; the parrots and Sánchez spooking around. Now, after my dramatic departure from *Comet*, I wasn't merely alone. I was isolated. I vegetated. I was invisible. I told myself over and over again how happy I should be, rid of Ribbeck and the whole bunch at the office, and best of all, able to sleep as long as I liked. But I wasn't happy. I couldn't understand it. Every journalist curses the rat race of his life and longs for peace and quiet, until he has it. In this profession you don't know what to do with peace and quiet. I guess I enjoyed the rat race more than I realized. On top of that, for the first time in my adult life, I was shy. I kept out of the way of my former colleagues, all of whom had envied my success and salary. I was a failure and couldn't get used to the fact. That this thing had happened between Ribbeck and me! Of course Frau Hannemann spread the word that I had left at my own request, which was true in a way, but nobody believed her. Hannemann, Kurt, and Lotte tried to ease the shock for me, but soon gave up. One afternoon, I saw Brenner and Fräulein Hoffmann wandering across the street arm in arm on their way from the archives to the Café Kranzler, where I was also headed. I jumped into a taxi and drove wildly through the city. I didn't want any more coffee, any more faces, any more questions, any more phony sympathy.

Everything went wrong. Now that I could sleep as long as I liked, I woke up every morning at seven. The empty day yawned at me, and I yawned back. Once I was halfway to the office before I remembered that Ribbeck had fired me. Albeit at my request...

Is there anyone who can explain human nature to me? Since Ribbeck took over, I had lived in a state of cold war with him. Now I missed the chronic vexation! Perhaps I even missed Ribbeck with his cruel sarcasm. Now nobody made trouble for me, not even Herr Bräutigam, at present in Uruguay. But he would return to Budapesterstrasse in triumph and fill my place until the next trip. I had always seen myself as a pleasant, kindly disposed person, now I was shocked to find myself wishing colleague Bräutigam the worst. In these difficult weeks I got to know myself, and I didn't like me. I stank of failure, and all the perfumes of Arabia and Chanel couldn't dispel it.

The silence around me finished me off. I played little memory games with myself, mostly scenes from the office. I would see Ribbeck standing by the window, and I broke out in a cold sweat. I could hear Edith Hannemann saying, "You've got to do something about it, Moll. He is not so..." But it was too late. The abyss between us grew deeper every day. He had probably forgotten all about me, unless he happened to watch *Carla Moll and her Guests*. He had no respect for anything that didn't require endless work, and these interviews looked spontaneous. These were the only times when I did my hair properly and got dressed up. It took a lot of energy to look charming and be witty. It was hard work. But I had no contract with the television people. The money was good, and now I needed it. I would have liked to propose a second series, but I would have to submit a theme to the director, and I couldn't think of a thing. Not a thing.

Ribbeck seemed to have disappeared from the face of the earth. All I saw was his car parked near the office. So he was still alive. Kurt Sommer kept telling me I couldn't go on like this, I had to do *something*. But I was in one of my blank periods. Kurt and Lottchen were worried about me. They were touchingly good to me, so I didn't go there as often as usual. But they helped. They were wonderful, and with them I wasn't at all shy. On the contrary! I knew Kurt was quietly looking for another publishing house for me, but it seemed to be more difficult than any of us had thought. If they turned Kurt down, he didn't tell me. Was I so quickly and thoroughly 'finished'? Of course I lacked a recommendation from Ribbeck, who had meanwhile become a bigshot. The subscription list of *Comet* had risen to five times its former count. He would probably have been delighted to give me a recommendation, after having got rid of me so easily, but there was no question about my asking him. "Calm down, girl," said Kurt. "If you don't want a letter from him—okay, okay." I yelled that Kurt of course couldn't understand it, and he said he could see my point but found it unrealistic. "You are the world's only unrealistic Berliner! You always used to know on which side your bread was buttered. Pull yourself together, Carlchen! *Do something!*" Kurt talked his head off. To no effect? To no visible effect. That I'd have to do something had finally sunk in.

Frau Hannemann behaved marvelously too, albeit with a sour face. I would have liked to ask her what the family in the Budapesterstrasse were up to, and if anyone ever mentioned me, but I'd rather have bitten my tongue off. Of course they knew that Hannemann saw me regularly, and since she never brought any greetings for me, evidently nobody was sending any. They didn't call me either. It was much worse than if I had a contagious disease—I was unlucky. And no one wants to come in contact with bad luck. One evening Hannemann's silence on this subject was just too much for me, and with false cheerfulness I asked her who was taking Bräutigam's place now.

"Herr Doktor Busch," Hannemann announced officially, like a funeral director.

"Is he new?"

"Yes."

"Nice?"

"I don't know."

"You must know if somebody's nice or not, Hannemann."

"He's often invited out to Grunewald. Dr. Ribbeck seems to find him nice." She never called him Oscar any more in front of me. It was stupid, but it hurt. I was out.

"You've got to do something, Moll."

"Yes, yes. But does it have to be right away? Why do you come to see me if I only annoy you?"

Hannemann was silent.

"You deserve a gold medal, Hannemann."

"When are we going to eat?"

"I'm not hungry."

"But I am."

We ate.

That I undertook something shortly after this conversation, was not my fault. It was the result of a letter from Venezuela from Wally Bendix. It was Wally's fault that I did something at last.

He wrote that he had never received an answer to his three letters from me. Was I still alive or had I simply forgotten him? He'd like to know. He was fishing in the fisherman's paradise again, in Samariapo, because he had wanted to take his vacation before the rainy season. He was staying at the Hotel Amazonas in Puerto Ayacucho, without Cooper, without the Padillas, without Gilbert Preston, deceased, and without me. He intended to stay two months, then the rains would start, and the green wilderness would turn into a huge tureen filled with spinach. And they say we Berliners have no feeling for poetry!

Samariapo. The Indian, Zongo. Big fish, little fish. Señor Wally Bendix. Sturmbannführer Bonnhoff. "I thought you were dead Tina." *El capitán. El viejo.* The fish glistening like glass. *El capitán* swinging his rod like a whip in his trembling hand. "Do you remember, Tina? I and you and Carlos?" On the Orinoco time raced, and at the same time stood still.

\* \* \*

Berlin *Beobachter*, March 1971:

*The journalist Carla Moll, world traveler, author of the best-seller* Caracas for Beginners, *valuable staff member of* Comet, *television star* (Carla Moll and her Guests) *is at present in the Orinoco area again. She has gone there to lead the German authorities to Sturmbannführer Bonnhoff, formerly from Berlin, whom the authorities have been seeking for decades. Now, as this item goes to press, she is very close to the house on the Orinoco in which Bonnhoff is hiding from the German courts. See the map of the green wilderness with a sketch of the so-called fisherman's paradise showing Bonnhoff's house in the background, almost hidden by tropical shrubs. When the journalist discovered Bonnhoff months ago, fishing along the shore, she made this sketch on the spot. Bonnhoff is a very old man today, but as one of Himmler's henchmen, he has the death of thousands on his conscience. Courageously, and with her usual vitality, Carla Moll undertook this dangerous mission to serve justice, and our best wishes accompany her. At the moment of her second confrontation with Bonnhoff, we will be bringing exclusive reports on Carla Moll's mission on the Orinoco.*

Press announcement. *Correction: Dr. Oscar Ribbeck, editor-in-chief of* Comet, *informs us that since last month Carla Moll is no longer on the staff of his paper.*

Letters to the Editor. Berlin *Beobachter:*

*Carla Moll deserves our admiration. "Death to the Nazis," my grandfather used to say, and he knew what he was talking about. (Lost a leg in World War I.) He was public prosecutor in the Weimar Republic, and spent years in the concentration camps of the Third Reich. I wish Carla Moll success in her mission. No punishment is too severe for SS criminals like Bonnhoff. To the gallows with him!*

*Democratic Associate Professor*

*Carla Moll should come home and darn socks, visit the sick, or do something for our orphans, instead of hunting down an old man in Venezuela. There are bigger and better things that need doing right here in Berlin.*

*Social worker*

*I am looking forward to Carla Moll's report on the Orinoco. I would like to know if the piranha (about 16 inches long, with bulldog faces, massive jaws, and knife-sharp teeth, can sense blood under the water,) lives his murderous life only in the Amazon or also in the Orinoco. Please pass my question on to Fräulein Moll.*

*Student*

*Three cheers for Carla Moll. Since* Caracas for Beginners *we are her fans. She looks terrific in her pants suit. We would like to know where she bought it.*

*Enthusiastic teenagers*

*Carla Moll should be ashamed of herself! We were never for the Nazis, but consider them misguided patriots. Carl Friedrich Bonnhoff comes from one of Potsdam's finest families. I am sure he meant well, but he lacked judgment. I hope Fräulein Moll comes back from Venezuela with a long face!*

*A general's widow, formerly Potsdam*

*Many thanks for the adorable picture of Carla Moll in her pants suit. She is a sight for sore eyes, whatever she may be up to. The girl has legs! Long and slim, just right for pants. Had a very sensible argument about it with my wife. For various reasons am not in agreement with Carla's intentions, but you won't find a smart girl like that again!*

*A well-meaning husband*

*Dear Sirs,*

*My partner and I hope that Carla Moll will come back with no traumatic damage. One can't be too careful in choosing one's enemies.*

*Two psychiatrists*

*I find the whole hullabaloo repulsive. Adventures like that are not fitting for a woman. I am sure Carla Moll doesn't even know how to boil an egg! I shall turn off the television whenever she is on.*

*Modern housewife and mother*

*The old man is alive, Carla! Don't let any spoilsport deter you from hunting him down! Hunter's luck!*

*A passionate big game hunter*

*Carla Moll should earn her daily bread in a Christian and decent fashion. Has she forgotten that we are supposed to love our enemies?*

*A priest*

*Keep up the good work, beautiful Carla! Where and when can we meet?*

*An admirer from the army*

*Has Carla Moll nothing better to do than to waste our money? If she finds old Bonnhoff, getting him back to Germany will cost our money!*

*Irate taxpayer*

*Al Carla Moll wants is sensation! All bluff and as little work as possible. She damages the reputation of today's career woman. I am canceling my subscription to your paper by the same mail.*

*Serious journalist*

Ribbeck put the Berlin *Beobachter* with its letters to the editor back on his desk; as he went on playing chess with himself he kept telling himself how happy he should be to be rid of this irresponsible woman. He read the letters to the editor again. The well-meaning husband, the general's widow, and the admirer from the army were amusing, but it really was no concern of his. He picked up his volume of Descartes. She'd get what she deserved in Venezuela. She would go to the wrong house in the jungle. She was always wrong about everything, including him. If people recognized their mistakes and apologized to him, he could relent. The Brenner case proved that. Ribbeck closed his book and threw the paper in the wastebasket. What would Moll do when she got back? You couldn't live on headlines. No one would employ her if it didn't turn out right. Her money couldn't last much longer. It was really none of his business.

He tried Descartes again. *Cogito, ergo sum.* Did one exist only because one thought? A lot of people lived for years without thinking. Or they thought with their instincts, or their feelings. Or with their sex organs. They acted first and thought afterward, if at all. What would Carla Moll live on if things went wrong? On an honorable defeat? On fresh air and the love of the army man? Ribbeck frowned. He would never have thought that she could keep a secret so many months. He wondered what had made her decide to go and look for the old fool. Of course there was the reward, but Ribbeck knew it wasn't the money that had tempted her. She wouldn't know that her account was overdrawn until the bank stopped payment on her checks. Frivolous! The "serious journalist" wasn't entirely wrong. He had fired her at just the right time. Nobody could make a fool of him!

He tore the paper with the readers' letters out of the wastepaper basket again and tore it up. Then he played another game of chess with himself. It was a pleasant evening. Would Carla Moll learn a lesson from her experiences? Highly unlikely. People who can't say they're sorry and don't see that they're wrong, dig their own grave.

At that moment the phone rang. "Ribbeck," he said, in his most discouraging voice.

"Frau Bräutigam speaking. Good evening, Herr Doktor."

"Good evening. What can I do for you?"

"I don't want to disturb you, but..."

"What is it?" asked Ribbeck, in a still more unfriendly tone. She had already disturbed him. Frau Bräutigam wanted to know if they had heard from her husband at the office. She had received only two postcards from Montevideo.

"Of course we have heard from your husband. That's why we sent him to South America. The gentlemen don't have much time for private letters. They're busy all day."

"And at night?"

"I beg your pardon."

"My husband has forgotten me. He is having a good time with other women. I mean...never mind. Excuse me for disturbing you, Herr Doktor."

Silly woman, thought Ribbeck. Of course men looked for a woman for the night when they were traveling. Not for every night, but when they needed it. And if they were married to Frau Bräutigam, an attractive, comforting young lady— not as fat as Frau Bräutigam, not as logical as jurist Wirth, not as shamelessly beautiful as Carla Moll, the devil take her! Ribbeck was not the well-meaning husband, but to his annoyance he too found that Moll looked simply enchanting in her pants suit. That was all she could do: drive men crazy! She had tried it on him, but he didn't pay high salaries for that. For the sort of money he had paid Carla Moll, he de- manded results. Of course he would rather see a pretty girl in the office than a scarecrow. But Carla Moll wasn't pretty, she was beautiful, and beauty sometimes obscured healthy judgment. Ribbeck had experienced the same thing with his first fiancée.

He went to the phone and told a girl he had met recently that he was coming. She was what he needed. Occasionally he forgot her, her first name, her face, her chatter. Pretty little thing. And not too simpleminded. She knew on which side her bread was buttered. And not from a bad family, not at all. She sold flowers in a fine shop on the Kurfürstendamm. Ribbeck knew everybody in and around Berlin and was often a guest. Then he bought flowers from . . . from . . . that's right: Hilda. Her name was Hilda. Just what he wanted when he needed it. She wouldn't make any headlines. She sold flowers, and herself.

# 28

# A Visitor from Berlin

Carla Moll:

Years after my last trip to the Orinoco, after my life and career had taken a totally different course, my husband called my obsession with this German-Venezuelan family my Bonnhoff Syndrome. My husband knew more than anyone else about this horrible period in my life, and what I couldn't talk about—for instance, the humiliating weekend with Sánchez in Palma Sola—he sensed. Because, to my astonishment, he loved me truly, deeply and constantly. And out of this he developed, in spite of his pragmatic spirit, the intuition of those who love. My stubborn, unrequited passion for Sánchez was actually inseparable from my search for Bonnhoff. As if my love-hate for the son gave my crazy hunt for the father an added, demonic fascination. My unquenchable thirst for sensation, my restlessness, my love for Venezuela and its combination of horror and beauty and the inner force that drove me, against my better judgment, to where I could expect nothing but humiliation and abuse, all were a part of this Bonnhoff Syndrome. Today, I can look back on all of it as if it had happened to another person. And in a way, it did. Bonnhoff brought an element of dubious fanaticism into my busy life, which was threatened by an inner emptiness. I was the journalist Moll and nothing else. A product of the times, dispensable to everyone except for my mother, Kurt and Lotte Sommer, and Frau Hannemann.

Sometimes, when the evening meal of my past lies heavy in my stomach, I see the old men at the river's edge in my dreams and wake up screaming, in spite of the fact that all this happened so long ago that it is barely true anymore. Fortunately my days now are bright and fulfilled. But I remain astonished about people in general. We dissect, analyze, and come to terms with our lives, but have no power over our dreams. And as long as we can't control them, we remain split personalities, confused and fearful. My husband helps me through nights like that. Gently but firmly he brings me back from Venezuela to Berlin. By the way, nobody ever found out that Sánchez was Bonnhoff's son. I kept silent about it for the sake of my dignity, not because of any consideration for the señor. I can't forgive him for the fact that in spite of all common sense and decency, I was madly in love with him.

My last trip to the Orinoco was intended, of course, to be a professional triumph, making headlines in the Berlin *Beobachter*. And Ribbeck was to realize what he had lost when he had fired me. I also wanted to avenge myself finally on Sánchez for all my humiliation. A pretty full program. But the whole thing turned out to be a nightmare, and as in all nightmares, what remains in one's memory are individual, unconnected pictures. The endless, murky river, the sinister woods, the broiling stillness of the afternoons, the Indian Zongo, my mute sentinel . . . A few people—I think they were Yanquis—were dragging a car out of the water with a crane. It dripped like a drowning man, and there may have been dead people in it. I don't know anymore. All I know is everything connected with the house on the Orinoco. Bonnhoff and his Indian, Tucu, and the young Venezuelan with the prayer book were not on the shore when Zongo and I arrived. I had arranged with the police and a cameraman that I would first celebrate my reunion with Bonnhoff alone. "Remember, Fritz? It's me. Your Tina from Berlin." On the

following day Bonnhoff was to be officially arrested. I would
not be present. A matter of tact.

The sketch of the house behind the bushes was as correct
as Wally Bendix himself. He was not in Samariapo yet; something must have intervened. But that suited me fine. I wouldn't
have liked to see his face when he realized why I had wanted
the sketch. Wally loved truth and clarity too much. My plan
for an unheralded confrontation seemed good. The dirty work
could come later; the arrest and deportation of Bonnhoff back
to Germany was something for harder souls.

Do all people feel so uneasy about seeing to it that justice
is done? Bonnhoff had more than enough guilt on his head,
and I had found him here quite by chance. I felt that my
cause was just. I had decided not to claim a cent of the reward.
I needed money, but that was not the way I intended to earn
it. Noble of me? Don't think about it, Moll, I told myself.
It's all A-okay and in the service of justice.

So there I was on the Orinoco, but where was Bonnhoff?
I left Zongo on the shore in our motorboat and walked up
the private path to the big white house behind the bushes. It
seemed to be deserted. All the doors were closed, and the
shutters were only opened a crack. There was no one in sight
in the big, slightly neglected garden. Not even a dog was
barking. I hate barking dogs, but at that moment I would
have welcomed one. Where was Bonnhoff? Why wasn't he
fishing? Or had I only taken for granted that he lived in this
house? That would have been a fine mess! But in this wilderness, this was the only private path, and the old man had
used it. With his Indian and his prayer brother. Through my
binoculars I couldn't see a second house anywhere, and the
hostile jungle stretched out to the horizon.

First I walked slowly around the house. No bell! Only the
big sign: Private Property. It sounded like Sánchez. The kitchen
quarters seemed deserted too. Was everyone taking a siesta?
It was Bonnhoff's hour to fish. He couldn't possibly be away.
He had said his son kept him prisoner. There! The door of a
veranda at the back was ajar. In my nervousness I must have
overlooked it. It creaked when I opened it and walked into

the house. Now I was standing in an empty, whitewashed hall with brown wooden doors, all closed, and shutters almost closed. The sun couldn't dance around in here. The doors were only three-quarter high so that the air could circulate through the rooms. The hall was not in the least inviting. A few stiff, wicker chairs stood against the walls. An old maize mill and a calabash bowl, the kind the Orinoco Indians use, stood on a wooden table in a corner. In front of it a woven mat. In another corner, near the stairs, stood a very old, empty trunk, open. It was terribly shabby, wobbly. My mother had had a similar trunk up in the attic, "In case we should ever want to travel." Was Bonnhoff planning to travel? But the trunk was dusty and looked as if it might fall apart any moment. The sight of the old hulk gave me a shock—crazy of course, no reason for it—and I had to sit down on one of the wicker chairs. It wasn't a very fortunate choice, because a horrible mask grinned at me from the opposite wall. Three Indian arrows with a bow hung beside the mask, and there was a silver crucifix. The hall was cold and as hygienic as a hospital. Bonnhoff might well be the inmate of an insane asylum in a green wilderness. Anything was possible on the Orinoco. But the trunk in the corner spoke against asylum rules.

I found breathing difficult. The wicker chair was hard, as if never used. As I tried to make myself comfortable in it, I was overcome by my old aversion to isolated, empty houses. Give me a big city with apartment houses and people standing around, newspaper vendors, pickpockets, natives, pedestrians, eyewitnesses. Give me Berlin! It's funny . . . you complain about Berlin when you're there, but you really can't stand it anywhere else! Of course the house on the Orinoco was exceptionally ugly. The high fence and bushes made it seem very far from the shore. I could sense that something was wrong. Why didn't they stand a few palms or plants in this funeral parlor? Even a crazy man appreciates a little green in his cell. The African mask glared at me as if ordering me to leave, but it didn't know Moll. I was here and I was going to stay here until *el capitán* or the prayer brother appeared.

Somehow the massive wooden mask with its puffy lips reminded me of Sēnor de Padilla from the Hotel Amazonas.
But not as he had been then: grinning, apparently foolishly
good-natured, proud of his checkbook and diamond ring. No,
no! This was Gilbert Preston's murderer glaring at me, lips
parted in maniacal rage and an ecstatic expression in his wide
open eyes with their slitlike pupils.

I looked up the stairs to the first floor. They led to a long
corridor behind a carved banister. The bedrooms and bath-
rooms had to be there. Here too, as far as I could see, all
the doors were closed. Somebody could easily jump out at
me from one of them. I could think only of horror stories.
And I was thirsty. Our thermos bottles with ice water and
fruit juice were down at the shore, in the motorboat. I envied
Zongo under its tin roof. He had peace and quiet and something to drink, and was probably throwing fish heads at the
crocodiles. Perhaps he was hoping that I'd stay in this house,
then I couldn't disturb him. Suddenly I screamed. A green
snake fell down the stairs and curled up at my feet. The snake
lay absolutely still. It was made of wood and was primitively
painted. I kicked it. I was trembling all over. Nobody had
responded to my scream.

Things couldn't go on like this. I couldn't stand around
here until Judgment Day, with the Padilla mask and the wooden
snake and the old maize mill. Museum pieces, undoubtedly,
but I had more important things to do. Anyway, I go to
museums only when forced to. Ribbeck had said that was
like me. And right now I preferred the Budapesterstrasse by
far to Padilla and the snake. I wondered what Ribbeck had
said to the headlines about my trip. Were they "like me"?

I called out loud, "Is anybody there?" The thought that
Ribbeck might be annoyed about it had restored my courage.
"Is anybody there?" My Spanish sounded strange, and my
voice was hoarse because my throat was dry. A door upstairs
opened. A man came down the stairs slowly. He wasn't fat
like Bonnhoff, nor emaciated like the prayer brother. He was
very tall and sinewy. Because of the closed shutters, the hall
was almost dark. Only Padilla's eyeballs and the silver cru-

cifix gleamed. The man threw open the shutters beside the stairs and laid the snake on the table with the maize mill. A mirror hung beside 'Padilla,' and for seconds we looked at each other in it: a lady with a very red face and straggly hair and the man who had come to set things right. I would have liked to run away—always the sensible thing to do in war—but I was rooted to the floor.

"Good evening," said Sánchez. "Did you have a pleasant trip?"

The way he moved had the same virility and charm for me that it had always had. Here he was not only the man of the house but the lord of the land. His assurance confused me. When he stood still, he was a statue. I stared at him, unflinchingly. Suddenly I knew that this was the last time I would see him, and I couldn't bear it. I tried to learn his face by heart, feature by feature, his bold, wonderful face with its deep-set Spanish eyes. For me he would always be El Greco's gentleman, with no jewelry or lace ruff. Perhaps he was to be envied. Right now he was looking at the silver crucifix and seemed to have forgotten me. He had more sources of strength than I. I had already recognized that on Margarita Island, where he had been my spring and my summer. How had Bonnhoff sired such a son? Carlos was the image of his Venezuelan grandfather.

Suddenly Sánchez looked at me sharply and an abyss opened before me. I forgot my mission, my career, the headlines, and Ribbeck's coldness. There was nothing in the whole wide world but Sánchez, standing in this empty hall. And I wanted him and he didn't want me. I had forgotten all about the London doctor, too. She might be here or even waiting in Caracas for the sēnor. Sánchez was perfectly calm. I found this incomprehensible. He should have been indignant about my intrusion, or at least in a state of suppressed panic. Bonnhoff might appear suddenly with his wide open, staring eyes, a fishing rod or a whip in his hands. Much later I asked myself why the flames of Sánchez's hatred hadn't burned me. Normally I am not tough-skinned, and in his presence I was never normal. I was blind, deaf, forward, desperate, and idiotic, with a passion nothing could destroy.

"What brings you here to me, señorita?"

His question was so unexpected, I could say nothing. I couldn't very well tell him why I was here. Rumors might have reached him from Berlin already. Not the headlines, which were still hot off the press, but friends of friends could have heard something. Ribbeck certainly wouldn't have talked about having fired me, but he knew all Berlin and told all Berlin through the press that I was no longer working for *Comet*. And Sánchez was the last person who couldn't put two and two together: a journalist out of work, side-tracked. He said drily that he had an idea why I was here.

"Really?" My heart was beating fast.

"But of course. You descend upon me quite regularly in one or the other of my houses."

"Is this your house?"

"Do you know of any other owner?"

"I can't understand Spanish when it's spoken so fast. I'm a little out of practice. Would you speak a little more slowly, please, señor?"

He said, exasperatingly slowly, "I am disgusted with this whole business."

So he was angry. Fortunately, by now I was too. Since Sánchez was turning to walk back upstairs, I said quickly, "Please don't go. Do you know what I am thinking of at this moment?"

"I have no ideas, and nothing could interest me less."

"I don't believe it. You are . . . you are . . ."

"Please speak a little lower. I'm afraid you're disturbing the other members of the household at their siesta." He looked at me in my sweaty, crushed summer dress with unbelievable arrogance. "Do you always barge into strange people's houses like this, señorita? Or am I the only victim of your eccentricities?"

How he despised me! He had found me attractive before Bonnhoff had come between us and ruined everything. I said, "I would like to ask you something, señor."

He said, "I consider you as having left the country. It is the best thing you can do."

"Is that a threat?"

"A warning."

Of course he knew everything and wanted to get rid of me as quickly as possible. All I had wanted was to ask him who the other members of his household were whom I was not to disturb. With that I might have won a little time until Bonnhoff appeared. And now I could hear voices and steps. The siesta was over. The game could begin. Suddenly I was perfectly calm. Nothing could happen to me, only Sánchez and Bonnhoff were endangered. Upstairs a chair fell with a clatter, and Sánchez frowned.

"May I have a glass of lemonade, señor?"

Now I could hear furniture being moved and Sánchez looked even angrier. Right then he couldn't be distinguished from his grandfather.

"Is it clear to you, señorita, that you are committing a felony? In this country forcible entry is a serious crime. Will you leave of your own accord, or must I ask the police to escort you out?"

"Do you really want to ask the police to come to this house?"

Sánchez laughed. It was so unexpected that it shocked me. Then he said coldly that I must have gone crazy. I again didn't know what I was talking about. The police and he were on excellent terms. At that moment a voice from above called out, "Do you have a visitor, Carlos?"

"Yes," said Carlos. "A visitor from Berlin."

I don't know why misfortunes never come singly. Not only was Sánchez barring my way to the stairs but suddenly Pilar Álvarez appeared at the top, and she was all I needed. The Indian wise men say that one shouldn't worry about bad luck because after three years it goes away by itself, but this was no help. I couldn't wait in this hall for three years, and Pilar wasn't going to go away.

I had been through all this before. This was how Pilar

Álvarez had stood on the stairs of Sánchez's house on Margarita Island and had tried to kill me with a look. All for Carlos! And now she was standing on the stairs again: tall, gaunt, in spinsterly black. I stared at her. What I might have said couldn't be said, not in this situation. She was a ghost in broad daylight, a starved virgin, who would devour her Carlos in good time. I couldn't tell her that.

"What does she want here?" Pilar asked harshly.

"I take it she wanted to see us again."

"This is no time for levity, Carlos. This woman always comes with a purpose. Tell her to go away."

"I have already told her."

"So why is she still here?"

"Why don't you ask her?"

"Because I don't want to listen to lies. In the old days liars and intruders were shot."

"That was long ago," said Sánchez, regretfully.

"Be careful, Carlos. This woman is a vampire."

"This woman is a journalist. Don't worry, Pilar. I have eyes in the back of my head."

I had to admire the way the two were talking about me while I was dying of thirst. Where was Bonnhoff? A man was coming down the stairs. It was the young prayer brother. Wherever he was, Bonnhoff couldn't be far away. The young man bowed to me, his eyes lowered, one person at least still practicing the renowned Venezuelan courtesy. He took the snake off the table with the maize mill, then he went upstairs again just as silently as he had come. So Bonnhoff was playing with wooden snakes now.

The silent young man had made the scene even more unrealistic, as if he were part of a mime play. He hadn't indicated by glance or gesture that he had seen me months ago on the shore with Bonnhoff. The only ones missing now were the old man and his Indian. I couldn't look at Sánchez, so I cast a sideways glance at Pilar. That finished me off, just as she had finished me off on Margarita Island. She was wearing a chain again, with the Hand of Fatima, a horrible little black hand that was supposed to protect against the evil eye.

She looked considerably older, but then all of us were getting older and less beautiful. Pilar's eyes and claws had grown sharper, probably because of the London doctor. Had Sánchez married her already? I imagined he had. He was furious with me but otherwise happy and calm. I looked at the Hand of Fatima again. Pilar wore this gruesome amulet like the League of Honor rosette. Nothing could happen to her, only to me. She was from another world. There were slightly arthritic swellings on her fingers and knuckles, and she was using a cane. But I knew she would outlive all of us, even Sánchez. Her hand grasped the cane so firmly that the knuckles showed white. She was tense, taut as a violin string. Until she had appeared I had had what you might call a moment of grace with Sánchez. Had she perhaps driven Teresa to her death? I considered her capable of anything. I hated her with my whole heart. She was bad for me because she made me bad.

Pilar murmured something about police, but Sánchez waved the suggestion away. He realized that sooner or later I would have to leave whether I wanted to or not. I would never get up those stairs. One look at his stony face told me that. As I stared at him I realized suddenly that he had power, influence, the best connections with the police, and the aura of a lord in his own kingdom. "Charm" had always been much too weak a word for him; he had charisma, extraordinary powers, and magnetism; he could command obedience. Men like Sánchez were admired for their radiance, not because of their intellectualism, not even because of their wealth, although it helped to make them splendid. At least in this part of the world. As a member of the oligarchy he was of course on the best of terms with the authorities. That was why Sánchez had laughed when I had mentioned the police. Sánchez was a Latin American phenomenon, and I had experienced him only as lover and private enemy. The realization hit me like a sudden fever. Whether Sánchez had sent his father deeper into the wilderness or was holding him under the surveillance of the young priest, Bonnhoff was out of my reach. I had been ridiculously naive when I had undertaken this final search. Ribbeck had been right not to send me back to Latin America. And since I grasped the situation at last in its merciless clarity, I said with the courage of those who have nothing to lose: *"Where is Bonnhoff?"*

Pilar leaned more heavily on her cane. Her amulet disappeared, as if frightened, in the folds of her black mantilla. She opened her mouth to speak, but a look from Sánchez, and she pressed her lips together again. The look said clearer than words that the señor wanted to settle this matter himself. I wish I could recall more precisely how he dealt with the matter, but it was too dreadful. I mean his cold fury and his finesse and his truly murderous look from which even Pilar drew back. She knew him better than I did, or the London doctor whom I no longer envied.

Sánchez said Bonnhoff was *dead*! And now he was through with me and the whole business. *Dead!* Then he was silent.

There the three of us stood, in the hall, in a cloud of hatred, threats and lies, and the empty trunk in the corner was watching us. Grimm's fairy tales flashed through my mind, all the gruesome ones, and I wouldn't have been surprised to see Sturmbannführer Bonnhoff rise out of the trunk, wrapped in a shroud. Three people and a myth. It all happened so fast. It may have been only five minutes, but to me it seemed an eternity. I stood there rooted to the spot and tried to put together the old picture of Sánchez, like a mosaic. I couldn't leave him like this! It had all been a terrible mistake, and it was Pilar's fault. I could read the gloomy satisfaction on her face. Sánchez was still standing at the foot of the stairs. Not a muscle in his face moved. He looked at me for seconds with unbelievable revulsion and boredom, and said, "You don't set traps for other people, only for yourself. How unfortunate!" Then he turned around and without another word walked up the stairs.

The hall was a devastated battlefield. Only Pilar Álvarez was left, the chatelaine, the guardian of the secrets. And she was enjoying the sight of my defeat. Perhaps she also wanted to make sure that before leaving I didn't try to go upstairs. The young lay brother, who looked like a Franciscan monk in civilian clothes, came up to me with a tall glass of lemonade on a tray. He bowed and said softly that Señor Sánchez apologized for sending the drink so tardily. I drank every drop of it and let the ice melt in my mouth, to please Pilar. After all, she had to wait until I left.

The lay brother led me through the patio and down the private path to the shore, silently. This too was on order of the señor. Of course—Sánchez wanted to know who was waiting for me in the boat, and if we left. I had lost the game. One should never let the falcon fly until one has seen the hare...

Zongo was waiting in the motorboat. His severe, birdlike face betrayed neither impatience or curiosity. He had caught a lot of little fish, and I had lost the big one.

# 29

## Ribbeck Speaking

Ribbeck had dictated his last letter for the day and Frau Hannemann rose. But he had something more to tell her. He held up Professor Locker's letter from Paraguay as if it had been an indictment. "Bad news, Frau Hannemann. This letter is from Asunción. Professor Locker has moved on to Bolivia."

"And Herr Bräutigam?"

"He was bitten by a crocodile! So stupid. He was swimming in the Paraguay River in a dangerous spot. Why didn't he ask Locker? Locker saved him, but..."

Frau Hannemann waited.

"Herr Bräutigam has lost a leg. They were on a river tour. König has taken wonderful pictures of the crocodiles from the shore. Otherwise there's nothing but tropical greenery all the way to the Brazilian border."

"Yes. And... Herr Bräutigam?"

"Dr. Wendt... I mean Frau Locker, took him to the hospital in Asunción. Without her he might have bled to death. What a mess! As soon as he can be moved, Dr. Wendt is going to bring him home."

"Will he be able to go on working for us?"

"He doesn't write with his leg," said Ribbeck. "I would appreciate it if you would inform Frau Bräutigam. Women are better at that sort of thing."

What he doesn't want to do we can do better, thought Edith Hannemann. She was astonished that Locker hadn't informed Bräutigam's wife. Ribbeck was astonished that she was astonished. Frau Bräutigam was much too nervous to be told such news directly. She had to have it broken to her gently. Ribbeck stared at his Indians on the wall. They could scent danger from miles away. Smarter than Herr Bräutigam. The silence between him and Hannemann became increasingly uncomfortable. "Anything else, Frau Hannemann?"

"Do you have a moment's time, Herr Doktor?"

"Three minutes."

"I would like to speak to you about Fräulein Moll."

"I *beg* your pardon!"

Anybody else would have bowed out then and there, but Frau Hannemann continued. If she wanted to speak to him about Carla Moll, he was going to have to listen.

"She isn't well. The doctor says work is the best medicine."

"I told her that and I'm not a doctor."

"Venezuela and the stupid headlines have made her ill."

"That was to be expected."

"She's unlucky too."

"In what respect?"

"This man Bonnhoff died before she got there."

"The most sensible thing he could have done."

Edith Hannemann hesitated, but then she said sadly, "What's to become of her?"

"I have no idea, Frau Hannemann."

"She is suffering from tropical fever. She is in Dr. von Hartlieb's clinic."

"All right, send a few flowers from the staff. But please nothing expensive as in Dr. Wendt's time. He must have had money invested in a flower shop. I'm willing to contribute ten marks. That's enough. In the summer . . ."

"Very well, Herr Doktor."

"I suggest you go to Fichte on the Kurfürstendamm. Ask for Fräulein Hilda and tell her I sent you. She'll arrange something pretty for us."

"I'll attend to it just as soon as I get away from Frau Bräutigam."

"Thank you, Frau Hannemann. Hm. I would have thought Bräutigam would have had more sense than to let a crocodile get his leg. Anything else?"

"Excuse me, Herr Doktor, but I thought . . . now that Herr Bräutigam is still in Paraguay, and then there'll be the transport . . . and . . . and . . . he won't be able to work right away, and who knows how long it will be . . ."

"Can't you make it a little shorter, Frau Hannemann?" Ribbeck looked at his watch.

"Under these circumstances," Frau Hannemann finished hastily, "couldn't Fräulein Moll come back to us?"

"I *beg* your pardon."

"She needs the money. She has inherited quite a bit from her mother, but she doesn't know how to handle money."

"My dear Frau Hannemann, that really isn't my concern." He raised one hand. "You don't have to apologize. I understand and appreciate your attitude, but I could never take anyone back who has left my office the way she did."

He watched Frau Hannemann leave. What a decent woman! Fräulein Moll could learn a thing or two from her. He could still remember every detail of the disgraceful scene in his office. "My work isn't appreciated here! I am wasting my time! I am very pleased with this solution." She could be pleased about it until Judgment Day. He had been exceptionally patient with her in spite of her arrogance, and what thanks had he got for it? He didn't want any thanks, but . . . And she threw away her talents in a shameful fashion. Lazy . . . yet she could write. What a waste! He thought of his one and only dinner with her at the restaurant on the Kurfürstendamm. He had tried to inspire her in a literary sense, and she had devoured Señor Sánchez with her eyes! He wondered if she had seen him again on this last trip. But no, Sánchez was in Caracas. In her lilac dress she had been the epitome of grace. He could remember it exactly. And the way Annemarie Schmidt had burst in on them. He was rid of her too. Eventually one got rid of all of them without having to do much about it. And Fräulein Moll was now left high and dry. Yes . . . Ribbeck enjoyed the fact that he had been right, and paid the price for it: unpopularity among his colleagues. He could take it. He still had his musical friends, and nobody ever refused his invitations. He had counted on Carla Moll's fiasco on the Orinoco. He was never wrong because he had no illusions. Not even about himself.

"Hello! Ribbeck speaking. *Comet*. I would like to speak to Dr. von Hartlieb. Thank you very much, Nurse Ullmann. I'll wait . . . Good evening, Dr. von Hartlieb. That's right. The name is Ribbeck. I would like some private information. About Carla Moll. What is wrong with her?"

"She has a rather nasty infection. Tropical fever. But we're counting on sending her home soon. However . . . and this is strictly confidential . . . we're worried about her. Nurse Ullmann does what she can but . . . I've spoken to my colleague, Dr. Schneider, about her too. He's Fräulein Moll's doctor. Has known her since childhood."

"What's wrong with her?"

"Serious depression. Doesn't go somehow with such a smart young woman. But you come across the strangest things in the course of your practice. I asked Ebers, my colleague from psychiatry, to have a look at her."

"Is it that bad?"

"In cases like hers everything is bad, my dear Ribbeck. You're working in the dark. Well, anyway, Dr. Ebers thinks it might be a personality disorder."

"And what's that in my language?"

Hartlieb laughed. "Yes, yes, these gentlemen have their secret language. It is what you might call a spiritual and intellectual breakdown which does not necessarily impair the core of the patient's personality. One might call it a neurosis on the edge of things, in the layers of the spirit. Does that convey anything to you?"

"No. Except that Fräulein Moll seems to be moodier than ever."

The doctor laughed again. "Why don't you visit her? I'm sure it would do her good."

"I'm sure it wouldn't. No, no, dear friend, I'm a better judge of that . . . What did you say? . . . No, I'm sorry, but Fräulein Moll's place at the office is taken. And very satisfactorily. And by the way, she left us at her own request. Right in the middle of things."

"She isn't reliable, I know, but she is extremely talented. Couldn't you find anything suitable for her? You have such wonderful connections, and a recommendation from you would have results, I'm sure. Fräulein Moll needs work. She isn't strong enough yet for television. Besides, after the fiasco on the Orinoco . . ."

"I'll see what I can do. The greatest difficulty is Fräulein Moll herself. No sense of responsibility whatsoever."

"Aren't you being a little harsh?"

"On the contrary. You don't know her at work. But all right, I'll see what I can do. Because you're such a fine Mozart player." Ribbeck laughed.

"Carla Moll's whole life lies before her, dear Ribbeck. But she is completely discouraged. Let's hope you can help her. By the way, the *Comet* articles on Paraguay and Uruguay are being read avidly in the clinic. Bräutigam is a good reporter. Not as amusing as Carla Moll, but he seems to be reliable."

"A crocodile bit off one of his legs. I wouldn't like to be there when they tell his wife. Your psychiatrists would have a life long job with her. It can only make one glad that one's a bachelor."

"My opinion exactly. When do we play again? . . . What's the matter, Nurse Ullmann? Carla Moll? I'll be there right away."

"Head nurse Ullmann speaking. Dr. von Hartlieb has been called away. He'll call you back. Thank you. We have your private number."

Carla Moll:

I must have collapsed, something like that. I looked in the

mirror and decided I was terribly pale. Should not look in the mirror again. And my whole body broke out in a sweat. My pupils were dilated. Frankly, I thought I looked enchanting. And I felt dizzy, because I'd had a nightmare. The Hand of Fatima, Pilar's black amulet, rose up on legs and came toward me. It is not nice when a gigantic black hand is laid upon one's face. I couldn't shake it off and I couldn't scream. Gradually it turned into a black cloud that pressed down more and more heavily on my chest. I wanted to ring, but that was impossible too. Pilar was in the room. I couldn't see her, but she was there. Unfortunately Nurse Ullmann looked in on me frequently. Didn't know what that was supposed to be good for. I wanted to stay buried under the black cloud, but that would have been too beautiful to happen in Hartlieb's clinic. They worked on me, hypoed cardiazol or sympathy . . . no, sympathol, and I opened my eyes again. I didn't ask the usual question: where am I? I knew damn well where I was. They were all standing around me as if beside a death bed. A deep faint . . . I suppose it's a sort of dress rehearsal.

Why don't they leave me alone? Nobody wants me, but I'm not allowed to depart this life either. Somebody explain it to me, please. One is part of a theater group, and the extras have to be there even if they only serve as a backdrop. So Hartlieb brought the extra, Moll, back on stage. There he stood, explaining things in whispers. Lottchen's father was there too, because Lotte had produced a baby girl the day before. And they wanted to baptize the defenseless little thing 'Carla!' Which left me speechless! Kurt Sommer, the proud owner of the defenseless little thing was standing next to Nurse Ullmann. He had on a new suit again. Evidently he wanted to make a good impression on his brand new daughter. The suit was light gray and so beautiful and not paid for— I was sure—like most things Kurt bought for himself. And there was Edith Hannemann, who usually visited me at five o'clock in the afternoon, asking me what I meant by all this nonsense. Nurse Ullmann and Sister Theresa asked me in whispers how I was feeling, and I told them I was feeling fine.

My voice was so low, it startled me. Only Lotte's father said nothing and asked nothing. My old doctor knows me. As a teenager I used to be able to faint whenever I wanted to, when I didn't want to see or hear anything anymore. Only this time I'd gone a bit too far. Somebody said once that I fell into all the traps I set for others. That's right. Sánchez said it.

Next day Hartlieb told me that my whole life still lay ahead of me. Exactly. But I know what lives behind me. I know a lot more than Hartlieb and his psychiatrists. He amuses me with his weekly bouquet of neuroses. That reminds me: *Comet* sent a modest bunch of flowers. It looked like Ribbeck and smelled of his principles.

A week after my collapse, Hannemann was sitting at my bedside again. I was feeling much better and I had seen my godchild. Lotte beamed, Kurt beamed, Dr. Schneider was radiant, and the baby screamed. I lay in my bed and nodded like a sibyl. The day before a few of my hairs had fallen out. My hair was always the best part of me. I told Uncle Schneider that if my teeth started falling out he would have to find the right old lady's home for me. He said he wouldn't. He said I'd quarrel with all the old women and turn all the old men's heads. Nobody overestimates you like your old friends. I couldn't even turn Ribbeck's head, in spite of the fact that I worked for him.

"What's to happen next, Moll?" Hannemann asked.

"No idea. First of all they've got to move all the broken china out of the way."

"How about your doing it?"

"The doctor said I mustn't exert myself." I began to brood. "I'd like to be somebody else, Hannemann. Somebody who bears no resemblance to me. A different backdrop, different experiences, different men. It would be nice."

"You think so?"

"Of course. Another name, too. And in no way different from all other women. Punctual, diligent, satisfied with everything, without any imagination whatsoever, and with a man just as dull as she is." Gradually I warmed up to the idea. "Nothing happens, and when it does she doesn't notice it. Now and then a little rape by a stranger, of course with mutual consent. How about it, Hannemann?"

"Does this new person sew on her own buttons?" This was Hannemann's only excursion into the realm of fantasy. But before I could say no, Nurse Ullmann sailed into the room. "Herr Doktor Ribbeck is here, Fräulein Moll. He would like to see you."

"Stay here, Hannemann!" I screamed, as in my best days, but before Ullmann had grabbed her, she had escaped. Ribbeck was standing in the doorway. He didn't ask if he might come in. He came in.

When I haven't seen someone for a long time I find him either stranger or more familiar. Sánchez on the Orinoco had been a complete stranger, whereas Ribbeck looked quite familiar. Perhaps because he is so consistent. I said it was nice of him to make this visit of condolence, and he said Hartlieb had told him I wasn't to talk too much. He, Ribbeck, had rarely come across such a sensible doctor. Pause. He looked taller to me, and seemed more sarcastic and self-assured than in the office. He was wearing a suit very much like Kurt's, and I was positive that he had paid for it in cash. Perhaps he seemed taller because he was so thin, almost gaunt. He evidently ate too little. Maybe he lived on air, on his work, and on sex? None of my business. His face was expressionless.

He was looking at me through his thick glasses. I knew that I was pale and that my hair was sprawled across the pillow, no sheen because I couldn't stand to have it combed or brushed, even though Sister Theresa was very gentle. Just then she brought in a small silver basket with orchids, which hadn't grown on a savings account. I asked Ribbeck if the flowers were from him. He said amiably that they could hardly be from anybody else.

"You're terribly pale, Fräulein Moll. That's got to change."

"It's not going to change."

"You must let time do that."

He took a book out of his briefcase. The *Persian Letters* by Montesquieu. "I hope the letters will interest you. You know Montesquieu was a city man, unlike Rousseau. And what you need is a return to the city, to your own element, Fräulein Moll. Differentiations. Individuality. Analysis. Change. The problems of modern society." With which Ribbeck was conveying to me that on the Orinoco I had been a phony Rousseau. Then he went on to say that Montesquieu was modern, a favorite of the psychiatrist Ebers. So he knew that too. I thanked him in the monotone I always spoke now, and he looked at me even more sharply. With his Montesquieu he had brought an intellectual draught into the room, but that only made me feel tired. I closed my eyes and began to tremble. When I opened them again gingerly, Ribbeck was standing at the window, and I saw his ramrod back, as in the office. Sister Theresa brought us coffee, and moved my bed to catch the last rays of the afternoon sun. Ribbeck carried me to a chair while Sister Theresa raised the back of my bed. I said I could get back to my bed alone, but he picked me up and carried me back and deposited me on it like a package.

"She's not supposed to walk alone yet," said Sister Theresa. "Thank you very much, Herr Doktor."

It was all as matter of course as his grim moods in the office. I drank my coffee and my tears dripped down into it. Pure weakness and shock that Ribbeck was being so nice. Because after everything he had had to put up with from me in the office, he was showering me with orchids! Was my condition that serious? Was I going to die? I couldn't make him out. But his calm, the cool matter-of-fact way he behaved, did me good, for the first time. He was the personification of reasonability. No passion, although he must need it sometimes. After all, he was only in his middle thirties and perfectly healthy. He had held me in his arms, but I had felt nothing. Or was I too weak even for that? Never mind. After Bonnhoff, Carlos, Pilar, and the Hand of Fatima, Ribbeck in the role of nurse was downright refreshing. But I shouldn't have thought of this little group of demons because my heart began to beat horribly fast. He put his cup down on the table and asked, "What's the matter?" He almost sounded worried.

"It was all so dreadful," I said.

"You mustn't think about it anymore." He had grasped at once that I was back on the Orinoco. He laid my Chinese robe around my shoulders because I was shivering. The robe was a present from Sánchez, his first present to me on the island, and I brushed it off. Ribbeck shook his head, picked up the robe and laid it over a chair. He was absolutely at home, as if he had shared a room and a bed with me for years. Odd fellow! Then he looked in the bureau for a hand-kerchief and gave it to me. He must have rung for the nurse without my noticing it, because she appeared with a hypo. "He won't believe that I'm going to bow out any day now," I said in a rather loud voice. Ribbeck said I should stop talking nonsense, and the nurse gave me the hypo.

When I woke up it was night. Sister Theresa was sitting at my bedside, and the room lay in the mild blue light of the bedside lamp. I asked where my Montesquieu was. I wanted to read in the night. Sister Theresa said that tomorrow was another day, and I said, "Unfortunately." Ribbeck didn't come again.

During the following weeks Hartlieb tried out all sorts of things on me and put on a great show of jollity. Since he is anything but a jolly man, I felt that things weren't going very well with me. But suddenly I began to feel better. I read the *Persian Letters*. If they and the little silver basket hadn't been in the room, I would have thought Ribbeck's visit had been a dream. The good man seemed to have vanished from the face of the earth. But that couldn't be either, because Frau Hannemann said one day that he had become utterly un-bearable.

Meanwhile it was August and I was at home again. I read, I called Kurt and Lotte, I let Frau Frosch wait on me, and wished, ungrateful creature that I am, that Edith Hannemann would stop visiting me, because she asked me every time what I intended to do now that I was well again. I didn't know. *Comet* was running the series on Latin America, and one day they would appear in book form with Hanns König's photographs. I was out. After so many years, *Caracas for Beginners* was a dated commodity. Hannemann said Busch was Ribbeck's current favorite, but he wouldn't drop Bräutigam. I asked how Hannemann happened to know that, and she said Ribbeck wasn't like that. She had evidently given up all hope of my returning to the office.

When I had finally made up my mind to phone Ribbeck and thank him for his visit and the orchids, Hannemann said I'd better write to him, he was in Paris. With a girl called Hilda. From the Fichte flower shop. That was all right with me.

"Maybe he'll marry the girl," Hannemann said grimly. "I order flowers for him from there. She's young and pretty, but that's about all."

"That's a lot, Hannemann."

"He can do better than that. The girl's not smart."

"He's smart enough for two. Why do you want to marry him off every six months?"

"He's in his middle thirties, has money to burn, and a big empty house in Grunewald. A woman belongs in it."

"How about you, Hannemann?"

"Don't be foolish. How about you, Moll?"

"Don't be foolish." Her lips tightened. We talked about Ernst Bräutigam and his crocodile, and I asked how he was getting along minus a leg. "He doesn't write with his leg," she snapped.

It sounded like Ribbeck. I learned that he and Hartlieb were friends. Ribbeck probably needed a pianist for his violin. But this explained his visit at the clinic to me. He was doing Hartlieb a favor. I didn't like the idea. But I had bigger and better worries. The television people hadn't called me. I couldn't run after them. They had already drawn up their winter programs. There were plenty of guests and plenty more interviewers. I had enough money for a while, but figuring how long it would last was beyond me. Fortunately. That's how I kept up my spirits.

One day in September I woke up and knew what I had to do. Whoever hasn't experienced this—the sudden revelation of what should have been obvious for months or years—will find it very funny that on September twenty-fifth I suddenly knew that I wanted to write a novel!

I didn't start writing at once. To begin with, I was much too excited, and then it wasn't my way to rush into hard work. Besides I knew absolutely nothing about writing a novel, but perhaps that was just what encouraged me. Only one thing was clear to me: I didn't want to write an anti-novel. I had the feeling that the first novel one wrote should be a pro-novel. Just as Picasso, before his abstractions, had been a master of the traditional. Perhaps that was why one believed in his abstractions.

I brooded about it while Frau Frosch cleaned the apartment, cooked for me, and told me blow by blow what her oldest son and her married daughter had said the night before. I didn't know why I had to know all this, but I could go on thinking undisturbed because Frau Frosch liked to talk and didn't expect you to listen. I stared at my wallpaper. It was alive with creepers and vines like the plants in Sánchez's garden in Altamira. Suddenly I heard a man's voice saying long forgotten things: "Fantasy that is rooted in reality... curiosity for the fate of the individual... a baring of the subconscious—they are the arms of the novelist. The journalist finds out, the novelist invents. Invent, Fräulein Moll!" He had wanted to further my development as a writer in the restaurant, while I had preferred to watch Sánchez.

At five o'clock in the afternoon, when Frau Frosch had finally taken off, I wrote the first sentence of my novel.

In October Frau Frosch called me to the phone. "A gentleman wants to speak to you." I closed the door in her face, but I knew she was listening.

"Ribbeck speaking. Hello, Fräulein Moll."

"Hello."

"How are you?"

"All right. But October is always cold."

"Isn't your heat functioning?"

"I'm not functioning."

"I want to suggest something. Do you have a moment's time?"

"That's all I have."

"It's about . . ."

"I'm not coming back to your office."

"I'm not asking you to. Could you have dinner with me tomorrow evening?"

"Thank you."

"Thank you, yes or thank you, no?"

"Thank you, yes."

"I'll come for you at seven. The conference with Frau Doktor Wirth and Doktor Busch is at my house. Of course I'll drive you home when it's over."

"Nice of you. But I can still afford a taxi."

"So, until tomorrow evening."


I recalled that everyone at the office always prepared themselves mentally for any conference with Ribbeck, and I decided I'd better do so too. I could have read Montesquieu or Jung, since they were Ribbeck's favorite authors, but I preferred to try on my cocktail dresses and do my hair up in five different ways. I decided to wear a black dress with an almond-green border, high at the neck but cut very low at the back, Sánchez' Margarita pearls, and my "Constant Nymph" hairdo which always went well with ultra-chic dresses. Susanne Wirth would be coming straight from work, and she didn't know how to dress anyway. Just the same, she had married one of Kurt Sommer's exceptionally nice colleagues. How did these unprepossessing women manage it? Susanne was undoubtedly a talented lawyer and journalist, but she bored me to death. I didn't know Gregor Busch. He was supposed to be just as musical as Ribbeck, Wirth, and von Hartlieb. So I was going to join a group of musically oriented people and wouldn't be at my best. Classical music and talk about music were as incomprehensible to me as psychiatrist Ebers. I hoped that the muses would be subdued this evening, and that Ribbeck would open up some new

source of revenue for me. I couldn't pay Frau Frosch forever
with a novel that might never be finished.

Who did not appear at seven, while I was trembling nervously, was editor-in-chief Ribbeck. Instead Bender appeared, Ribbeck's chauffeur and factotum in Grunewald. I
knew his uniform and sly face from the *Comet* parking lot.
Ribbeck was still at a conference he hadn't been able to
postpone (nothing new about that) and Bender, who had been
born without a first name, was to drive me to Grunewald.
He covered my knees with a rug, which was evidently what
Ribbeck's ladies expected. After that I stared at his back. The
Mercedes was nothing to be sneezed at, neither was Ribbeck's
house. It was large and furnished in excellent taste: reception
room, music room, dining room, and behind it the library.
Rows of books up to the ceiling, a glass cupboard with rare
stones, two tables with chess boards, comfortable chairs. The
music room was empty except for a grand piano and built-
in cupboards for sheet music, and lamps. His violin case
stood on a long table beside the piano, as closed as Ribbeck
and the cupboards.

It is always strange to come to a house for the first time
and to find only the guests, not the host, present. But Busch,
Susanne, and I waited only five minutes in the reception room
with the tasteful furniture, and porcelain in glass cupboards,
when Ribbeck came tearing in, apologized for being late,
and Bender served drinks. In white gloves. Ribbeck was
wearing a dark suit and looked like a benevolent patrician
who just by chance happened to be editor-in-chief of a paper
with subscriptions in the millions. The portrait of an exceptionally unsympathetic man hung in the dining room. There
was a strong resemblance to Ribbeck. His old man, no doubt.
If there was a portrait of Ribbeck's mother, it wasn't visible.

If anyone could have ruined my appetite, it was Public
Prosecutor Ribbeck, whose sharp eyes seemed to look through
me and did not approve of my low cut dress. Frau Doktor
Wirth asked if I didn't feel cold, especially after such a long
illness. I said no, although it wasn't very warm in the dining
room. With two Ribbecks in the room, that wouldn't have

been possible anyway. As a woman, Susanne is so chaste that she thinks clothes were intended to cover the body, which her dress did in a depressing fashion. It was of non-descript length and sagged at the shoulders. Her hair was clean, which was really all that could be said for it. She looked freshly pressed and there was a waxy smell to her perfume. Perhaps I judged her too sharply because Ribbeck was so pleased with her. He was much nicer with Gregor Busch than he had ever been with me. Edith Hannemann had told me everything about Gregor Busch. He came from Munich, and had the natural warmth and good humor of the South Germans. He had a wonderful bass voice, had wanted to be an opera singer, but his restless intellect had drawn him to the world of publishing. When he was suddenly called to the phone I got to know Ribbeck from a different side.

He frowned. He hated interruptions while dining, and he didn't like the calls Busch received. They came from Theo, according to Hannemann, a depraved fellow with inclinations to blackmail. He was Busch's lover. Busch had left his wife because of Theo, and they now lived together. Hannemann would have been happy to throttle Theo. Busch was a fine, clever, hypersensitive man, and the mask of a good-natured Bavarian didn't sit well on his full, pale face, his prematurely gray hair, and lively, round, slightly astonished eyes. I decided not to think of what Ribbeck would do to Theo if the young man ever crossed his path.

Ribbeck kept the conversation going, but his frown deepened. Busch came back, white as a sheet, and excused himself. Bender had kept his food warm on a hot plate and refilled his wine glass. Busch didn't touch the food but downed his wine nervously. His lips were trembling. The others didn't look at him, but I did, and Ribbeck didn't like it. He steered the conversation on to immediate problems and ignored Busch so cleverly and sympathetically that the latter gradually recovered and was able to express his unconventional and precisely worded opinions in a normal voice. As we walked into the library for coffee and liqueur, Ribbeck patted his friend on the shoulder. He must have asked Busch in a low voice if he would rather leave, but Busch, in his penetrating bass, said he preferred to stay. "Very good," said Ribbeck. "Doktor Busch always has several invitations in one evening. We're lucky that he can stay with us. Your health, Gregor!" Busch raised his glass and looked at Ribbeck gratefully and somehow shamefacedly. "You're much too kind," he murmured. He was still breathing fast. What had Theo done to him? I liked Gregor Busch, although he now had my well-paid job at the office, plus a few other assignments.

When I think that on this evening Ribbeck saved me from the financial bind I was in and got me a job on television, I could really have been nicer to him. He was the only one who could do something for me, and did. The conference ran smoothly and was fruitful. I was to interview important women: politics, economy, art. Busch would write a questionnaire and act as moderator. I was to visit the women in their own homes and the television show that resulted was to be as spontaneous as *Carla Moll and her Guests*. Susanne was to discuss the position of the career woman from the legal aspects. Finally there would be a round table discussion between Busch, Wirth, Moll, and the guests. If the series was successful, Ribbeck was planning a German-French collaboration. "Paris would be fun," I said, but received no response to that from Ribbeck. He wasn't interested in what I found fun.

When it came time to say good-bye, I found myself suddenly alone with him for a moment, and I thanked him sincerely for what he was doing for me, but he waved my thanks away. No reason for it. He wasn't a charity organization. I had mass appeal, that was all there was to it. Did I want an advance? I didn't. What would I be making? Ribbeck didn't know. My throat was dry. A while ago I had been so animated and could have tossed ideas around like confetti. Busch would have liked them. But Ribbeck seemed to prefer a lecture by Susanne Wirth. When he needed sex he evidently got it from Fräulein Hilda in the flower shop. In the meantime I'd had a look at her when I'd sent Lotte flowers. She had a snub nose and was thick around the waist.

Suddenly the evening was over. Bender had disappeared. Gregor Busch wanted to drive me home, which was nice of him, but he lived at the other end of West Berlin. Ribbeck said he would take care of it, which was even nicer.

Susanne slipped into her cloth coat and I waited for Ribbeck to help me into my fur. Who would put on her own coat with two men standing around? As Ribbeck raised the coat around my shoulders I felt his hands on my naked back. "What did you say?" But he was only warning me not to get pneumonia. I was careless, and we were not in Venezuela. "You certainly notice everything," I murmured, and he said, "Fortunately."

The shrubs in the garden rustled like thousand mark bills, a pleasant sound. God, was I broke! The dress I had on wasn't paid for. Just like Kurt Sommer.

On the way home Ribbeck was silent until he asked suddenly whether I thought I'd enjoy the new job. "And how!" I said. "I can hardly wait."

"Why are you trying to fool me, Fräulein Moll? You're not in the least interested in women."

"That's not true."

He stopped in a quiet side street and stared at me. "Of course it's true. I know you a lot better than you realize."

"You don't know me at all!"

"At any rate, better than you know yourself, my dear." His long fingered, graceful hands lay on the steering wheel. Why didn't he drive on? As if I didn't know why! After midnight and a lot of drinks, there was only one thing he could possibly want. I was only half dressed in this dress anyway. He needed it. Annemarie was gone, his Hilda was not available at the moment, he wasn't Gregor Busch, and he was in his middle thirties. "If you want to kiss me, I don't mind."

"Your enthusiasm is catching, Fräulein Moll," he said, and drove on.

He had made a fool of me again. I studied his sharp, arrogant profile. His maneuvers were as distasteful here as any he had ever subjected me to. There was nothing more to say, but I found his silence just as unbearable as it had been at the office. "I didn't mean to make you angry, Doktor Ribbeck."

He laughed softly, not unpleasantly. "You make me laugh. For the moment we are partners, that's all. You need me to pay your bills and I need you for my television show. Did you think you had to sleep with me because I was improving your financial position?"

"Doktor Ribbeck! I forbid you to..."

"To what? And by the way, when I want to kiss a woman, I don't wait for permission. Who do you think I am?"

A small residue of caution warned me not to tell my benefactor what I thought of him. Suddenly I was dead tired. That still happened to me sometimes since my collapse. I closed my eyes. In my precarious situation and after Carlos and Pilar, I needed friendliness. The tears poured out of my closed eyes. All of a sudden I felt desperate.

"Don't... don't..." Ribbeck murmured in a completely changed voice. Evidently he couldn't stand tears. Whereupon I sobbed. Ribbeck said his only consolation was that I wasn't crying because of him but, as usual, because of myself. "So, there we are. Good night, Fräulein Moll."

A week later he sent me a velvet stole that matched my cocktail dress with the almond-green border. A single green-silver flower was embroidered on it. Beautiful! Did Ribbeck feel he had been too harsh with me, or didn't he want me to catch cold in my low-cut dress and ruin his well-laid plans? I thanked him in writing for the present and the nice evening. After that I didn't see or hear anything from him for weeks.

My novel would not leave me in peace. My characters became more real to me all the time. All of them bore the characteristics of people I had met, people who had either uplifted or degraded me. But they were not photographs. They were new people, and to some extent bigger than life. Much later I found out that the characters in a novel only seem real when they are stylized, when the daily monotony of their lives is reduced to a minimum.

Ribbeck's television series was a success, like everything he undertook. The television people accepted his proposals and he remained the clever manipulator in the background. And he liked the role. Just as he had prophesied, the prominent women bored me to death. Perhaps they would have bored the audience too if I hadn't thrown my confetti around. "You bring life into our hallowed halls," said the director. Too bad that Ribbeck couldn't hear him.

I thought of him often. After all he was the one who had given me the idea to write a novel. I was wonderfully busy and missed no one. But sometimes I felt weak at the knees when I wondered what would happen when these television interviews came to an end. Nobody had suggested a new series to me. I had been stamped as a world traveler and I wasn't traveling. Frau Hannemann continued to keep me in the know as to what Ribbeck was doing. Bender had told her that he was fixing up a second bedroom in his house. In pastel colors. So he had to be planning to marry. One afternoon, when I was sitting at my desk in my pajamas, he turned up. He had come with a suggestion. I put on Carlos's Chinese robe.

Ribbeck asked if he could have a cup of coffee. He had come straight from the office and could do with one. "Don't I know that Chinese thing from the clinic? Beautiful embroidery."

"It's a souvenir from Venezuela."

"I thought so."

I hastily removed my manuscript from the desk, ran into the bedroom and hid it under my pillow. I didn't want him to see or criticize it. While I got the coffee, he looked at the picture of my parents on the desk. "Are these your parents?"

"Yes."

"Your mother looks like Potsdam."

"She always did. I take after my father."

"You look a lot like him. Are you like him?"

"Since when are you studying family history? Black coffee?"

"Yes, please."

"Hartlieb says that's bad for the heart."

"I don't have a heart. At least that's what you think."

"I can't think anything about total strangers."

"I was talking about myself."

Since the conversation was again threatening to derail I asked him why he had come. He said that several papers were inquiring about me, through his intervention, and wanted to know if I'd write some short stories about Venezuela for them. The fee was generous. "It's something you can do with your eyes closed," he said. "And you need the money."

"Now I'll have to thank you again!"

"Do you find that so difficult?"

"Short stories will be even more difficult."

"Why?"

"Because I happen to be writing a novel."

"*What?!*" He jumped up. "When did you start?"

"Shortly before your dinner in Grunewald."

"And you didn't tell me!"

"I was going to tell you on my way home, but you were so . . . so . . ."

"Horrid. I always am, even when I want to be nice. Where is the manuscript?"

"In my bed."

"I *beg* your pardon!"

I went and got my grease and coffee-stained manuscript. He sat down at my desk and began to read. My heart beat so loudly, I was surprised he didn't hear it. But he heard and saw nothing. I put on a dress and did up my hair because now things were getting serious. If he found my work bad, then it was bad. I could see him take his red pencil out of his briefcase. He made notes. "It isn't any good, is it?" I asked. He didn't answer and went on reading. He hadn't noticed that I had come back into the room. I think that I began to know him in this one hour between day and night, hope and despair. He was the only one who had recognized that there was something in me that demanded expression in a form new to me, and now he fell upon it. It had grown dark. I turned on the desk lamp. My hands were ice-cold.

When he had read it to the end, he got up and gave me a strange look, but he didn't say a word.

"So it's no good," I said.

"It's great!" he said. "You have people who live and ideas that will mature. Of course there are parts that will need cutting and a few awkward places, all typical of a beginner. But we can fix that. I know exactly whom I'm going to interest in the manuscript." He mentioned the name of a well-known West German publishing house. "What's the matter, girl? Don't collapse on me!"

As he had done in the clinic, he carried me to my bed. He rubbed my temples with eau de cologne. The room was swimming in front of my eyes and everything went black. But I was aware that he took off my dress and listened to my heart as I gradually came back to my senses. His head was lying on my breast. I threw my arms around it. I had to. "I'm so happy . . . about the book." He kissed me gently. Incredibly gently. Then he asked if I had anything to eat in the apartment. Yes, there was a chicken Frau Frosch had cooked in the refrigerator. He disappeared into the kitchen. He was just as at home in my apartment as he had been in my room at the clinic. Then he sat down beside my bed, and we ate and drank whiskey. It had been afternoon when he had come. He stayed all evening. He stayed the night. I lay in his arms as if in a solidly-built house. Nothing could fall on my head. He was the roof over me. He whispered that I was the most beautiful girl he had ever known.

In the night I woke up. His right arm was lying across my body and he woke at once when I moved. It was a bright, moonlit night and I hadn't drawn the curtains. My head lay on his shoulder. I murmured, "Oh Ribbeck, who would have thought it . . ."

"I did," he said, "for quite a while now."

# 30

# Five O'Clock
# in the Afternoon

Carla Moll:

Ribbeck came to see me fairly regularly, usually at five in the afternoon, a lousy time, the bridge between morning and evening. He worked until five, and at seven he inevitably had to leave again. He knew everyone in Berlin, and twice a week played trios and duets with his musical friends. He tried to spend all his weekends with me, but that wasn't always possible. I hadn't realized the scope of his professional and social obligations. At the office he had seemed just as lonely as I was. Again I saw how strangely different the life of a single man was from that of a single woman. He was so much in demand. Gradually I found out how modest and lacking in illusions he was. He never attributed the many invitations to the magic of his personality but to the prestige of his position. He was an influential man in the public eye.

He didn't become enchanting overnight; when he was unpleasant he continued to be hard to deal with, but he had fine qualities that he hid as other people hid their vices. He was the best and most reliable friend one could wish for, but he was not a lover, like Sánchez on Margarita Island. He had told me once that I was beautiful, and that was that. He never said that he loved me or needed me or couldn't do without me. I suppose he loved me in his way. He needed me when he needed sex, or so it seemed to me, but he could evidently do very well without me; he never refused an invitation because of me. He couldn't even manage a couple of weeks off for an illicit honeymoon. Sánchez had been a busy man, but he had spent three weeks with me on his island and lived only for me. He had even sometimes done what *I* wanted. Ribbeck did what he wanted, or felt he had to do out of a sense of duty. But when he had time for me, he was all mine.

I was fairly unhappy when I was alone. It's a funny thing, but I could live for a long time without a man and not seem to miss anything, but when I had a man, I missed him when he wasn't there. I always wanted a man who could steady me. And now I wanted Ribbeck!

As usual, other men sensed that I was no longer alone. Suddenly the program director wanted to go out with me. I was alone so many evenings. Why didn't I do as Ribbeck did? Because now, idiot that I was, I wanted only him! He rarely spoke about his invitations. I didn't even know if he was still seeing Hilda. I didn't think so, but I couldn't be sure. I never asked him where he was going.

He gave me many beautiful things. I never said he didn't have to. That would have been a mistake. He didn't have to be taught thrift; it was part of his nature. That was why his exquisite gifts means a great deal to me. Once Kurt Sommer said to me, "You look adorable, Carlchen. Are you in love?" I said "No," and it was the truth. I was not in love with Ribbeck. What I felt for him was deeper and calmed rather than excited me. One evening I asked him if he couldn't stay with me. "Work on the novel, Carla. I'd only disturb you, and you're so easily distracted."

"So you care more about the novel than about me?"

He said we were one and the same thing, and that's why we both meant so much to him. He was the only man I could believe, but I would have liked it better if he had preferred me to my novel.

It was crazy: now I wanted to be with him day and night, and of course I kept this possessive urge to myself. He would have said, "I *beg* your pardon!" We were independent bachelors. He also never asked me where I went evenings.

Perhaps Ribbeck made such an impression on me as a man because he was so different from Carlos. That's why he was so good for me. Sánchez caught fire at the coolness of a woman, or at least her reserve, whereas Ribbeck told me one night that my responses were what made him happiest during our lovemaking. I caught fire slowly, but then it was a prairie fire! One night I lost all control and was depressed when it was over. I was lying in his arms, but I freed myself. I lay like a piece of wood beside him, and he noticed it. He always noticed everything about me. "What's the matter? Why are you unhappy?"

"I'm very happy."

"That's what I thought," he whispered, and drew me close again.

"No. Not now."

"Yes. Now."

I couldn't deceive him, not seriously, not in fun, not in bed. And one day he would have had enough of the prairie fire, of my dreadfully changeable moods, of me. Five in the afternoon is not my hour. He came, kissed me, read what I'd written, discussed it with me, drank coffee. The only thing missing was that he didn't drink it standing. Then he left, latest at seven-thirty, and I could stare at the moon.

Nobody knew anything about our relationship, not even Lotte, who always knew everything about me. I simply couldn't talk about it even though I had talked to Lotte a lot about Sánchez. Yet basically Sánchez had always been an alien force in my life, whereas with Ribbeck I felt perfectly at home, as if I had known him forever. I told myself that I must have dreamed up Sánchez, and he had turned into a nightmare. Ribbeck gave me the security I needed to live.

The more his afternoon visits annoyed me, with their abrupt departures, the louder I laughed over coffee. But I guess I overdid it. I overdo everything. One afternoon he said, "Don't work so hard at it. I don't want that."

"I don't know what you're talking about?"

"I'd like to stay with you and you know it," he said patiently, "but I have a dinner invitation I can't turn down."

"I know, I know, I know."

"Repetition weakens the effect, my child. Keep that in mind when you're writing."

Something snapped in me. Surprising that he didn't hear it. I was wild with rage or disappointment or God knew what. I threw my coffee cup at him. "Go!" I screamed. "I've had it! And don't look so surprised! You're sick of me. You've had what you wanted. You don't have to come and see me out of a sense of decency!"

"In your place I wouldn't mention decency. You don't know the meaning of the word." He picked up the shards of the Meissen cup and threw them in the wastepaper basket. If there was anything I felt sorry about at this point it was Mother's cup. His iron self-control told me it was over. A funeral at five in the afternoon.

I was trembling. But for the life of me I couldn't shut up. Carlos had told me I talked too much. But unfortunately I don't learn by experience. I asked if he was still there. He was standing in the doorway. I was tempted to say, as I had done once in the office, that I was pleased with the solution. I could feel cold air on my neck, as if he had opened a window. "I'd like you to know that I despise you!"

"You must calm down, Carla!"

"You don't owe me a thing! After all, you didn't seduce a virgin."

"Who'd want to? Now listen to me . . ."

"I don't want to listen!" I ran into the bedroom and locked the door. He knocked on it impatiently. So he was still there. I didn't move. "Let me in, please!"

That did it! I opened the door and threw myself on the bed. I closed my eyes because I couldn't stand the sight of him another minute. He was pale, and there were drops of sweat on his high forehead. Even his thin blond hair seemed damp. He leaned over me and turned my head so that I had to look at him, then, abruptly, he let go. "Now you listen to me! You're overworked, and anyway you're unpredictable. I'm willing to forget all this nonsense!"

"Go! For God's sake, go!"

"Right away. I'm late anyway. Only one thing more: I don't want any scenes. I expect a minimum of respect." I stared at him. To have and receive respect was not courtesy for him. It was his basic law and it determined his behavior. But right then, as he said it quietly and with devastating impact, I saw red. I didn't even give him his lousy minimum of respect, which he needed like the air to breathe, like work and relaxation, like love and life. I must have gone crazy.

"I'm stupid, that's what I am," I said. "What you want from me you can get from your whores! I . . . I . . . give you all I have!"

"Half a portion of you is all I need."

"You come and go as it suits you, and I sit here like an also-ran. What do you take me for? You stay overnight only when you need it."

He looked at me with such fury, I closed my eyes again. He had never shown me this face before, not even during our last scene in his office.

"You never had any idea what I want from you, or rather what I wanted from you. You never know when you've gone too far."

He walked to the door. I jumped up. I wanted to say I was sorry, but I couldn't utter a sound. He was one of the few people who had ever taken any trouble with me. He worried about me and helped me, was helping me toward an entirely new career, patiently, and absolutely selflessly. In tender moments he brushed my long hair, which for some reason or other fascinated him, and dressed and undressed me like a child. It wasn't true that he only wanted *it*. When he found me pale and tired, he would sit me down on his long-legged lap and stroke my hair off my forehead and speak quietly and lovingly to me. He could get supper and serve drinks just as adroitly as Bender.

"Stay!" I ran over to him and clung to him. I sobbed and coughed and wouldn't let go. "Forgive me!"

I had never asked forgiveness of anyone, not even of Mother. He freed himself gently, very gently. But then he grasped my shoulders in an iron grip. "Don't destroy what we have!" he said. Threat? Warning? Exhortation? He had said once that I trampled on other people's feelings but was a shrinking violet with myself. I should try things the other way around.

I had black and blue marks for days where he had grasped me. Next day he called from Grunewald: he had to go away suddenly. I felt cold. I wrote him two letters which he didn't answer. Frau Hannemann told me later that he'd only been gone two days. He still had the keys to my apartment. I didn't have the keys to his house. But anyway Bender was there, and the housekeeper, and his many guests.

One afternoon when I came home he was sitting at my desk, reading the latest chapter. He jumped up and looked at me. "If I could write like that," he murmured. "What would you do then?" I asked. He said crossly that the trouble was he had no imagination. He asked where I had been. I had had lunch with Lotte. I was still standing in the doorway. He had walked back to the desk and began putting the new chapter, with his comments, back into my green folder. "Why don't you come in?" he said, as if it had been his apartment.

I came in gingerly. I didn't want to do anything to disrupt the mood between us. "Closer." He opened his arms wide and I ran into them as if into my house. Oh dear God in heaven, how I had missed him! "Oh, Ribbeck, do you still like me a little?"

"Unfortunately."

I always called him Ribbeck. Later I found a nickname for him. When I told him my second name was Ulrike, after Grandmother Moll, he began to call me Rieke, in special moments.

Everything was all right again. I asked him if Bender made better coffee.

"Yes."

"Why didn't you bring him along?"

"Bender is easily shocked. I don't know what you might throw at his head."

We laughed. He sat on the big Gobelin wingchair he had bought for himself, and I sat on his lap with my arms around his neck and kissed him wherever the kisses fell—on his forehead, ears, nose, lips.

"Rieke, Rieke, you bad girl."

"Oh, Ribbeck, you must never leave me again!"

"As far as I can recall, you threw me out."

"But I love you!"

"You have strange ways of showing it."

"And you don't show it in any way at all!"

"I *beg* your pardon!"

He carried me into the bedroom. He stayed the evening. He stayed the night.

The manuscript got thicker and thicker and I got thinner. Ribbeck wanted to go away with me as soon as the book was finished. I said that was too good to be true. It was too good to be true.

I learned a lot from him because he knew how to sweeten his criticism. I was still very unsure and easily discouraged. He wrote most of his comments in the manuscript, or attached notes. To this day I find blunt criticism hard to take, but at the time it would have discouraged me completely. He chose his words carefully.

"You still explain a little too much. Readers like to think a few things out for themselves and form their own opinions. Quite often they are just as intelligent as the author. We laughed. But I kept his advice in mind. He brought me books which I was to read for some specific reason, he discussed all sorts of technical problems with me, although he was nearly always worn-out by the time he got to me, and he taught me the most important thing of all—to work systematically. I began to rewrite pages when they didn't please me or him. When he said, "Good," I was happy. Then I knew it wasn't bad.

"You really think something's going to come of it?" I asked every now and then.

"Something's already come of it. But you must go on

writing. Afterward we'll go away." I went on writing, but we didn't go away.

It was my book, his book, our book. When it was three-quarters done wild horses plus Ribbeck couldn't have dragged me away from my desk. We decided to take our holiday later. Later . . .

I had strange experiences at my desk. My characters and their backgrounds became increasingly lively as Venezuela and its characters grew more shadowy. Until a letter came from Wally Bendix. A thick airmail letter. Not because Wally had suddenly become an ardent letter writer but because a newspaper clipping was enclosed. "Remember him, Carla Moll?"

Of course I remembered him. The shadows came to life again. Cooper's dinner in Puerto Ayacucho. Cooper, the Prestons, Sánchez, and the Padillas in the bushes. It was all so long ago! Headlines from Venezuela are never amusing, but this one was gruesome.


FIERY DEATH IN MARACAIBO.
*Special report by Juan Picado, Caracas, Venezuela, 1971*

*A few days ago a tragic event took place on Lake Maracaibo. César Pérez, a petroleum worker from Puerto Ordaz, was killed in the fiery gas that had escaped from one of the pipes. He had dropped a burning rag into the oil while close to the scaffolding and was burned alive in the gas-filled air. Workers and foremen dragged the huge man away and poured water over him, but it was too late. He died on his way to the hospital. Before he lost consciousness, he screamed for a woman called Anna. She is a gray-haired European who has meanwhile reported to the authorities. Her name is Anna Carlovac, a cashier in a Chinese restaurant in Maracaibo, and she revealed something sensational to the police. The deceased César Pérez was actually Camilo de Padilla, an Orinoco guerrilla, whom the police have been looking for for months. Padilla and his band of terrorists were responsible for the kidnapping and murder of the North American Gilbert Preston.*

*Señora Carlovac and Father Antonio Valdivia were the only ones who walked behind the coffin of the murderer.*

*Padilla's mother in Puerto Ordaz recently died, shortly after Padilla's young wife and her lover burglarized the poor woman's house and disappeared. Señora Carlovac, who for some time lived in an elegant pension in Puerto Ordaz, saw Padilla again by chance in Maracaibo. She recognized Padilla one night as he was lurking around the restaurant. She took pity on the unfortunate man and did what she could for him. At nightfall Padilla would wait at the back door of the restaurant until Señora Carlovac brought him something to eat. Señora Carmen Tsung, née Chang, the owner of the restaurant, looked the other way. "We Chinese think three times and breathe ten times before we deny an unfortunate man food and comfort," the highly respected owner of the restaurant said. She is a true daughter of the church and the happy mother of three sons. Her husband is the successful manager of a famous hotel in Maracaibo.*

*Father Valdivia explained that Pérez-Padilla had been one of his parishioners, like many of the petroleum workers. The huge man never missed mass and often burst into tears. During the last months of this life he suffered from hallucinations of hell fire. Padilla went around in rags and begged for food in spite of his good salary. Every month he gave it to the priest for the members of his flock.*

"A strange continent," said Ribbeck, when I read the article to him. "Did you know the Padillas?"

"I met them at the Hotel Amazonas, with Cooper, the Prestons, and Wally Bendix."

"And Sánchez?"

"And Sánchez."

"How would it be if you finally told me everything. From beginning to end."

So I told him all about it. The only thing I didn't tell him about was the dreadful weekend with Sánchez in Puerto Cabello.

Ribbeck's reaction to my experiences in Venezuela had always been sour. He didn't have to be in the office for that. He didn't interrupt me once, but the expression on his face became increasingly stony. That's the worst thing about self-controlled people, they hold everything back. When I was through, Ribbeck jumped up. "Come on, let's go home."

He was always alone over the weekends. His housekeeper went home to her family and Bender to his girlfriend. Yes, Bender (no first name) had a girl.

I looked for my white coat which Ribbeck loved, but couldn't find it because Frau Frosch had taken it to the cleaner. Ribbeck was standing in the foyer asking, "Well, are you coming or not?" like an old husband.

On the way to Grunewald I looked at him out of the corner of my eye. He looked a lot like editor-in-chief Ribbeck, the beast. His lips were closed tight and the frown between his eyes deepened. He was finding Sánchez hard to digest. I swallowed and coughed because there was a lump in my throat, and he said it was too late for crocodile tears. I said, "Drive me home! You're terribly unfair. I detest Sánchez!"

"That doesn't mean a lot where you're concerned," he said, and drove on, direction Grunewald. Maybe he was remembering how I had watched Sánchez at the restaurant.

"Shall I tell you what's burning me, Carla? You can't say no. You lack . . ."

"Shall I tell you what you lack?"

"Do."

"Another time," I said wearily. I was working very hard, and here was Ribbeck with his demands. I was supposed to be a beautiful, elegant, talented girl, with the temperament of a Cleopatra, and the modesty of a violet!

He stopped at the garden gate. "With whom do you go out in the evenings when I'm not there? How often do you say yes? Answer me!"

He grabbed me by the shoulders. He must have gone crazy, and I'd been crazy to tell him the truth about Sánchez. "Well— out with it!"

"Don't destroy what we have!"

He looked at me like Lazarus risen from the grave. His cheeks were hollow. He buried his face in my hair. "Give me time! For God's sake, give me time!"

*  *  *

My novel was accepted and Ribbeck worked out a wonderful contract for me. In answer to the publisher's first percentage offer he had said, "I *beg* your pardon..."

I asked him if he would take me to a concert some time, something for beginners. "You mean it?" He looked radiant.

"Of course," I said. "If you're with me I may get used to music."

"If you could get used to an old bastard like me, you can get used to anything."

Five o'clock was our hour for coffee and confessions. That's how I found out one day why Ribbeck had been engaged twice, unsuccessfully. Number one had been a lesbian, and number two had had a child which she kept hidden in a foster home outside Frankfurt. Ribbeck had found out easily—the child had been playing outside. "If I want children, I'll make my own." He never spoke a truer word...

"Who is the fellow? I'll give him a piece of my mind until he hears the angels singing!"

"He'll love that. He's very musical."

"Who is it, Carlchen?"

"I can't tell you."

"You can tell me anything girl. Is he...hm...married?"

"No, please let's not talk about it, Uncle Schneider. I make enough money for twins. Don't be so old-fashioned!"

Lotte's father sighed. He had brought me into this world and since then felt responsible for me because my father had been so unreliable and had done so many peculiar things. "Why doesn't the fellow want to marry you?"

"Who says he doesn't want to? I don't want to. He even more so. A dyed-in-the-wool bachelor."

"A dyed-in-the-wool bastard if you ask me."

"I didn't ask you. He is *not* a bastard. He is...he is..."

"Let me speak to him, girl."

I shook my head. I didn't want to be a leech. Ribbeck would hate that, and me. It was a quarter to five and I didn't dare keep Ribbeck waiting. "Why do you want me to take so much medicine, Uncle Schneider?"

He mumbled that I wasn't all that strong, and I'd had a collapse only a few months ago, and . . . and . . . "You mean I'm going to die in childbirth?"

"I mean the child needs a father, you little fool!" There were tears in my eyes, quite often now, and Lotte's father had to console me again. He didn't say that he was glad Mother hadn't lived to see this, and that was decent of him because I knew it was on the tip of his tongue. "Think it over carefully, girl. Drink a lot of milk. Go to bed early. And drive carefully. I'll see you next week. If you want to talk to me before that, call me. Anytime."

I kissed him hastily. "I must go." He asked if I had such a pressing appointment that I couldn't take time to button my dress.

Ribbeck arrived three minutes after I got home. "What's the matter with you?"

"Nothing!"

"Don't you feel well? Do you want me to leave?"

I shook my head, ran out of the room to the bathroom, and vomited. He came running after me when he heard me groaning. "Go away!" He supported me, held up my head until I'd given up all I had, and, trembling and sweating, drank a glass of water. "Oh, my dress! Get out! Everything stinks! I do too!" I wept. I was in my third month and either wept or vomited in the morning and afternoon.

He undressed me and ran a bath for me. He rubbed me down with eau de cologne. He put my soiled dress and underwear in soapy water to soak. Bender couldn't have done better. I felt dizzy, and he lifted me into the tub. He was wonderfully adroit. He dried me and helped me into my pajamas and robe. I had never loved him so much. He carried me to the couch, and I thought how wonderful it would be to die at that moment of his complete love and care.

"Now you smell like Rieke again."

"Weren't you disgusted?"

"Nothing about you can disgust me. But what on earth's the matter now? Please don't cry! What's wrong, child?"

"The lobster salad didn't agree with me."

"That was the day before yesterday." He gave me a sharp look, then he asked how far along I was. I told him.

"And *this* you kept from me?"

"Forget it. Forget it right away. Thousands of women bring up their children alone, and I will too."

"The poor child!" He turned his back on me and studied the titles of the books on my shelf. Then he swerved around abruptly and asked what did I have against the name Ribbeck?

I stared at him. "You think you've got to marry me."

"So?"

"You think I set a trap for you."

"So?"

"Stop saying *so*!"

"Don't give me orders. We're not married yet. Your rooms have been ready for ten days now. Bender is just hanging the curtains."

"He can do that, too?"

"He can do anything. And much better than any woman."

"You really don't have to marry me."

"I'm not marrying you because you can't hang curtains."

"Oh Ribbeck!" I jumped up and hugged him. "Careful!" he said. "Have some consideration for the little one."

He made me lie down again, but I wanted to make the coffee. I felt at least I owed him that. He said I should stay put. "Uncle Schneider said having children was healthy." Ribbeck ignored the remark and brought the coffee and the pretty little colored petit fours he often bought for us. "Why aren't you eating?" he asked anxiously.

"I don't feel like it now. Maybe later. But listen—we don't have to get married right away. It won't be noticeable for quite a while and a wedding right now will disrupt all your plans."

"Do you want to wait until the boy can strew flowers at the wedding?"

"So you really mean it? And you'll have the two of us on

your hands at the same time? Do you realize what you're taking on?"

He was looking at my books again. "If it's a daughter, she's got to look just like you, or we'll send her back."

Lotte Sommer:

I wouldn't like to know how this marriage would have proceeded without Bender. Because in spite of the fact that Carlchen was crazy about Ribbeck, she remained unpunctual, inconsiderate, indolent, and unsociable. Nobody could have been more considerate than Ribbeck, but right after the wedding he was already entertaining on a grand scale. The guests were Bender's department, and he was allowed to hire as much help as he wanted. Ribbeck wanted a very beautiful, very elegant mistress, with wedding ring. And Carlchen played her part when she felt well enough. Unfortunately this was not always the case during her pregnancy. She went on behaving strangely and unpredictably, only we didn't really notice it because we'd known her for such a long time. But Ribbeck noticed it and ignored her after every quarrel, which she chose to call "differences of opinion." Father had always said she was half-cracked. Sometimes she was twelve years old, other times she seemed much wiser than her thirty-one years. But I think Ribbeck adored her periodic childishness and her need for his support. Sometimes these differences of opinion ended with Ribbeck being served dinner in the library while his wife ate in her room.

The planned honeymoon never took place because in her fourth month Carla hemorrhaged. Father and Dr. von Hartlieb prevented a panic and ordered her to bed, and no excitement! At five Ribbeck came home. Father said he turned green when he saw Carla lying in bed, deathly pale. The unborn child seemed to be robbing her of all her strength and blood, and I was afraid Ribbeck was beginning to hate it. Father said I shouldn't talk nonsense, but he didn't sound very convincing. Frau Hannemann said he had become unbearable at the office.

When Carla was feeling better, she visited us often in the afternoon because Ribbeck didn't get home until five. She was always afraid of being late because, just as at the office, he never waited more than ten minutes. She looked at her watch so often that Kurt asked if she was Carla Moll or Ribbeck's slave. She didn't laugh, but said seriously, "You know, he expects a minimum of respect." Kurt cast his eyes heavenward. But then we chatted and laughed as in the good old days, and before we knew it, it was seven. Carla turned pale, I was horrified, even Kurt looked worried. Bender's "Miss Hertha" said that Ribbeck and Bender had left the house long ago, destination unknown. At that moment the bell rang three times (Ribbeck's signal) and Carlchen and I started. "Courage, girls!" said Kurt as he went to open the door. Ribbeck came into the living room without taking off his coat and exuded a glacial air. His ability to make you feel uncomfortable and guilty was magical. He greeted me frostily, looked at Robert's teddy bear on the floor with undisguised disgust, also at the pieces of his toy train on the table, and asked Carla why she hadn't let him know that she was coming home two hours late. She said she didn't know.

"I *beg* your pardon!"

"I mean, time passes so quickly here with Lottchen and Kurt."

I could tell by Ribbeck's expression how much this explanation pleased him. The situation was funny, but nobody laughed. Ribbeck asked if Carla was ready to come home now or should Bender come for her later. She said he should leave her in peace, and he said she could depend on it, he would do just that. He was on his way to an evening of music with Hartlieb. He didn't say how he had spent the time between five and seven. As he left he explained that Herr Doktor Schneider had advised bed rest for his wife after six P.M. It only occurred to me later that he meant my father. I disliked him as much as my peaceful nature permitted. I kissed Carlchen, and she shook hands with Kurt. He had given up kissing her good-bye after Carla, slightly embarrassed, had told him Ribbeck didn't like it. By the way, she never called him "Oscar." He was either Ribbeck or "he."

Bender was waiting downstairs in the car. By the light of the street lamps his face was smooth and expressionless. He

had never done me any harm, but I couldn't stand him either.
I realize this was irrational and horrid of me, but Bender was
so perfect. Perhaps that was what irritated me. "I would be
grateful, my dear Sommer, if you would draw my wife's
attention to the time when she visits you again. In pleasant
company she tends to forget everything." Kurt said that took
talent, and Ribbeck said that he had put off a conference in
order to be home at five. Great!

Carla, Kurt, and I had been a happy trio; gradually we became a trio with an easy conscience. Ribbeck didn't notice it,
or he pretended not to. He was waiting for the day when Carla
would stop visiting us, but that was one of the few things he
didn't succeed in. Except for Gregor Busch, Carla didn't make
friends with any of his friends. Women didn't interest her, and
she had lost all interest in men. She no longer had her bit of fun
with them. Ribbeck condemned everything that could remotely
be termed "flirtation." Kurt got along well with him, especially
when he saw him at Susanne Wirth's house without Carla. Ribbeck could be a good friend when he felt friendly. He couldn't
possibly be as arrogant as I thought he was. His cold features
and his aloofness probably caused this distance between him
and me. Kurt spent too much and I had to get rid of his secretary
twice because he was susceptible to women's charms, but he
exuded warmth and good humor. Sometimes he told Carlchen,
when a crisis between her and Ribbeck lasted too long, "You
must be more considerate."

"You have no idea how horrid he can be!"

We tried not to laugh. Kurt voiced the opinion, cautiously,
that Ribbeck could be very pleasant when one lived up to his
expectations. "He expects too much of me," Carla said with
sudden insight. "I can't change completely on order."

"But Carlchen, he fell in love with you as you are!"

"Don't be silly, Kurt. He had illusions about me."

"That's how all men are, silly." Kurt grinned. "Would I have
married Lotte if I hadn't first remodeled her in my dreams?"

"With Lottchen that wasn't necessary," Carlchen said
darkly. "She is always right. But I am..." She sank into a
brooding silence. This she had learned from Ribbeck.

She wasn't only Father's problem child, she was Kurt's and mine too. She should not hurt Ribbeck, or let him down. He had staked everything on this marriage. He loved her deeply, but he hadn't changed overnight either. He remained editor-in-chief Ribbeck, the beast! But I felt sure that he was totally different with her when all was well between them. Carla had always said you only knew a man when you had slept with him. I am not in complete agreement, but I can't prove the opposite.

When he picked Carla up and Bender drove them back into their world, it was always a real separation for me. As soon as she was sitting with Ribbeck in his car and he laid his arm across her shoulders, the outside world sank like a heavy stone in a pond. Lately Carla had been suffering from severe headaches. She grew increasingly pale and more dependent on Ribbeck's strength and energy.

It must have been strange in their big house, with Bender who saw and knew everything, with Public Prosecutor Ribbeck in the formal dining room, with the housekeeper, and Bender's "Fräulein Hertha" (a girl without a second name) in the kitchen quarters. From the music room you could occasionally hear great music. After "differences" Ribbeck sat like a leafless tree in the library and let Bender serve him dinner, while Carla, in her pretty rooms, wrote, dreamed, and brooded. She had a bedroom with bath, a studio, and a small salon with a Gobelin armchair that had been made to Ribbeck's measurements. I had seen the chair in Carla's apartment in the Hansa quarter.

Her first novel was at the printer's and the child was on its way; everything was as it should be. Why were all of us so depressed? Kurt said he would thank God when the child was finally there. He was sick to death of Ribbeck's black looks and Carlchen's pregnancy.

One afternoon Bender and Ribbeck brought her to the Hartlieb clinic. At last! Father was there already because she had to hold his hand as she had done in every previous crisis. A heart specialist was present too, a top ranking man who looked like a melancholy giraffe.

Ribbeck, Kurt, and I waited in Hartlieb's private office. To wait with Ribbeck for anything is no fun. The baby seemed to take after its mother—it was not punctual. I didn't try to talk to Ribbeck; I found that difficult in the best of times. Ribbeck read *Comet*. He read with clenched fists. Sister Theresa burst in on our idyll with a tranquilizer for Ribbeck, which he refused to take. Later head nurse Ullmann served him the same pill, with friendly greetings from Hartlieb, and Ribbeck laughed, or gave a good imitation of same, and took the pill. "To please you, Nurse Ullmann." Christina Ullmann always reminded me of Carla. She must have looked like Carla when she was young. Ribbeck asked if he couldn't see his wife for a moment. "Not now. Later."

"When she's dead?" Ribbeck asked hoarsely.

"For God's sake, Ribbeck!" said Kurt.

At six Bender brought his famous platter of sandwiches, and Mosel. "Please eat, Sommer. And you, Charlotte," said Ribbeck.

"And what about you?" asked Kurt.

"I'll eat when she eats," Ribbeck said stonily. How I would have liked to help him in his suppressed agony, but one might as well have tried to comfort bedrock. At least he drank some of the Mosel with us. Suddenly Hartlieb appeared in the doorway. We jumped up. He looked worried. "Listen, Ribbeck. I'm going to have to operate."

"What did you say? Nobody's going to cut her up! She couldn't take it. Birth is a natural event. I won't allow . . ."

"We've got to do a cesarean," Hartlieb said calmly. "Something perfectly simple."

I knew through Father what was endangering her life. Her doctors were worried about her heart. Just like Carla, you couldn't rely on it. Ribbeck said with an eerie calm, "Don't try to fool me. She's dying."

"We're doing all we can and you know it, Ribbeck. We have the best heart specialist, we . . ."

"What are you standing around for, man?" Ribbeck interrupted him gruffly. "Save her! It's up to you. I . . ." With a characteristic jerk he pulled himself together. "Forgive me, Hartlieb, I'm behaving badly." For a moment he couldn't speak. Then he said with pitiful formality, "It won't happen again."

The doctor patted him on the shoulder. "I must go now." Sister Theresa said that Dr. Bode, the anesthetist, was ready. Frau Ribbeck was on her way to the operating room. Hartlieb nodded to us and left. Ribbeck was standing by the window again. He must have forgotten Kurt and me because he murmured, "Oh, the poor child..." Was he thinking that his mother had died when he was born? His cheeks were hollow, his face bloodless. He put his glass of wine on the table. He didn't want anything anymore. Was he thinking of a life without Carla? I didn't want to know what he was thinking, and he wasn't about to tell us. He didn't look afraid, not even desperate, only absolutely without hope. A man in the desert who has left the last oasis behind him.

"I want to thank you both for putting up with me," he mumbled. "But now I must be alone. Please excuse me."

We met Sister Theresa in the hall. "He wants to be alone." She nodded. I wanted to speak to Father again, but it wasn't possible. All of them were in the operating room, Nurse Ullmann too. We could still see Ribbeck in his private hell. We didn't share anything with him, nor he with us, but now we were bound by the same anxiety. It established a closeness between us which no one ever mentioned later and we hadn't consciously sought. Our relationship didn't grow warmer because of it, but at least there was a relationship where there had been nothing before.

A few weeks later Ribbeck sent me flowers via Bender, and a small package. An emerald ring. I had never owned anything so precious. Once I had mentioned that I loved emeralds. There was a card. "With best regards, O. Ribbeck." I had always been under the impression that he didn't know I existed.

Later, when it was all over, Nurse Ullmann told us how she and Hartlieb had gone to Ribbeck and told him, "A healthy boy!"

Ribbeck had stared at them blankly. "And my wife?"

"She's all right. Very weak and still unconscious..."

Ribbeck had wanted to rush into the room, but Hartlieb had held him back with an iron grip. "I'll call you when she comes to. You can only see her for a minute. And don't say anything, you understand?"

"I've got to see her! I won't say a word, I promise you!"

Ribbeck saw Carla for the promised minute. He spent the night in a small room next to hers. Every fifteen minutes he asked the night nurse how his wife was doing. Next morning he was allowed to be with her for five minutes. Ullmann told us all he did was look at her. Then he went to his little room, and she brought him a small bundle. "Your son. Don't you want to take a look at him?"

Unpredictable as usual, after scaring us to death, Carlchen recovered quickly. But she had to stay in the clinic another month, and Ribbeck went to see her in the morning, at noon, in the afternoon, and then drove home reluctantly. I was allowed to visit Carla ten days later. I went there in the late afternoon, Ribbeck hot on my heels. Carlchen was quite lively, almost her old self, but she looked ethereal. Then Sister Theresa brought in the baby. It looked grim, with a deep frown on its little face, "Like your father," said Carlchen, and Ribbeck said consolingly, "That can change." But it didn't change, and they called him the little public prosecutor. Sister Theresa handed him over to his father, and Ribbeck nodded happily when his son tugged at his tie with his tiny hand. But then he held the infant away from him, horrified. "He's wet," he said helplessly, and laid the baby down on the bed like a package, and wiped the damp spot on his jacket vigorously with his handkerchief.

"Kurt Alexander Ribbeck," Carlchen said sternly. "Show your father a minimum of respect!"

# 31

## Epilogue

Carla Moll:

It is summer, and I am sitting under a big pear tree, not on a patio with an unlimited horizon. Yet the Orinoco flows sometimes through my slumber, but so far away it can do me no harm. The little prosecutor is playing on the grass. My son is two years old and very difficult when he doesn't get his way. Bender is the only person he adores and obeys promptly. Again one of Bender's silent triumphs! He appears with lemonade and cookies, and Kurt Alexander Ribbeck stretches out his arms to him. He never does it with me. Bender rocks the blissfully crowing boy in his arms and whispers with a complacency meant for me, "Kurt must have his bath now, and his supper." Of course he's right. Upstairs the nursemaid is waiting because I'm supposed to write another book, and Kurt's father is a very important man. Ribbeck will end up in politics, and that will be the end of me. I hate people around me, the Sommers excepted. "Recluse!" says Ribbeck, shaking his head. "And you get more and more beautiful all the time." I tell him my beauty is going to end up being unbearable, and he says, "That's possible. What do you do all day?" Nothing at all!

"Pull yourself together, Moll," Frau Hannemann says as in the good old days. She visits me often in the evenings when my husband is busy with his musical friends and I am alone. I never did make friends with his Stradivarius. I tried, but my love for Ribbeck isn't enough to make me love Bach.

Ribbeck helps me over the many daily defeats in his house. It is not my house. It remains his, with Bender, Fräulein Hertha, the housekeeper, baby nurse Marianne, Public Prosecutor Ribbeck in the dining room, and the Stradivarius in the music room. Everyday life had always been my enemy, and that hasn't changed. The housekeeper suggests a menu, and when I think of Bender's white gloves, I lose my appetite. Lottchen does too. She's on my side. Kurt likes to dine at our house. Good old Kurt!

I wish Frau Frosch were here, telling me what her old man had to say last night while Ribbeck discusses politics with his guests. They are his guests, not mine. And I sit opposite him at the oval table and play the hostess. Then, at night, I'm too tired for him, and he's got something to forgive me for again. Sometimes I ask him when we are finally going away, and he says he has to consult his calendar. "Burn it!" I tell him. "Yes, yes. One of these days." He will never burn it. It's my bad luck that I love him. He is touchingly proud of me. My first novel, *Picnic with Demons*, is a success, and now I'm resting on my laurels as I did after *Caracas for Beginners*.

Ribbeck is the only one in the house who loves me. When he comes home, his son screams bloody murder. Ribbeck frowns when he sees his screaming son in Bender's arms. "I'll show you a thing or two, you little brat!" he says, and he will. He will be a wonderful father as soon as he can talk sense with his son. And his son will be sensible much sooner than his mother. The boy is extremely intelligent. "You'd think Bender was his father," says Ribbeck. Exit the indispensable Bender and our obstreperous Kurt. I ask, "Would you like to exchange your wife, Ribbeck?"

"I *beg* your pardon!"

"You could do so much better. A lively, businesslike, energetic, diligent, punctual woman, who does everything she can to please you."

"I want Rieke."

"Anything else?"

"A second child and a second book," he whispers.

"And if I don't oblige?"

"Then you don't. Come, drink your lemonade."

"You can talk like that to your baby son."

"I have two children."

"You're soon going to have three."

I hadn't wanted to tell him at night. I wanted to see his face. I am the only woman who knows his true face.

This time things were a lot easier. One night I said to Ribbeck, "I have an idea for a book."

"High time," he said. "We'll talk about it tomorrow. By the way—how far along are we?"

"If Hartlieb's count is reliable, six months."

"You know that I've ordered a daughter. But someone to follow me on the paper would be all right, too. I'm afraid Kurt is going to be a jurist. He keeps his books on file already." We laughed. Ribbeck laid his hand on my stomach as gently as on his violin. "Rieke, what do you and the child talk about in the dark?"

"Oh, mostly about that beast, editor-in-chief Ribbeck." He laughed softly. "I'll show the two of you . . ."

"Do that," I said sleepily. "Show us."


Carlos Domingo Sánchez (Caracas) to Ellen Driscoll (Brighton, England)


Altamira. Villa Acacia. In the cool season.
My dear charming Ellen,

Many thanks for your letter. I hadn't heard from you for such a long time, I began to wonder if you hadn't noticed that the English mail strike was over. I was all the more pleased to have a sign of life from you and to hear of your marriage. Please congratulate Dr. Ambrose Prior for me.

Why should this news have surprised me? I would have been surprised only if such a pretty and smart young woman like you had remained a bachelor!

That's not the right thing for a woman in spite of all efforts at "liberation" that you read so much about in the Anglo-Saxon newspapers. In Latin America it is mostly women without charm, whose freedom no one would dream of curtailing, who cry out for it. Here we men are still pretty well off in this respect and prefer even a disagreeable family to no family at all! I am a lone wolf, as you know, but of course I don't know what lies ahead of me.

Of course you and your husband will be welcome guests in Altamira. What an honor for me that you still want to carry out this plan, made so long ago! Unfortunately my enterprises have become increasingly far-flung, and I am away from Caracas for months at a time. But my sister-in-law, Pilar Álvarez, will be delighted to receive you. She sends you her best wishes. You write that Dr. Prior has never been in our part of the world. He will like Venezuela if he has a capacity for leisure.

You say also that he is an ardent fisherman. I can understand that because I occasionally fish on one of our lovely islands in Nueva Esparta. That's where I relax among the fishermen, in my grandfather's house. Unfortunately the house is a kind of memorial to him, and we receive no guests there. A while ago I had a country place on the Orinoco, very close to the so-called fisherman's paradise, but I sold it recently. Too bad!

In a few days I am flying to Chicago where I shall stay with Mr. Cooper and dear little Naomi in their new house. Later they are coming to Venezuela because Mr. Cooper and I are interested in building residential houses around Puerto Cabello. I have a house in Palma Sola, where you could meet the Coopers. How about it? I remember how all of us met at Fräulein von Strelitz's house. I am sure you must have felt her death keenly. A wonderful, loyal human being. It seems so long ago! In the meantime,

I hear from quite a few Berliners. Naomi sent me the first novel of a Berlin girl I met briefly: *Picnic with Demons*, by Carla Moll. A very interesting book.

I hope that circumstances will permit me to welcome you and your husband at the Villa Acacia, in spite of all my business trips. When it comes to coincidences, I am lucky. That is Venezuelan. For us uncertainty has a certain poesy. I spoke to you in London in this vein, but charming Ellen didn't want to hear anything about poesy ... The weather was dreadful, but I forgive you. I nearly always forgive my friends. It's the sensible thing to do. Apart from fiestas on a moonlit night, we Venezuelans are worshipers of reason. Otherwise where would we be? No, I won't be going to Berlin again. That chapter is closed. Nobody is there anymore whom I want to visit. With very best wishes,

Sincerely yours,
Carlos Domingo Sánchez

Ellen Driscoll tore up the letter, exactly as Sánchez had intended she should. She told her husband that Sánchez was away and there was little point in visiting Caracas when he wasn't there. Dr. Prior nodded happily. He had never intended to go to South America and visit the *caballero*. He could sense that Ellen was upset by the rejection, but he was much too smart to talk about it. He knew his wife very well and had drawn the correct conclusions from the affair. Ellen had never noticed that Sánchez had developed a silent passion for her. Prior had had to point it out to her bluntly when he had told her that they really should finally get married.

"I only wanted to find a new place for you to fish, Ambrose."

"I'd much rather fish at home. Then I don't have to speak Spanish, which I can't speak anyway."

"Do you really love me?"

It was the first time she had ever asked him, and it was

somehow connected with Sánchez's letter. He said that was the first stupid question Ellen had ever asked him.

"I love you, Ambrose."

"I should hope so. Are you going to answer the letter from Caracas?"

"In time. There's no hurry."

"That's my girl." He kissed her lightly.

Ellen didn't know much about men. She had a lot to learn in that respect, but there was no hurry about that either. Prior was pretty satisfied. Marriage naturally brought its conflicts with it, but a bachelor's life became boring as time went by.

"So are you going to Venezuela?" Ellen's sister-in-law asked three days later.

"Ambrose says he doesn't want to speak Spanish, and England is good enough for him."

"Can he speak Spanish?" asked Miss Prior, who was the dietician at the Brighton Clinic.

"Forget it," said Ellen. "That chapter is closed."

For Sánchez, too, the chapter was closed. He stood under the huge acacia tree in Altamira. The tree was a parasol of red, festive blossoms. Sánchez watched the clouds. They were playing an ecstatic game with the wind, and moved on. For months he had thought Ellen Driscoll was the cool, calm angel he had been looking for all his life. But she was more than cool and calm. Her letter had bored him because in every third sentence she had chosen to inform him of Dr. Prior's needs. Prior, by the way, would have been the first one to agree with him. But Ellen hadn't shown him the letter she had written to Sánchez. His involuntary and one-sided ecstasy was over, and like the clouds, he was moving on. He had the ability to shake off memories like dust. And they were dust. Only Carla Moll's *Picnic with Demons* had substance. Sánchez wouldn't have thought her capable of it. But he never thought much of anyone until they had convinced him that he should. Perhaps that wasn't right, but no one is perfect.

For the most part very little good came from marriage anyway. Camilo de Padilla's hasty marriage, for instance.

The young woman had robbed his house and run off with her lover. Anna Carlovac still wrote Sánchez grateful letters from Maracaibo. He had gotten her the job in the Chinese restaurant. Decent of her never to have mentioned his name when the press had interviewed her. Suddenly he realized too that the journalist Moll had never mentioned him in public whenever she was searching for Bonnhoff. Strange girl. He thought kindlier of her now, but he still didn't understand her. Was she Carlita? The journalist Moll? The author of *Picnic with Demons*?

Sánchez considered how much his acacia tree knew about his life. More than any person did. All his quarrels with his deceased wife had taken place under this tree. Odd . . . he and Cooper had almost forgotten Teresa. They were good friends today, in business and privately. Poor Teresa. It had to be depressing to make so little impression and be forgotten so soon. God would show more mercy to her violent and confused soul than Sánchez, Cooper, and Pilar. Pilar . . . Sánchez knew that she was watching him from a side veranda. She had been happy when he had come back to the Villa Acacia without a wife. He had never mentioned Ellen Driscoll again, and Pilar would never ask. But there was a vague pain where Ellen was concerned. Pain became much more attached to one than joy. But he would think of Ellen less and less, and in the end she would dissolve like smoke in a forest fire.

The wind stirred in the acacia leaves, and Sánchez breathed in the evening air. It was cool and pleasant after the rain. The tree was witness to his freedom. Bonnhoff had died shortly before Carla Moll's second visit to the Orinoco. With his persecution complex, the old man had run away from the house without his hat while the others were having their siesta. All he had taken with him was an old Indian basket. Sánchez and Brother Fernando had found him on the shore, dead. Later Sánchez had examined the contents of the basket. He locked the picture of his German grandmother in his desk, together with a dog-eared, dirty volume of Rilke and a journal. He threw the gold party badge into the river. Father Alonzo laid Bonnhoff to rest in the cemetery of the Franciscan mission. The headstone read: Carl Friedrich Bonnhoff. Born in Potsdam 1890, died in Venezuela 1971.

And now Sánchez was free. He thought once more of Christina, Carla, and Ellen. Had there been a pattern behind these encounters? Something must have drawn him to these German girls. Was it his German heritage, which he had consciously ignored and tried to extirpate because of Bonnhoff? If this was so, then this heritage of blood and nostalgia was much older than Bonnhoff; it was rooted in the collective memory of a nation. Yes, these primeval memories in his subconscious had driven him to find pleasure and torment in these women. But now they were dead for him, as dead as Bonnhoff, and he was free of them too. Now at last he could walk out into his own future out of the limbo of the past. The tree was his witness.